HOW TO DATE A SUPERHERO

(And _Not_ Die Trying)

HOW TO

A SUP

DATE
ERHERO
(And *Not* Die Trying)

CRISTINA FERNANDEZ

KATHERINE TEGEN BOOKS
An Imprint of HarperCollins Publishers

Katherine Tegen Books is an imprint of HarperCollins Publishers.

How to Date a Superhero (And Not Die Trying)
Copyright © 2022 by Cristina Fernandez

Library of Congress Cataloging-in-Publication Data
Names: Fernandez, Cristina, 1999– author.
Title: How to date a superhero (and not die trying) / Cristina
    Fernandez.
Description: First edition. | New York : Katherine Tegen Books, [2022]
    | Audience: Ages 13 up. | Audience: Grades 10–12. | Summary:
    "When Astrid discovers that her boyfriend is a superhero, she must
    learn how to survive their relationship, college life, and figuring out
    who she is"— Provided by publisher.
Identifiers: LCCN 2021061345 | ISBN 9780063114302 (hardcover)
Subjects: CYAC: Superheroes—Fiction. | Dating (Social customs)—
    Fiction. | Universities and colleges—Fiction. | New York
    (N.Y.)—Fiction. | Youths' writings. | LCGFT: Novels.
Classification: LCC PZ7.1.F46 Ho 2022 | DDC [Fic]—dc23
LC record available at https://lccn.loc.gov/2021061345

Typography by Molly Fehr
22 23 24 25 26   PC/LSCH   10 9 8 7 6 5 4 3 2 1

First Edition

FOR ANYONE ELSE WHO'S FELT
LIKE A SIDE CHARACTER.

HOW TO DATE A SUPERHERO

(And _Not_ Die Trying)

SOPHOMORE SPRING
WEEK ONE

M
T   Cell Bio Lab Safety Quiz
W   BioChem Syllabus Quiz; Orgo 2 Syllabus Quiz
Th BioChem Lab Safety Quiz
F   Physics Syllabus Quiz

ASTRID HAS A SUPERPOWER.

Nothing exciting, not caused in any usual way by lab accident or genetic mutation, but for as long as she can remember she's had a perfect sense of time.

She knows it's exactly 5:34 in the afternoon when she sits down at her desk and begins to work on the master schedule for her semester.

She doesn't have any fantastical, magic powers that let her play with reality like an Etch A Sketch like the heroes she sees in the skies on a weekly basis, but she has her schedules. Big schedules and small schedules, rough outlines for the next five years framed above her desk, and meticulous to-the-minute plans for her evening scribbled on Post-it notes. She has sprawling flow charts and stacks of bullet journals, and a carefully maintained Google calendar synced to computer, phone, tablet, watch. An endless detailing of her reality in spreadsheets and lists.

For a moment, she takes it all in: her small planner directly in front of her, the thin stack of the four syllabi she's picked up so far this week, the colored markers at her right hand, colored pencils behind them, and highlighters behind them. At her left, the cup of cart coffee Max had grabbed for her slowly cools. In front of this sea of syllabi and schedules, her computer open, her sleep tracker on her phone, her five-year plan in the corner, her ten-year plan behind it, she feels completely at ease, on top of the world, untouchably powerful.

It's 5:36 when she takes a deep breath and dives in.

She can't fly like Captain Jericho or even jump really high like Kid Comet, but she can take this leap, feel like she's soaring just a little as she flips open to a fresh page in a new journal. It's not superspeed, but she can know in an instant that Sunday morning has never been a productive time, so she should get her BioChem homework done Saturday night between reading for Orgo 2 and grabbing dinner with her roommate, David.

She blocks in classes first in thick Sharpie highlighter lines, makes little dotted lines on either side of them for her walking times. Office hours in colored pencils, club meetings in thin markers, then volunteer hours at the hospital, her commute to and from. Her English class has mostly small and thin books, easy to commute with. She draws a careful pink line along the green commute. She uses a yellow pencil to sketch out hours for pre-labs.

Her eyes trace over the page and this is where her powers thrum beneath her skin, as she feels it out with her eyes, poking around until she can find that one little gap of time where her Orgo 2 homework can slip right in. Her fingers fiddle with the orange highlighter, letting it thrum in the air like a plucked violin string, until the marker itself can find its place on the page.

Monday looks good as is, feels right. Tuesday is packed tightly, barely room to budge or shift without knocking things over. Wednesday looks complete, but . . . Wednesday nights, technically early Thursdays . . .

She smiles and lets the highlighter skate over the page.

"You're so fucking weird," David says from where he's sprawled across his bed, and through some contortion of his arm he manages to throw a pillow at the back of her head.

She bats it away wildly; it nearly takes out the coffee cup before flopping to the floor. Max, where he's sitting on her bed, laptop in his lap, hides his laugh behind his hand.

"I think it's cute," he says, which he is required to think as her boyfriend. She blushes at it anyway, busies herself with tossing the pillow back to David—who mimes gagging at their flirting.

"What are we doing for dinner?" she asks, mostly Max, and mostly for show because it's Tuesday and approaching 6:00, which is on her schedule in a neat little box: dinner with Max and David at the nicer dining hall across campus.

"Uh, nothing," David says, wiggling his phone in the air. "There's some super bullshit going on right now by 125th. The dining halls closed early."

Astrid lets out a deep groan and drops her head to the desktop, cushioned by her thick planner. If only her superpower could predict the real superheroes, the way their nonsense always seemed to hate her specifically. If they wrecked another precariously scheduled Monday . . .

"What, uh . . . what kind of super bullshit?" Max asks.

"Some giant blue beam of light," David says. "Twitter thinks it might be aliens, but Tumblr is saying it's an alternate dimension thing."

She really hopes it's an alternate dimension thing. Those usually involve weird time shenanigans that put things back exactly as they were, which is a lot more schedule-friendly than the usual alien fare.

"Whatever," Astrid says, sitting up and closing her planner. She sets it on top of her textbook stack. "We can just have a ramen night."

David pumps his fist, tossing the book he'd been "reading" messily to the windowsill and hopping off his bed. "Why do we ever eat anything *but* ramen?"

"I'm not going to dignify that with an answer."

"I should probably get going," Max says, slipping his laptop shut. Astrid frowns. If he leaves now, she'll have to find another night for them to have dinner this week, since they try to get in at least three, but she's already booked for every night except tonight and . . .

She really doesn't want him to leave.

"I mean," he continues, "if they're already shutting down the dining halls, they're probably going to do the dorms next."

"You can stay the night," she says quickly. David shoots her a look. His ramen is already in the microwave, even though she didn't see or hear him get water for it from the bathroom.

"I don't have pajamas," Max says.

"You can borrow mine," Astrid offers. It's grasping at straws, but worth a shot.

"Yeah, if you're into ratty sweatpants and band camp T-shirts," David says.

"Science camp," she corrects.

Max is already standing by her desk, backpack over both of his shoulders. "As much as I'd love to, I should really head back." He presses a kiss to her forehead. "Breakfast tomorrow?"

"I have physics at nine," she says. "So, if you can be up that early."

He presses a hand to his chest, right over his heart. "For you? Absolutely."

"He's not even crossing his fingers behind his back," David adds helpfully. The microwave beeps and Max heads out, the door swinging shut soundly behind him.

5

Astrid sighs and leans back into her seat.

"C'mon, nerd," David says. "Ramen."

The schedule is already outdated by 7:39 Wednesday night when the email comes in.

She's in Max's room, and Max is swinging his legs back and forth off the side of his bed. It makes her think of the first time she let him sit on the twin in her freshman dorm, hands folded neatly in his lap, back stick straight while her heart fluttered like a nervous bird and her fingertips tingled because the sight of him there on her bed was too much, too intimate, too right.

She's just as nervous now, but not because it's Max and a bed. She's used to Max and beds, currently in a very PG-13 way (even if they've slowly been testing the limits of the rating). She sits on the edge of his desk chair and clicks on the email.

Max leans forward, still maintaining some space, resolutely not peeking over her shoulder as she opens it.

"I got the interview," she breathes. She closes her eyes and lets herself feel the victory in every molecule of her body.

"I told you," Max says, his head falling back against the wall with a solid thump. "I told you. Nothing to worry about because you are a genius and amazing and any lab on this campus would be lucky to have you."

She opens her eyes, smiles without thinking. It feels light and right—*she* feels light and right—like a kite on a breeze. She shuts her laptop and shoves it away from the edge of his desk.

"Okay, I can take fifteen minutes," she says, standing and practically floating over to the bed.

"Really?" he says, eyes widening. She nods and his cheeks go pink.

Her heart thumps, her hands reach for his knees without thinking. He's so beautiful and it makes the room brighter, the world smaller and simpler and breathtakingly whole. Looking at him feels like lying out in the sun on a carefully scheduled day off and basking.

He twists, facing her when she tries and fails to leap up onto his goddamn lofted bed. His nose wrinkles and she wants to die.

Instead, she brushes her thumb along the line of his jaw, pulse dancing painfully when his inhale jerks, when his eyes lock onto hers. There's a little bruise beneath his chin. And he can make fun of her for failing to get onto his bed all he wants, but she's not the one who fell down a staircase two days ago. It's about the only mark left, which she chalks it up to letting him use her vitamin K cream.

"I'm dating the smartest person on this campus," he whispers, leaning forward, resting his forehead against hers. His hair tickles her skin and her whole body thrums with nerves, like she's holding a live wire and it might kill her but God, she can't imagine letting go.

I'm dating the most beautiful person on this campus, the most heartachingly breathtaking person maybe in the entire world.

She doesn't say as much because it wouldn't feel real if she said it, it would just feel like some easily parroted line, to go along with his.

She kisses him instead, feeling triumphant, untethered in a storm, unbelievably breathless.

"Wow," Max says against her lips. Her heart is going to explode. She's going to die before the semester even really begins, halfway standing-sitting on his bed. His hand tangles itself in the hair at the back of her neck.

"I think we're getting better at this," she offers in agreement.

He laughs, eyes crinkling, chest shaking. In a move almost too incomprehensibly smooth, his arm wraps around her waist and he lifts her right up onto the bed.

She pushes him down to the mattress, straddling his lower waist at a careful position that is still certainly PG-13, but the kind of PG-13 that's weird to watch with your parents.

She likes being on top. This surprises no one.

His hands run along her back and he tugs her down gently, craning his neck up to kiss her again and again and again. Astrid can feel the countdown of those twelve remaining minutes, but goddamnit, they're going to make those twelve minutes count. The hand she has against his chest shakes a little—but it's not the bad sort of overwhelming everything else is.

Because everything else is. She really has to get back to her physics pre-lab readings. And she should add some extra time into tonight's plans to put the interview in this week's schedule, which is a terrifying thirty-nine hours away. Not to mention some hours for practice questions and re-researching everything Dr. Vaughn has ever done in between then and now, looking for spaces in her schedule to potentially fit ten to twelve lab hours a week in her schedule, if she somehow manages to get the position.

But she can spare a little more time for this. For Max. For another eleven minutes.

It's 3:04 on Thursday and she's back at her desk, a little sweaty from walking in her thick winter coat from her first Orgo 2 section.

It's week one work. Recaps and setting baselines and warming up. She can do these kinds of chemistry problems in her sleep. She can eat them for breakfast.

David stumbles his way into the dorm room, big, clunky headphones blasting eighties rock so loud she can hear it from her desk. She rolls her eyes at the sight of him, toeing his shoes off and banging his head around.

"It's freaking freezing out there," he announces, yanking his hoodie off over his head.

She knows he thinks he's the coolest thing since sliced bread, since rock 'n' roll, since Ferris Bueller.

"What?" he asks loudly, when he's finally standing and looking back at her. She rolls her eyes again because he is that cool. He came in hot this semester, back from vacationing over winter break with his warm brown skin glowing like he'd captured some of the tropical sun deep inside.

"Where the hell have you been?" she asks. She's perfected

the exact intonation on the question, so she doesn't sound like her mother. Extra emphasis on the *where* and *you*.

"Out," David says, throwing himself down across his bed, spread eagle.

"I haven't seen you in like two days, dude," she says, spinning her chair around.

"Really?" He frowns, pulls his wrist up like there's a watch there. There isn't. "Hmm. Guess so. How you been, nerd?"

She kicks her feet up onto the foot of her bed.

"Fine," she says.

"Ah," David says, snapping his fingers at her. "Syllabus week. You're having the time of your life, aren't you? Getting all horny for your schedules?"

"We've done this how many times, David," she says, sighing. "Four? I can't make my official schedule until next week when I have an accurate read on the time requirements for each course. Right now, I have a preliminary—stop smiling like that."

"Like what?" He has the audacity to tilt his head. She rolls her eyes.

"Smarmy," she says. "You're smiling all smarmy because you think I'm being ridiculous."

"You are being ridiculous," he says. "Just a little. In a very endearing and quirky way."

She glances around her desk for something to throw at him. Everything is too valuable to risk losing right now.

"Get out of my room."

"It's our room now, darling," he says. The bed creaks and squeaks as he sits up, scooting until his back is against the wall.

It is their room. She takes a second to marvel at it. Two years ago, she shuddered so hard at the thought of having a roommate that she went through every step she could to ensure a single for freshman year. Yet here is David in their room, with his neon-green bedspread that actively clashes with her gray one, with his messy desk and concerningly cluttered drawers, his overflowing laundry basket and his collection of old takeout boxes arranged on the floor like a postmodern art installment.

It's unfair that he just waltzed into her life last year like the brother she never had, her freaking platonic soul mate in the form of the most annoying person she's ever met.

"How's Max?" David asks, hoisting his ankle up onto his knee.

"Good," she says, shrugging.

"Y'all cuddle last night while I was gone?"

"Nope," she says. "Because you were supposed to be back by ten thirty." And because Max canceled last minute on dinner with a twenty-four-hour stomach bug. She feels bad that she was relieved, just a little bit—more time for interview prep.

David smiles again. "Still wanna know where I was?"

Well, *now* she doesn't.

"No," she says. "I was curious on Tuesday night. And last night. Did you die? I didn't know. You know we live in the age of the internet; you could have texted once."

"Well, obviously I wasn't dead," he says. "I tagged you in

that thing on Instagram yesterday, the one about . . . the tag which dining hall frozen yogurt are you." He squints like he'll remember it better with his eyes almost shut. "Strawberry was like 'perfectionist, has cried in a Walmart more than once, knows the exact time and place of their own death.'"

"I've never cried in a Walmart," she says.

"I was there, Astrid."

"That was a CVS."

"Okay, okay, Tuesday I was at a SigEp mixer," he says.

"What was her name?" Astrid asks. Now she gets to tilt her head and act all smug.

"Helen," David says with a lovelorn sigh. "Journalism major. She's on the dance team, too."

It's one of the great David-isms, how he can rattle off facts about each notch on his belt so fondly but can't pass a science test to save his life.

"Which dance team?" Astrid asks, in the interest of cyber stalking the girl, putting a face to the name even though she has already breezed through David's life.

"There's more than one?" David asks, eyebrows scrunching together.

"Aren't you in the musical? Shouldn't you know that?"

He shrugs. "I'm dedicated to my craft and my craft alone."

She's not sure if he's talking about theater or girls.

"And how was your 'craft' last night?"

"Magnificent. I mean, we're just setting everything up right now," he says, so they're talking about theater, "which is why your untalented ensemble boyfriend didn't have to come, but it's looking pretty good." He smiles, shaking his foot. "That girl who always wears her slippers in the dining hall asked me to *hang out* after practice."

She rolls her eyes. "I don't know how any of you have all this time to hang out on weeknights."

"I'm sure you and Max could make time," David taunts. English major. He loves his double entendres twice as much.

"Max and I will not be making time," she says. "Not with the way my semester is shaping up."

"Oh my God, you're gonna schedule losing your virginity in your planner, aren't you?"

She decides her orange mechanical pencil is a sacrifice she is willing to make. It bounces off David's knee, and he laughs.

"You wanna grab lunch?" he asks, rolling off the bed in a disastrous flailing of limbs and sheets alike.

"It's three in the afternoon," she says.

"And?"

She rolls her eyes and jerks the highlighter in her hand at her schedule. "Have fun."

He salutes, slips back into his sneakers, and is off again. She probably won't see him for the next three to five business days.

There's a strange sort of serenity that passes over her at times like this, in the postmidnight haze of working. David's out at rehearsal or whatever rehearsal after-party he's come across, so Max has stayed late, sitting on her bed while she hunkers down at her desk. His breathing is a soothing white noise as the swirling pattern of his laptop's screensaver splashes color across his shirt.

There's a rhythm to doing problem sets like this, her pencil scrapping across a page, the pop of a marker cap when she needs to draw something out on her whiteboard, the squeak of the eraser after.

Outside the window, the city is almost quiet.

It's been exactly forty-three minutes since she started her Orgo 2 problem set when Max jolts out of his spot on her bed by picking that moment to wake up.

"Whoa," he says, blinking rapidly. He shakes his head out, glancing around her harshly lit dorm room and orienting himself. She lets herself lean back in her desk chair to watch him as he wakes his laptop up as well and winces, running his hand through his tangled curls. "Oh man, when did it become this time?"

"This time" being 2:34 in the barely-even-morning. She raises her eyebrows.

"Do you want me to be pedantic about it?" she asks. He closes his laptop and slides it off his lap.

"Always," he replies, hopping down from the bed in a movement unexpectedly smooth for her clumsy, accident-prone boyfriend. And then he's standing behind her chair, elbows on the top of her seat back, making her crane her neck to continue to watch him.

"Well then, it became this time just now," she says. "And

now it's no longer this time. And now it's no longer this time, and now—"

"Oh man, it's too late to get this existential," he says, pressing his hands over his eyes.

She allows herself to smile now, while he's not looking.

"Hey, buddy, you knew what you were getting into with me," she says.

He lets his hands fall and smiles at her, even more disgustingly fond than she'd ever dare to look. Her heart pounds anyway, even at 2:35 in the morning, even months and months into this relationship, even though it's literally nothing new as he bends down and kisses her chastely and comfortably.

"Yeah, I did," he says through that smile. He sighs long and belabored, pushing back from her chair and stretching his arms out above his head. "Well, I should go and try to get some real sleep." He grabs his laptop from her bed and shoves it unceremoniously into his backpack.

She decides she's allowed a short study break.

"You could stay," she says, nonchalant, suave, a picture of poise. "You know, since David's still out."

Max shrugs his backpack up and turns back to her with a wince.

"I'd love to, but I, uh . . ." He bounces on his toes for a few seconds, panic growing steadily in his eyes. "Uh . . ."

"It's alright if you don't want to," she says quickly, twisting her mechanical pencil between her fingers but not looking away. And look, she's not going to read into this because she doesn't have time to do non-class-assigned readings, but this is kinda twice in one week that he's ducked out of staying over, which is not a novel concept for them. And twice is almost three times, and three times is a pattern. And maybe it has something to do with that time last week shortly after the staircase incident when they were making out and he didn't want to take his shirt off, which she didn't think was a Thing but maybe it's a Thing and they need to talk about it or something.

"I'd love to, really," he says with all of his Max earnestness, that soothing sweetness to his voice that smooths right over the jumble of panic in her head. "I just . . . I can't tonight."

"No worries," she says, releasing her shoulders. Honestly it might even be better. She's 14.7 percent more efficient at problem sets when Max isn't in the room being all cute and Max-like, and she's not allowed to sleep until she gets this problem set done. "I'll see you tomorrow?"

"Lunch? After your lab interview?"

She grimaces. "Oh, please don't remind me."

His hands shoot up in surrender. "Sorry!"

He sweeps back into her space like he never left, kissing her forehead and tucking some of her flyaways back toward her ponytail.

"I mean, you're going to do great," he says as he backs slowly toward the door. "But I can tell you all about that at lunch tomorrow."

She waves him off and he flashes her one more of those beaming smiles before turning and leaving.

The room feels a little less with him gone, but she gets back to work, break over.

She finishes the problem set at 2:47 and leans back in her chair, glancing over at her bed instinctively, even though Max isn't there anymore.

She climbs into the bed at 3:14, with the lights off and the room in dark midnight blues and stark pale moonlight from the one little window between her bed and David's. She closes her eyes.

And then it's exactly 5:22, and her dorm room window shatters.

She forces her eyes open, squinting into the dark, shoving at her mountain of pillows and blankets until she's sitting up in the middle of her twin XL. Her brain boots up slowly and fires off concerns as they're processed.

One: if it's 5:22, she's only had two hours of sleep and she was really counting on four and a half to be functional tomorrow.

Two: the other side of the room is dark and quiet. David is still gone, which is potentially A Problem because that means he's probably at a frat party making more poor life choices.

Three: the room looks different, the moonlight casting through the room at strange angles and shadows because the curtain rod is hanging askew.

Four: the window is shattered. The university doesn't provide renters insurance.

Five: a bulky form in a bright green spandex suit and black domino mask is climbing through the broken window.

She's found the most pressing concern.

"I swear my dorm was so much smaller than this," he says, voice booming in the small space of her room.

She screams.

A signal for someone to do something, maybe contact someone else who professionally handles situations like this.

However, her roommate is out and her neighbors on both sides of the paper-thin walls choose this moment to finally mind their own business. The intruder drags her from her bed by her arm, blankets tangling around her legs, pillows tumbling to the floor.

It's up to her to take action in this escalating situation, which is ridiculous. She's wearing a pair of ratty pajama pants that have three holes along the inseam and fuzzy socks with glue dots on the bottom that she bought to avoid slipping on the hardwood floor.

She's dragged up and toward the window, still blinking against sleep and the tired headache pounding at the space between her eyes. It's hard to remember the semester of self-defense she was required to take in high school, mostly because she had Chemistry right after it that year and spent most of the period drilling formulas into her head.

She tries kicking out; she tries going limp. She screams again.

The guy trips over her plushy green area rug, then rams up against her IKEA nightstand. It slams into the wall.

"Careful!" she says, speech slurred from her retainer.

He regains his balance, one arm still wrapped around her, and yanks the dusty curtain rod off the windowsill entirely. She wonders how many of the repairs she could make herself so she won't owe her goddamn college any more money . . . except she's being kidnapped from her bed in the middle of the night so who's to say whether she'll even make it back to her dorm room ever again. At least if she dies she won't have to pay back her student loans, but she's at college for a reason: namely, she wants to be a doctor, so dying right now would be a little counterproductive.

Her brain is on fire, ignited with adrenaline and anxiety. But she's still so tired; it feels like she's too deep underwater to actually think of anything useful. The man hoists her out the window and for a moment she thinks that's it, he's going to drop her out of her shitty dorm like some karmic justice for how many strings she pulled to get a double on the tenth floor. She'll just die, splattering on the grimy New York sidewalk, her last day spent poring over excruciating Orgo 2 homework she won't even get to turn in.

Instead he comes out the window with her, holding her by the back of her faded high school robotics club T-shirt, and floats over the quiet side street below. She blinks, rubs her eyes, tries to make sense of the city lights around and below her, all blurring together. Her contacts are still in her room and her brain is still in some half-REM hybrid sleep.

Maybe this is solvable. Gravity is just a physics problem.

And then the guy lets go of her. Her stomach, lungs, and

heart slam up into her throat in that order, as she falls for about half a second before she crashes into something firm, but gratefully not sidewalk firm. Everything lurches, and, like a sickening carnival ride, starts going up again. Another spandex suit, this one a navy blue, holding on to her and holding on to a windowsill.

"Astrid!" a vaguely familiar voice says. "Oh God, are you okay?"

And this is just a lot for her to be expected to process at this time, between the property damage and the dangling sixty feet above the city street in her ratty pajamas and fuzzy socks and being thrown around like a rag doll, with her headache pounding her pulse in her forehead and her eyelids so heavy and her brain half asleep but still flooding with adrenaline.

She passes out.

AN ORIGIN STORY
IN THREE PARTS

PART ONE

When Astrid Rose was twelve years old, she was left truly alone for the first time in her life. Her sister was already off at college, so she sat in the living room of her family's Woodside apartment while her mother ran off to reach the post office before closing, her father to deposit paychecks at the bank.

She wasn't a rambunctious child, just the right side of precocious, not much of a risk once they locked a few choice cabinets (namely the one with the cleaning supplies and the one with the snacks) and parroted off some trusty lines about responsibility (namely that responsibility means not breaking anything and not jumping on the couch and generally following the preestablished rules for appropriate behavior).

All of it would prove to be unnecessary since they also left the TV on, and for her first half hour of glorious independence, she watched a PBS documentary.

As the documentary explained with colorful graphics and soothing narration, Jonathan Jones, PhD, also known as Dr. Lightwave, was technically the first person officially classified as a superhero.

People argued over the technicalities.

Technically, by the time his experiment went right-wrong, leaving him with the ability to fly and shoot beams of light from his fingertips, there had already been three extraterrestrial landings on Earth, with little alien babies already being raised in different corners of the world: Ultrasonic, the Seer, and Miss Venus.

Dr. Lightwave, though, was homegrown, a World War I vet, a scientist off the beaten path, playing with UV radiation in a little lab in Morningside Heights when a sparking outlet changed his life and changed the world. By 1938, Dr. Lightwave was making headlines across the country, rescuing cats from trees and ladies from miscreants.

And then the war, and then the aliens in their bright uniforms from their home worlds, and then not too shortly after, more experiments, more happy accidents, more superheroes. At the root of it all was biology, chemistry, and more, ingredients in a great big melting pot of science and magic and a little bit of luck.

The history was well known enough, so the documentary spent most of its time on Dr. Lightwave's research. Astrid ate it up. Every little model of light waves, their distractingly simple equations, their color-coded variables. She fell in love for the first time watching a little photon bounce along the screen. She fell in love with the world beneath the one she could see, full of tiny, perfect systems and mechanisms that made the world work the way it did, things that could be understood and then used to do amazing things like create superheroes or save lives.

And for a moment, following the lines of logic and explanations, absorbing the information like a sponge and wanting more, she lost track of time.

PART TWO

Astrid Rose met Max Martin her first week of high school.

They existed in neighboring but distinct social worlds. She'd already garnered quite the reputation as an annoying, know-it-all freshman, pushing her way into the advanced STEM courses and correcting teachers at every turn. Max had managed to establish himself as a Hot Mess: klutzy, nerdy, lonely.

She knew enough about who he was before they met face-to-face. To the point where it wasn't a surprise that he crashed into her on the stairs at the single most inopportune time: Tuesday, fourth period, her five-minute fun run up six flights and down two halls between Geometry and BioLab.

"Oh God," he said in the second before they collided. But it was too late. Her stuff went sprawling. For a second it looked like he might tumble down the steps as well, but she grabbed him by the long sleeve of his T-shirt as he babbled on. "Sorry. I'm sorry, I can't believe I just—I should have been looking."

Max Martin was as short and weedy as the rumors had advertised. All bony angles, shaggy short hair, a golden tan, and little patches of acne along his temples and cheekbones. He looked like a walking apology. She found it hard to be mad at someone so earnest and depressingly contrite.

She gathered up her binder, three folders, and history textbook by the time he regained his balance and bent down to help. He rescued her pencil case from three steps up before it could get trampled underfoot; like anywhere else in New York, the pedestrian traffic inside refusing to slow or stop. She grabbed his glasses from where they'd fallen, a step below his Converse, and shoved them toward his face.

"No worries," she offered with a tight smile. "Try not to die out there." He took his glasses back. She took her pencil case.

"Right," he said, flushing and stuttering. "Yeah."

And she moved around him to continue up the stairs, praying she never would so much as see him again because if there was one other thing everyone seemed to know about Max Martin, it was that he was bad luck.

PART THREE

Their biology class took a field trip early in their sophomore year to a research lab up at City College.

Biology was easily Astrid's favorite class that year and maybe ever. For the forty minutes a day she was in the class things seemed to click together, sudden amazing understandings about the universe were drawn out on their squeaky whiteboard, and questions she hadn't even known to ask were being answered. Here's how your body produces sugars, here's how cells reproduce, here's how the immune system keeps you alive despite the million things that could kill you.

She photocopied the textbook page with the Krebs cycle on it to hang in her room.

So she was just a little excited about this field trip.

It might not have seemed that way from the outside, since she usually was at the front of the pack of students as they were led meanderingly through the labs, nodding along and answering all the prompting questions from their tour guide when no one else would. But it felt different as her head swiveled between the test tubes and the microscopes and the artfully organized project posters lining the hallway walls.

During their lunch, with all her class sitting in a line down a half-deserted hall with their brown paper bags, some of the boys trying and failing to have a discreet food fight in the corner, and one of the chaperones searching for Max who probably got lost looking for the bathroom, Astrid filled out notes in the flimsy notepad that came in the field trip bag, as many terms as she remembered from their tour to research when she got home.

A shadow fell over her, a pair of navy ballet flats on the linoleum in front of her.

"Mind if I sit?" their tour guide asked, holding her own paper lunch bag. Astrid nodded her head, feeling ridiculously starstruck considering the woman was only an undergrad researcher. "I'm Stacy, by the way."

"Astrid," she offered, tucking her pen into the notepad and sitting up straighter.

"Let me guess," Stacy started, pulling a sandwich out of her bag. "You want to be a doctor?"

In all honesty, Astrid hadn't thought that far ahead. Sure she had never experienced full joy as deeply as she had in her sciences classes, but aside from making it a lot easier to get perfect grades in those classes, there didn't seem to be much else to it.

"Uh, yes," she said in the moment, because suddenly it seemed like another miraculous answer to the universe's questions.

Stacy smiled. "I could tell. You've got all the passion and excitement down," she said. "Which is good. You'll need that because it's a *lot* of work." She took a bite of her sandwich and nodded. "But . . . you know, with all that work, comes some really incredible accomplishments."

Astrid wanted to write that down too, but it felt rude. So she committed it to memory instead, and when she got home that afternoon, opened a new notebook and traced out the first of many tentative life plans in careful cursive.

SOPHOMORE SPRING
WEEK ONE

M
T ~~Cell Bio lab safety quiz~~
W ~~Orgo 2 syllabus quiz~~
Th ~~BioChem lab safety quiz~~
F VAUGHN LAB INTERVIEW; Physics Lab Safety Quiz

ASTRID SQUINTS AGAINST THE BRIGHT SUN-
light that floods the room, taking it in one eye at a time. She's curled on her side on what is immediately identifiable as a dorm mattress, hard and unforgiving. It's definitely not hers since she invested early in a mattress topper. There's an ache that twinges at her neck as she sits up; an alarming crack when she rolls her head around.

"Hey."

"Jesus!" Astrid says through her retainer, her soul slipping out of her skin for a second as she spins toward the foot of the bed. Still no contacts, she stares apprehensively at the vague, blurry outline of a person sitting there with legs crossed, too close to pick apart specific details.

"Sorry," the blob person says, and it's the most familiar noise in the universe, Max apologizing.

"Max?" she asks as a part of her relaxes, just a little.

"Here," Max says, leaning forward, holding something out to her.

Glasses. She closes her fingers around them, places them carefully on the bridge of her nose. It's a power move: she's regaining control of the situation now that she can actually *see* the situation.

There's Max, slightly slouched, hands folded between his thighs, smile sheepish, deep purple bags beneath his eyes.

"What the fuck?" she asks, and then turns discreetly to pop out her retainer. There isn't a place to actually put it so after a moment of existential contemplation she holds it carefully with two fingers and turns back to Max.

"Yeah," he says, rubbing at the back of his neck like he does when he forgets to meet her for lunch.

"It's 9:43," she says. "I'm gonna miss my interview with Dr. Vaughn. Why am I in your room? What . . . happened last night?"

He scoots forward, his knees bumping against hers.

"Okay, so remember when we were hanging out last Saturday when you got back to campus, and I kept trying to tell you something, but then didn't?" he asks, pressing his lips together.

She nods.

He inhales shakily, exhales sharply through his mouth. His hand goes to his back pocket, tugging something out and dropping it in between them on the bed.

A clump of fabric, navy blue with thin gray stripes. She flattens it out on her lap, sees diamond-cut eyeholes.

"Um," she says. "What exactly am I looking at?"

"I'm Kid Comet," he says.

She blinks.

She sighs.

She rubs at her eyes.

"Kid Comet?" she echoes. "The superhero?"

She stares at him as he nods, tilts her head just a little because maybe a change of angle will help everything slot into place. He doesn't really look like a superhero. He doesn't really look any different than he's always looked, the soft slope of his nose, the curve of his lips, the cut of his jawline. She wouldn't necessarily call it a heroic jawline, but it has a little bit of an edge to it.

He's still just looking at her with his puppy dog eyes, earnest and apologetic and tired, like he hasn't slept in three years.

He's still just Max.

But sure. Sure. He's a superhero.

"Okay," she says, scratching at her nose. "Care to elaborate, just a little?"

He nods, bracing his elbows on his thighs.

"Do you remember that field trip we went on in sophomore year?"

◆ ◆ ◆

So apparently Max did not accidentally lock himself in the bathroom as he explained to their teacher, but instead ended up in a private lab, tripped over an extension cord, got pumped full of radiation and other unidentified chemicals, and then hit the biggest growth spurt of his life overnight.

She just thought he was a late bloomer.

Also apparently Max's weird roommate from last year who got expelled for blowing up a research lab is his nemesis or something, and knew where her dorm room was, but it's totally fine because he's locked up now and probably won't break out until well after move-out at the end of the school year so everything should be good.

They don't really have enough time to cover much else before she has to run back to her dorm to change. The room is still in ruins, glass sprinkled over the rug and her bedsheets, the sharp winter wind rhythmically gusting through the place where the window used to be. But she only has time to reach into her dresser and grab the first collared blouse she can get her hands on, and then run off to her interview with Dr. Vaughn, head pounding, sorely in need of a coffee, some ibuprofen, and a six-hour nap.

The tension behind her eyes makes her feel blurry even with her glasses as she hurries up the stairs of the lab building, trying to figure just how fast she can go without arriving at the office completely out of breath.

Astrid feels the time ticking on, a slow death crawl toward the start of the interview. Without this position in Vaughn's lab, she'll have no chance of doing any independent research this semester, which means it'll be impossibly harder to get a position at a lab this summer, and without a position in a lab this summer she'll have a gap in her résumé when applying to med school that she'll have to explain and won't be able to and there goes her five-year plan. And her ten-year plan. And everything else with it.

She makes it to the lab right on time instead of five minutes early like every article and career center handout says. But she's sitting across from Dr. Vaughn at 11:02, and she's barely panting so she'll take what she can get.

"Astrid Rose," Dr. Vaughn says. Astrid takes a deep breath, smiles professionally, sits up straight. "It's great to put a face to the name."

"Yes," she says, nodding. She still feels frazzled and sweaty. "I just wanted to thank you again for taking the time to talk to me."

"Of course," he says. He looks at peace in the lab, his lab, grad students and lab techs buzzing along in the background. "How's your semester going so far?"

"It's been alright," she says. Her cheeks are starting to hurt a little from the smile she's maintaining but she's not quite sure how to relax. "I'm taking a lot of courses, but the material is all very interesting."

"Probably pretty busy too," he says. "From looking at your résumé. You have been doing some impressive work this year. When do you sleep?"

She laughs politely to mask the way her heart stops for a moment, wondering about whether or not he can see the deep, deep purple bags under her eyes poorly hidden by half a tube of concealer minutes before in the bathroom.

"It is a bit of a challenge to make time for everything," she says. "But it's also very worth it."

Very worth it. She's never going to get this position and also maybe he's going to tell the other professors that she said "very worth it," and none of them will let her do research with them and will fail her on principle and she won't get into med school.

Dr. Vaughn sets her résumé aside and looks up, smiling. "Alright, I just have a few questions about your interest in my lab."

"Of course," she says.

"So, as you know, my lab conducts a lot of research on telepaths' stem cells, but that has a lot of crossover with other super abilities. What draws you to the study of enhanced people?" he asks.

"Right," she says, blinking a few times. The past twelve hours are all still right at the forefront of her brain along with the dozen articles about lab interviews encouraging her to "find a personal connection." She bites her tongue hard. *Don't talk about your boyfriend, don't talk about your superhero boyfriend, don't expose your boyfriend's biggest secret to your dream research lab.* "Well, we live in exciting times." *Don't think about your window shattering at five in the morning.* "Science is evolving faster than ever, both in the study of extraterrestrial biology and in mapping the full extent of the human genome, and I think everything we learn about the range of life on our planet and in the universe is another thing we can then use to create lifesaving techniques and technologies."

Dr. Vaughn makes a note on the yellow pad in his lap. Astrid does not try to make out what he's writing and takes a deep breath.

"And what in your classwork here so far do you think has prepared you for work in a lab like this?"

When Astrid finally gets back to her dorm after what's shaping up to be the longest day of her life, there's a woman standing there. She looks vaguely familiar—something about her straight medium brown, medium-length hair, her clear eyes, the cool undertone of her skin. She's clean and polished like the main character of a forty-minute drama on NBC. Or the antagonist in a CW show.

Astrid stays very still in the doorway, keys still in hand, and tries to decide if this is something she should run about.

There's someone else just outside her room fixing the window. By the way the woman glances over, it seems like she's there to oversee the work.

"Yes, I have the files," the woman says into her phone, like she's reading from a snappy Sorkin screenplay. "Uh-huh. No, no, I told Peter, I told him I'm picking the photos. It's very important." She shakes her head and sighs. Astrid tries to picture the person on the other end of the line, someone half as stressed as she is who is definitely losing this argument. "Look,

I'm still on my break, okay, I'll, yes, I'll be back within the hour to handle whatever . . . Alright, alright, talk to you later."

The phone drops away and the woman lets out another sigh, shaking her hair out even as it falls perfectly back into place.

She finally turns and smiles politely at Astrid like she's inviting her into her own dorm room.

"Sorry about that," she says. "Honestly, if I take a break for five seconds . . ."

"Uh, who are you?" Astrid asks, even though she's thoroughly exhausted her question limit for the day.

"It's wonderful to finally meet you, Astrid," she says, stepping away from the window. "I'm a *friend* of Max's, Eleanor—"

"Olsen," Astrid finishes, like it was a question being posed to her. The name had been right there on the tip of her tongue the entire time. "From the news."

Eleanor smiles, lips pressed together tightly, just the appropriate amount of humble.

"The news by me or the news about me?" she asks, and her tongue might literally be in her cheek.

"Both are hard to miss," Astrid says tactfully.

Personally, Astrid's never been in a love triangle before, and doesn't have the faintest clue how they work, but she's especially unsure of how it works for Eleanor Olsen, who's somehow dating a superhero with a ten-pack and the ability to fly and/or his megalomaniacal mad-scientist archnemesis.

"So," Eleanor says and leans against the side of Astrid's desk, gesturing for her to come closer into the room. Astrid tucks her keys back into her pocket but doesn't step any closer.

"I heard you had an interesting night."

"Um, yeah," she says, trying hard not to wince. Thinking about last night right now makes her feel sore and scratchy, like she's been scrubbed over with sandpaper, especially now that Max isn't in front of her.

"The Conversation is always pretty hard," she says, nodding sympathetically, and Astrid can hear the capital letters. "I remember . . . both of mine, very well. But just know that the fact that he told you, it means that he trusts you a great deal."

"Well," Astrid says. "He told me because I got yanked from my bed last night so . . ."

Eleanor's smile is starting to get a little grating.

"I know this can be overwhelming," she says. "But that's exactly why I'm here. For years, people like us, regular people who get caught up in all this superhero stuff, we've been on our own trying to figure it all out. And it was dangerous. So, I created a network, for those of us who straddle the line between worlds, to talk, to share tricks, to protect ourselves. A Pre-venge training program. To *prev*ent the need for anyone to seek revenge over our untimely deaths."

It's practiced and careful. Eleanor's voice is gentle but firm, gliding along the air like a plane taking off.

"I'm not following," Astrid says, for the first time in her life. She doesn't even feel the burn of humiliation with those words, she's too overwhelmed.

"You, Astrid Rose, are not the first person to date a superhero, nor will you be the last," Eleanor says. "But luckily, I am here, and this class is here, so that if anyone out there thinks they can break down your window in the middle of the night again, you will know what to do."

Astrid tries to imagine herself as someone who's prepared for a midnight kidnapping.

No, better yet, Astrid tries to imagine herself as someone who dates a superhero.

She's seen the bodice rippers, the articles, the BuzzFeed quizzes. She even liked the one documentary they made back in the nineties, even though all those girlfriends in the interviews were very fifties with their red lipstick and hoop skirts. And that's not Eleanor Olsen, investigative journalist and superhero expert.

And that's certainly not her.

Astrid is missing a day of working on homework and she can already feel the panic attack building, can already see herself this weekend: not sleeping, not showering, greasy hair and hormonal acne and dark, dark under-eye circles.

She's not cut out for this.

"So . . . am I like, going to some hidden underground base until I can kill a guy with my thighs or something?" she asks. "Because I have a class in an hour and forty-three minutes and I really can't miss it . . . There are clicker questions."

Eleanor laughs a little. "Think of it more like an extracurricular. Just two or three hours a week."

She's already in eight clubs and she's vying for leadership positions in most of them next year for her résumé. Plus, she might get that position in Vaughn's lab.

"I don't think I have time for that," she says. "Do you have like an abbreviated curriculum I could check out? An online seminar maybe? Summer session?"

Eleanor presses her lips together again in a tight, polite smile.

"No, not exactly."

Astrid scratches at her nose, longs for her planner and a spreadsheet, but they're over on the desk.

"Okay," she says. "Okay, and if I don't participate?"

Eleanor is frowning now.

"Um, well . . . I'd have to highly advocate for you and Max to end your relationship."

Astrid did not spend a year pining, four weeks planning, and nine months learning the ins and outs of a relationship to break up with Max because a world-class journalist recommended it.

"And if I decide to not listen to you?" she asks.

Eleanor drums her fingers on her arm. "Then you take your life in your own hands, Astrid." Which is what she's been doing so far. She barely goes outside to begin with, she can invest in some dead bolts maybe, move her bed away from the window . . . But Eleanor seems to see the gears turning. "Look, I know how stressful college can be and I know how intensive your double major is, but I have to recommend you find the time. If not for the training, then for the network. We're . . . We're like a family in a lot of ways. We look out for each other, protect our own. There's strength in numbers and—"

She thinks of Max. Of how she spent all of last semester studying everything about him like there was a final on the other side worth 45 percent of her grade. He's wonderful. Annoyingly wonderful, a hearth through the short days of winter, a breath of fresh air in her dusty dorm room, a ray of sunshine breaking through gray clouds.

He's a time-saver, too, bringing her the same amount of joy and dopamine in half the time of anything else in the known universe. She's never found anything nearly as efficient.

"Alright," she says. "I'll try to make the time."

After her last class, Astrid returns to her dorm room to mentally review her emergency backup plans. She invites Max over so she doesn't have to be alone with her thoughts, but ends up overthinking everything anyway.

Like tall buildings and healthy relationships, a good schedule needs to be flexible to keep itself from crashing to the ground. She has been prepared for years in case of any number of natural disasters, supernatural disasters, plagues, and broken bones (ideally her left arm below the elbow, the most useless of her four limbs).

So, losing the first half of the day to earth-shattering revelations about her boyfriend is actually not the end of the world.

She just has to call in some favors, text Emily Rosenberg and Jason Song and Ben fucking Barnes for Cell Bio notes (in triplicate to cover all her bases), send out some apologetic emails to professors and club leaders, and get to work catching up on deliverables.

Which she will. In another second. She can hardly use her time efficiently if she's not in peak mental condition and right now, she's not.

She does some breathing exercises, lying flat on her bed, running her fingers along the soft downy comforter, tracing the pattern of vague rudimentary shapes. It feels good, simultaneously plushy and solid.

"Okay," she says, once she's finished the guided meditation on her phone. She scoots up her bed until her back is pressed against the wall.

Her dorm is exactly the same. The blinds have been rehung, the window replaced, the nightstand readjusted, her bed made. Eleanor Olsen's work, apparently. It's like nothing had even happened the night before. Everything on her side of the room is very precise, bed and desk side by side, perfectly fitting along the longer wall, dresser pressed tight in the corner next to the door. She didn't bring any of her own furniture last semester because it all fit so perfectly already in the space. But now the empty surfaces and neat corners feel unsettling.

"Okay?" Max echoes, leaning up against the window, hands in his pockets, head tipped down.

David is out at musical rehearsal until 10:00 so Max has elected to stay with her.

She pats the free space on the bed.

"Couldn't clear my brain out," she says. "But we can talk again. I have more questions."

"Okay," he says again, and climbs up onto the bed next to her. He's never struggled hopping up onto the half loft. She always felt self-conscious about her little stool but now it feels unfair. He could probably jump higher than a half-lofted bed. Like, much higher.

Max leaves a foot of space between them, tilting his head to look at her.

She thinks of her freshman dorm room, finding peace and happiness while they sat across from each other doing homework on the cold wooden floor.

"That time in junior year when you had the flu?" she asks. She moves closer, much closer, head on his shoulder, arms around his waist. He's warm and his Pokémon T-shirt is as scratchy as always. His arm slips around her back, hand settling between her shoulder blades.

He whispers, like he used to when they were on the floor and speaking too loudly felt illegal. "Uh . . . broke my leg, hairline fracture in my skull . . . I think that was one of my first big fights with Stormwind."

She remembers reading an article about it in the hallway after she finished the Spanish test they had that day. Max had asked her for notes two days later, studying for the makeup test.

"Hmm . . . end of junior year. You missed prom," she says.

"Alien attack in Greece," he says. "No big injuries, but it was a rough two days." She watched the news coverage on her phone while the debate team drove to McDonald's for some midnight milkshakes, idly wondering if the world was about to end. "I wasn't gonna go to junior prom anyway."

She rolls her eyes. That's what everyone on the debate team said.

"The senior skip day trip to Six Flags," she says and doesn't even let him answer because yep, she can recognize this goddamn pattern. "That fight downtown with Mystic-Man."

He nods, brushing his fingertips against the bottom of her ponytail.

"I'm an idiot," she says, closing her eyes.

"You're not," he says with intent, squeezing her just a little.

"Six years," she says. "Six entire years. Coincidence after coincidence and I didn't suspect a thing. I'm an idiot."

"Astrid," he says, voice pitching upward, pleading.

"Every time something went down at school, you were never there," she says. "That trip to Rockefeller Center, the homecoming game, the . . ." She rubs her knuckles into her forehead. "The School Bus Incident. You were there and then . . . and then you weren't and five seconds later, there's Kid Comet and I . . ."

Nose scrunched up, she groans, reverberations from deep in her throat and deeper in her soul.

"You weren't supposed to know," he says. "*No one* was ever supposed to know."

"I should have put it together," she says, shaking her head, pressing her face against his stupid scratchy T-shirt into the space where his neck meets his shoulder. "We've been dating for nine months, and I didn't even notice."

His hand rubs circles on her back.

"You couldn't have," he says. She raises her eyebrows even though he can't see her face from this angle. "I stopped for a little while. Like all of freshman year and most of last semester. I only started up again . . .

"Remember that breakdown I had a few months ago, right after we got back from Thanksgiving break?"

Ah, the Breakdown.

He'd had a panic attack right on her dorm room floor, like a full hyperventilating, shaking, crying kind of messy panic attack. She'd never seen one from the outside before, let alone from Max who always seemed to take everything that fell onto his shoulders like it weighed nothing at all. She had almost had her own panic attack trying to figure out how to calm him down, ended up holding his hand as tight as she could and stroking his hair, which felt so strange because just the thought of someone touching her during a panic attack made her feel nauseous. But for him it mostly did the trick, or at least it got him breathing again.

"The Chemistry test?" she says, even though it's not a question. They both remember that night well.

He exhales a shaky laugh. "I got like an eighty-six on that test, I was fine. But, uh, well, that was when I found out about my roommate, Kyle. There was that explosion in the Stephens lab, all those stolen chemicals, and those people died." He sighs. "I can be a little paranoid about these things sometimes, but he was my roommate and it's not like there weren't signs. I just kept telling myself there was nothing wrong and I shouldn't do anything about it because I was out. But . . . I should have done something about it. Before. So I put the suit back on and I went after him. And then I kept putting it on over winter break. Because then there was Mystic-Man again, and then Velocity and then I kinda just fell back into it."

He sighs and shrugs, tipping his chin way up toward the ceiling.

"And you were with your parents for the holidays, and it didn't feel right to tell you over the phone. Like, I always knew I'd tell you. It just didn't seem as urgent before. I could just bring it up in a few years like it was some silly thing I did in high school and we could laugh about it. But . . . it's not just some silly thing I did in high school, I guess."

"Oh my God," she says, closing her eyes. "When you said you fell down a staircase on Monday?"

He has the decency to look guilty about it. "I kinda got thrown off the Chrysler Building." Her face must do something alarming, because he rushes to clarify. "I'm just a little rusty right now. It wasn't even that bad, just some broken ribs and a concussion, I wasn't even in the coma for more than ten hours."

"Coma," she says. "Right."

He grabs her hand, lacing their fingers together on top of the duvet.

"I mean, those are nothing for me," he says, like it's reassuring. It might be. She isn't sure yet. "Literally nothing. I've got a thick skull and some pretty accelerated healing. I was fine. Am fine."

She squeezes his hand. As hard as she can.

He still feels the same under her fingertips: warm skin, long fingers, delicate and sharp wrist.

Right. She's decided she hates this.

She thought she knew him down to his bones. Because he's Max, with his easy smiles and his terrible sleep schedule and his dorky T-shirts. And because worst of all, it makes sense. It makes perfect sense. He's still Max, he's not different, but it's like all the puzzle pieces have snapped into place now. She was only seeing a photograph of him before and now here he is in Technicolor 3D.

She swallows again and lets go of his hand.

"I can't believe you didn't tell me," she says, tilting her chin up, trying to channel Eleanor Olsen as best she can. "You know, trust is the foundation of any healthy relationship."

His smile goes away. Unfortunate. It was the only thing making sense.

"I know," he says. "I'm sorry. I—"

"I mean, I get it," she says quickly. "For all you knew, I was some conniving minx set upon you for a long con to steal all your secrets."

He gnaws on his lower lip, rubbing his palms flat along his thighs, but she can read the faint hints of a smile in the lines of his face. "You're no conniving minx, Astrid."

"How dare you."

They've been laid out on her bed for way too long and she's legitimately behind now. Tomorrow is going to be hell and she still hasn't penciled in a panic attack—she probably doesn't even have time for a panic attack, not even an itty-bitty one in the shower or in a bathroom between club meetings.

She hums. She still doesn't want to move. He's warm and her bed is soft and the wall behind her is real and solid and it's like being cradled gently by the entire world.

"So?" he asks. "Eleanor's program?"

She resolutely does not want to think of Eleanor's Finishing School for Superheroes' Girlfriends. In her mind spreadsheet she's already pushing and pulling and shifting her week around to squeeze in time for this stupid program. It's not going well.

"What about it?" she asks.

"You're, uh, you're doing it?" he asks. His heart is skittering along when she needs it to be sure and steady and calming.

"Well, she didn't make it seem like I had much of a choice," she says, patting his side. "It's gonna be hell when midterms start, but she made it pretty clear it's this stupid training program or I can just die."

He squirms around, scooting away just a little like he wants to talk face-to-face. She tips her head back and blinks at him.

"I guess I'm trying to ask . . . like, you want to do this?" he asks.

"Absolutely not," she says, grimacing. "But apparently there's no option with a gentler time commitment; it's full-on boot camp or nothing."

"But like, you're willing to make the time, because . . . you want us to . . . we're going to keep . . . um . . ."

He's floundering. It's cute.

"I would like to continue dating you," she says. "Despite the curveball, despite the extra time commitment. I've invested a lot of time and energy into locking this down and it's not like I actually need more than four hours of sleep a night."

"Right," he says, nodding. "Right, the, uh, investment."

She rolls her eyes.

"Are you fishing for compliments?" she asks. "Cuz you don't get to do that today. I'm still kinda pissed at you."

"No," he says, shaking his head. "No, no. I'm just . . . I would understand, that's all I'm trying to say, if this is too much for you. You didn't sign up for this and it's a lot to ask and I just wanted to make sure that you know that you don't have to do this."

"I know," she says. She turns so she's on her back again, staring up at the ceiling. "Trust me, I've done the calculations, I've weighed the pros and cons. I like you, Max, and I like what we have. And I'm not a quitter." His hand finds her, squeezes tight. "I'm majoring in BioChem and BioPhysics. I'm premed. I don't give up on things I want because they're hard."

"And"—his voice is thick—"and you want me."

"Don't be coy," she says, bumping her shoulder into his. And then because (despite some unforeseen developments) she knows him truly and deeply, and knows when he needs some extra encouragement, some things spelled out as clear as possible. "I want you, Max. I want us."

He squirms around again, wraps his free arm around her waist. "Cool," he says, like he's not sniffling. "I want you, and us, too."

She's knows. She's not an idiot and he's as easy to read as a book. Well, usually.

"Plus, a lot of superheroes are MDs," she says, tapping her fingers on the back of his hand.

"Yeah?"

"Well, if I had known dating you came with all of these amazing networking opportunities," she says, whistling through her front teeth.

"Okay," he says, grumbly, elbow bumping into her side.

"We would have been making out since sophomore year of high school."

Astrid doesn't tell Max that she tries not to think about super-heroes.

She's never had the time to focus on it for too long, and after the School Bus Incident, she actively avoided the subject when she could.

Even before the Incident, she had always hated school buses. Hated having to pick someone to sit with and trying to maintain a conversation for an hour. She hated everyone else talking because the bus was not that big, and the chattering just filled it all up with sound and made her skin crawl. She hated when everyone would start chanting and screaming because she had never, not once in her life, been a fan of loud noises. And there was nothing quite as understatedly terrible than not knowing whatever song everyone was singing, stumbling along with consonants and vowels tripped up on her tongue, voice feeble for fear of sticking out.

There were also no seat belts on school buses, or if there were, they'd be so beat up and draped oddly across the seats it was impossible to actually figure out how to put them on. They went on the highway and bridges so she always felt like it was probably illegal.

And then the Incident happened, deep into sophomore year during a field trip to the Museum of Natural History. Some asshole in a skintight black suit started throwing shit around on the Queensboro Bridge, and she didn't see any of it because she was fifteen rows back. The bus swerved and everyone screamed and she got slammed up against the window and then thrown into her seat partner, Sophia Halbert. And it was all noise and violent jerking and she couldn't breathe and she was going to die. There was a moment where the bus almost flipped over, and then there was a moment where the bus almost fell off the bridge.

And then it all stopped. Because Kid Comet, out of the ether, was hanging from the bridge by his knees and holding their bus up with one hand, muscles quaking with the effort. Suddenly the lack of seat belts was a fucking godsend because everyone could slip on out of their row and up toward the bridge, and toward Kid Comet, who held his free hand out and guided them off one by one, grunting with the effort.

It was a miracle that she didn't push and shove her way to the exit, anything to get herself on solid ground, out of the goddamn bus, out of the goddamn bus, out of the goddamn bus.

She just breathed and waited her turn and then Kid Comet

grabbed her hand, his palm warm and sweaty, pulled her up with an arm around her waist, and she squeezed her eyes shut and didn't dare to breathe until her knees hit asphalt. She curled up on the ground and stayed there.

She stayed there for a while. And then a little longer.

One of the faculty chaperones kept doing a head count, kept asking after Max but also after Peter Jenkins (who stayed home "sick" and would later boast that his Xbox saved his life). But Astrid wasn't really there for that. She just stayed there on the ground, losing her mind, losing track of time entirely. All her seconds and minutes and hours bobbed in the East River with the remains of the bus. She didn't know how long it was until everything finally went quiet again, inside and out. She lifted her head and it was all over and Max Martin—no longer short and weedy but just as clumsy, and perpetually absent from their shared computer science elective—was hovering around her like he wanted to pat her back or something. He was breathing heavy and there was a deep scrape that ripped his jeans and a few layers of his knee. She chalked it up to the crash at the time.

The School Bus Incident still lives in a space of its own in her mind entitled Near-Death Experiences, a small dusty box that sits in a dark far corner where it can gather cobwebs. More often than not she barely dares to look at it, doesn't mention it or buses or superheroes.

But after Max leaves that night, kissing her once at the door, deep and tender, she opens the box, carefully, carefully.

She takes the Incident out and holds it in her palm and

stares at it, a moment crystallized. Max in that costume, his hand in hers, sure and steady, his arm around her waist, lifting her up, guiding her to safety.

She exhales, puts it back, and gets ready for bed.

Astrid is good at three things: planning, studying, and compartmentalizing.

So, it's on the walk back from her last club meeting on Saturday, finally switching out of school mode for the rest of the weekend, that she thinks about Max.

Everything with Max is casual and easy. On the outside at least, while inside it feels like roller coasters and somersaults and Central Park in July, romantic feelings all tangled and warm and threatening to expand until she bursts at the seams.

He brings her coffee in the library, and it makes her heart pound not just from the caffeine. She finds him another ridiculous video game T-shirt, and he lights up with a supernova grin and the sky in his eyes.

Max has always been about the little things, remembering details like her favorite cookie from the place she loves on Amsterdam. He helps with little problems that other people overlook. Granola bars for people asking for food on the subway, smiles for babies in grocery stores, a steady arm for old ladies crossing the street.

It's what she lo—*really likes* about him, how good he is, all the way down to the bones, all the way down to the small things.

So, while cutting across the quad, she confronts the big thing. The superhero thing.

It's not just the little things. His world is so much bigger than she thought. He exists on this larger scale that's more than she expected. But just because it doesn't fit in her brain the same way doesn't make it a bad thing. What else would he be doing but helping other people in any way that he can?

Flexibility, she reminds herself. Essential to reaching any sort of real height. Making the adjustment won't be a problem. For Max, it's not even a choice.

JUNIOR YEAR
HIGH SCHOOL

CHOOSING MAX NEVER FELT LIKE A CHOICE, not even the first time.

Max's parents died. That was a thing that happened. A few weeks after the end of junior year in high school.

He looked . . . He wore a suit at the funeral, the funeral she attended when she should've been studying for the extra credit summer classes she was taking at St. John's. She wasn't entirely sure why she went because she was never that close to Max Martin, not parents'-funeral close. They were sharing-class-notes close, occasionally sitting-at-the-same-table-in-the-library close, very, very rarely after-school-study-session close. He had changed since freshman year, with his wild growth spurt and far-away eyes, but also not changed at all, because he was still painfully awkward and uncomfortably earnest Max Martin.

She barely saw him during the funeral proper.

He sat in the front row with people she presumed were his grandparents, aunts and uncles, family. She sat closer to the back with a few of her classmates, some kids from their debate team, half of the robotics club, a straggling teacher or two.

She stared at the back of his head and tried not to think about her parents dying or how statistically likely it was she'd probably end up in a car crash one day (77 percent based on recent statistics) and might even die in one.

She had to tune out most of the ceremony, to keep herself from spiraling in thoughts of death and eternity and how she might not be a person at all just a facsimile created by millions of chemical reactions in an ever-exploding, ever-expanding universe that no one understands, and one day those chemical reactions would stop and everything she was would be like dust in the wind.

There was a bus a ten-minute walk away that left thirteen minutes after the funeral ended, and she spent most of the eulogy debating whether or not she should try to talk to Max before she left for it. Three minutes wasn't a lot of time and there were a lot of people who would probably be lined up and waiting to say something, and she wasn't sure if she even had something to say that would mean anything.

Sorry you're an orphan. Sorry the universe is a dick. Sorry tragedy doesn't care how old you are.

Sorry both of your parents died.

She ended up having to pee so she decided a better three minutes spent would be to use the restroom and leave the condolences to others, adults who maybe had some great wisdom she didn't, or maybe just a better turn of phrase.

Two large caskets were carried out of the church and she caught a glimpse of Max's face as he followed the procession down the aisle. He looked pale. And tired, with painful-looking bags under his eyes like bruises. Like always, like Max, but worse somehow. Much worse.

She checked the time even though she didn't need to, she checked on her bus, and she waited for the crowd to thin before slipping off to the side to seek out a bathroom.

There wasn't proper signage, wasn't anything that looked particularly like a bathroom and her three-minute window was closing, closing, closing fast.

She pushed open a door in the back corner of the building and, well, appropriately enough prayed.

And it was a bathroom, but it was not unoccupied. Of all the ways a bathroom could be occupied it was either the best-case scenario or the worst because Max was on the toilet fully clothed but crying into his palms.

There was a moment where her future branched into two distinct paths, one where she closed the door, left him be, made her bus, and another where she stepped in and closed the door behind her.

It was not a black-and-white choice.

For example, if she was crying in a bathroom it would probably be because she wanted to be left alone and not have anyone see her cry, especially not a random classmate she'd done maybe five group projects with. However, she'd been told that she was "standoffish" and "aloof" and tended to "isolate herself from any meaningful human connection."

But she thought about closing the door between them and walking away, leaving him to this moment, and it made a voice in her head scream, "Astrid Rose, there is a member of the human race crying in front of you because both of his parents are dead. Do not leave him in this church bathroom alone."

So in the end, there was no choice, just this sudden calm in her chest as she closed the door and stepped toward him.

"Hey," she said.

He did not look pleased to see her. Which was expected. His eyes were red-rimmed, cheeks flushed and stained with tears. It was . . . hard to look at him. Astrid came from a long line of stoic, repressed people with poor, substance-related coping mechanisms. She'd never seen someone look so broken before, wearing hurt so plainly.

His mouth hung open, trying to work itself around a response, but he was a little too busy hiccupping through sobs.

Comfort, her brain instructed, even though she had never really developed those skills.

"I can . . . go," she offered, still frozen by the door, staring at him while he stared back. This was mortifying. This was the wrong choice. This was hurting more than it was helping. "Or . . . um . . ." *Comfort.* Say something comforting. Only she'd spent the past hour trying to think of something worth saying about the terrible day he was having and she still didn't have words to fix this. "Do you . . . want a hug?"

He was still staring at her, looking mildly traumatized.

It felt like another branching moment in the universe, but blessedly she didn't have to make the decision this time. He stared and stared, while the last seconds of her three minutes ran out. Even if she started sprinting now, that bus was pulling away without her.

She thought vaguely of moral obligations, of the bus she missed, of how many cars crash a day, of how many ways she could die. The universe felt wild and disastrous, all chemical explosions and increasing entropy, and in a version of the universe maybe her parents both died in a car accident on a sunny June day and she would be the one crying on a toilet while Max Martin stood awkwardly in the doorway asking if she wanted a hug.

Finally, he nodded.

She stepped toward him slowly, giving him a chance to change his mind, giving herself some time to acclimate to the idea of hugging an acquaintance at his parents' funeral.

It wasn't a comfortable hug. There was relatively no way to make it comfortable. She perched awkwardly on the closed toilet seat next to him and placed her arms loosely around his shoulders. He was sobbing again, chest heaving, shoulders shaking. There were odd pockets of space between them, and she was doing most of the hugging while he just pressed his hands over his face and cried and cried.

She readjusted a few times to get a better grip on him, started moving her hand in small circles on his back.

It didn't feel real. The whole moment felt like something she was watching from afar, like she was out of her body, just looking down on herself holding Max Martin in a church bathroom. All the thoughts about tragedy and death and the universe paused.

Her mind went blank, and she sat there, balanced precariously on her sit bones, feeling the smooth fabric of his button-down shirt (she wasn't sure where his suit jacket went), his scruffy curls tickling against her cheek.

Time stopped, seemed to form a little bubble around the bathroom. The faucet dripped steadily and his sobs came in waves before they slowly dropped off. He shifted and peeked his head up, peeled his hands away from his face like something small and timid and innocent coming up for air after a terrible storm.

He glanced over at her. It was hard to look at his face, especially this close up.

"Sorry," he said, squeaking over the words, voice ragged. He cleared his throat. "I'm sorry."

She extracted her arms very carefully and time started again.

"It's okay," she said, nodding. She patted his shoulder.

"I have to—" He stood and his knees buckled. She offered a hand to steady him. "I have to go."

She nodded. "I'll . . . uh, see you," she offered. "At school." He stared at her for a moment, looking like he might start crying again.

"Thank you," he said and rushed out the door.

Her legs also ached a little when she stood. She shook her knees out, went over to the door, and locked it.

While she peed, she looked up the next bus, and checked the time.

SOPHOMORE SPRING
WEEK TWO

M Cell Bio Problem Set 1; BioChem Pre-lab
T Cell Bio Pre-lab; Physics Pre-lab; Orgo 2 read ch. 15
W BioChem Problem Set 1; BioChem read ch. 1
Th Orgo 2 Problem Set 1; BioChem Lab Report; Women in Lit read
     Woolf, *A Room of One's Own*
F Physics Problem Set 1

TIP OF THE WEEK

"Don't try to be the hero. Your greatest skill will always be your ability to get out of a place as fast as possible. I've found you can't go wrong always having bobby pins on your person."

—Eleanor Olsen

"HEY," MAX SAYS, BLINKING AT HER IN SOME-thing between surprise and delight. She doesn't usually show up at his dorm room after dinner unprompted.

She also usually doesn't slam into him, chest to chest, hands on his shoulders, up on her toes to kiss him.

He staggers back into his room, his hand slipping around to the small of her back, something like a gasp and a laugh sparking against her mouth where it's on his.

"Hi," he says again when she decides he deserves some sort of explanation and steps back. Without looking he toes the door closed and beams at her.

"Hi," she replies and pulls her phone out of her back pocket. "Look at this."

He blinks again, eyes still stuck on her face before she all but shoves the phone into his face, email queued up. His eyebrows knit together, his hand brushing her wrist as he reads. She feels like a launched firework, a quiet, high-pitched buzzing as she soars up and up, about to burst into fire and color and noise.

"I . . . don't know what this says," he says after a second, because her hand is shaking in place like she is, but he's grinning because she is so it doesn't matter.

"That's an email from Dr. Stanley Vaughn," she says. "Who officially wants to offer me a position doing research in his lab this semester."

"And this is good!" he says, nodding.

"Very good!" she agrees and lets herself explode, beaming and breathless. "I mean, it's not a guarantee I'll get to do my own research project anytime soon, but it's a start."

Max plows into her, arms latching around her waist as he hooks his chin over her shoulder. She presses her smile into the side of his head before pulling back at a sudden shock of red along her peripheral vision.

"Hey, uh," she says. "Is that blood?"

"Hmmm?" he says, his chest vibrating against hers. "Oh, I was out . . . doing the thing. It's not mine, don't worry."

"Right," she says.

"That's incredible, Astrid," he says. "You're so fucking smart."

She closes her eyes and feels, for one single second, the entire electrifying universe.

"Thanks for coming over to tell me," Max says, his hand on hers, a tether to her physical form so she doesn't fly out into the expanse of the galaxy.

She had gotten the email and felt her whole body go cold but in a good way, like a glass of iced water after a long day or that first plunge into the deep end of the pool in the middle of summer. And her room had been so empty. She looked out at it and it felt weird, that she was going to have to wait for David to return, if he ever did, to have a witness for this overwhelming wave of validation.

And then, just like that, she remembered Max was just a street away with his beautiful eyes and warm arms.

The thought of losing this is more than ridiculous. To lose what she has with Max would be the most inefficient thing she could do.

"I'm taking the rest of the night off," she tells him. "As a reward."

His eyes widen. "Oh?"

She leans in. He closes his eyes and waits, eyelashes fanned down his cheeks.

"Oh," he says again.

When she kisses him, everything in the world slows down.

Once a week, she allows David to drag her out to work in the library even though it messes with her entire system of deliberately and precisely rationing her time.

Thankfully the need to set alarms is negligible—she never gets too caught up in things, always is aware of both the time, how long she's been doing something, and how long she has left to complete that task. It saves her from setting her phone loud enough to actually startle her out of some deep trance of work in a public place.

It's a fun little game though, always glancing at her phone a second or two before the little ping that tells her to move onto the next thing. Her itty-bitty superpower.

"You're a robot," David says. "A weird little robot person."

"I'm organized," she says.

"You're neurotic."

"I mean, yes, but being productive isn't really a part of the things that are wrong in my brain," she replies. She opens to a new notebook page, carefully writes down her heading: name, date, subject.

David hypothetically has a five-page essay due tomorrow at noon analyzing a novel that he's only fifty pages into. In the three hours they've been in the library, David has gone on four coffee trips and two bathroom breaks. When he's actually sitting at their table he has oscillated steadily between watching Vine compilations on his phone and watching book reviews on his computer.

"Tell me, robot," he says, setting aside book, phone, and computer to fully engage in conversation with her. She continues taking notes on her Chemistry reading. "Do you dream of electric sheep?"

"I never got that," she says. There's a table she probably has to memorize on page 113. She reaches for her pen and starts copying it over.

"Literature?" he asks. "Art?"

"People don't dream of sheep," she says. "They count sheep."

"People can dream of sheep," David protests.

"Yeah, but that's not how the saying goes," she says, shrugging. "It's not, 'Go dream of sheep.' It's, 'Count sheep.'"

David kicks her shin under the table.

"Not everything has to be so literal," he protests. "Robot."

"I'm not a robot," she says. Would that she was. No sleep, no meals, no panic attacks. Just ultimate efficiency, endless productivity. The uncomplicated life.

Granted, being a robot would limit her ability to enjoy the simpler things in life, like overpriced library coffee and the tingly feeling she gets in her chest when making out with

Max . . . but science is improving rapidly.

"You're so rote and mechanical," he sighs dramatically. "Where's the art? Where's the passion, Astrid?"

"Like the art of wasting hours on YouTube? Or your passion for sporty girls who forget your name in the morning?" It's a metaphorical kick under the table. She feels smug as she copies in another line of the chart. "Beep, boop. Does not compute."

"Fuck off," he says. "It's not my fault David is a bland name. I didn't pick it." His hand goes to the table, brushing for a second along his book before closing around his third latte of the day.

"Becoming a doctor is my passion," she says. There's not a particular need to defend herself. David makes robot jokes, and she ribs him for wearing socks with sandals in the dining hall and on and on until the day they kill each other.

But at the same time, she wants to tell him all the weird, original things that swirl around in her head so he'll think she's cool. Like issues she has with iconic science fiction titles and her hopes and dreams and all the secret gushy things she hates that she feels.

"Life is only so long," she continues as he sips his coffee. "So, it's important to optimize the time I have so I can accomplish everything that I want to before I kick the bucket."

"I can't believe you say things like 'kick the bucket,'" he says, shaking his head. "Why are we friends?" He grabs one of her highlighters and starts twirling it over his knuckles. "And you have no interest in seeing what life might have in store for you?" he continues. "Feeling it out, exploring, letting the wind move you."

"Nope," she says. "Feelings are messy and unreliable. I am more than satisfied exploring the different ways I can become a doctor as soon as possible."

"You're boring," David decides.

"Well, then find a more exciting friend and steal *their* highlighters."

David goes to the bathroom, or maybe to buy another coffee, or maybe to chat up the girl across the atrium he knows from his Zombie Fiction class. She takes a moment to appreciate the blessed loneliness, a quick respite from the need to constantly argue with him and actually get some—

"Hey, Astrid!"

She's never letting David talk her into coming to the library again.

"Hey, Ben," she says, and carefully tucks her Cell Bio notes away before looking up to face Ben Barnes with his carefully tucked polo shirt and thickly packed backpack hanging loosely off his shoulders.

"I heard you got into Vaughn's lab," he says.

How? "Uh, yeah. I start tomorrow."

"That's so exciting," he says. "I was in his lab last year. Changed my life. You know the application process is *super* competitive. It's *super* impressive that you got in without previous experience. Are you sure you're up to it? It can be pretty overwhelming if it's your first lab."

"Oh," she says. Ben fucking Barnes. He probably means every backhanded compliment. "Uh, I'm a fast learner."

"Right," he says, nodding, tugging on his backpack straps. "Well, let me know if you need any more notes. Cell Bio looks like it's gonna be pretty killer."

"Yeah, definitely. Same."

"Hang in there," he says, standing perfectly straight and still in front of her table. "Heard that the first Orgo Two midterm is next week, yikes, right?"

"Yep," she says and hopes he can't see how just hearing the word "Orgo" makes her entire stomach turn over.

"Man, I heard Professor Sousa is a hard grader too, no curve," he says, shaking his head. "Glad I got that out of the way freshman year with Douglas."

"Yeah, that was . . . probably smart." She wonders what superpower would be best to get her out of this moment: invisibility, teleportation, superspeed? She makes a note to ask Max about it later.

"Anyway, I've gotta run," he says. "I'm working at the Watts Lab this semester."

"I thought you were in the Heath Lab," she says.

"Oh, I still am. You know, I've also been thinking about doing another semester with Vaughn, too. It might be nice if he has someone actually experienced around. You might need an extra pair of hands."

"Right," she says, exhaling slowly. "That's awesome."

"Well, I'll see you in class tomorrow," he says.

He walks off before she's unclenched enough to nod politely, and she does not think about how he's a prodigy or how he's three years younger than she is and will graduate this semester and apply to med school and become a doctor years before her, because his brain is wired to absorb molecular structures and biological processes like a sponge, or how he doesn't even have to study for more than an hour to ruin a curve and subsequently her entire life.

She drops her head to the cool marble tabletop instead.

"Jesus fuck," David says as he returns to his seat. "What was that?"

"That was Ben Barnes," she says. "Child prodigy and human manifestation of my impostor syndrome."

"Oh, the guy from Calc Two last semester who gave you wrong answers when you were checking your problem set."

"Yep. But I did crush the curve for the final and bumped him down a half letter grade, so there's that."

David takes a sip of his drink, staring deeply into it.

"Fucking premeds."

She shows up for Eleanor's program orientation three minutes early thanks to an uncharacteristically cooperative subway.

The brownstone looks like every other brownstone she's ever seen, tasteful greenery by the side of the quiet street, and some flower beds alongside the steps leading to the front door. There is no buzzer at the door but after a few moments of floundering, a robotic voice sounds from one of the potted plants and takes her fingerprint before sending her inside.

The inside is more what she expected, a long minimalist hallway leading to an elevator. Sleek steel and glass doors show the ropes and walls of the tube. It moves so smoothly, for a moment she barely feels like she's moving at all.

The door opens directly into a thin, little gray room with a white desk that's all angles, perpendicular to the elevator. Equally full of angles, Eleanor types away on a desktop.

"Astrid," she says before she even looks up.

"Hi," Astrid says, stepping out of the elevator onto the hard marble floor of the office.

"Perfect." Eleanor stands and walks over, eyes moving ceaselessly from the screen to meet Astrid's. "Welcome to the Fridge." She gestures at the room. "I have a few more things to take care of out here but if you head down the hall you can join the rest of your class in our little waiting room before the tour starts."

"Right," Astrid agrees and moves slowly toward the hall.

In the waiting room, three younger teens sit uncomfortably at awkward stranger-distances on the long black couch: a small girl with pale skin and pale blond hair, straight and long down her back, bright eyes and a pink headband; a boy with sharp red hair, a healthy smattering of freckles, and more muscle than he seems to know what do with; another girl with warm bronze skin and thick black curls that cascade over her shoulders, wearing a long pendant necklace and an oversized flannel shirt.

"I'm Molly," the blond girl says after a few seconds of awkward silence. She leans forward. "That's Thomas and that's Lucy. Not that we know each other. We just met a few minutes ago, too."

"Um, I'm Astrid," Astrid says when Molly continues to stare at her. "Nice to meet you."

Molly nods eagerly and opens her mouth, a look in her eyes like a runner at the starting line, waiting for a gun to go off.

"I'm a sophomore in high school. I just started dating my boyfriend Arthur around a month ago," she says. "Arthur is, you know, a superhero. I don't think we're supposed to tell each other all the details for safety and everything, like we should probably pick either their civvy names or their hero names just to keep from getting confused. I personally feel more comfortable with using civvy names since I dunno about you, but it feels like it's probably better for security reasons than referring to my boyfriend by his hero name."

"Right," Astrid says slowly. Though everything feels slow in comparison to how Molly speeds along. "That makes sense."

"So, your boyfriend?" Molly asks. "Or girlfriend? Or partner?"

"Boyfriend," she says. "Max."

"That's such a cute name," Molly decides, eyes wide and serious. "I'm pretty sure it's on my baby name list; I love it. When did you two meet? How long have you been together?"

Lucy clears her throat.

"Right," Molly says, closing her eyes for a second and leaning back in her seat. "Right, you guys should go, too."

Lucy grimaces like that was not what she meant.

"Um," Thomas says. "I'm Thomas. My girlfriend's name is Allie." He pressed his lips together. "She's an alien . . . um, apparently."

"Arthur's an alien, too," Molly offers before clapping a hand over her mouth. She looks enthused.

Thomas . . . does not.

"Well, I'm Lucy," Lucy says. "As has been established. My girlfriend is not an alien, so . . ."

"And her name is Jane," Molly adds. "Which is another name I love. It's *such* a classic."

"Why do you remember that?" Lucy asks, raising an eyebrow.

"Well, I'm like great with names," Molly says. She points at herself and moves clockwise. "Molly, Astrid, Lucy, Thomas. Hey, if you take our initials it spells MALT. That's cool."

Lucy looks like she has a lot of things she wants to say about that. Molly looks like she has even more to say back.

Thomas looks like he's slowly contemplating his existence in the universe, eyes miles away. Astrid gets it, wishes she was there with him, except not with him of course, just miles away, preferably in her room with a to-go box of dinner and her problem set.

"Okay," Eleanor says, stepping back in. "All set. We're ready to go. Follow me."

The computer lab in the Fridge is huge, but the computers are huger. The four of them each get their own wide table toward the front, the rest of the room empty and sleek gray, cold from the unending hum of air-conditioning. Eleanor stands at the front of the room and clicks through a PowerPoint that lists out code words and safe house locations.

Astrid was forced to leave her phone outside, and she's not allowed to take notes. For security. They have been assigned a mandatory online quiz following Eleanor's lecture to ensure they have everything memorized.

She should be worrying about the BioChem homework she needs to go over a few more times but there's something thrilling about the challenge of memorizing information without notes for reference.

"You can take as long as you need," Eleanor says at the end of her lecture.

Astrid leans forward, presses her feet flat against the marble floor.

At the table to her right, Molly shifts in her seat, pushing her hair behind her ears.

It's not a competition. It's not a competition, this is not a real class, and there are no grades. But when you earn the title Astrid the Great and Terrible Curve Destroyer in sophomore year of high school, it becomes a mindset, a way of life.

While Eleanor's heels click solidly on the marble as she walks out of the room, Astrid is already clicking past the first two title slides and diving into the material.

She doesn't need a notebook or a planner. She is evolved. There's a piece of paper in her head and she can turn it into a to-do list as she quickly scans through the PowerPoint.

Things to memorize: *Locations and addresses, passwords, security levels, emergency protocol levels (i.e. Code Green = rampant, full-bodied, shape-shifter invasion), other examples include—*

"Hi."

Astrid flinches, jerking back from the computer screen, the imaginary pen in her head scraping against the imaginary page.

Molly stands next to her desk, leaning up against the side of it and smiling brightly.

"Hi," Astrid says, after a moment of intense eye contact.

"Do you want to work together?" she asks, tilting her head so her hair spills over her shoulder.

Astrid glances carefully at the row behind them. Thomas is leaning back in his chair, eyes glued on his screen, eyebrows drawn together. Lucy props up her head with one arm on the table as she clicks through the slides.

Molly still watches her, grin unwavering.

"Uh, sure," Astrid says.

Molly claps twice, fluttering in place like a small bird. She drags her chair over from her desk, a squeaky wheel cutting through the stillness of the room.

The other two glance up from their monitors.

"Sorry," Molly says. "You guys wanna work together, too?"

Lucy shakes her head. Thomas starts to pull his chair over.

"So," Astrid says, shifting her attention over to the PowerPoint, leaning back so the two of them can watch over her shoulder.

"You go to PS 130, right?" Molly asks, spinning her chair to face Thomas's.

"Um, yeah," Thomas says. "How do you—?"

"I'm a cheerleader for Jones and I'm as good with faces as I am with names," she says. She bounces a little in her chair. "You're tight end for the football team, right?"

Astrid follows the conversation mildly, glancing between the two of them. Molly, small and stick thin and practically vibrating with energy. Thomas and his bulging biceps and triceps, squared shoulders and steady posture.

She reaches carefully for the keyboard and uses the arrow keys to subtly flip through the PowerPoint, facing the two of them but watching the screen out of the corner of her eye.

The chatter is kinda nice. Their voices are smooth and bounce in the air lightly. It feels a little like being on the top floor of the library during rush hour or listening to white noise generators while trying to fall asleep. She should record them and play it back while she's studying for Orgo next week.

"Where do you go to high school?" Thomas asks.

The chatter drifts off.

Oh, he's facing her—he's asking her. Molly's facing her, too. She abruptly remembers that she exists on this physical plane and is not a floating piece of brain matter memorizing addresses.

"Um, I'm in college," she says, and shrugs. Her fingers hover over the arrow keys.

"You're in college?" Lucy says from her desk. She was

listening in from afar. Astrid, considering picking up a minor in self-isolation, feels a vague kinship with her.

Molly has stopped bouncing. Thomas's eyebrows raise, wrinkling his forehead.

"Yeah, I'm a soph—" she offers before all three interrupt:

"Where do you go?"

"Are you living in a dorm?"

"What was your application essay about?"

During the interrogation, Lucy has dragged her chair closer.

Astrid would text Max to let him know she's going to miss dinner, but it looks like she won't get her phone back for a while.

After the quiz, they all walk down the one very long hallway. Molly finished first and insisted on waiting for them—and then Astrid, who finished right after her, felt weird trying to leave alone. Despite the past hour and a half talking, they still stand at that stranger-distance, an awkward clumping that suggests they're walking toward the same place but that's the limit to what's sustaining the conversation.

"You already know so much about this," Lucy says to Molly. Her voice barely reaches Astrid, who is nearly dissociating in her stress. "I'm surprised you failed that bizarre kidnapping test Eleanor sprung on us."

"Uh," Astrid says. "What bizarre kidnapping test?"

Molly turns to her, practically walking backward, head tilted and eyes wide. "Eleanor's test? You know how she gets her hero friends to volunteer and surprise attack to see how well you're prepared for real threats."

"Oh . . ." Astrid pauses, considering. "Uh, I just got regular kidnapped then."

"Wow," Molly says, swinging her backpack on her shoulder. On a second glance, Astrid realizes that her backpack is not a backpack but a large pastel shoulder bag she's somehow fit all her books in. "I think I might have done better if my test had been the real thing. One of the heroes who kidnapped me was Green Hawk, and I had such a crush on him when I was like eight. I was. . . starstruck."

"What about you, quarterback?" Lucy says, jerking her head toward Thomas who is wearing his backpack off one shoulder and watching his feet like he's about to trip over something. "You failed your test?"

"Yeah," Thomas says.

"How?" Lucy asks.

He shrugs. "I don't wanna talk about it."

"Well, you'll get the chance to take it again," Molly offers. She keeps zigzagging across the hallway, getting close to whoever she's speaking to. "You know, at the end of this whole thing."

"Why would anyone want to do that again?" Lucy asks, shaking her head. Off Molly goes so she's walking in stride with her.

"I'm pretty excited to try again," she says. "And I think it's a really cool way to show that we've learned enough, like if you can pass this test you're good to go."

"Wait," Astrid says, even though the elevator is in sight and she can almost get away from this conversation without having to say anything more. "So if we take this fake kidnapping test and pass, we get out of the Program?"

And then Molly is right by her elbow, nodding frantically. "Well yeah, the whole philosophy is that if we could avoid getting kidnapped in a safe, simulated experiment of it, we could avoid getting kidnapped in the real thing. So, if we can't pass then we probably need to keep trying at it until we can."

"Right." Astrid nods slowly, and lets Molly press the button to call the elevator. The thing is, she knows what a shortcut looks like, and more importantly, knows that you should never ever pass one up, scenic route be damned.

Max is in her dorm when she gets back, sitting awkwardly on the edge of her bed, like he's never been there before, like they haven't made out against every surface on her side of the room.

"Did you superhero your way in here?" she asks, rolling her bag off her shoulders and setting it down against the side of her desk.

He hops off her bed and up to her.

"No, uh, David let me in," he says, rubbing the back of his neck.

"But you could totally superhero in through the window if you wanted to?" she confirms.

"I mean, it's only the tenth floor, so yeah, but your window is on the street side so I probably couldn't without exposing the whole double life thing I've got going on."

It's a little bit infuriating the way her body just leans toward Max every time he's near, like a plant to the sun. His soft, dopey eyes have a gravitational force strong enough to wrinkle the space-time fabric.

She steps toward him and rests her forehead against his shoulder. His lips brush against her temple, arms slipping around her waist. It's too easy to close her eyes, take a micro nap against his T-shirt. It's the most sleep she'll get for the foreseeable future.

"How'd it go?" he asks.

"My head is a Jackson Pollock of color-coded emergency protocols," she grumbles. "And I gave a lecture to a bunch of scared high schoolers about the college application process."

"Oh?" he says. "That sounds . . . um . . ."

"I think I'm tutoring one of them for PreCalc on Tuesdays now," she says. "Add it to the schedule. I'm not even sure what highlighter colors I have left."

"Sounds rough," he says, bone-deep empathy in the way he reaches for her hand. She shrugs. Being near Max makes anything remotely stressful feel distorted and distant, fuzzy so it can't hurt her. "I grabbed you a to-go box from the dining hall."

Heart aflutter, stomach a-grumble, she lifts her head and kisses him soundly.

He's smiling when she pulls away, a small, proud thing.

"Steamed broccoli?" she asks, spotting the cardboard box on the foot of her bed.

"Of course," he says, moving over to claim her empty chair while she reaches in her desk for her collection of reusable plastic forks.

"How do you feel about a July wedding?"

It's not an outright confirmation or confession of any kind of gooey feelings, but they don't need that. They just need this. Quiet nights where she eats over a problem set, and he plays a DS ROM on his laptop next to her.

But then he jumps to his feet, eyes wide before she's even pulled open all the tabs she needs on her laptop.

"I, uh, just remembered I have a, uh . . ." He blinks, head tilting. "Wait, you know," he says, like it's the most amazing thing. And then exhales with a little grin that makes her chest go warm and her toes go numb. He reaches into his pocket, holds out something that looks like a higher-tech version of the pagers Astrid knows from *Scrubs*. "Team-up alert. I gotta—" He gestures at the door, still looking so relieved and amazed.

"Uh, have fun," she says. He hops backward with a little skip step and smiles one more giant, bright smile before swinging the door open and shutting it behind him.

She stares at the door for a second and wonders if there's some sort of pamphlet or color-coded guide for what she's supposed to feel about this. Maybe a chart to match the strange, sinking feeling in her stomach and the deep sigh that weighs on her chest to a category of emotion. At the very least, with

Max gone, she can get some work done. Pushing her feet off the frame of her bed, she lets her desk chair spin around and then scoots her chair in, grabbing a fork with one hand and reaching for her laptop to send an email to Eleanor Olsen re: The Test.

FRESHMAN FALL
ORIENTATION WEEK

HER FIRST WEEK OF COLLEGE, ASTRID RETURNED to her dorm from the mailroom, struggling up the narrow staircase with two Amazon boxes balanced in front of her, a care package from her mother tucked under her arm, and a cheap, unassembled nightstand between her chin and the other boxes.

Somehow, she made it to her hall and inched along, every breath and every step a careful, measured movement. Which didn't help at all when she spotted a person rushing down the hall seconds too late to do anything about it.

The crash was explosive.

"Oh my God. Oh, I'm so sorry. I can't believe I wasn't looking. That was so dense of me."

"Hey, Max," she said, because of course it was Max, miles and months away from high school and the last time she had seen him, talked to him, thought of him. For a moment they stood in the middle of the hallway, most of her boxes still tumbling over each other on the floor. It was hard to be surprised. It was hard to imagine anyone else causing such physical chaos. Like the second she had been placed on a path where a horrific crash was inevitable, Max was summoned from a different corner of the universe, the god of mild pedestrian disasters.

He seemed surprised to see her, though, enough to stop stammering through his apologies, stop scrambling to grab all her stuff. He just blinked at her with his wide, deep brown eyes.

"Hi," he said and blinked some more. Something was different about him.

"Hey," she repeated, carefully retrieving one of her boxes he had caught somehow. Their fingers brushed and she wanted to roll her eyes because she was legally an adult now. The time to have a fluttering crush on Max Martin had come and gone along with all four years of high school.

"We should, um, probably stop meeting like this," he said, handing over a few more boxes. His hair was the same, tufty curls, a deep brown. His eyes, his nose, the shape of his eyebrows.

He helped her carry her stuff back to her door and it was very gentlemanly and a bit of a godsend because she didn't have a plan for getting her keys out of her back pocket before.

She dropped her boxes onto her bed while he shuffled around dopily in her doorway for a few seconds.

"It's really great seeing you," he said, like it hadn't been only

81

a summer since they were last in class together. The bags under his eyes, always deep purple and puffy, were gone. Faded like he'd been sleeping the whole four months since the last time she saw him, grabbing a coconut macaroon at a graduation party.

And more than that, when she looked at him, he was looking back. Something about him felt settled and present, his eyes focused like he was actually here and not on whatever planet he spent most of high school.

"Well, now you know where to find me," she said, shrugging.

In her great big life plan, she was supposed to start dating in med school, get married somewhere between then and her first residency.

College, like high school, was about school, grades, and résumé building, no time for anything else.

So she pretended she didn't notice how wonderful he looked, how full and happy and here, and how it made her want to smile and move in closer and put off the schedule building she had to do that afternoon to ask him about it. Instead she closed the door behind him without watching him retreat down the hall and tried very hard to shake it off.

Friends never just happened to Astrid. In high school, she mostly stumbled into them, not literally like with Max, but in her smaller clubs and classes when it was impossible to not know everyone in a room. College was a different beast. There were so many people in her classes, and they were all lectures so the only people who talked were the professors and know-it-alls, like her.

It took a few days, but she identified three freshmen with the most potential to fit well with her and she worked through every ensuing anxiety attack about whether she's even worthy of human attention and why she was even born. She took a breath, marched herself down to the dining hall, made herself a plate of rubbery pasta, and assertively dropped herself down next to the first promising candidate.

Well, that was the plan anyway.

She did sit down next to the redhead from her Biology section only to find her already deep in conversation with three other girls farther down the table. It was the wrong angle to get her attention, and Astrid decided in seconds to stop staring and leaning in before she made a fool of herself.

She busied herself trying to puncture a piece of pasta with her plastic fork, ignoring the churning mess of insecurities in her chest, blocking out the endless chattering of the cafeteria, trying to breathe because everything was fine, really. She was not overwhelmed, she was not bursting at the seams with icky feelings of humiliation and shame and dread. She was just breathing and trying to eat some terrible pasta.

And then a boy with a dark buzz cut, dark brown skin, and bulky wireless headphones sat across from her, an ideal position to strike up a conversation.

"You're braver than I am," he said.

Which was ridiculous, she wasn't brave. She was just sitting here in the cafeteria, and yeah, it was kind of gnawing at her—but since when was surviving a public outing considered brave.

He had gestured to the pasta though.

She shrugged, tried a little harder to skewer a single piece with her fork. "A life of fear is a life half lived."

"Here," he said, holding out his fork, actual cutlery. She'd been avoiding the silverware for two days, ever since grabbing a metal spoon still crusty with day-old yogurt.

It would be rude to reject the gesture, so she traded him.

"Thanks," she said and jabbed the fork into her mountain of pasta.

"You're in my Calc lecture," he said.

"Oh," she said. The pasta was ridiculously dry, and she chewed it for approximately five years.

"You ask too many questions," he added.

"Thank you."

He grinned but tightly, like he didn't want to, like he was trying not to break and start laughing.

"David," he said.

"Astrid."

SOPHOMORE SPRING

WEEK THREE

M Cell Bio Problem Set 2; BioChem
Pre-lab; Beth Israel Volunteering 5-7

T Cell Bio Pre-lab; Physics Pre-lab; Orgo 2 read ch. 17; LAB 1-5

W BioChem Problem Set 2; BioChem read ch. 2

Th Orgo 2 Problem Set 2; BioChem Lab Report; Physics Lab Report;
Women in Lit read Rowlandson, *Narrative of the Captivity*; LAB
1-5

F ORGO 2 MIDTERM 1; Physics Problem Set 2; Cell Bio Lab Report;
LAB 3-5

TIP OF THE WEEK

"Your partner will not show up on time. Not to dinners, not to dates, not to meeting with your friends, not to family events, and maybe not even to your rehearsal dinner for your wedding. And it's easy enough to rationalize this to yourself, and to get used to it, but no one else in your life will understand. So prepare for a lot of

arguments with your mom about whether or not you're throwing your life away for some good-for-nothing who isn't even a lawyer."
—*Wally Watson*

ASTRID DOESN'T GET ANGRY A LOT. SHE DOESN'T have the time to.

But her blood is starting to boil, sitting in Vaughn's lab, staring at the back of Ben Barnes's head as he continues to hog the only microscope.

It's been an hour. And if she could run a different experiment right now, she would—but she also came in to find that someone had used the last of the pre-poured gels. She doesn't know if it was him. But at the same time, she knows it was him, it was absolutely him, she can feel it in her gut.

There are schedules. Vaughn explained all this at orientation last week, and Astrid found it all very comforting. Schedules are sort of her thing. But schedules mean that there are things she needs to do today in the four hours of lab and there's only so much longer she can flip through last week's graphs before someone realizes she isn't doing anything.

She still can't believe Ben actually did it. But sure enough, she showed up this morning and there he was, with his own desk and computer and that condescending smile. It seems like he did it just to spite her, but now he's here, in her space again, and the only other person in the room, a postdoc named Raj, doesn't seem like the type to notice anything outside his own cell cultures. So, she swallows her pride and her fear and reminds herself that asking for help when you need it is a sign of maturity.

She stands and walks over to Raj's desk.

"Hi," she says, hands folded in front of her. His shoulders tense and he looks up slowly.

"Yeah?"

She clears her throat. "Do you know where the other microscope is?" she asks, shifting her weight carefully to one leg and then back.

Raj sighs. "Uh, no," he says. "It went missing a few nights ago."

"Oh?" she says. "Missing?" She's not exactly sure how a microscope goes missing—how do you lose track of something that weighs approximately thirty pounds?—but at the same time, she's also not sure how someone would steal something that's approximately thirty pounds.

"You didn't see anything, did you?" he asks, scanning her up and down.

"Me?" she squeaks. She didn't see anything last time she was in because she was too busy having a panic attack that her first round of cell culture plates would be anything less than perfect.

"Well," he says. "I think one of the post-bachs propped the door open. Did Dr. Vaughn give you the rundown on lab safety and security protocol? 'Cuz it's really important."

She nods vigorously, feeling her teeth clack together. She stands there for another second, palms sweating.

"So . . . just the one microscope then," she finally tries.

"Unless someone steals that one too," he mutters, and turns back to his computer.

"Well, thanks," she says and steps back awkwardly. He presses his lips together in a grim smile without turning from his screen.

She exhales hard, running a hand over her face before heading for the back of the lab.

"Hey," she says from a few feet away. Ben snaps up from the microscope and leans an arm over his desk.

"What?" he asks, sharp enough that Astrid winces.

"Uh, are you gonna be done with the microscope any time soon?" she asks.

He shrugs. "How am I supposed to know?"

"Well there's only one now," she says. "So, uh . . . I need that one, like, sometime soon to stay on schedule with my cell cultures."

"Oh," he says, leaning back in his seat. "Don't worry about it. Vaughn just has you doing the basic stuff. He barely needs your results so, like, it's not a problem if they're a little late."

He smiles briefly and ducks back down to peer into the microscope.

She stands for a second, staring. Her hand is in a fist she doesn't remember making. She briefly contemplates grabbing him by the back of his Vineyard Vines shirt and throwing him out the large glass windows.

He doesn't look up again and she finds herself walking back to her desk on autopilot. The same three graphs are still up and she stares at them for a second before letting her forehead fall to the cool desktop, and squeezing her eyes shut.

So apparently there is one perk to her new weekly training session at the Fridge, and it's that this week they're learning how to properly hit people with baseball bats. And swinging with all her might at a foam dummy is a lot more effective than screaming into a pillow, which is going to save her maybe fifteen minutes after dinner tonight. (She's not pretending the dummy is Ben Barnes. But she's also not *not* pretending it's Ben Barnes.)

The dummies themselves have some kind of high-tech gizmos that register how effective each hit she lands is because there's apparently a right and wrong way to hit someone really hard with a baseball bat.

Down the line, Lucy swings hard and gets three hundreds in a row. The program gives a little celebratory ding and she gets to leave early.

Which is fine. Astrid is absolutely fine with not being the best in this class and not getting a little celebratory ding before everyone else or leaving early to study for her Orgo midterm on Friday or maybe take a shower because the hygiene situation is honestly starting to get a little desperate. It doesn't matter at all.

Molly hits a bunch of hundreds as well a couple of minutes later and goes off to find Eleanor to ask her additional questions about the syllabus. But Thomas, in his corner of the room, keeps swinging away as hard as he can, the little screen in front of him flashing high sixties or low seventies.

After a score in the mid-fifties, he drops his bat to the ground with a resounding clanging noise and lets out a deep guttural groan. Astrid winces in sympathy, feeling the pressure of her own deep guttural groan that's been sitting pretty on her chest since the first day of the semester and also probably a million years before that.

She tries another half-hearted swing at her dummy but feels bad about it when Thomas doesn't pick up his bat and instead drops to a crouch, burying his face in his hands.

Astrid takes a step back and leans her bat up against the back wall.

"Um, hey," she says, inching toward Thomas, and immediately wants to hit herself in the face with a baseball bat. "What's . . . up?"

"I'm on the baseball team," Thomas starts, so Astrid hasn't done the worst job in the world at starting this conversation. "I don't know why I'm so bad at this! I shouldn't be."

Right. Okay, she can do this.

"Maybe . . . there's something wrong with your sensor," she offers. "Like it's not registering properly. You could try one of the other—"

"It's not my sensor," he says, shoulders slumping. "It's me."

"Oh," Astrid says. She wonders briefly if she should try placing a comforting hand on his shoulder or something. "I'm sure that's not true."

"This isn't how things are supposed to be," he says. He stands again, crossing his arms tightly over his chest. "This isn't how our relationship was supposed to be. We were—we were supposed to be . . . bowling and playing mini golf and—and having movie nights. And I'm supposed to, like, give her my jacket when it's cold, but instead she's, like, never cold because she has some internal heating thing. And we're supposed to be, like, going to homecoming together and instead she's on a spaceship somewhere with all these other super-tough alien dudes and . . ." He trails off with another groan.

Which means that he's done talking and she should probably respond, but she doesn't know how to. She never had any expectations of her relationship with Max, not like that, cutesy dates and dances and any of those milestones. She finds her romance in the way they move in close to hear each other in the dining hall, the way he always takes her hand when they're walking together across campus and waits until the last second to let go when they part ways, the way they have to squeeze to sit next to each other on either of their twin XLs, the way they try and fail to hold conversations while working until they give in to a break, sitting on the floor and sharing secret doubts and fears.

Or well, the way they used to . . . it's been a busy semester. For both of them.

"I, uh, get what you mean," she offers Thomas. "Like, I didn't exactly expect to be spending my Tuesday afternoons learning to hit people with bats. If I think about it too long it makes my brain want to melt."

Thomas doesn't fully relax or anything, but his eyebrows knit together like he's thinking.

"And I think it kinda sucks to have to limit things to what you think they should be," she adds. "I mean, just because I'm dating a superhero, it shouldn't mean I have to be just like Eleanor. First of all, I don't think I could even come close to being like Eleanor, and also I hate pencil skirts so"—she gestures vaguely to the bat on the ground—"you can know how to hit a baseball but it might not help you hit a person."

It gets Thomas to pick up the bat again, which makes her feel briefly triumphant as she heads back to her station. The feeling does fade when he finishes before her and she spends fifteen minutes completely alone in the gym.

On the subway back to campus, she reschedules her entire night in the schedule on her phone. She ends up eating dinner in the shower.

Wednesday nights are Roomie Nights this semester. David has musical rehearsals Tuesdays and Thursdays, she has Women in Medicine meetings Mondays and homework for most of the weekend while he hits up frat parties. So, Wednesdays.

They put on a movie (an Oscar-nominated biopic about Captain Jericho with a throwaway line around the forty-five-minute mark about Kid Comet that makes her choke on her ice cream), but like always they mostly ignore it to talk in the dark. It's a little classier this year, now that they share a double and each have a bed to stretch out on instead of the floor of her cramped freshman year single.

"I just really wasn't prepared for the culture shock," David says in that strangely quiet voice he pulls out during Roomie

Nights. "And I didn't grow up in some super rural town or any-thing—it was a relatively populated area—but, like, our big attractions were the open plaza where we sometimes had live music and the good Culver's by the highway. It was a big deal when the lake rose an extra foot. And now, it's like I went to see a show at Lincoln Center for a class last week and we had to evacuate because Mystic-Man tried to blow up the building with a magic spell."

She tries not to tense as she suddenly realizes why Max missed dinner last week, and just nods along. "That's New York."

"I love it," David says. "But it, like, terrifies me just a little."

"I was on a school bus that almost got thrown off a bridge," she says. She doesn't even have to think about saying it. It's Roomie Night. Any and all traumas are fair game.

"Jesus," he says. He laughs a little, the way you do when you hear something shocking and don't know how else to respond. She almost joins him.

"It was bad. One of the most terrifying moments of my life," she says.

"Yeah," David says. "I sure hope so."

On his tiny laptop screen across the room, Captain Jericho holds together a severed cable on the Throgs Neck Bridge, muscles bulging in spandex as he strains to keep the roadway from collapsing.

"I think it kinda made me who I am," she says. Which doesn't make as much sense out loud as it did in her head. "I dunno. Things like that, you survive them and then take stock of yourself. I felt like I could count every minute of my life in that moment. So after, I . . . stopped wasting time."

"Yet, here we are," David says.

"This isn't wasting time," she says. "This is building necessary social connections so I don't completely lose touch with humanity."

"So you're saying if not for me and Max you'd go full Dr. Midnight?" he asks.

She fights the wince, again, and tries to not think about Eleanor Olsen's love life.

"More Max than you," she says. He shakes his head.

"And how is Max these days?" David asks, and she can tell he's grinning in a way that she hates, moving his eyebrows all around the way he can because he's something of an actor. "How's the meticulously scheduled sex?"

"There's no Max sex," she says, already grimacing.

"By choice? 'Cuz that's cool—"

"Not by choice. I'm too busy. I haven't done the proper preparatory research anyway."

"The proper preparatory research," he echoes. "Astrid, if you need to learn about the birds and the bees I would be honored to tell you all—"

"Stop," she says, gagging just a little. "I know how sex works. It's just . . . you know, it would be my first time, and his from what I can tell, and so I feel like we should make a whole occasion of it and take our time and stuff, and that's just not something I can do between classes and lab and volunteering and the Prog—probably . . . d-dozens of other things I need to do." It's maybe the clumsiest attempt at a save in the world but David doesn't bat an eye.

"It doesn't need to be a big deal," David offers. "Like my first time was just a Saturday my junior year that I spent with this girl I really liked from my PreCalc class."

"I know," she says. "But . . . it's Max and it just felt right to take things slow at first because we've known each other so long and didn't want to jump into anything before we could find our footing. Like if we weren't going to work and had to find a way to be friends again, it would be way weirder. And then over the summer with my parents moving to Maryland, we were basically long distance. And anytime during the semester I'm always thinking a little bit about classes all the time, even when we're making out, and I really don't want to be thinking about classes when we're that physically intimate."

"Oh my God, please just say sex," David says. She kicks a throw pillow at him. It doesn't bridge the divide between their beds, just flops to the floor between them. He actually looks serious for once when he asks, "Do you love him?"

Yes.

Except it's a lot more complicated than that, and she's never been the best judge of how she's feeling at any given moment. She falls back on facts and schedules and lists; she compartmentalizes to the point where it warps back around into an unhealthy coping mechanism.

"What is love?" she says before the silence becomes incriminating.

"Baby, don't hurt me," David says blandly. "Look, I know this might be actually impossible for you, but don't overthink it. He makes you happy and that's a good thing. That can be enough."

"I thought you said you don't have any relationship advice," she says, even though the panic in her chest is calming.

"That wasn't relationship advice," he says. "That was Astrid advice. I'm pretty good at that."

She smiles and feels her eyes get a little watery, but it's okay because they're in the dark so he can't see and she doesn't have to explain it away.

She gets a call from Max as she's leaving the lab on Thursday after four excruciating hours of reading through introductory materials and watching different machine tutorials while Ben Barnes hogged the rotovap and wouldn't even let her watch because it was "classified intellectual property."

"Hey," she says, leaning into the phone, feeling her shoulders drop just like that, just at the thought of talking to him. "You know, thanks for calling. David keeps making fun of me for using my phone to make actual phone calls to people besides my parents."

"Are you outside?" he asks. He's breathing heavy and there's a static over the line like a car rushing by.

"Yeah, I'm walking back from Dr. Vaughn's lab right now," she says. "I think I've decided Ben Barnes is my nemesis.

Convince me to not stop in the cafeteria and grab some doughnuts."

"Just . . . uh, I'm dealing with a thing," he says.

"A thing?" she echoes. There's another whooshing sound
and then something like a boom. "Oh, a . . . Thing. What's
going on? Are you alright?"

"Uh, ask me in like an hour," he says. "Shit! Hang on."

She presses her lips together, quickly approaching the fork
in the road that will lead her toward the dining hall. On the
line there's more whooshing and static and heavy breathing
and then quiet.

"Hey," he says after a particularly stressful second of silence,
and she exhales. "Okay, I just . . . I'm up at City College and
I'm dealing with this new guy, he's calling himself Rat Boy.
It's a long story, basically he wants to release this bioweapon
that'll turn everyone in a fifty-block radius into a rat person,
and campus is within fifty blocks from here so you should
probably get inside."

"Oh," she says. "Okay . . . uh, should I warn other people?"

"They already have one up on local news. I just know you've
been in lab all day."

It's sweet, but she's still a little caught up on the whole bioweapon, rat person thing.

"I've got it under control," he says, like he can hear her
stress. "I'm pretty sure I've got it under control."

Right. Well then. That confidence won't really do much for
her anxiety, but at least he's feeling strongly about it.

"I guess no doughnuts then," she says and speeds up a little, tightening her grip on her backpack straps.

"It'll be fine," he says. "I just wanted to let you know."

"Well, thanks," she says, because it is a nice gesture at the very least, even though her plans for the afternoon now include calling David and boarding up the windows to their dorm with old cardboard boxes.

"Oh, shit," he says, and something on his end makes a loud, ugly sound. "Okay, I gotta go. Love you."

The call ends, and she should keep heading to her dorm but instead she almost trips over her own feet as she comes to a stop in the middle of the walkway.

He's never said that before.

It's been implied several times, but he's never actually said that before.

She exhales, shoulders slumping, and stares up at the sky, steadily darkening even though it's only 5:34.

"What do I do with that?" she asks the sky and the campus and the squirrel scampering across the path ahead of her.

She dials David and speeds back to the dorm.

FRESHMAN FALL
WEEK THREE

SHE WASN'T SURE WHEN EXACTLY SHE AND David had decided to spend every weekend night in her room watching movies on sketchy websites that were slowly poisoning her laptop, but it had been a few weeks so it basically counted as a part of her routine.

Which meant she was particularly frustrated when he stopped the movie one Friday night and hopped to his feet.

"Let's go out," he said petulantly. "I want to drink shitty alcohol and break a law."

"We're watching this movie illegally." She pushed up onto her knees to level the playing field a bit against his height. "Isn't that exciting enough for you, David?"

Apparently it wasn't.

So she got changed and they went out. David could somehow sense a party at fifty yards and managed to convince a tipsy frat bro that he knew someone who knew someone who was a pledge.

"I hate this," she said, stepping into the noisy, crowded room.

"Don't be a stereotype," David replied, holding her hand. He had to shout a little to be heard over the ruckus.

"I don't hate parties," she said. "But it's too hot in here, everything smells like booze, and I can't even hear the music, but I know it's bad." It was also dark and damp, a sea of bodies she could barely keep from drowning in. The floor was cold, craggy basement stone littered with plastic cups and napkin corpses and . . . great, some unopened condoms. There was the opposite of fresh air—stale, old, used air—suffocating the entire room. The flashing rave lights made her worry about epileptic seizures and had her feeling like time was jerking along in short tugs. It only sort of made her feel like she couldn't breathe. Otherwise, the overstimulated buzzing in her brain was almost soothing.

"If you let go of my hand, I'm never speaking to you again," she said, shoving forward to shout in the direction of his ear. A body she recognized by build alone as a lacrosse player stumbled into her, sending her bumping back into someone else.

"Is that really all I have to do?" David teased but pulled her along anyway.

He turned right sharply and again she had to wonder what he was looking for, what the purpose of this exercise in misery was.

They rounded a pillar and David pushed off just as someone stumbled between them. Astrid slammed into another stranger except this time it was a head-on collision and not a stranger because—

"Max," she said, his face illuminated for a single second by bright white light before it flickered out again.

"Astrid," he said, bracing his hands on her shoulders before struggling to take a step back. She hadn't seen him since that day in the dorm and found herself shocked all over again, by how different college Max looked. David stopped and turned and was now staring at her in amusement. "Hi. Hey. Wow, I'm sorry 'bout that. We always just kinda"—he bumped his hands together—"don't we."

"Are you drunk?" she asked. He was so loose and uninhibited, his shoulders void of tension, his smile wide and free, his eyes alight. She wasn't sure what to do about it. Well, there was nothing to do about it, but her sober, high-strung brain kept spinning wheels like there was something there to work through.

"I don't think so," he said. "Can't really get drunk because of my . . . um, high tolerance. Yeah, I've got a super-high tolerance. For alcohol. It's the noise and everything, really does a number on the senses. My completely normal senses." He winced, nose wrinkling up.

"Hi," David said, stepping in a little closer and tugging on her arm.

It felt too weird seeing them next to each other like this, in this dank, dark basement with music so muffled and loud she could feel the bass shake in her chest. David and Max belonged in different universes.

"Um," she said. "David, this is Max. Max, David."

"Oh, hi," Max said, spinning back to smile at David, holding his hand out at the most awkward angle she'd even seen.

He was wearing a tank top and for another millisecond she saw him lit up, saw a bicep so defined it was counterintuitive to everything she'd ever learned about Max. Another flash from the lights traced a drip of sweat along his jaw. She swallowed hard.

She averted her eyes quickly. Which was ridiculous. He was just sweating. And sweat was just the body's response to heat, water droplets that evaporate to cool the skin, simple as that, nothing . . . more to it.

"Astrid was going to waste away in her dorm watching *Aristocats* so I dragged her out here," David said. God, why were they trying to hold a conversation? It was too loud.

"It's a great film," she said for lack of anything else to say. This conversation was an eight-hour international flight out of her comfort zone.

"What?" Max asked, eyebrows creasing. He leaned in and she was going to have to repeat the most foolish sentence she'd ever said aloud.

"It's a great film," she said into his ear, wincing slightly. She thought she saw, for a split second, a shiver pass over him when her breath hit his neck.

"I'm trying to get me and Astrid some drinks," David said. "Do you know . . . ?"

"Yeah," Max said, nodding. "Yeah, keep heading straight, take a left at that couple, uh . . . doing . . . that . . . against the wall and it's right up ahead."

David squeezed her hand and nodded. "Thanks," he said, and then super casually, "Hey, do you want to come with?"

She tried desperately to mouth a subtle *Fuck you*. She doubted he could make it out, but for a second she thought she heard Max snort.

"Sure," Max said, bouncing on the balls of his feet. She pinched David's thumb and carefully plotted his murder.

Somehow Max was even better at navigating the room than David, stumbling along, clearing a path with his wide shoulders and overflowing apologies. They ended up against a plastic foldout table littered with empty bottles and broken cups.

She carefully measured out three cups of the dollar store tequila David decided to poison them with before she's dragged back into the fray of the dance floor. They stood in a little triangle and swayed and jumped to whatever beat they could make out. Astrid couldn't distinguish a single song, only able to follow along because Max could apparently hear everything and knew every song well enough to hum along.

She looked up from her feet for the first time in maybe an hour when David touched her arm and pulled her closer.

"Hey," he said. "I'm gonna go have sex with a cute girl."

"What?" she said, blinking up at him.

He gestured over his shoulder at a tall girl next to him, swaying a little off beat to the music. "Her name is Sarah. She's on the softball team," he explained. "We can walk you home first. Or . . ." He tilted his head at Max, who was busy apologizing to a much taller guy behind him.

"Or?" she demanded.

"Stay," David said, shrugging. "Enjoy the party a little longer. Let someone else walk you home."

She watched Max for another second, how he spun and jerked to the beat, bumped into Sarah not two seconds after he got back into the groove.

"He's cool, right?" David asked. "Like if you wanted to stay?"

"Yeah," she said. "Yeah, he's fine." *He's Max*, she almost said but that wouldn't have meant anything to David, who had absolutely no context for the inherent goodness of Max Martin.

"So, I can go?" David asked, stepping back toward Sarah.

"I hate you," she said. "I missed the best part of *Aristocats* so you could have sex."

David laughed, which probably meant he was a little drunk, but everyone else here was, too.

"Hey, I'm sure Max wouldn't mind watching *Aristocats*," he said, wiggling his eyebrows. "If you know what I mean." She wanted to punch him in the face.

He escaped with Sarah before she could enact any of her violent fantasies.

"Oh, hey," Max said, blinking. There was no triangle now.

She had to turn and face him head-on and she'd only had two shots of terrible tequila.

And Max was thoroughly more interesting than her feet, with the look on his face right now, so . . . happy and untamed as he bumped into person after person and apologized with a smile, then kept dancing to the godawful music.

He was a bad dancer, but in the stop motion of the lights it almost looked poetic.

Someone bumped into him from behind and he moved forward, closer to her, stumbling a little and she had to touch him, his arm, to help him steady himself. He was so warm like this. She could feel the heat from his body, and it was different from the oppressive heat from the rest of the basement. He was so . . . sweaty. She could still see the weird, crooked unevenness of his jawline, the way his nose had a little bump on the ridge like it'd been broken even though she knew Max had never been in a fight in his life.

He was so beautiful.

She choked a little, the thought bouncing around inside her like a reckless, disastrous pinball.

"Hey," she said hoarsely, hating every second. "Hey."

"Yeah?" He blinked at her.

"I'm not . . . I'm not feeling well. I think I should go."

It was like night and day. He was still just like that, loose-limbed and light on his feet, but with a single sentence he was focused again. "I'll walk you home."

"No," she said, shaking her head. "You're having fun. It's okay, I'll be—"

But he had already sprung into action, taking her hand gently and guiding her out of the basement, back toward fresh air and open spaces, leaving the heavy freedom of the party behind.

The cool air hit her harder than any drink had; a sudden clarity settled over her. The boundaries of her body existed again, out on the sidewalk where the cars and trees and buildings were lit by the warm, dim streetlights. What she was and what Max was reorganized themselves in her mind and it felt reassuring to be away from whatever swirling, churning void she was being dragged toward down in that basement.

Horribly, Max looked better out on the street, whole and uninterrupted, glowing and bright, his eyes clear and on her.

"Better?" he asked with this gentle intensity, like her being better was the most important thing in the world to him.

"Yeah," she said, feeling safe and grounded and overwhelmed and terrified and happy. But it made him smile, and then more than anything else, she just felt alive.

SOPHOMORE SPRING

WEEK FOUR

M Cell Bio Problem Set 3; BioChem Pre-lab; A.J. Fraction
Scholarship Dinner

T Cell Bio Pre-lab; Physics Pre-lab; Orgo 2 read ch. 16 & 18; LAB 1-5

W PHYSICS MIDTERM 1; BioChem Problem Set 3; BioChem read ch. 3

Th Orgo 2 Problem Set 3; BioChem Lab Report; Physics Lab Report;
Women in Lit read *Jane Eyre* pps. 1 - 153; LAB 1-5

F Physics Problem Set 3; LAB 3-5

TIP OF THE WEEK

*"Face your fear of large heights. And falling. And falling from large
heights. And you know, when falling from great heights, always
extend your limbs to increase air resistance. You will most likely
be caught, but it always helps to buy your partner some extra time
on the way down, just in case."*

—Daphne Dane

"I CAN'T BELIEVE YOU INVITED MAX TO YOUR super-special scholarship dinner and not me."

"He's my boyfriend, David."

"Oh, is that what we're calling it now?" He's throwing her stress ball at the ceiling. She watches it bounce and ricochet off the wall and his bed, as she waits for it to be an appropriate time to leave that will get her to the building exactly two minutes early.

"That's what we've been calling it, David," she says, wincing when the ball careens toward her desk. David lunges to catch it, almost braining himself on his desk chair. "Anyway, if he doesn't show, which he probably won't, you're my backup."

"Aw. She loves me."

"No, I just need an extra pair of hands to steal the food with."

"And why wouldn't Max show?"

"He's a total flake."

David snorts. "Max? Max Martin?" The disbelief is jarring. She has to remind herself that David didn't know Max in high school. Most of the time that David's known Max, Max hasn't been heroing. Something about that makes her stomach twist. "Drop-everything-for-you-in-a-heartbeat Max?"

"Yeah. He's been pretty busy this semester." She sighs. David doesn't say anything so she keeps going. "He was like this in high school. Absent and flighty and directionless."

"Well," David says. "That seems ridiculously out of character. The Max I know has one direction: you." He hums under his breath. "Do I have to have a talk with him?"

"No," she says. "No. He has good reason to be busy all the time. He, uh, he's doing a lot of work that's like really important for his . . . future, like, career-wise. It's fine."

David doesn't look convinced.

"And," she says, sitting up straighter, "we talk on the phone sometimes, when we're both too busy."

And they both are very busy. She's talked to Max on the phone more often than she's seen him this week, which has been strange because it kinda feels less like talking to Max and more like talking to Kid Comet, who is very Max-like but also is a lot more energetic and said he loved her that one time so . . .

"You live a block away."

"Our schedules aren't super compatible," she says, before frowning at the word choice.

David starts shaking his leg, his foot tapping an annoying beat against the wall. "That sucks."

She blinks at him. "That's what you've got. 'That sucks'?"

He tilts his head and blinks for a moment. "Yep."

She flips him off and stands, wobbling a little in her heels as she grabs the small wristlet from her desk. It bulges with all her IDs, a free froyo card, a debit and credit card. While David stares, she shoves in some assorted flash cards in case she has time to sneak in a bit of studying. Mercifully, he says nothing. With that, she's ready to go.

"Well thanks," she says. "See you never."

♦ ♦ ♦

Amazingly, Max is there waiting outside her building when she gets down. His hair is wet and wild like he just showered. His smile is contagious, and his button-down is a wine red that he looks so good in she almost suggests Kid Comet try a new color scheme.

"Hey," he says, breathless. "You look . . ."

"Yeah, same to you," she says. She slips her hand into his as they start down the street.

"Did you, uh, get my text?" she asks.

"Yes," he says. "There's a plastic Tupperware in every pocket."

She presses her lips together to shove down the beaming bright smile that aches in her cheeks.

"I love y—" She coughs, choking for a moment, her brain finding itself in a very sudden and very violent war with itself. "Love that for us."

She stares straight ahead at the sidewalk and doesn't even dare a peek out of the corner of her eye. She's been pretty resoundingly avoiding this line of thinking in the few times they've spoken this week since the Phone Call.

He hasn't even said it yet. Not really. Not in person. And she certainly doesn't know if it's something she wants to say first, and definitely not like this, not over Tupperware.

"Love this for David, too," she says. It's been too long since somebody spoke. Max's hand is still in hers, just holding on, not too loose, not too tight, and she's not sure if he's thinking so loud she can hear it or if that's just her brain. "We did some research and made an educated guess that the caterers that did that freshman brunch last December are doing this event too, and he's been fantasizing about the spinach puffs since then. So we will be stocking up."

"Well," Max says. She dares to look over. He's smiling same as ever, like it wasn't even a blip on his radar. "Happy to be of service."

It's not late when they walk back to the dorm. Well, college late is easily three in the morning. But it's not even normal people late; it's only ten.

The dinner went well. They were professional and classy, and she did the casual-bragging-while-rubbing-elbows-with-professors thing, and Max did the charmingly-talking-her-up thing and then the lookout thing when she stole as many spinach puffs as she could. He even let her stuff the extras in his blazer pockets. A resounding success of a night.

It was almost a proper date, their first one since Thanksgiving break. If you count going to the Museum of Natural History to buy fifty dollars' worth of astronaut ice cream a proper date.

She wants to take the long way back. Only Manhattan is a grid, so the long way is circling blocks, deliberately going out of their way. It feels like freshman year, and leaving one of the three frat parties they went to, or getting bored just sitting in one of their dorm rooms and going on an adventure with milkshakes or hot chocolates, depending on the season, walking until they got tired.

She moves so fast all the time, but something about tonight, something about Max, makes her feel like slowing down and wandering the side streets, and actually holding hands instead of letting their knuckles awkwardly brush like they used to when they were still stumbling around what they were to each other.

Only as she reaches for his hand while they're waiting at a crosswalk, he freezes, head cocking to the side. His hand shoots out without looking, landing on her shoulder and squeezing.

"Hang on," he says. "One second."

He pulls a piece of blue fabric out of his back pocket and goes running off.

The light changes and even though it goes against every New York instinct that's been drilled into her since birth, she stays at the stoplight, swaying from heel to heel to give her feet a break.

The light changes two more times before Max comes running back.

"Sorry," he says. "Mugger." There's blood dripping from his nose. He swipes at it with his jacket sleeve.

He misses a little spot by the crease of his nose but she's not really sure how to bring it up. They end up walking straight back to her dorm.

Astrid is not smart.

Well, no, Astrid is smart. She is not a genius. Things like a deep, profound understanding of the inner workings of electromagnetism don't come naturally to her. She has to work for it and that work takes a lot of time.

Time she doesn't want to spend in the Fridge with their new instructor talking about the "Psychology of Dating a Superhero."

So she shows up a little early to the Fridge's rec room. There's a man there, standing by the couch, with short blond hair and a round face, and he grins when he turns to her.

"Hi," he says.

"Hi," she replies, smiling politely back. "So I was reading over the syllabus—"

"Syllabus?" the man echoes, raising his eyebrows. "Oh, you must be Astrid."

And she absolutely doesn't know what to make of that. "Uh . . . yes."

The man nods slowly, and Astrid desperately tries not to think about if Eleanor has talked about her. "Right. I'm Wally."

He holds his hand out. Astrid shakes it tentatively.

"Uh, well, I was reading the syllabus over and I saw that we're supposed to talk to you about psychology every other week now. I took Intro to Psych last semester," she says, too quickly and unpolished but she's slightly thrown off. "So I was wondering if there was a way I could . . . transfer those credits to, uh, count toward these lessons."

Wally smiles like he knows something she doesn't. "You're premed, right? At Columbia?"

Oh God, Eleanor has totally talked about her.

"I get it," Wally says. "I remember how busy I was in undergrad."

"You're a doctor?" Astrid asks. It's a bolt of lightning through her brain, and she stands a little straighter.

"Yep. In pediatrics over at Mount Sinai," he says. "I've also been dating a superhero for ten years now, though Henry gets testy when I still refer to it as dating since we got married last spring. If there's anything I've learned, it's that this lifestyle is about more than just safety procedures and self-defense. There's a lot of personal and psychological issues that come with the territory for both you and your partner."

He moves around the couch to perch on the black La-Z-Boy across from it.

"Well, Max and I—" she starts slowly.

"Did your Intro Psych class cover . . . I dunno, debilitating hero complexes? Survivor's guilt? Any practical applications of things beyond the Stroop Effect?"

She's saved from answering by Molly who bounds into the room and sets up on the couch immediately. Astrid reluctantly takes off her backpack as Wally introduces himself again to Molly who somehow already knows exactly who he is.

"I think this is going to be a pretty interesting year," he says. "We've got two people dating aliens. Hell, we have two people dating heroes who are women which is pretty rare."

"Is it?" Molly asks, tilting her head to the side.

Wally nods. "Surprisingly yeah. I'm a really big stats guy when it comes to these things. The numbers are fascinating. Did you know around seventy percent of the women usually end up dating other heroes rather than civilians whereas only twenty percent of the men and nonbinary heroes date in-house?"

"Wow!" Molly says, and her eyes might literally be shining. "How do you find that stuff out?"

Wally shrugs and Astrid takes her seat next to Molly on the couch. "I just ask the right questions."

On principle she tries not to check her email while she's in lab. For one because every email she receives undoubtedly means another homework assignment or some project for a club she'll have to take on to better her case when she runs for office at the end of the year, and sometimes it's better to portion out the amount of stress spikes she has in a day. And also she wants to be alert, to seem attentive and hardworking.

Except there's only one microscope again. A newer, nicer one arrived over the weekend and has already managed to disappear.

This time it's not Ben but Raj looking at his slides, so she can't do the work she needs, but at least she's not listening to Ben brag about how he's managing to balance work in three different labs on campus, or winning a Nobel Prize, or curing a rare blood disease, or whatever it is he's been doing these days. She isn't sure. She tries not to pay too much attention to him for her own mental health.

Speaking of her deteriorating mental health, she decides she will check her email in lab just this once and inevitably does find extra readings for her Cell Bio, a new event that needs to be publicized for Women in Medicine, and the grades for her first Orgo 2 exam of the semester.

She opens that one last, to really savor the anxiety since it's been too calm today.

And the thing is, it's not like she even did bad.

The raw score is 90.35, which on its own might be completely disastrous, but there is a curve in the class. Only the mean score on the exam was an 89.75 and the highest score was a 98.45.

Which means she did not get in the top ten percentile of the scores and only the top ten percentile in the class will get an A at the end of the semester, so . . .

It's one test, she reminds herself as she resists the urge to bang her face against the cool lab table in front of her a few dozen times. It's just one test and she can come back from it. It's not even that bad.

But there's an itch beneath her skin that says to start scheduling in study time even earlier for the next midterm, maybe three weeks ahead of time instead of just two. Maybe four-hour study sessions instead of three-hour ones. Maybe she should go to every review session instead of just the one for her section, and maybe she should make her TA her new speed dial on her phone; she's sure her parents will understand.

She's still mostly dissociating while she stares down at the open email on her phone, when a new text comes in. It's from Max: *giant squid in fl!! Missing dinner sry :'(*

Which makes her blink, think of the Program, and wonder if giant squid is code for something.

The worst part is, she half forgot they were supposed to have dinner together tonight. She has BioChem office hours right before it and a club meeting right after.

The second worst part is, she's also half relieved he's canceled because she needs to do some serious schedule reconfiguring to make up for this Orgo thing. She doesn't really deserve Max time tonight, no matter how much she might need it.

Astrid is a creature of habit and this is a habit, marching down a side street in the Village on her way out of her volunteering session at the critical care unit of Beth Israel. She doesn't even need to look to know that Union Square is ahead, the entrance to her train stop, the light rush of people, mostly tourists bustling about.

And she doesn't see someone in a black ski mask appear out of literal thin air and grab her by the arm.

She screams, not even to get attention from any passersby, just because she's having a heart attack and maybe peeing, just a little.

There's a rushing sound and a pop and suddenly she's not on a side street downtown; she's standing in front of Eleanor's desk in her office.

"Easy peasy," the girl in the ski masks says, releasing Astrid's arm and stepping up to the desk. "Anything else you need?"

Eleanor smiles. "No, that's all," she says. "Thanks, Susie, I owe you."

Susie waves her hand, tugging off the mask and dropping it

on Eleanor's desk. She winks at Astrid on the way out, walking with that athletic bounce in her step that Max does before and after a night out.

Finally, Astrid's brain catches up with her from wherever she left it by Union Square.

"That's not fair," she says. This was the Test. Eleanor did get her email. And she failed. Again.

"How so?" Eleanor asks with a sigh, like she was expecting it. Astrid decides she wants to die and then reminds herself Eleanor is not a professor; she doesn't have to care this much.

Astrid gestures vaguely to where Susie just left. "She came out of nowhere!"

"Supervillains can teleport, Astrid," Eleanor says. "People have superspeed."

"I was perfectly aware of my surroundings," she says. "I have superglued my window shut; I have reinforced the glass. I'm on top of everything we've covered."

"Well, you clearly aren't prepared for a teleporter," Eleanor says.

"How can anyone prepare for that?" Astrid says.

"I guess you'll have to stay in the Program to find out," Eleanor says.

Something like a scream builds in Astrid's throat. Maybe it's just a panic vomit. But it feels like a scream, not the sharp, short one of being snatched off the street that was torn out of her throat on instinct—this is a building wave of frustration and exhaustion and anger that might crash for days.

She chokes it back down and eases her face into something calm.

"I'd like to take the Test again, please," she says.

"Astrid," Eleanor says, like she's disappointed, and Astrid doesn't care, doesn't care, doesn't care. It doesn't matter what Eleanor thinks about her. She'll be out of this soon enough and it won't even nudge her GPA.

"Can I not take the Test again?" she asks evenly.

"There's nothing saying you can't," Eleanor concedes slowly. "But just because you can keep taking it—"

"I'd like to take it again please," she says. "And I'd like to be teleported back to my dorm room, please."

"If I killed someone would you arrest me?" she asks, flopping back against her bed, too tired to try to even step up onto the half loft. Max continues unpacking their takeout, handing her a fork.

It's actual takeout, not just dining hall food, because he wanted to celebrate whatever big victory he had down in Florida yesterday, despite the black and blue under his left eye that's already fading to a nasty green. And she certainly isn't going to turn down food or Max, especially not with the scream still building under her collarbone after another exhausting day in lab.

"Uh, I don't really arrest people," he says. "And I don't usually deal with non-super homicides."

"Cool," she says, pushing off the bed and making her way

to the desks. She steals David's desk chair because Max always feels too guilty to take it himself, insisting on sitting on the floor instead. But floor sitting is such a freshman thing and they are firmly sophomores now, sophisticated and mature, so he takes her chair and she takes David's. "Anyway, I'm gonna kill Ben Barnes."

Max smiles, biting his lip, cheeks chipmunking in that little Max way.

"Well now that you told me that I might have to arrest you," he says, leaning back into her desk chair. "I have a very strict code of ethics, Astrid."

She rolls her eyes and steals a piece of his sushi.

"Is this the Ben Barnes who kept correcting the professor in your Orgo 1 class last semester?" he asks.

She nods. "He's so . . . ugh. Anyway he's in my lab this semester, right, with Dr. Vaughn, except he wasn't supposed to be, he stopped working there before break but came back because he thinks I'm incompetent or something, and he's always hogging the stupid microscope, which is whatever, alright, I can deal with that, but today, today, he freaking left the reagent bottle empty while I was right there next to him waiting for him to finish."

"Right," Max says, nodding. "The reagent bottle, which is very important and . . . hard to refill?"

She spins David's chair around, letting her socked feet hit his knee.

"It's just, like, rude," she says. "Ruder than the microscope. But it's all these little things too, like he keeps telling me he'll show me how to use the incubator. I know how to use the incubator!"

Max is sitting very still suddenly, eyes wide, head tilted, chopsticks hanging loosely in his hand.

She kicks him lightly. "Max?"

He blinks, licks his lips quickly, and turns back to her. "Do you hear that?"

She doesn't.

"Uh, no."

He pushes out of the chair and leaps over her knees to the window in an easy, seamless movement that reminds her he's built of lean muscles and has the grace of a cat when he wants to. He hovers by the window, eyes tight.

"I have to go," he says, glancing back briefly. "I'm so sorry. I think that was an explosion and I . . . I need to go."

"Oh," she says, because they have dinner together on Thursdays because David has rehearsal on Thursdays and she only has one problem set due on Fridays so it's kind of an ideal night to have dinner and talk and maybe make out a little after.

But obviously this is more important.

"Well, be careful," she offers, twisting David's desk chair to face him. She's not sure what the protocol is here, should she get up and . . . what? Show him the way out? He seems to be figuring that out, pushing the window up as high as it'll go, absolutely ruining her glue job.

"I'm so sorry," he says again, turning back to her.

"Hey, no worries," she says. "You gotta do what you gotta do." She winces.

He doesn't seem to notice her fumbling as he hoists himself up onto the sill.

"Uh, are you going like that?" she asks.

He pauses and flashes her one of those heart-stopping, beaming smiles. "Right!" He pulls his long-sleeve T-shirt off over his head, revealing dark blue spandex, and drops it on her bed. "I'll grab that later."

He says it like a promise, pulling the cowl over his wild, wild curls and pushes himself out her window. Her heart still jumps to her throat, even though she knows he's fine. That this isn't even the dangerous part of his night.

She coasts David's chair over to the window and peers out.

"Were you wearing that all night?" she calls, but he's already gone.

She slumps back into the chair and scoots slowly back to her desk, dropping her fork into the takeout container and sighing. Glancing over at her laptop, she reaches for her planner and finds something to study while she eats.

FRESHMAN FALL
WEEK FOUR

DAVID NEVER RESPECTED HER SCHEDULE.

It wasn't like she hid it away or anything; it was posed up against her desk and next to her bed. She'd even offered him a copy for reference. He just didn't care. While she was trying hard not to slouch in her desk chair and pound out this week's Chemistry problems, he just kept staring at her from where he sat on her bed, playing with her stress ball. It was becoming increasingly unclear what the point of even having a single was considering David continued to stop by and bother her at any and all hours of the day.

"So," he said. She ignored him. This was the fifth time he'd tried to capture her attention and he could see—she knew he could see—that she still had three problems left and they were multi-parters. She didn't have time for whatever he was doing.

"So," he said again, not even waiting this time. "Max."

Her hand jolted on the page because that was . . . not where she thought this conversation was going. She didn't even think David remembered Max after everything else on Saturday night.

"Hmm," she said, a weak attempt to play it off, act like she forgot about Max, like it's somehow scientifically possible for her neurons to un-fire off his sweat-damp curls and his red burning cheeks and how he closed his eyes and leaned back into a song, moving with it like he was . . .

"We went to the same high school," she said, and prayed, prayed that David would suddenly develop a new personality that would let him drop it.

"High school boyfriend?" he asked.

"I didn't date in high school," she replied.

"You were a bridge troll back then, too? I thought you just let yourself go."

"Get fucked," she said, carefully reaching for her textbook and adding it to the mix of laptop, notebook, scrap paper. "I was taking three APs a year."

"God, you must have been the worst." He started throwing the stress ball around, bouncing it off the ceiling. If she didn't have only the next forty-five minutes to finish this problem set, she'd murder him.

"So, what is it?" he asked. "Did you have a crush on him or something? Make out at a weekend debate tournament?"

I hugged him for fifteen minutes at his parents' funeral.

"We ran in the same circles," she said, and prayed again for silence.

"Why do you talk like my mother?" The ball hit the ceiling at the wrong angle, went bouncing against the windowsill and nearly killed her succulent.

"David," she snapped.

"Apologies," he said, sliding off her bed to grab the ball. He patted her plant pot soothingly. "It's nice. Knowing you've been actually socialized like a normal human."

"At least I'm house-trained. Give me the ball," she demanded.

He remained by the window, tossing it from hand to hand. But she was not about to get up and grab it—not when her stupid titration problem had the audacity to go up to part k.

"It's sweet," he continued with a sigh. "See all this time I thought you were some insanely advanced AI but you have a cute little human crush on a real boy and now I don't have to worry about your programming going terribly awry."

"Get out of my room," she said. "And leave my stress ball." She was gonna need it. The other two problems on the page also went up to ridiculous letters.

"Fine. I have to go grab dinner," David conceded. "Should I fetch some oil so you can refuel?"

She threw a pen at him. He tossed the ball back.

"This is why you're a humanities major," she said, like the greatest insult she could bestow.

He patted her head on his way out the door.

"Don't worry, dear Astrid. I know a girl in the Comp Sci department who can code you some game."

SOPHOMORE SPRING

WEEK FIVE

M BioChem Pre-Lab; Beth Israel Volunteering 5-7

T Cell Bio Pre-Lab; Physics Pre-Lab; Orgo 2 read ch. 19; LAB 1-5

W CELL BIO MIDTERM 1; BioChem Problem Set 4; BioChem read ch. 4

Th Orgo 2 Problem Set 4; BioChem Lab Report; Physics Lab Report; Women in Lit read *Jane Eyre* pps. 153 - 272; LAB 1-5

F WOMEN IN LIT PAPER 1; Physics Problem Set 4; LAB 3-5

TIP OF THE WEEK

"Practice your grip strength. You don't need to have the best upper body strength. I mean, it certainly helps, but just make sure you can get one pull-up in and you should be good in most life-and-death situations. Don't forget about the grip strength, though, sometimes you just gotta keep holding on to whatever ledge you're holding on to."

—*Lydia Roth*

"JEEZ, YOUR PHONE'S BLOWING UP," DAVID
says, snatching it from the table between them.

"Asshole," she says, but keeps chipping away at her five-page reflective essay on *Jane Eyre*.

"Who's Molly?"

"High schooler I'm tutoring," she says, and holds her hand out. "Phone, David. Now."

"Molly has sent you ten red exclamation marks and those worried-face emojis. The one that look like the Chrissy Teigen meme," he says. "And, um, Wally, is telling you to quote 'breathe through it.' What does that mean?"

"Phone, David," she says again, turning away from her essay since her brain is already shouting at her that this seems like something that is going to have to take precedent.

"Who are these people?" he asks, tossing her phone back. She flinches and her heart jumps, scrambling to grab hold of her phone as it tumbles into her lap.

"Just . . . people," she says slowly. David rolls his eyes.

She does have close to fifteen texts from Molly, mostly emojis. One says, "channel 4." Another from Wally says, "You don't have to watch. Trust me."

"What's up?" David asks, leaning his shoulder against hers.

In a new tab she googles channel 4 and clicks over to the sign-in for the live news feed.

"No, Astrid," David says over her shoulder. "I can't believe . . . you have an account? Who are you? Next thing I know you'll be reading the morning paper."

"I already do and you know that," she says, swatting at his arm.

The feed boots up. "Oh no, some super bullshit downtown," David says with a disinterested sigh.

That's the Flatiron Building in the background. She really hopes it isn't about to get destroyed—it's a really nice building.

There's a man in black, with a flowing cape and a sharp red mask.

She should know this. He's . . . a Doctor something. He's flying and thin beams of light are shooting from his fingertips. Dr. Supernova. Maybe. Dr. Radiation?

The camera swings wildly as a skintight blue suit shoots across the screen.

"Kid Gorgeous," David says.

"Kid Comet," she corrects, rolling her eyes. And then he crashes into a parked bus and her brain reminds her, ever so helpfully, that's *Max*.

Her blood runs cold.

"I thought he died a few years back," David says. "Like right before college, right?"

Wait wait wait, her brain says. *Wait, that's Max. Wait, that's* our *Max*.

He crashes into the black figure and they both go tumbling through the sky. The camera isn't fast enough, spinning around to trees and pedestrians jogging out of the way, and not focusing on Max and what Max is doing and what is going on with Max.

"Astrid," David says, tugging on her ponytail. "Hello."

"He went to my high school," she says, batting his hand away absently. The camera jerks again, centering on the fight, centering on Max as he flips through the air, moving like nothing she's ever seen before, like an acrobat, like a bird, a human bird except that human bird is her boyfriend in a blue and gray super suit.

He arches through the sky, tumbling across the ground and coming back up in a crouch.

"How do you know?" he asks.

"What?" she asks. Max goes up again, launching off the ground like he weighs nothing, like gravity can't hold him.

That's Max. Her Max. And he's doing that. He's flying through the air, he's soaring and twisting and dancing over the rooftops of the Flatiron District.

"How do you know he went to your high school?" David asks. "I thought the whole point was that they're unknowable heroes of the night."

"Incidents," she says. She scrambles for an explanation. "There were all these . . . incidents. He was in my grade or the grade below."

Dr. Radiation or whatever sticks his hand out. A burst of light streaks through the sky and smacks Max right in the chest.

She gasps sharply, and it cuts into her throat, still slightly sore from screaming the last time she failed the Test.

"Hey?" David asks. His hand brushes her shoulder. "You good?"

She nods, drags her eyes away from the screen as Max

climbs his way out of a crater his body just made on the corner of Twenty-third and Fifth.

"Yeah, I'm just a really big fan," she says. "He saved our gym from exploding like three times."

David shakes his head but is apparently satisfied by the answer. "You know I learn something weird about you every single day," he says, leaning back into his seat.

She rolls her eyes, glancing back at the livestream quickly. The camera is unfocused again, the action lost in a cloud of dust.

Her heart is hammering, like she's been sprinting on the treadmill, like she's misplaced her planner, like she's taking a final and there's a question she hasn't prepared for.

"Astrid," David says. She blinks. "Your phone."

It's ringing. Wally. She picks it up and takes a breath.

"Hey," he says, his voice is like an ocean breeze, cool and calming.

"Hi," she says, and oh great, she sounds as panicked as she feels. She can feel David's eyes on her, concerned and confused.

"Alright, so you're watching it then," Wally says with a little laugh of a sigh.

"I'm . . . fine," she says. The dust is clearing, and she may or may not be on the literal edge of her desk chair, waiting to catch a glimpse of him.

"Yes, you are and so is he," Wally says. There's a little rustling on his end, a bus wheezing in the background. "He's doing fine. If things were going bad, he'd be calling in some backup. I don't know if they're catching it on channel four, but he's joking around, smiling for the crowd."

"Where are you?" she asks. The camera catches hold of the action again.

Max is still whole and moving. Her eyes lock on his pixelated shoulder, part of his ridiculous costume torn away and stained red.

"I'm grabbing lunch," Wally says. "But Henry texted me. He's in the area, by total coincidence, for a work thing. If it gets too bad, he'll tap in."

"It didn't look that bad at first," she mutters.

"Looks kinda cool, right?"

Max and his shoulder land on the street again. His whole body moves up and down as he breathes heavily.

"I mean before he got shot in the chest," she says.

"It's just Dr. Proton," Wally says. Right. Dr. Proton. She should probably flip through that set of villain index cards again. "It's like a hand buzzer. Just a tickle really."

"Do I want to know how you know that?"

Max pushes off the ground again, a perfect quadratic toss into the air.

"Probably not."

The camera zooms jerkily. For a second Max's covered face engulfs the screen.

That's his mouth. She should know. That's his smile.

"That's really him."

"That's really him," Wally echoes. She starts to breathe again. "I gotta get back to work. Remember, you don't have to watch it. He's fine. Henry is there. Everything is fine. This is what every day looks like."

"Right," she says.

"I'll see you in class," Wally says. "Or text me later if you need."

David clears his throat as the line goes dead. "I thought you've seen him in action before?" he asks, raising his eyebrows. He's confused, maybe even concerned, but trying to play it off, like she's just being weird again.

"He never gets on the news," she says. Dr. Proton gets thrown into a park bench and the camera starts to jump around again.

She holds a deep, meditative breath. Like Wally said, this is every day. So she should go back to her every day. She reopens her essay, but doesn't close out of the tab.

Ben is heading out of the lab as she's heading in. Thank God, because, believe it or not, she needs to actually use the equipment in the lab that she's working in.

"Hey, Astrid, heard that Cell Bio midterm was rough," he says. "Hopefully there's a good curve."

She's so tired she doesn't even try to respond, just hums under her breath and continues her dreary trudge to her desk. Especially after watching Max get pummeled on live TV, and then spending three hours last night checking him for symptoms of a concussion. And maybe she's even more tired than she thought because what she thinks is her desk is occupied.

"Uh," she says, stopping at the edge of her desk and

squinting. The post-bach is in here, the one whose name she always seems to forget, like she's finally hit an information capacity. She clears her throat. "Greg?"

He flinches hard, spinning to face her. "Jesus, you're so quiet," he says. His hand stays on the desktop mouse, quickly clicking out of tabs before she can get a good look at them. "What's up? What are you doing here?"

"Uh," she says. "This is my desk?"

"Shit," Greg says. "It's one already?"

"Yeah," she says. He shakes his head and pushes her chair out, hopping to his feet.

"Sorry about that," he says. "My desktop hasn't been loading MATLAB all week so I've been using yours until I can get anyone from IT up here. Anyway, it's all yours."

She nods and watches him make his way to the other side of the lab. He drops down into his desk chair and pulls his phone out of his pocket.

It's not her business. He's a grad student, he knows what he's doing. But chalk it up to Eleanor making her paranoid and skittish. Plus, Dr. Vaughn made it clear there were protocols. Assigned computers. He shouldn't have been using hers. She checks the history in her browser once she's sitting down and settled, but there's nothing there.

She exhales and shakes her head out.

"Uh, hi," Raj says. Astrid looks up quickly.

"Hi," Astrid says.

"Well, just so you know, you really shouldn't leave cell

cultures out overnight," he says. And she nods because she totally does know, but it's nice of the older members of the lab to take time to give her advice.

"You need to put them in the incubator to keep them warm," he continues, speaking slowly. "Because if not, they're likely to be exposed to contaminants that they're sensitive to and it kills them, ruining the whole culture."

She nods again.

"I cleaned them up for you this time, and I didn't tell Dr. Vaughn, but it's really important to be careful about—"

"Um," she says. "I put all my cultures in the incubator before I left on Friday."

Raj tilts his head. "Well, there were a group of them left out on a tabletop when I came in this morning."

She shakes her head. "They weren't mine then, because I put them in the incubator."

Raj shrugs and steps back. "They were labeled as yours. Look, it's fine but just be more careful in the future."

She's built a whole personality around being careful, but sure. She stumbles into the next room. Her cultures aren't on the table anymore, but when she peeks into the incubator, she sees a whole row missing.

She lets her head fall back, breathing out heavily as she stares at the ceiling. A weeks of work, gone.

"Why?" she asks the heavens, any gods or superheroes over-head at the moment, before swallowing hard and marching over to grab some gloves and start over again.

◆ ◆ ◆

"Hey," Max says practically the second she answers his call. "I'm missing dinner tonight and I'm very sorry. Something came up and actually something is still coming up."

"Okay," she says, and doesn't say that she already grabbed an early-dinner late-lunch to-go box and is halfway through scarfing it down in order to get back to this Orgo 2 problem set before her club meeting later. She also doesn't bring up that he's missing the good chicken wings in the specials station because that would just bum him out.

"Unless, uh, you wouldn't know how to demagnetize a gravitorium machine, right?" he asks.

"What?" she asks. "No. No I would not. I'm not that kind of STEM major, Max."

"Right," he says. "Right, just thought I'd ask. I'll, uh, go figure it out. Maybe stay inside."

"Alright," she says. "See ya."

"Yes," he says. "Yes, I will absolutely see you later."

She braces herself but he hangs up without saying anything else.

Her shoulders slump. And then she frowns because she's not sure why she's sad that he didn't say it again since she still hasn't fully figured out what it means that he did say it the first time.

She stabs her fork into the next grilled carrot and sets aside two chicken wings for him if he saves the city and makes it back sometime tonight.

◆◆◆

He doesn't. She doesn't see him at all the next day either which already has her on edge before she gets knocked out on her way back from volunteering at the hospital.

"Hello!" she screams, tugging at the ropes around her wrist. She's never been tied to a chair before. She always thought it looked easy enough to wiggle out of, but she's not having that much luck in action. "Eleanor! Eleanor, seriously. Safe word, okay? I'm . . . fuck, I'm missing a club meeting! I need to get out of here."

She's never been in an abandoned warehouse before either, and the sound echoes a lot more than she thought it would, sending her own scratchy voice back at her a million times until she winces.

There is a brief second where she wonders if maybe this has nothing to do with Eleanor at all and she's actually tied to a chair because of something Max related and there *is* real danger, and she should maybe be panicking for a much greater reason than the fact that she's missing a pretty essential Women in Medicine society meeting.

"You put on your schedule that you were free during this time," Eleanor says, emerging from the shadows at the end of the room with a pair of scissors.

The ropes are pretty thin. Astrid thinks maybe she should be embarrassed that she can't break them, but she's still caught on the meeting she's missing.

"I usually am," she says. "But we have a special event tonight and attendance is mandatory and if I show up more than fifteen minutes late they're gonna put me on probation and if I'm on probation I probably won't qualify for board elections and I need to be at least secretary next year so I can have a platform for president or vice president senior year."

"Astrid," Eleanor says. "Breathe."

Right. Breathing. Astrid tries it out. Not bad. Pretty helpful actually.

"It's not the end of the world," Eleanor says, and cuts through the ropes. Astrid springs to her feet.

"Where's my backpack?" she asks, feet itching to run for the nearest bus, nearest train, maybe just sprint back to campus from here, except she doesn't really know where here is.

"By the door," Eleanor says and leads her over.

Astrid feels like she's about to explode out of her skin.

"Where am I?" she asks. "What trains are nearby?"

"I'll get you a car," Eleanor offers. "Astrid, I know you want to keep retaking the Test, but this is why I suggest against it."

"It's after five," Astrid says, shaking her head. "Traffic'll be worse than anything else. I could walk faster, probably. Where are we?"

"West Eighty-seventh," Eleanor says, tapping out a code on a keypad and pushing the warehouse door open. The late afternoon sunlight stings in Astrid's eyes after the past few dozen minutes in the darkness.

"I can work with that," Astrid mutters to herself, scooping her bag off the ground, slinging it over both shoulders.

"Are you sure you don't need—"

"I can make it from here," she says, all but tripping back out onto the streets. She'll have to run. That's probably the best bet; it's only around forty blocks. She can maybe waste up to ten minutes waiting for a bus. No five. Five minutes at the nearest M11 stop before she'll have to just suck it up and start running. Fifteen minutes late. Jeez.

"Astrid," Eleanor says, before she can dash off. "You, uh . . . you failed the Test, by the way. We have Knots Week around a month and a half from now, so—"

"I'd like to take it again then, please," she says. Maybe she should just accept defeat at this point. So far, despite being run ragged, she's been able to keep up with everything and the Program, especially since the independent work is mostly just memorization and takes half the time Astrid has originally scheduled for herself. But it's the principle now. She doesn't fail tests. She can't just start lowering the bar.

"I'm sorry," Eleanor offers diplomatically. "I didn't realize you had a conflict today."

"It's fine," Astrid says, digs her fingers into her backpack straps, and starts running.

She shows up to the auditorium twelve and a half minutes late, out of breath and dripping sweat. The talk has already started so she does her best to duck into the closest available seat, at which point her knees essentially give out.

She gives herself a couple of seconds to micro nap in place before she tunes back into the world. The speaker is still thankfully only a few years into her life story, just covering the tail end of her junior year of undergrad, so Astrid hasn't missed anything too important. The thought of leaning over just to grab a notebook makes her entire body feel like it will explode from the molecular level, so she takes notes on her phone instead and only briefly worries about how out of shape she is if a forty-block run does that to her. A forty-block run with a backpack and business slacks. Well, she's not a super-hero.

It takes her seven minutes to remember the other essential component of being here right now.

"Uh, hey," she whispers under her breath, leaning forward to the person in front of her. "Do you know where the sign-in sheet is?"

"Astrid?" Ben whispers back, practically turning around in his seat. "What are you doing here?" Like it's somehow more surprising that *she* is at this Women in Medicine society event. "Did you just get here? Because you missed a lot of interesting stuff."

"Yeah, I'm sure," she says. "Have you seen the sign-in sheet anywhere? Like do you know who might have it?"

"Nope," he says. "Haven't seen it since I got here."

She slumps back in her seat even though Ben continues to whisper loudly something about all the exciting things she missed.

The talk is a tight hour, and while she doesn't exactly learn anything new about the med school application process or residencies that she hasn't already heard in dozens of other accounts; she does cry briefly when Dr. Yang describes her first day running her lab at Johns Hopkins.

To make up for being late, and to try to hunt down the goddamn sign-in sheet, Astrid helps Jenny Chen clear the stage after the event, even though she would give anything to just be in her room right now taking the longest shower she can conceivably excuse.

Jenny's nice, though. And she's working at the Heath Lab so Astrid gets to ask questions about how she managed to get her own research project in the lab.

"It's really exciting," Jenny says, after the table has been folded away and they're walking back to the lobby of the building. "The hardest thing though has been scheduling time with the equipment. We keep having these cell cultures and slides go missing."

"Really?" Astrid asks. "We've been having that problem in Vaughn's, too."

Jenny shrugs. "It's pretty typical. The more prestigious the lab, the nicer the equipment, the more likely it is that someone will hit it up for their own little experiments."

She says it so nonchalantly. Astrid wonders if she'll be that cool and collected by the time she's a senior, enough to brush off lab thefts and supervillain origin stories.

"Do you think it's someone in your lab?"

"Nah," Jenny says, pushing the front door open for the both of them as they step into the cool night air. "We didn't take on any new people this semester so it's probably just someone else breaking in."

Astrid's stomach drops. This explains Raj's questions, Greg's weird looks. She's the someone new. The obvious suspect.

Astrid opens her mouth to ask Jenny what to do but then stops short.

"Max?"

He snaps his attention away from his phone, nearly dropping it to the ground. "Hey!" His smile shines in the darkness.

"Bye, Astrid," Jenny calls, turning down the right fork in the path ahead. "See you next week."

"Bye," she says weakly, almost physically unable to pull her eyes off Max, who's right there underneath the streetlamp. "What are you doing here?"

He shrugs, stepping toward her way too slowly. "I was in the neighborhood. Thought I might make myself useful and walk you home."

She remembers to move herself out of the doorway at last, the ache in her feet forgotten as she meanders over to him. Closer she can spot the faint circle of purple under his left eye.

"You can make yourself even more useful and walk me to the dining hall," she says. "I heard it's doughnut night."

He gasps. Like actually, out loud, lips parting.

Oh no, her brain says. He is overwhelming, just like this, miraculously here and miraculously Max as always.

"You know, I keep missing doughnut night this semester," he says.

Their hands find each other in the almost dark, fingers slotting together as naturally as . . . God, as water molecules forming hydrogen bonds.

"How was your day?" he asks as they start down the left side of the path that curves to the dining hall.

"Terrible," she says, even though she's starting to forget why.

"Hey, Astrid, can I talk to you for a second?" Eleanor asks.

Astrid can talk for maybe a literal second. It's been a rough week.

Eleanor's not really asking, though, already gesturing to the chair across the desk, like Astrid should come sit down.

Astrid does not have sit-down conversation kind of time.

"We got cut off yesterday," she says. "Discussing retaking the Test?"

"Uh, yes," Astrid says. "Do you need my schedule for next week because I—?"

"Look, I don't think you're taking this seriously enough," Eleanor says. Just like that. Voice tipping downward, disappointed in that way that moms and high school teachers always are.

It's annoying how effective this tone has always been on Astrid. She's not sure why she needs every authority figure she's ever met to shower her in validation. She's not even sure why her stupid lizard brain has decided that Eleanor is an authority figure to impress. Probably the desk and the heels.

Astrid shifts in her seat and bites down on the anxiety and shame rising in her chest. She wants to tell Eleanor about how much of a sacrifice this has been. How much time she's giving up. She wants to show her just how seriously she's been taking it.

Instead, she stares at her hands, the way they interlace in her lap.

"Come on," Eleanor says finally, like she understands. She walks around the desk and toward the door. "There are some things I think you need to see."

"Oh," Astrid says. This is going to be a moving meeting. Even longer than a sit-down conversation. She stands and follows Eleanor out to the hall. It's a bit of a battle to not calculate the exact number of pages in her BioChem textbook that she has to review tonight. Roughly it's a lot. A lot of pages.

Eleanor turns off down a corridor Astrid has never seen before.

She'd hate to go exploring here without Eleanor. She'd probably never see the surface again, just trapped forever in these sprawling underground catacombs.

The hall ends in a blank wall. Astrid knows better to accept it at face value by now. "Hailey, access to the Rotunda, please, for me and Astrid."

"Yes of course, Eleanor," the automated response system calls from above. "Voice and facial scans confirmed." A panel pops out of the wall with a touchscreen, lighting up a PIN pad.

Astrid looks up at the ceiling while Eleanor punches in the pass code.

The wall opens itself up down the middle like a sliding door, a little whoosh as it reveals a round room in green marble.

The ceiling is all windows, the burnt late afternoon sunlight streaming in, from where Astrid has no idea.

There are names and dates chiseled into the wall, arranged in neat lines and painted in gold.

Eleanor has already moved deep into the room, facing the wall next to the door, her expression drawn tight and solemn. Astrid shuffles up beside her.

"Every year I see people I know and care about, friends so close they might as well be family, die. Sometimes permanently. And it's everyone." She closes her eyes, her head tipping back. "My elders. The women who gave me tips and tricks, who warned me about hard nights and long falls." Astrid reaches out, running a finger over the closest name. *Olive O'Neil: January 17, 2003.* "And people that I've tried to train. Kids who want so much, could be so much, who never get the chance to find out the half of what they're capable of."

There's empty space toward the back of the room. A whole chunk of the wall that's blank, the pattern slowly encroaching. Like the list isn't done; there are more names to come.

Astrid's stomach turns over just a little, the back of her neck and the base of her skull turning suddenly cold and stiff.

Eleanor continues around the circle of names. There's a break, a clear glass door in the middle of the left side of the room. Eleanor stops, eyes going soft as she sighs.

Astrid follows her over, feeling like her feet aren't actually touching the ground, like she doesn't physically exist in the space, like she's watching a movie of Eleanor, reacting to this room. There's a hospital bed, a woman with long and large orange curls lying across it while the heart monitor beats out her pulse.

The woman looks familiar, just like Eleanor had that first day.

"Is that . . . Kat Robinson?" Astrid asks. Eleanor nods.

Kat Robinson, child star turned hot mess turned intrepid space reporter, married thrice, lastly to a known Martian superhero, Miller Mason.

"My best friend," Eleanor says with a sigh. "This program was her idea, more or less. She always said we needed to consolidate our information, help each other in order to survive." Eleanor takes a step back, glances up at the skylights. "She's been in a coma for seven years. She got kidnapped, taken off world for weeks. When Miller found her, she was . . . The doctors barely managed to save her, and she's been out ever since. We waited. Weeks and months and . . . well, years now. Miller died two years ago, sacrificed himself to stop the Time War on Asper. One of the last things he said was that he wanted me to be the one to give Kat the news when she wakes up." Eleanor grimaces. "So, I have that to look forward to."

"That's terrible," Astrid says, ever the paragon of comfort and compassion.

Eleanor finally turns back to her and the intensity in her gaze nearly knocks Astrid over.

"It is," she agrees, blinking the wetness out of her eyes. "I'm trying to do what I can to save lives. I want to give you a fighting chance in this great big war that we've been roped into."

It all sounds like so much when Eleanor says it like that.

Which is the point, isn't it?

Astrid grimaces. She doesn't have time for a war—she has midterms to study for. She needs a little sign, or a quirky T-shirt: "Please do not involve me in your silly superhero stuff, I'm premed."

"I don't want to scare you," Eleanor says, drawing back. Astrid doesn't feel scared, just stressed. There's a difference, she thinks, a razor's edge of difference. "I just want you to understand why it's this important that we make sure you're prepared."

Astrid nods. "I'm good at that," she says, even though the deeper she gets into this semester the more she thinks she isn't good at half the things she thought she was. "I'm good at being prepared."

FRESHMAN FALL
WEEK SEVEN

THERE WAS NOTHING PARTICULARLY BAD ABOUT the week. Just generalized stress, that one problem on this week's Calc problem set that took too long and was undeniable proof she was the stupidest person alive, and that look she got from that TA when she gave the wrong answer to a practice problem in her review section.

Astrid never tried to suppress emotions—she just rescheduled them. When a reason to be angry or panicked or sad or anything else cropped up, she carefully and tactically put a pin in it, made a brief note in her phone and let it out in discreet packets during predetermined times later in the week.

Thursdays have always had a weird sort of cursed energy, so every other Thursday night after dinner she would pull up her list and ride it out for twenty minutes.

It was always a scary moment at first, pulling on that little box full of sad and hurt and letting the contents spill out, slow and then fast like a newly opened gallon of milk. Breathing got harder, and she pushed down every instinct to hold on to the tears that welled up. There was fear always that once she let it all out, she'd never be able to pull it all back in and together.

Eventually she got in the groove of it, exhaling sobs, not bothering to wipe the tears away, just letting them trickle out, wringing herself dry. Her chest felt tight and she dug her fingers into the meat of her thighs, kneeling on the floor between her desk and her bed, a comfy little corner, perfectly framed by solid walls as if made for crying.

The crying slowly became about her anger and anxiety and deep unwieldy existential dread, the pressure to not screw up that has consumed her on a daily basis for about as long as she could remember, the weight of every weird thing she'd ever said and every single point she'd ever missed on any test.

She scheduled fifteen minutes for this, and planned to use all of them, in the corner, on the floor, sobbing it out, but two minutes in there was a knock on the door.

A sob caught in her throat as she sat up, craning her neck to stare at the doorframe in abject horror.

Another knock came, slower. The knocker was uncertain, but persistent.

Astrid wiped her face off with the edge of her gray comforter, blew her nose into the hem of her T-shirt, and climbed her way to her feet, clawing at her desk and the bed frame on her way up for support.

She checked her face in the long mirror she had pressed up to the back of her door. Yeah, she definitely looked like she'd been crying.

Whatever, she decided as she swung open the door, it wasn't like she cared what her RA thought about her anyway.

"Hey," she said, opening the door a careful 35 degrees to shield the mini toaster she was absolutely not supposed to have.

Only it wasn't her RA, it was Max Martin in the same over-sized Columbia blue sweatshirt he had been wearing at dinner a few hours ago, shifting his weight from foot to foot, fist hovering where the door used to be.

"Hi," he said.

Shit.

It would be rude to close the door in his face, wouldn't it? She shoved her flyaways behind her ears and leaned up against the doorframe.

"What's up?"

Max blinked at her, wide puppy eyes taking her in, snot and dried tears and already in her pajamas at 8:30.

"Are you okay?" he asked.

She nodded, pressing her lips together and clenching her jaw.

"Oh yeah, I'm good," she said. She decided on a tactful, forceful and quick thumbs-up. "Do you need something or . . . ?"

"Um," Max said, forehead wrinkling up. "Yeah . . . are you sure you're . . ."

She gestured vaguely. "Fine. I'm fine. College, you know. Just one of those nights."

"Um," Max said. "Do you want like . . . a hug?" An echo across time and space. For a second she was in that bathroom again, at his parents' funeral, feeling his grief in her chest. Unsurprisingly, it sounded more genuine and reassuring when he said it.

"It's nothing serious," she said.

"Okay," he said slowly.

He didn't look convinced.

"Did you . . . need something?" she asked because now they were just staring at each other in the door of her dorm and she only had another four minutes left before she had to get back to homework.

"Uh, no, I guess not," he said.

Weird. But a seemingly normal kind of Max Martin weird. She decided to not be concerned about it since it probably wouldn't affect the rest of her night.

"Cool," she said. "I'm gonna . . ." She stepped back, wiggling the edge of her door.

"Right," he said, and he stepped back, too, ducking his head. "Uh, if you ever need anything, I'm, like, right below you so . . ."

She had half a heart attack before reassuring herself that there was no literal way that he could have heard her a floor down, thin walls be damned.

"Okay," she said, feeling tingly in her scalp and shaky in her knees. She was starting to regret not accepting the hug, starting to imagine his arms around her, warm and firm and sure. Maybe she could cry into his shirt a little. He'd rub circles along her back because of course he'd be good at knowing exactly how to comfort someone, with all that wiry strength that he used to hold up those in need. She didn't really need it, had no claim to Max Martin. She looked away, letting her eyes settle on the dirt-stained tips of his sneakers. "Thanks, Max."

"Anytime," he said, and she could tell that he meant it so deeply, the way only someone like him could. His shoes twisted and turned off down the hall.

She waited maybe a little too long to close the door, watching him leave if only because he walked so weird, half limping, half tripping over his own feet, like he wasn't sure how fast was normal. It was a miracle he got anywhere at all.

When she stepped back into the room, she'd run out of time for crying tonight; it'd take too long to get back into it. Whatever, she had better things to do.

SOPHOMORE SPRING
WEEK SIX

M Cell Bio Problem Set 4; BioChem Pre-lab
T Cell Bio Pre-lab; Physics Pre-lab; Orgo 2 read ch. 20; LAB 1-5
W BioChem read ch. 7
Th Orgo 2 Problem Set 5; BioChem Lab Report; Physics Lab Report
F BIOCHEM MIDTERM 1; Physics Problem Set 5; LAB 3-5

TIP OF THE WEEK

"One piece of advice I wish I got when I started dating a super-hero: stop buying expensive heels. You can find some really cheap options at Kmart. Actually just stop buying expensive anything. Clothes get ruined so easily. Necklaces are just choking hazards. And if you ever see an emerald stud earing somewhere about Union Square, let me know, because it was my great-grandmother's and I've been told finding it is the only way I can repair my relationship with my mother."

—*Ivy Everson*

"HEY," MAX SAYS, BREATHLESS, STATICKY. IT'S 9:00 at night on a Tuesday and he missed lunch and dinner and hasn't responded to texts, which she was too busy to worry about because Tuesdays have her dashing back and forth across campus from 9:00 a.m. to 8:45 p.m. So when her phone starts buzzing when she finally drops her backpack and slouches back in her desk chair, she already has an idea about what's going on.

"What's going on?" she asks.

"Uh, are you anywhere near Times Square right now?" he asks.

"Why would I be anywhere near Times Square, Max?" she asks. "It's a school night. I just got back to my dorm and I'm starving. I had to run from physics lab to Vaughn's lab because my experiment would not work—"

"Right, uh, and that's supercool but could we pivot for just a sec?"

"Yeah sure." Even though they haven't really talked since last week because he's been busy and she's had a midterm and a physics lab report kicking her ass.

"You were in that serums class last semester, right? It was your two hundred level BioChem elective?"

"Yeah."

"Okay, well, let's say this guy I'm dealing with hypothetically injected himself with a serum that's carbon-based according to this whiteboard he has in here, and it turned him purple and made him like three times bigger and maybe ten times stronger."

"Dude, it was a class at the undergraduate level. I'm not some expert—wait, did you say carbon-based?"

"Uh, yeah, yes. Does that change things?"

"Just, uh, read me what the board says really quick and I'll see if I can make sense of it."

"God, you're a genius, okay, I'm texting a picture."

She drags a notebook from her backpack and starts copying over numbers from her phone screen in the corner of the back page.

"Okay, this sort of makes sense. What do you want me to do here?"

"Could I make like an antiserum or something?" he asks. "I'm in his lab right now and I don't have a lot of time. But this guy's way stronger than me and I need to turn the tide before someone gets hurt."

"Uh," she says, glancing between her phone and the notebook. "Okay, gimme a second."

"You're a lifesaver. Literally."

"Okay, yeah, here we go," she says, the equations and numbers just coming together on the page. It's practically a practice problem from her Orgo 2 study sheet for next week. "Okay, I'm gonna send you a picture. It's the boxed equation."

"What do I do with the equation?"

"Uh . . . well it depends if he used rotovap or something like a fractional distillation. I should get a look at his setup."

"Don't come down here, okay? Whatever you do, don't come down here, he's still out here and causing chaos and—"

"Why in the world would I go down there? I don't have a death wish. Just send me a picture, and I'll . . . I'll run down to Vaughn's lab really quick and talk you through this over the phone. Hang on." She drags herself out of the chair, slips her sneakers back on, grabs her keys from her desk, and heads to the door. She sticks the phone between her shoulder and cheek like an early-2000s rom-com protagonist and carries her notebook and water thermos with her as she speed-walks down the stairs. Her phone pings with another photo from Max, and she checks it as she waits at the crosswalk.

"Okay, that's a glassware setup, which is a little more complicated."

Half the reason she wanted to work in Vaughn's lab was because it was in a building only three minutes from her room. She quickly swipes in and makes a beeline for the back of the lab, where the practical stuff happens. She really shouldn't be doing this. Vaughn has been super particular about protocols and lab safety and protecting classified information. But desperate times.

She glances around to make sure the lab is empty before grabbing the necessary pieces from the back cabinet. She sets them out on the lab table and double-checks the equation on the page.

"Alright, we're gonna start with a round bottom flask," she says, and listens to him shuffle along on the other side of the line.

Max is a good listener and a better learner. It reminds her a bit of helping him with chem lab homework in freshman year, and a little like those two weeks they were lab partners in AP Chemistry back in high school.

She's not actually using any chemicals, but she builds her own setup along with him. She doesn't know what his serum looks like as they go along, but it's almost a part of the challenge. Her brain is firing on all cylinders as she thinks and explains and asks him clarifying questions. If her brain was a laptop, the fan would be buzzing away.

"And that's it?" he asks, when she determines that the serum is ready and he should turn off the Bunsen burner right now, *like right now, Max.*

"That should be it," she says, and feels amazing for one second before being flooded with uncertainty and the knowledge that if she's wrong about anything and it doesn't work, it doesn't mean points off on a homework or a lab report, it could mean him getting hurt or someone else getting hurt or—"Wait, but . . . maybe I should double-check my equations again. Or, like, do you know any actual scientists that could try to—"

"You're the only scientist I know," he says. "Astrid, I trust you. You are the smartest person I know, okay?"

"I've never done this before," she says. "And I'm not even a doctor, Max. That was all really hypothetical and basic work that I did that might not—"

"I trust you," he says again and his voice is quiet and sure and soft. She exhales and stares down at her fake setup. "I trust you more than anyone. I've gotta go now, okay? I'll see you later tonight."

"Okay," she says. "Uh, good luck, I guess."

"Thanks," he says. "Love you." And hangs up.

That's twice now.

"Fuck," she says, reaching up and fixing her ponytail and squeezing her eyes shut.

"Astrid?"

She almost screams, reaching for the nearest glass to throw.

It's Ben Barnes, standing frozen by the entrance of the lab, hand reaching for the light switch. For a moment, they stare at each other.

"What are you doing here?" she asks.

"What are *you* doing here?" he asks, an equally valid question. That she should really think of an answer to, fast.

"Uh," she says. "I . . . forgot my . . . water bottle." She grabs her thermos from the desk and holds it up, nodding.

"Is that a fractional distillation setup?" Ben asks, stepping further into the lab.

Shit. "Uh . . . What are you doing here?" she asks.

He stops and shifts on his feet. "Okay, don't tell Dr. Vaughn, but I got pretty busy last week with my other labs and a Fulbright Scholarship interest meeting and I fell behind on lab work," he says, eyes darting around the room. "So, uh, I'm catching up now."

"Right," she says, nodding. He looks super uncomfortable, but also like he might ask more questions, so she steps around

157

the lab table and starts heading for the exit. "I totally get it. And I won't tell Vaughn."

"Thanks," he says, and she steps carefully around him and makes a beeline for the door. "Hey, Astrid?"

She turns, tightening her grip on her thermos, tucking her notebook under her arm in case there's anything incriminating he might spot on the page.

"Are you a superhero?" he asks and it's such a ridiculous question she literally barks out a laugh.

"Oh God, no," she says, waving her hand like she's batting the idea aside.

"Are you sure?" he asks, squinting suspiciously at her. "Because it's cool if you are. I won't tell anyone."

"Ben, I'm premed, when would I have the time?" she says. He glances back briefly at the setup still on the lab table. Like somehow he's conceiving of a world where this is the time she has to do superhero stuff . . . which it isn't entirely not, but really she should be working on that physics lab report right now. This is merely procrastination.

Ben nods, relaxing back into his posture. "Right, yeah. Well, see ya."

"Yep," she says, and turns on her heel, exhaling steadily as the door sweeps open in front of her and she hurries for the stairs.

So here's the thing. She knows she has no good reason to dislike Ben Barnes.

He's a little sneaky and rubs her the wrong way and he did

send her redacted notes and wrong answers. But premeds are competitive creatures. The med school application process leaves no room for errors and the smallest leg up can make all the difference.

So the next time she goes into lab on a cloudy but not rainy day and sees Ben Barnes at his desk in the otherwise empty lab, head buried in his arms, she feels almost sorry for him.

And there is that part of her that still has no idea how to make meaningful human connections or help other people emotionally, that does remind her that he has not seen her yet and she can still make a run for it and not have to do anything about it.

"Ben?" she asks, walking carefully through the lab and dropping her backpack off by her desk.

Ben sits up straight and his eyes go wide.

"What are you doing here?" he asks.

"Um," she says. She always comes in after class on Thursdays and he's usually not here at this time, so she's not entirely sure how to reply. "I'm here to work. Are you okay?"

His eyes dart between her and the door, and he presses his lips together tightly.

"I'm fine," he says. And she doesn't need to be an expert in social cues to know that he doesn't mean it.

"Look," she says, because he looks particularly young right now, reminding her of Molly and Thomas and Lucy. "I know we're not close or anything, but I'm here if you want to talk about stuff."

A very uncomfortable moment passes where he just looks

at her, thinking hard, and she debates just heading back to her desk and/or leaving the country.

"I'm just feeling very overwhelmed," he says. "I thought since I'm mostly retaking classes this semester to up my GPA and study for the MCAT that it wouldn't be as hard. And I just started this independent research that I've been struggling with."

He looks very sad, which is the only reason her head doesn't literally explode with jealousy right in the middle of this conversation from the fact that he has an independent research project.

"I think I must be dense or something," he says, voice growing sharp. "Because I can't make this make sense."

She nods and exhales solidly before wandering slightly closer to his desk.

"I can take a look if you want," she says.

He scoffs. Hard. His eyebrows draw together, and for a second his face shows such deep contempt and dismissal she almost steps back.

There's a shift, and almost as quickly as the look came, it's gone, settling into something contemplative and calm.

"Uh, yeah," he says. "That would be . . . helpful. Thank you."

She walks the rest of the way over to the desk, and he shifts back so she can study the microscope photos on his desktop screen.

"What's the project about?" she asks, even though she's

already taking in the cells in the picture and the numbers on the spreadsheet.

"Uh . . . ," Ben says. "Can't tell you. Lab policy."

"Right," she says, and really fights to not roll her eyes. "Well, uh, I know nothing about what you're looking for, but . . . those cells in the corner there are abnormally tight. Like they're probably going through mitosis faster than the others. But I don't know, maybe you've already picked that up."

He leans back into his chair and stares up at her, eyes inscrutable. He shrugs.

She sighs and grabs a chair from the desk next to his. "And walk me through what this column is measuring. Why's the formatting look all weird like that?"

He frowns. "I don't know," he says. "I don't care about the formatting, the numbers are what matter."

"Yeah, well, if you don't label what the numbers are . . . ," she says, grabbing the mouse from his side of the desk and making the file full screen. "Here, I'll help you."

It's easy to zone out at the lab, especially once Ben has left and it's just her and her work. Now that it's been a few weeks and she knows how to use all the machines, knows how to run the functions, plug in data sets and write out code, now that it's all so rote and makes her brain feel like a stalling engine sometimes, she barely has to think.

"Astrid," someone says, and she's violently thrown back into her body, blinking heavily like she's waking up. She turns and

Dr. Vaughn is standing across from her.

"Yes," she says, sitting up straighter.

"Can we talk for a second?" he says, gesturing to his office in the back of the lab. And her brain, which is whirring back to life, says *research project*, and her heart starts thrumming.

"Of course," she says, and slams her knees on the underside of her desk in her rush to stand.

Dr. Vaughn's office is as cluttered as it was the day of her interview. He has a three-monitor setup and a wall along the back with various degrees and scholarly awards that make her yearn for a wall of degrees of her own.

She takes a seat across from Vaughn and places her hands in her lap carefully, trying not to let her leg bounce or her smile grow too wide.

Vaughn presses his lips together.

"So you've been here for a while now," he says, and she nods because it is true and she's been waiting for this moment since she started. "I know there's a lot of responsibility that you've been taking on. And I also know that you've been doing a lot of other work around campus, without even counting the rigorous coursework. But that's no excuse for not being attentive and thorough." He leans back in his desk chair and sighs. "I came in this morning and found a series of your cell cultures overcrowded or mostly dead. Look, for the most part, your work here has been very well put together, but these cell samples don't grow on trees, okay? There are only so many telepathically inclined people out there, a small minority of which are human, and even fewer willing to donate biological samples. If we run out, we might not have more to work with for years. So it's important we don't waste them with careless mistakes. And apparently this has been a bit of a continuous problem with you."

"Uh," she breathes, and it feels like a wave crashing over her, like a riptide pulling at her gut, dragging her down and out to sea to drown. "But I didn't—" she starts.

"I don't care, alright. If it's just that you've been uncareful, then I'll ask you to be more careful in the future," he says. "If it's more . . . Science is a complicated field that draws a lot of people to it for a lot of questionable reasons. There's great power in knowledge, and power has the tendency to corrupt. I've watched several colleagues of mine use science to take that power for themselves. But more often than not what science gives, science can just as easily take away. So really question why you're pursuing a medical degree. Because if it's not for the right reasons, I'd encourage you to not pursue it at all."

She feels cold all over, like her body has died, but she's somehow still alive, still sitting in Vaughn's office, sitting very straight and staring across his desk.

"Is that clear?" he asks.

She doesn't have words to respond with, but she does manage to move her neck and nod.

"Okay," he says. "I'm going to have to ask you to just work on running the MATLAB programs for now, and take a break from the cell cultures until we feel you're ready to take on that responsibility again."

He dismisses her and turns back to his computer screens and she pries her cold, shaky body out of the chair and out of the door.

It takes a full night's sleep and then a few extra hours in the morning while she goes to class, but she makes it all the way to around 1:34, doing a physics pre-lab in her room when she sits up straight and says to the room and herself and the world, "I didn't do anything."

Obviously. She didn't leave her cell cultures out; she would never do something that reckless, especially not with lab equipment.

She made vague attempts to communicate that much to Dr. Vaughn, but in the haze of visceral fear at being in trouble with maybe the most important authority figure in her life right now, she forgot that meant someone else did.

She didn't do anything, someone else did, and as long as Vaughn thinks it was her, she's not allowed to do any serious work in lab, which most likely means she's not getting her own research project anytime soon and he might not even take her back next year.

But someone else did it.

She stands, physics pre-lab abandoned, and hops up onto her bed, kneeling so she can carefully peel the corners of her mitosis poster off the wall and set it down on the windowsill. She flops down on her stomach and reaches for her notebook on the corner of the desk and her thickest black pen.

She's got a mystery to solve, and hypothetically she knows how to solve things.

Max stops by her room late, after dinner late but not quite David late. She's converted the wall on her side of the room into a proper spiraling conspiracy board, even though it felt really unnecessary to head all the way to the library and pay seven cents a page to print other pieces of evidence.

There's notebook pages covered in mostly sensical ramblings. Arrows and color coding and charts. A rough timeline of everything that has gone missing in lab, every time something weird happened to her cultures and any other small discrepancies she could remember.

"Wow," Max says, tilting his head. He sets his to-go box dinner on her desk and wanders over. "What's all this?"

"An investigation," she says, sliding off the side of her bed to view the wall from a farther distance, take it all in at once. "A lot of things have been stolen from my lab and now someone is ruining my experiments." She tilts her head like the angle might help. "They may be unrelated."

"No shit." He moves so he's standing next to her, crossing his arms like her, blinking up at the wall. "There's this guy I've been following, when I'm in the mask. He's been stealing stuff from bio labs all over campus."

She turns to look at him. "Really?"

He nods.

"Well," she says. "What do you know?"

He walks over to his backpack and pulls out a thick, black spiral notebook, stuffed with various papers. He flips through it, and she catches a glimpse of a catalogue of investigations, suspects and incidents and newspaper clippings. She's thoroughly impressed with how well researched it all seems to be and decides not to examine too closely the way it makes her feel a little flushed.

He pulls out a paper-clipped collection of papers from toward the back and spreads them out on her bed.

"That's what I've got," he says, stepping back so he's standing next to her again. He glances up at the wall. "What do you know?"

A grin twitches at the corners of his mouth. She's overwhelmed by the need to kiss him immediately and for a prolonged period of time.

But apparently, they have work to do.

"So," she says, eyes darting over the pages he's spread out. "Our guy has hit up every single biology research lab on this campus that does studies with enhanced DNA."

He nods.

"What next?"

He pauses for a moment to think about it. "Well, uh, it never hurts to check out the scene of the crime."

He stares at her for a moment before stepping toward the door.

"Whoa," she says. "Where are you going?"

"Uh . . . We should check out your lab? For clues?"

She shakes her head. "I can't. I have my BioChem midterm tomorrow."

Max frowns and gestures over his shoulder with his thumb. "But . . . mystery."

She presses her lips together, considering deeply for a second before she heads to the desk. "Okay, I think I'm free next Tuesday at seven, how about you? David'll be at rehearsal."

He follows her over, grinning widely. "So will I—we're rehearsing with the full ensemble for once."

Her eyes skim over her schedule for next week and she can feel him watching her, leaning into her, his smile beaming brighter than the fluorescents.

"How about the evening of the eighteenth?"

"It's a date."

FRESHMAN FALL
WEEK TEN

THIS TIME SHE WAS PREPARED FOR THE PARTY, had it penciled into her schedule, *frat party 11:00 p.m. to 2:00 a.m.* in David's blue Paper Mate.

"I literally hate you," he had said at their Thursday lunch after he had broached the topic and she had agreed and pulled out her planner. But it was significantly nicer to have it boxed in and to meet up with Max before walking over.

This time, she also got properly drunk. Not excessively, just a few sips past tipsy.

"Jesus, Astrid," David said.

"I've been drunker," she replied, barely slurring. She was fine.

"I don't want to know," he decided.

"You have never been to a debate party," she said, wincing

at a particularly loud, squeaky bass drop. "Those motherfuck-ers know how to party."

"You're scaring me," David decided, stepping away from her.

Max was there though, so she grabbed his arm for support.

"Hey," he said. She nodded, patting his arm. Her hand lingered for a second, her fingertips stuck to his soft, warm, perfect skin like magnets, explicitly against her wishes, and . . . oh . . .

"Shit," she muttered. "Shit, I drank too much."

"Told you," David said, shaking his head. It wasn't fair at all actually, because he'd actually been drinking more than she had.

"Shit. I didn't," she hiccupped, pressing a hand tight to her chest. "I didn't schedule in time for a hangover tomorrow."

David rolled his eyes. "You're killing me."

"Do you . . . you really schedule in things like that?" Max asked, grinning a little too widely.

"She schedules everything," David said, meeting Max's eyes over her head. Her brain was a little slow, but it decided pretty quickly that she did not like that at all. No, not a fan of whatever it was going on between David and Max right now. "Conversations, bathroom breaks, long yawns."

She shook her head violently. "Lies."

"I wanted to watch a YouTube video with her on Wednes-day," David continued. "Had to schedule an appointment. The only opening was two weeks from now."

"David," she protested, swinging at his arm. He batted her hand away, then wrapped his arm around her shoulders. He was warm and comfortable. Solid.

She felt a tsunami wave of something big and fuzzy as she stood between him and Max, felt whole and happy and . . . what was that other thing? Loved, maybe.

David found a girl to spend the night with. "Anisha," he said. "She's a physics major." And then he was off.

It was just her and Max, and the music was loud, and the people were louder and she was sweaty and tired, and likely more dehydrated than she'd ever been in her life.

She leaned up against Max, ended up babbling to him, the words just pouring out even though whatever she was saying was probably pretty inane, and he probably couldn't hear her anyway. But there was a layer of something like clear plastic wrap between her brain and her body and she kept getting tangled in it.

"Evolution is so cool," she found herself saying. "Do you ever think about that? About how cool evolution is? Like, by some miracle of science all these chemicals came together and made a teeny tiny little organism, and then that organism died and then the chemicals did it again and then again and again and again until the organism didn't die, and then somehow made me and you and you and me and we're just—" She broke off laughing and he laughed back, eyes a little wide. "We're at this party. Millions and millions of years of chemicals and things dying and changing all so we can be at this party right now, destroying our brain cells with alcohol and ruining the eardrums that our ancestors developed to survive in the wilderness, because—because it's fun, and . . ."

"Yeah?" he asked, right into her ear, loud so she could hear. His breath was cool against her skin and her heart thumped along so hard it almost drowned out the bass for a moment.

"What?" she asked.

"You were saying . . . ?"

"What was I saying?"

"Never mind," he said. He was smiling—he was always smiling at her.

He didn't used to smile like this. She remembered high school, he always looked so sad. Not quite frowning, but his eyes were always somewhere else and always a little watery. College looked so good on him, and this T-shirt looked great on him, and the lights were glistening off his skin.

She liked this for him, with him, liked him dancing and liked him smiling. She kinda wanted to press her mouth to his just to feel that smile, just to know what it was like even closer.

She leaned forward and crashed a little awkwardly into his chest.

"We should go?" he asked.

She nodded.

It was all a little fuzzy when she thought about it the next morning, but it was almost nicer that way. The walk back under the orange streetlights with the whole world around them quiet. The soft noise of New York, the buses and cop cars buzzing while her ears were still ringing from the pounding of the speakers. Her head swimming in the bad beer, but like a pleasant breaststroke across a clear lake.

Max held her hand. They talked about high school.

And she said something, something witty and clever hopefully because he laughed afterward, his feet still stuttering across the smooth sidewalk. At one point, he threw his head back and everything, and she stared as his neck for, like, a second too long.

They ended up walking in the street and she wanted to kiss his hand like she was a proper wealthy gentleman in a Regency drama. She was no proper wealthy gentleman though. It probably wouldn't work for her—it'd probably just look ridiculous. So, she kept her Austenian fantasies to herself, just swayed a little toward him as they wove through the thin pedestrian traffic.

He walked her to her door, offered to help her with her key, and then smiled, small and rueful before leaving her there, in the doorway, longing for things she couldn't even name.

SOPHOMORE SPRING
WEEK SEVEN

M Cell Bio Problem Set 5; BioChem Pre-lab; Beth Israel Volunteering 5-7
T Cell Bio Pre-lab; Physics Pre-lab; Orgo 2 read ch. 21; LAB 1-5
W BioChem Problem Set 6; BioChem read ch. 10
Th Orgo 2 Problem Set 6; BioChem Lab Report; Physics Lab Report;
Women in Lit read Chopin, *The Awakening* pt.1; LAB 1-5
F Physics Problem Set 6; LAB 3-5

TIP OF THE WEEK

"It can be a pretty lonely and emotional kind of thing, dating a superhero. Just remember that patience is a virtue and you're going to need a lot of it. There will be intergalactic trips that go on for months, dramatic breakups after long, ugly fights, and a lot of nights you spend wide awake, staring out the window, waiting for your partner to come home. But, once you get used to the waiting, it all seems worth it."

—*Alice McCartney*

THE FRIDGE GYM IS JUST A GYM. THERE'S apparently no way to make gyms that much higher tech. The equipment is sleek and metallic. The walls are mirrors, which kinda sucks because Astrid does not want to know what she looks like right now. It's been four days since the last time she washed her hair and her stress breakouts are becoming A Problem. All she really has time for is studying and stress eating. She hasn't made direct eye contact with anyone in two days thanks to Max's superheroing and David's musical theatering.

She's here anyway though, in her yoga pants and an old debate club T-shirt, to run on a treadmill, which honestly is pretty sexy of her.

Working out is always, always, always the first thing Astrid cuts from a schedule, because while endorphins are good and make your brain work better, she hates it so much. Just repeating the same motions over and over, and purposefully getting sweaty. But if she's going to prove to Eleanor that she's taking this seriously for a chance of retaking the Test again or getting enough credit to bow out of this by the time spring break rolls around, she'll put in the time.

Even if it means running and running and having nothing to do with her brain but worry about all the work she has to do when she stops running. She counts the time in her head, second by second, and wipes sweat out of her eyes.

"Hey."

Astrid nearly trips—she has to grab the side of the treadmill for balance. It takes a second to figure out how to not go flying backward while turning to see who's there, but, well, she gets there, spotting Thomas and Lucy by the door.

"We're heading out," Thomas says, thumbing over his shoulder toward the door.

"Cool," she says. A bead of sweat rolls along the line of her nose. "See you next week."

Lucy nods at her once and slips out the door. Thomas follows and Astrid listens to them fade away, their chatter and footsteps echoing along the hall.

This week was Running Week. Apparently, there are right and wrong ways to run away from someone who wants to kill you. Eleanor also gave them all referral discounts to a cheap shoe store in the Village since Rule Two is Lose the Heels. (Rule One is still firmly Don't Be the Hero.) Neither are a problem for Astrid, who has been wearing the same pair of gray Converse since senior year of high school.

They're supposed to run four times a week, starting at five-minute sessions at a time and working up by two-minute increments each week to "build endurance and stamina."

She approaches the end of her five minutes, and now the sweat is rolling steadily down her face and cooling there under the harsh blow of the AC. Her brain is still buzzing, frustrated at its own disuse, thinking about all the things that are due later this week, wondering how in the world she's going to fit in trips to the campus gym without showing up to all of her classes a disgusting, sweat-encrusted mess.

"Hey, Hailey," she calls, letting herself slow, heave for air, down half her thermos of water in the space of a breath. "Can you add another ten minutes to the timer?"

"I'm not sure that's the best idea, Astrid," Hailey calls back, the cool crisp British voice of God. "Your BPM has been pretty elevated for the past twenty minutes. Might be best to take a rest and get back to it tomorrow."

"I'm alright, Hailey," she says. She is. She's fine. Sweaty but she's resigned herself to showering tonight. "I'll stop if I'm tired."

She's not lying. She's really not that tired. Or else, she's forgotten what it feels like to not be tired. Either way she'll be fine. In all honesty, the dining hall is most likely going to close by the time she gets back to campus, but that's fine. This has been a ramen week; another bowl won't kill her. She thinks she might even have a soy-flavored one, which might be a nice Friday treat that she'll pretend she deserves despite making no progress in her investigation at the lab and wasting an hour longer than she wanted to yesterday on her physics problem set.

"Alright," Hailey calls down and Astrid finishes her water. The treadmill starts speeding up again. "Ten minutes, starting now."

She gets back to her dorm, an hour and a half later, feeling raw and tired, the sweat dry on her skin, her hair so frizzy and tangled she's been considering just shaving it all off instead of attempting to make sense of it in the shower she can't wait for.

David is there, which is a little surprising because it's a Friday night.

She grunts at him as she crosses the twelve steps to her bed. Even stepping up onto the stool makes her thighs ache, and she barely presses herself up before collapsing facedown into the mattress.

The rest of the world falls away.

Unfortunately, her nose and boobs don't like being smushed into the mattress very much, so she rolls onto her side to breathe.

"Hello," David says, and she's ready for the mockery, she knows she looks like shit warmed over. Upon inspection he doesn't look even vaguely amused. If she didn't know him better, she'd say he looks annoyed, but it's David and David doesn't get annoyed.

"Hi," she says, stepping out onto a frozen lake, testing carefully the step ahead.

"What have you been up to?" he asks. He's sideways when she looks at him with her cheek smushed against the pillow, his back against the wall and his arms crossed.

"Working out," she offers. It's hard to get the words out right when her neck is at this angle. "What're you—"

"I thought yoga workouts are in the mornings? Tuesday, Thursday, Saturday?"

"New schedule," she says. She'd wave vaguely at her desk, but she doesn't think she'll ever be able to move her arm again.

"Right," he says, nodding. "I'm guessing you forgot to put

Roomie Night in this new schedule."

"Roomie Nights are Wednesday," she says. He's frowning at her.

It's weird and serious.

"Today is Friday," she says.

He shakes his head.

"It's Wednesday," he insists, which is ridiculous, she would know if it was Wednesday.

"No, it's not," she says. "I have a perfect sense of time, David, it's Friday."

He shakes his head again, tilting his head.

"That's not . . ." Except it is. It *is* Wednesday. She has Thursday class tomorrow. She has Thursday work due tomorrow. She can't remember if she did it or not.

And that's just unacceptable because half of her classes automatically submit a zero for any overdue assignment, and a third of her classes this semester don't even drop lowest assignment grade, so if she actually forgot an assignment she's looking at a big hit to the highest homework grade she can actually get, and homework grades are anywhere from 10 to 30 percent of her final grade, and that's a sizable dent if she's looking at a highest homework score of 85 instead of 95. She'll have to get a near perfect score on every midterm to make up for that kind of number, which is ridiculous because she's supposed to be using her homework grade to boost her midterm grades. She puts the time into her problem sets, hours and hours, so no she can't have forgotten to do an assignment.

"Are you okay?" David doesn't look angry anymore. He's leaning forward, frowning.

"I'm fine," she says, even though her head is still rattling off numbers and calculating percentage losses. "Just tired. I have to take a shower. And work on Orgo for a sec, I guess."

"Astrid," he says. She very slowly, very carefully, uses the wall to leverage her body back up into a sitting position.

"Whoa," she says, stars clouding her vision, things going dark and loopy.

"Hey," David says, and his hand is on her shoulder. "Why don't you lie down?"

She blinks hard and long until she can start seeing again. He has a furrow in his brow, right above his nose.

"Gotta shower," she insists. "I'm gross." It's good that he's standing next to her bed. She can use his arm as a little ledge to brace herself against as she swings her legs back over the side of the bed. "Sorry for missing Roomie Night."

"Whoa," he says. She sways, and he holds her steady by her shoulders. He's a good friend. She doesn't think she's ever had such a good friend. "Careful. What were you doing?"

"Workout," she says. "Long one." She slips off the bed to stand next to him.

Her knees buckle for a second and she claws at the comforter. David wraps an arm around her waist.

"Did you eat?" he asks, and she fists her hand in his T-shirt. "I know you were too busy for lunch, but you ate something, right?"

She nods. "Ramen. I'm gonna have some ramen." He's still frowning but it's fine. She can fix it, just make room for another Roomie Night, maybe on Friday. No, she's studying all night Friday for next week's Orgo midterm. Maybe . . . she might have an hour to spare next Tuesday morning. "I gotta shower first."

"I don't think that's a good idea," he says.

"Well, I want to," she insists. "I have to . . . I have to work on Cell Bio, too."

"What's happening?" David asks. "You haven't been sleeping, you're missing lunch or skipping dinner, you're always working, and now you're working out multiple times a week."

"Just got busy," she says, pulling her hand out of his shirt, staggering a step back.

"I've seen you busy, Astrid," he says. "Last year. This is . . . different."

"It's fine. I'm fine."

She just has to keep her hand on the bed, just hold on to the sheets and step toward the desk, and then she can balance with that.

"Okay, um," David says, trailing after her, grimacing. "You know that . . . Astrid." He catches her elbow and steps around her, meeting her gaze with wide eyes. "You are my very good friend and it's important that you know that you are beautiful. Um, very beautiful and thin. Or, well, not thin, but healthy and beautiful and Max also thinks you're beautiful, I'm sure. And there are things more important than weight, like weight doesn't even matter because you're also very smart and . . . funny."

He looks so very uncomfortable.

"What is happening?" she asks because she feels light-headed, but this is something else. This would be weird on a good night, she's pretty sure.

"Do you . . . have an eating disorder?" he asks slowly.

She's too exhausted to process the statement at first, just exhales sharply and blinks at him.

"And it's okay if you do," he continues. "Because there are . . . services on campus. I think. And if not, we have the internet and we can . . . um, figure out what to do to help you get better."

She swats at his arm. "Please tell me that's not how you'd actually approach me if I had an eating disorder."

"What?"

"Well, I don't have an eating disorder," she says. She leans heavily against the side of the bed. "But if I did, you are being way too confrontational right now. If you really wanted to talk about your concerns, it's better to not center the conversation around weight at all because eating disorders are usually about more than just weight. You should try to talk toward the root of the problem for the individual instead of just the way it's manifesting in the person's treatment of food."

He blinks a few times and then takes a deep, deep breath. "Are you . . . correcting me right now?"

She nods. "You're doing it wrong."

"Why do you know that?"

"I've done the research, David. It's important to know these things so you don't barrel into conversations like this and accidentally hurt people."

He's gnawing on his lower lip, massacring the area. She knows he's going to steal her lip balm tomorrow. Which is unfair because she needs that; it's dry season.

"Okay," he says, huffing out a breath. "Okay, sorry, I probably should have done some research." He rubs his fingers into his forehead. "So . . . if you don't have an eating disorder, what's wrong with you? Are you . . . dying?"

"Oh my God, that's still so confrontational," she says, shaking her head.

"Alright! Okay, you can trust me, you know that, right?" he says. "You know that I love you and I support you and I just want to help. So just . . . tell me how I can help."

"David, I'm fine," she says. "It's just been a rough week and I didn't have time to get dinner at the dining hall. But it's fine. I've got enough ramen to last me to Sunday. I'll be fine by Sunday."

"But the workouts all the time? And the skipping meals? You're never here anymore, you're always out," he says. "You thought it was Friday?"

"I'm just busy." She tries to move around him, but he steps in front of her again.

"You're always busy," he says. "Not like this. You keep canceling plans or forgetting to cancel plans."

She shrugs, pushing at his chest a little. He doesn't move.

"It's nothing," she says. "I'm fine. Just distracted." He's still frowning at her, still standing in her way with his shoulders tense and his hands at his sides. "I've been trying to spend more time with Max." Yes, perfect, Max. She hasn't seen him in three days because of some alien invasion that was happening down in DC, but that means David probably hasn't seen him either. "You know, things are getting more serious and it's just been an adjustment."

"Hanging out with Max and doing what?" he asks.

"None of your business, perv," she says.

"Astrid," he says, still serious, not playing along. She's too tired for a conversation this serious.

"I'm fine, David. I don't need your permission to do things." It's supposed to still be a taunt, she thinks, just another little nudge to get him back on track. It might come out a little snippier than she intended.

His mouth drops open. "Wait. Wait, hold on. I never said—"

"I'm sorry I missed Roomie Night, but it's literally nothing."

"You don't need my permission. I'm just worried about you."

"Well, you know, I worry about you, too. You're never here. I go days without seeing you at all. You're out on weeknights, partying who knows where and sleeping with who knows who, but I don't get on your case about it."

"If you have a problem with how I spend my time—" There's an edge to his voice that would make her take a step back, if the world still wasn't weaving around.

"I didn't say that."

"I text you anyway. When I'm out. Where I am. You know, most of the time. And I'm not the one who's been canceling plans and forgetting responsibilities."

Forgetting responsibilities? Forgetting responsibilities! Like she would ever let herself do that. Like she'd rather die than lose any more ground than she already has this semester. "I am working very hard to stay on top of my shit so I'm sorry if your feelings are hurt that we didn't get to talk over some movie tonight. I've got bigger fish to fry right now."

"Can you go one conversation without a stupid idiom?"

"We get it, you're an English major. Sorry my dialogue is riddled with clichés. Have fun with your consulting career."

He steps back suddenly, eyebrows furrowing. "You're not better than me."

"I never said that I was."

"Oh no, of course not. You just work so much harder than me, don't you? You're always working so goddamn hard and I'm just out partying every night so what do I know, right?"

"You don't know half the shit I'm going through."

"Well, apparently it's none of my business."

"There are a lot of balls I'm trying to juggle."

"Again with the stupid—"

"Shut up about idioms! Shut up about idioms!"

"And you make time for Max so it's pretty telling—"

"What? What, are you jealous of Max?"

"I'm . . ." His face falls, mouth drops right open. He rocks back on his heels. Astrid takes a step back. He looks like he's been slapped. "No, I'm not! I guess . . . I thought I had a best friend but if that's what you think—"

"David," she says.

"No," he says, stepping away when she reaches for his arm. "I gotta go, actually." He steps back again and then again, reaching for his desk, hand closing around his wallet.

"Wait, I didn't—"

"Please don't die in the shower," he says. "And just . . . eat something." And then he's out the door.

She wishes he'd at least slam it.

She misses the days when Max lived right below her. When she could just march on down and be at his door in her slippers. When she didn't have to hope that he was in the same state as her and not off somewhere saving the world.

Honestly, she's just spent an unscheduled thirty-five minutes crying in a shower, it should be illegal for her to have to put on sneakers after something like that. She hovers at the door for a moment of hesitation about whether it's worth it to brave the cold with her hair still wet, and risk anyone of significance seeing her cross the street in her pajamas.

The moment passes, so she does it anyway.

Arms crossed over her chest, just a straight march down the stairs across the street and up to his room.

She knocks, tapping her foot, shivering just a little because her hair is freezing over now and yet still somehow will be frizzy tomorrow.

There's a series of crashes and thuds and then footsteps and when Max opens the door, he only sticks his head out, hair tangled, face flushed, a gash above his eyebrow dripping blood down the side of his face.

"Oh," he says, smiling when he sees her, opening the door fully. "Hey."

"Jesus," she says, stuck in the doorway. At least, the rest of him looks fine. (His shirt is off too which . . . yeah, yeah, okay, that's a thing. She's dating like a whole ass superhero and that's a thing.) But there's something about the way the blood looks so bright against his skin, red and dripping along his temple and down his cheek.

"It's just a scratch," he says. "Head wounds bleed a lot."

She knows. There was a whole talk about it with Wally, about accelerated healing and head wounds and setting broken bones and what actually constitutes a medical emergency for superheroes. Not much, as it turns out.

"Astrid?" he says, reaching out for her hand. "You okay?"

Right. Right, she marched over here with purpose, with questions and doubts and her ears still waiting to hear a door slam.

"Steve Page," she says, pointing at him. He blinks.

"Do you want to . . . come in?" he asks, stepping back.

"Yes," she says, and closes the door behind her. It doesn't slam, just closes solidly and she's in his messy room, a blue spandex suit covered in dirt and blood lying across the floor. "You and Steve Page. In junior year."

"Yeah?" he says, kicking the suit along with the rest of his dirty laundry into a more cohesive pile by his bed.

"You guys got super close and were always flirting when we were doing that project for history," she says.

"Um, yes," he says, pulling out his desk chair and offering it up. She all but collapses into it, her legs are still aching.

"You asked him to winter formal and then never showed up."

He winces, settling down on the floor next to her, leaning his head into her knee. "Yeah, um, that was . . . Killer Bee had a bunch of explosive devices scattered through the city. Are you okay?"

No, Astrid doesn't think she's okay.

But like whatever. She's probably fine. This is just her being dramatic and fatalistic. *Don't make me take out the School Bus Incident, Astrid*, the little voice in her head warns, *pull it together, you're fine.*

Her life is just like a Jenga tower. Except she's very good at Jenga. Or she thought she was—David was supposed to be a secure piece and that was just yanked out abruptly from the core of her. Now the tower is wobbling, just a little. But she's very good at Jenga, so this is fine. Nothing is actually going to fall over. It's fine.

"You never told him?" she asks. "About . . . your thing."

Max shakes his head and it jostles her knee, drags her back into her actual physical body and all its sore, exhausted pain.

"No, you're the first person I told," he says. He grabs her hand, laces their fingers together. "Or . . . well, the first person I've voluntarily told."

"He was so sad," Astrid breathes, and tries very hard to not think about where David might be right now. Max rubs at her hand, kisses her knuckles.

"Yeah," he says. "He was."

"What did you tell him?"

"That I was sick," he offers. "That it was a stomach thing and I was in the bathroom all night."

She shakes her head. "Is that just your go to?"

"People don't really ask many questions after that," he offers.

"I emailed you those articles about IBS last year," she says in a flash of sudden embarrassment, bringing her free hand up to rub at her forehead.

"Yeah," he says, drawing the word out carefully. "I . . . That was pretty funny. And very sweet. That you were concerned."

She swats lightly at his shoulder.

"Was he . . . What did Steve say?" she asks.

"Why?" he asks. "What happened? Are you—?"

"Max, please," she says. "I know it's none of my business, but you told him that you were sick and what did he say?"

He sighs, eyes dropping away from her. "Uh, that he didn't believe me. That I was a liar and he didn't think he could ever trust me again and that I could have at least texted and . . . and that he didn't want to talk to me anymore."

His hair is so tangled and so dirty. It feels gritty under her fingers, dirt and dust and other debris, and she just showered, but it's soothing, to be touching him like this, to have his breath steadily against her, like if she can give him this calm right now, keep him out of his own head, it means there's something calm in her to give.

"And you didn't tell him?" she asks. "Even then?"

He shrugs. "I dunno if he would have even believed me. And it would have put him in danger. And we had only just started flirting, and it was only high school."

"So, you just let him walk away instead?"

"Yeah, but that's why I told you," he says, eyes locking onto her, deep brown, deeply serious, enthralling, impassioned. "Because I don't want to lose what we have, and I didn't want to keep lying, and I didn't want you to keep worrying about whether or not I had IBS. I wanted to tell you the truth and share this with you and I trust you with it."

She nods, waves her hand. "Yeah, no, I got that part." She sighs.

"Oh," he says. "Then . . . um, what's going on?"

"I got into a fight with David," she says, and stands, powering through the pain and ache, closing her eyes against it. "And I couldn't tell him the truth, and I . . . I guess I just don't know how you've been able to do it."

"Astrid," he says, thick as cough syrup. "I'm so—"

"Don't," she says, grabbing his hand and pulling him to his feet. "Please don't do the thing where you apologize and blame yourself and blah blah blah. It's just gonna . . . piss me off right now and I don't want to get in a fight with you, too, tonight."

"Okay," he says, squeezing her hand. "What do you need me to do?"

She glances around his room. His stack of textbooks, his unmade bed, his artful Pokémon concept art posters with pastel landscapes and soft brushstrokes.

Her room is so empty, and David didn't say when he would be back.

But she doesn't need to go back to her room right now. Max is here, actually here, in the state, in the room, in front of her. And that feels like a sudden stroke of good luck that she does not want to take for granted.

"Where's your first aid stuff?" she asks, turning back to him, taking in all the grime and blood on his face. She pushes his curls behind his ear. "Let me get that cut for you."

"So . . . 'Voluntarily told'?" she asks, quoting his words back to him later, when they're crammed into his twin XL, her head on his shoulder, his hand on the small of her back.

"Sometimes villains tend to rip my mask off when we're fighting, even though it's generally frowned upon," he explains. "So like Mystic-Man, Red Dawn, Dr. Proton, uh, Dr. Deadnite now. Some people from high school."

"What? Who?"

He shrugs. "Uh . . . Richard, Kali, Artie, Logan C."

"Uh," she says. "That was our entire AP Chem class."

"Hmm," he says. "Is it?"

"You told our entire AP Chem class and not me?"

"First of all, Dr. Lim also does not know," he says. "And I didn't exactly tell them. I would just change out of the suit sometimes behind the dumpster at the back entrance of the lab, and I got caught a lot."

"Four times?"

"I've gotten a lot better at this."

"I sure hope so."

She turns into him a little more, pressing her nose into his collarbone. His soft pajama T-shirt smells clean and fresh, not like dirt or blood or sweat, hers or his.

She hopes she'll get better at this, too.

FRESHMAN SPRING
WEEK SEVEN

FRESHMAN YEAR, IT SEEMED, WAS ABOUT LYING
flat on her back, down on the floor of Max's dorm room. His
roommate was absent once again, apparently a permanent res-
ident of the library's lower level.

So she was on the floor and instead of sitting awkwardly at
his desk, he'd decided to join her, head next to hers, legs in the
opposite direction.

It was also approaching three in the morning, her scheduled
break from studying to philosophize. She'd never really been
around someone else at three in the morning. She'd probably
have to head back to her room before her next agenda item,
the 3:40 panic attack.

The floor was hard and unyielding, but other than that it
was pretty nice. She didn't have to look at him like this. She

didn't have to look at anything because he had turned off the harsh overhead fluorescents and turned on his dorky little Christmas lights. She could stare at the delightfully plain tiled ceiling and listen to his hushed whispers and respond whatever and whenever she wanted.

"You know I almost didn't come here," he said, his voice ever softer, ever gentler, like he was afraid to disturb the air.

"This is your room." He did this thing a lot where he forgot other people weren't in his head, hearing all his thoughts with him. She could usually read him well enough that she might as well be in his mind anyway, but it was harder when she couldn't see his face.

"No. To Columbia," he said, and then exhaled a laugh that didn't feel like a laugh.

"Waitlist?" she asked, because she knew he didn't get in anywhere better (because she didn't get in anywhere better).

"No," he said. "No, I put down the deposit and everything, I just . . . kinda didn't want to do it."

Out of the corner of her eye she watched him rub at his nose.

"What?" she said, and her skin crawled at the sentiment, but it felt like it was okay to not understand right there, right then.

"The college thing," he said. "I didn't want to do it."

"That's ridiculous," she said. "You're lying."

"I'm not lying," he said, through a smile—she could hear the smile. It had a distinctive sound. Her brain was slowly

193

becoming littered with endless facts about Max. Which wasn't concerning in and of itself, facts were just facts whether they were about Max or David or calculus, but was concerning in moments like this, when she realized that little inflection in his voice always made her smile and was also maybe her favorite thing in the world.

"Why would you not go to college?" she asked.

"Didn't feel right," he said.

"What does that even mean, Max?" she said. "What would you do instead?"

He shifted around, his side bumping into hers briefly before he finished readjusting.

"I dunno. I just felt like . . . why was I doing another four years of sitting in classes and struggling to make time for homework when I could be . . . helping people, really helping people?"

"How could you help people without a college degree?" she asked, turning her head so she could watch his face in profile, the slope of his throat as he breathed. It was dangerous to do when she was working on anything else, because looking at him always felt like such an active thing. He was too distracting. She lost all focus.

"I can't tell if you're being sarcastic. . . ."

"I'm being dead serious," she said. "What would you do without a college degree? With minimum wage what it is and rent in the city, you'd be too busy just trying to keep yourself afloat. How do you help people like that?"

"There's a million ways to help people," he said, his shoulders rubbing against the floor as he shrugs. "Like . . ." He exhaled for a moment, before he let his head fall to the side to look at her. It made her blush almost immediately with how close he suddenly was, how consuming his gaze was when it was turned onto her like that. "Do you remember my parents' funeral?"

"Oh," she gasped before she could catch herself. Despite how close they'd gotten these past few months, they'd never talked about it. Honestly, she hadn't been sure he even remembered it was her. "Um . . . yeah. Yeah, I do."

Something bright flickered behind his eyes, like relief or hope, like he was worried she didn't.

"That was one of the nicest things anyone has ever done for me," he said. His nose wrinkled and he blinked until his eyes stopped watering. She felt like maybe she couldn't breathe anymore, as if some giant weight had been placed on her chest.

She oscillated wildly between responses, ranging from questions about how that could have possibly helped him to explanations of how completely useless she had felt in that moment.

"But . . . that wasn't . . . ," she started. She closed her eyes. "That didn't change anything. That didn't actually . . . make a difference." Not like curing cancer or discovering new antibiotics or any of the million things she's daydreamed about for the past decade of her life.

"It did though," he said, and he's Max and it's 3:00 a.m.

and he wouldn't lie, he wouldn't say something like that and not mean it. "It helped so much, and I think that's more than enough. I think that has to be."

And there was something about it all, the gentleness of his voice and the quiet of the room and the warmth of his shoulder that she could almost feel, that just cut right into her, right to something deep that she didn't even know was soft inside her. It was so Max of him, to be able to do that, to be able to say things like that.

She kinda wanted to crack open the front hood of his entire life and get elbow deep in there, push things around, tune everything up, get grease smeared over her arms and forehead maybe, lean back with a relieved, triumphant sigh when she finally figured out how he worked.

"I want to be a doctor," she said. "It's . . . I don't know. It's the only way I see where I can help people in the big ways. Make a difference."

He tilted his head, facing her head-on, something soft and wonderful and welcoming in his eyes, in the soft slope of his smile. She sat up and cleared her throat.

"And it's 3:35 so I need to get back to my chem problem set."

He looked small now that she was sitting over him, just lying there on the floor of his dorm room, his scruffy curls sprawling across the rough carpeting.

"Wow, 3:35 exactly," he said, eyes down on his phone, which was good because she wasn't sure she could handle direct eye contact with him for a second longer.

"I have an impeccable sense of time," she said, and stood, crossed the room back over to his roommate's desk. She pushed aside a disgustingly old cup of coffee, leaned off the side of the chair to drag her backpack over. "It's like my superpower."

SOPHOMORE SPRING
WEEK EIGHT

M Cell Bio Problem Set 6; BioChem Pre-lab
T Cell Bio Pre-lab; Physics Pre-lab; Orgo 2 read ch. 22; LAB 1-5
W BioChem Problem Set 7; BioChem read ch. 11
Th Orgo 2 Problem Set 7; BioChem Lab Report; Physics Lab Report;
Women in Lit read Chopin, *The Awakening* pt.2; LAB 1-5
F ORGO 2 MIDTERM 2; Physics Problem Set 7; LAB 3-5

TIP OF THE WEEK

"In general, the woman who sleeps with a weighted baseball bat hidden in the baseboard of her bed is a fool every night but one. Or twenty-seven, in my experience."

—*Blythe Blake*

SHE STANDS STOCK-STILL IN THE DOORWAY OF her dorm. She's sweating through her second heaviest coat because even though it's chilly out, lugging her textbooks around campus is still an exhausting exercise in misery.

David is in the room.

He's never in the room at 2:00 on Monday. She leaves him still asleep in bed on Monday mornings and goes to her block of morning classes, back and forth around campus, and then comes back to study for the four hours he's in his English seminars before they grab dinner.

Only they aren't grabbing dinner this week, are they? And he's not at class, is he? He's sprawled out on his bed making out with a girl she can't even see.

This is a line crossed. An unspoken rule broken.

He has never brought a girl to the room, and frankly she wouldn't mind if he did so long as he gave her some notice so she could work around it, like she does with any Max time that doesn't take place in his room. But this? This is intentional and provocative, and she won't stand for it.

She clears her throat.

Nothing.

She's going to kill him.

Well, she can't stand in the doorway sweating all day. She steps in, lets the door shut loudly behind her, drops her backpack to the floor. David and his partner separate, and he glances over at her with a serious, bad, not-amused expression that she does not care for. It makes her stomach turn over and she promptly decides that she hates arguing with him, she doesn't want to fight with him, she doesn't have the time or emotional energy to fight with him.

And yet he continues to stare her down with his eyebrows

tipping at an angle that reads frustration and sourness.

"Whoops," the girl says, brushing her braids behind her ear. "I'm so sorry." She smacks at David's shoulder. "You said she was out."

"Well, she was," David says, shrugging. And Astrid's not even sure this was intentional anymore either. Like maybe he just doesn't even know her schedule half as well as she knows his. Like he doesn't even care at all to try to understand her life and the things that matter to her. He just flies around, doing whatever he wants whenever he wants with whoever he wants.

"C'mon, there shouldn't be anyone in the common room," the girl says, sitting up. "Sorry, we'll get out of your hair."

"It's fine," Astrid says. It's not. She can't even bring herself to smile politely. She feels like she's going to throw up—there's all this terrible anger and sadness churning in her stomach with the three coffees and the questionable dining hall salad she had for lunch. "I'm heading out anyway."

She grabs the closest notebook off her desk and doesn't even bother throwing it in her bag, just tucks it under her arm, and grabs her bag and leaves.

She doesn't let the door slam, on principle.

Max is stripped down to a pair of briefs when he answers the door.

"Jeez," she says, blinking at the sudden eyeful she gets.

"Hi," he squeaks. Over his shoulder, his room is a mess.

Like more than usual, everything is everywhere, like his closet exploded, like his bed was attacked by a mountain lion, like—

"Oh my God, what happened to your outlets?" The plastic casings are cracked, the wires are just hanging out in front of God and everyone. "Max, we don't have renters insurance!"

He places a hand over her mouth and shoves his way out into the hall, shutting the door behind him. She contemplates licking his palm.

"Now is a really bad time," he hisses, glancing over his shoulder.

"What's going on?" she says. It's muffled by his hand.

"Look, you can't be here right now," he says in a whisper. "I've been tracking that guy who's been stealing tech from labs and I'm starting to think that he might be in my Ab Psych section. And he came over to work on that project last week so . . . my whole place might be bugged."

She briefly considers mentioning that she can work quietly and on the floor, but logistically she'll probably still be in his way since there's no way not to be in his cramped little single. So that's strike two. Not her room, not Max's room.

She swats his hand away, and plants a kiss on his cheek before she leaves, calling back, "Check your lamps."

So, she heads down to the Fridge early.

For the first time. At the very least maybe it'll get her some brownie points with Eleanor, and she won't have to waste a half hour this week being reminded about how she could die horribly if she doesn't take the Program seriously.

She doesn't expect Molly to be there, too. She doesn't know why Molly is here early or why she's so interested in Astrid studying.

"Your flash cards are so cool," Molly says. "But like weird."

"Well, I just fold them in half," Astrid explains. "That way they have four sides, so I can quiz myself four ways, like given one, fill in the other three."

Molly gapes. "That's amazing. Jeez, you're a genius."

Astrid shakes her head fondly. "I'm not. But this is how I trick people into thinking I am."

"Man, I wish I was half as good at studying as you are. Like I suck at math and science and all that stuff."

"Math and science aren't the only ways to be smart," Astrid offers, nudging Molly's shoulder. "I mean, you're almost as good as Wally with these superhero stats."

Molly smiles with one half of her mouth, popping a dimple and shrugging.

"I'm just really passionate about it," she says. "I think I spend an unhealthy amount of time reading up on them, Wikipedia and documentaries and old news footage and stuff."

"Still," Astrid says. "That's cool. That you're passionate about history."

"Yeah," Molly says, getting an almost dreamy look in her eyes. "I just think . . . I mean everything they do is so . . . selfless and good. And people like Eleanor, who report on it and everything, who tell their stories. It's incredible. I would be so lucky to get to do the same thing."

"Are you sure you don't want to be a superhero?" Astrid asks, glancing at her out of the corner of her eye. Molly's hair is back in a ponytail, the kind of ponytail that actually looks like a horse's tail because of how straight and sleek her hair looks. Astrid's always puffs out, frizz and tangles.

"Oh no," Molly says fervently, shaking her head, eyes wide. "I could never." She shrugs, folding her hands together on the tabletop.

"You can do anything you want to," Astrid says, because it feels right, feels like the sort of thing her parents told her whenever she was doubting herself in high school.

"I don't want to," she says. It sounds earnest. "I am more than content to sit on the sidelines and watch. We can't all be heroes."

"No," Astrid says, twisting a blue fine-tip marker between her fingers. "I guess we can't."

"Hey," she says, stepping up to Wally. It felt so very weird to wait her turn to talk to him, like he's a real professor or TA or something. But Thomas had also sidled up to him and started asking questions right after class. Granted, it was about where he could learn more about the kind of alien his girlfriend is and the best way to be culturally sensitive about their differences.

Astrid hangs back, trying not to eavesdrop too much and refreshing Twitter on her phone too many times.

"Astrid," Wally says. "What's up?"

"Well, you know how you're here to emotionally support

us and stuff?" she asks, fitting her thumbs under the straps of her backpack.

"Please don't make me regret that very genuine and loving offer," he says.

"I won't," she says, rolling her eyes. "I just need a little favor."

Wally's apartment is so nice.

Hardwood floors, a wonderful kitchenette with a marble island. The color scheme is rich dark browns with an occasional pop of vibrant red. The windows are sweeping and let in so much natural light it almost brings a tear to her eye. This deep in the trenches of a semester she hasn't seen this much sunlight in days.

"How do you even afford this place?" she asks, setting up her laptop, notebook, scrap paper, and textbook in front of the wide clean window overlooking Madison Avenue. Jesus, she wants this. She wants to be a rich New York City doctor and bask in front of beautiful windows for the rest of her life.

"Oh," Wally says, chuckling. "I don't."

For some godforsaken reason, he sits at the kitchen table, away from the windows, doing paperwork. This apartment is wasted on him. He doesn't deserve it.

Astrid will rescue it from him, love it properly.

"It's all Henry's," he says. "He has some trust fund his parents set up for him."

Why wasn't she born rich?

"So, you're, like, a gold digger," she says, flipping open to

Chapter 18 in her Cell Bio textbook.

He scoffs, the same way David does. She tries not to think about it too much.

"You know I'm literally doing you a favor, right? Letting you study here. I can still kick you out," he says.

"You wouldn't dare," she replies, unafraid. "You need me to make you feel cool. I bring a bright youthful energy that lights up your life."

"Mmm-hmm," he says.

Chapter 18 is a joke. One that she gets to laugh at for once since something this week about DNA replication is just clicking with her.

"You never told me your great love story," she says, carefully penning in her heading on some loose leaf.

"What?" he asks.

"You and Henry," she says. "How did you end up dating a superhero?"

"Hey, remember how you asked me to study here because your roommate sucks and it's too busy at the Fridge?" he asks, humming a little.

"Yep," she says. "Good times. Luckily I can multitask. So, your passionate love affair?"

He shakes his head.

"Henry and I met in high school," he says. Pages flip. He types something up on his computer. "We were in the same English class. I fell in love with his insights into Gatsby's tortured psyche."

"Ugh, basic."

"Well, I was young and impressionable as well, and boys with dark hair and a classical literature fetish were my one true weakness. That and doughnuts from the bodega on Thirty-third."

She glances over. Either Wally's paperwork is exciting or he's a disgusting sap, grinning like that just thinking about high school and his husband.

"So, I strategically court him," he continues. "Casually bump into him after class, just so happen to glance his way when I make a particularly strong point about Nick Carraway's sexuality."

"Subtle."

"It was an incredibly skillful seduction," he insists. "Highly effective. Two short months later we almost kiss in the back corner of the school library."

"Almost?" she asks.

"Almost. He gets all flustered and tells me he's no good, I should stay away from him. My goddamn *Twilight* fantasy come to life."

"Oh please, *Twilight* was not out thirty-five years ago," she says.

"You're a terrible, disrespectful youth," he says. "I am thirty-four. And you don't deserve to hear my wonderful story."

"Fine, somehow I will turn off my dazzling wit."

"So, he tells me to stay away, and I don't because I fancy myself some tragic romantic hero. I trail after him like a lovesick puppy. I'm not an idiot, though, so I know he's hiding something and I'm just desperate to find out. There was a week where I actually did some pretty intensive research into vampires. I'm very casually stalking him all around town when I actually stumble into something I shouldn't. Next thing I know, I'm tied to a chair in a warehouse in Red Hook, being threatened by some Mafia goons."

Her head snaps up from her notebook.

"You got kidnapped by the mob?" she asks.

"And held at gunpoint," he says, chuckling a little. "Man, I was so fucking careless. I think I shit my pants."

"You got abducted by the Mafia?" she repeats.

"I mean, everything was fine, obviously. Henry showed up with his impeccable timing and little red cape. Did you know he used to wear a cape? Ridiculous. So, he saved the day, swept me away like I was some nineteenth-century damsel. We had the big tearful confession, he kissed me under an ornate streetlamp on Twenty-fourth, and now we're married in this beautiful apartment with two loving cats and date nights on Friday," he says.

"You got together after you found out?" she asks, trying to imagine that, trying to imagine getting kidnapped and then being rescued by Max in a mask and cape before she had even scheduled him asking her out.

"Yep," Wally says. He looks up, surprised to find her staring. "You good?"

"Yeah, I just . . . You were really kidnapped and held at

gunpoint," she says, shaking her head. "In high school. And Henry was saving people from being held at gunpoint when you guys were in *high school*."

Wally nods, slowly. "I mean . . . the first abduction is always the worst. And they were just some nameless goons, so it wasn't as . . . Sometimes when it's a major nemesis you get to know the other person, start to build up a rapport. Plus, if they've gone in for a costume you know they're willing to have fun with it."

Her mouth goes a little dry.

"You regularly get kidnapped by supervillains." She's not sure if it's a question or not. It's just something she feels the need to say out loud.

"That's the gig, kid," Wally says. "But that's also what we're training you to prevent. These days I can get myself out of a pair of handcuffs like nobody's business."

"But that's . . . that's for the big leaguers, like Eleanor, who date the super-duper superheroes," she says, grabbing her nearest pen and spinning it viciously between her fingers. She glances down at her textbook again, but the words there slip through her brain like water.

"Are you saying Henry's not a big leaguer?" Wally asks, squinting. "Because I think maybe I should defend my man's honor."

"That's not what I'm—*is* he a big leaguer? Is Max?"

Wally shrugs. "Kinda. I mean I've got nothing on Eleanor, of course, who does, but I'd say it's been . . . yeah, fifty-three times I'd say, over the whole run."

"Oh, just fifty-three," she says. She thinks her left eye is twitching and turns back to her laptop to avoid the look Wally's giving her. "Well, that's . . . that's nothing then."

"It's not nothing," he says. "It's never . . .There have been some rough ones, some close calls, some really, really bad nights for both of us. There's therapy and nightmares and some pretty loud fights about it. But it's . . . I trust him with everything I've got. He's got me. I know he does. Every single time I need him, he's there."

She can't make herself write another number on the page.

"Hey," he says. She can hear him slowly get up from the table, play with some papers, take a step toward her. "Are you okay?"

She nods violently.

"Astrid—"

"That's ridiculous. That's . . . fifty-three times is ridiculous. That's multiple times a year, how can you just . . . ?" And she turns to face him, she has to see him so she can reevaluate everything she thought she understood about him. Eleanor is supposed to be the one who's nonchalant about these things, kidnappings and aliens and the Mafia, with nothing more than an unimpressed raised eyebrow. Wally is supposed to be rational and real and *normal*. "That's wild. I can't imagine having a relationship like that. That's not what love looks like, not for me."

Wally blinks at her.

"Sorry, I'm sorry," she says, closing her eyes tight, shaking her head out. "Sorry, I'm not trying to . . . I—"

"That's not our relationship," he says carefully. "Those

moments . . . The danger and the enemies, that's not our relationship. That's not why I love Henry, and that's not why Henry loves me. That's not who we are. I love Henry because he's smart and sharp and he makes me laugh and he sings in the shower and he holds our cats like babies when he thinks I'm not looking. There are a million things every single day that make me love him and make me want to be here with him and . . . remind me why I'm here, despite the fact that any day I could have a gun pointed to my head for the fifty-fourth time. I don't . . . We're not together *because* of things like that, we're together *in spite* of those things."

His face is drawn tight. He's dead serious and she can feel it, feel this deep, powerful energy of his love for Henry.

"I just . . . I don't think I could ever love someone that much," she confesses. "To put up with all that." Spending hours being kidnapped when she needs to be studying or having her life be on the line multiple times a year. Wally's expression twists again, into something that looks like pity. After a moment, he looks like he wants to say something—his mouth opens a little and she can only imagine the kind of things he might say, all things that she really doesn't want to hear, not when she's having dinner with Max tomorrow, not when she's still reeling from her fight with David, and not when she has another midterm looming on the horizon.

She turns back to her numbers. "I'm glad you do love him that much," she says. "It is a good story."

◆◆◆

It's 3:36 in the morning when she wakes up alone in Max's bed to the sound of hardwood creaking. And once she's awake, she's *awake* awake, blood pounding and synapses firing quickly. Think, think, think.

Use what you have, Eleanor would say.

It's okay to play dirty, Wally would say.

She inhales and reaches, grabbing the tiny cactus Max keeps on his windowsill by the base. She hurls it in the direction of the intruder.

The dark silhouette ducks faster than her eye can track and the pot shatters on the wall behind them.

"Shit," the shape hisses and her tired, panicked brain at the very least recognizes it as Max's voice.

She sits up and her head spins a little, still adjusting to being awake and moving so quickly. "Oh my God, Max." Her retainer feels sticky in her dry mouth and her tongue twists over itself.

"I'm so sorry," he breathes into the dark of the room. "I was trying to not wake you up."

She exhales and shifts over as he hops up into the bed. He's warm and a little sweaty and normally she'd be a little grossed out if she wasn't so tired and coming down from that spike of adrenaline. She folds right into him and slumps back down onto the stiff bed.

"Where have you been?" she asks. He sighs and the pads of his fingers run along the back of her shirt, one of his thinning graphic tees.

"Midtown," he says. "This guy Tectronic was trying to rob a bank. He has, like, rock powers. And, you know, most of the city is made of rock so that was interesting."

She exhales a laugh, suddenly not tired or terrified, but feeling fuzzy and bright and like her skin isn't the border between her and the world anymore, that she's seeping out and mixing with the bed and Max's sweaty, sticky skin.

"Did you throw Brian at me?" he asks.

"Is Brian the cactus?" she asks.

"Yeah."

"Then yeah. Sorry about that, I thought you were a dastardly villain here to kidnap me. Or Eleanor trying to test me again."

"Good instincts," he says, turning his face into her hair and settling in.

"I'll buy you a new Brian," she offers.

"Thanks. He was already, like, Brian Twelve though."

"What?"

"I dunno. He keeps dying."

"It's a cactus, Max."

"I know. I think I'm cursed or something."

She laughs for real, uncomfortably loud in the dark of the room. His shoulders shake like he's laughing, too. The bed creaks under their weight and she props her head up on his shoulder.

"How was your day?" she asks, fumbling for his hand in the dark.

"My day or my night?" he asks.

"Either."

She wakes up at 7:26, four minutes before her alarm is set to go off, opening her eyes to a whole sightful of Max.

He has his arms around her waist, one hand fisted in the loose fabric around the small of her back. His face is smushed hard against the pillow, his mouth half open, huffing small breaths that gust over the wispy flyaways at her temple. His chest rises and falls again and again, lifting her head up and down like she's floating in a gentle ocean.

She sometimes forgets how good it feels to be in the same room as him, to be touching him, to be looking at him, even if he's asleep. It's like he has this other superpower, this little stupid specific one, that he can make her heart swell and her breath catch and her soul relax just by existing, just by being near her.

She spends so much time every single day trying to convince herself that things are fine, and that if for some reason they aren't, they will be, and without even trying, without even being awake, he does it for her.

It's the best she's felt waking up in literal years. She closes her eyes and stays very still for the next four minutes.

"I can't believe I've never been to your lab before," Max says as she leads them up the stairs. This was the earliest gap she could find in both of their schedules to pencil in the investigation (which she did, literally), and despite the circumstances, it's nice to see him twice in one day for once.

"I can't believe I need to break more rules to prove that I haven't been breaking rules," she says. He smiles his very best Max smile. There's something wonderful and illicit about sneaking around here with him, like high school but not like what they were like in high school, because she never did any sneaking in high school. If he did (and he probably did, considering), he certainly never invited her.

She swipes them into the lab and opens the door, and she's so on edge, when Max's arms wrap around her waist, she nearly has a heart attack.

"This is fun," he says, bouncing on the balls of his feet. "Right?"

"We just got here," she says, pushing him away so she can lead the way to the side room and the incubators. Max's eyes dart around the room.

"So which desk is yours?" he asks, and she points over to the corner by the window, biting down on a smile as she pushes the next door open. "Wow."

"Okay," she says, intimately knowing Max in all his complexities and contradictions. "Don't touch anything."

He holds his hands up, fingers out and wiggling. She rolls her eyes.

"This is the incubator," she says, swinging the door open. "I keep all my cell cultures here because they need to be warm. But they've been going missing or left out and stuff and . . ."

She freezes and pulls out the top shelf of the incubator,

squinting at the rows of samples.

"These are mine," she says.

"Okay," Max says slowly, stepping closer.

She picks up one of the closer gels, rubbing her finger over the tape label. Red.

"They were stolen a few weeks ago," she says. The cell culture is overcrowded, just like Vaughn said, but they shouldn't be—at least not this overcrowded, not if they were left the way she was treating them.

"So . . . someone put them back," Max says. "After they did something to them."

"Whoever's been stealing stuff is working in my lab. And experimenting on the stem cells."

Astrid is distracted—with this week's Eleanor lecture and quiz, the way that Max was out basically all day and all night yesterday, the fact that she now has evidence that someone is messing with her cell cultures—so it takes her a few extra minutes to notice.

Molly is late.

Which is strange enough. But then Eleanor starts the meeting without her.

"Molly isn't here yet," Astrid offers, raising her hand.

"Molly isn't coming today," Eleanor says, passing her clicker between her hands.

Astrid didn't know that was an option. She stops herself from saying as much, pressing her lips together and sitting back in her desk chair.

Eleanor runs a hand over her forehead.

"Look," she says, her voice taking on a lower, buzzy quality. "Molly is missing. It's been around twenty hours, but everything will be fine. Her boyfriend is looking for her. I have a lot of trustworthy people working right now to find her. So don't worry about it."

Don't worry? It's like Eleanor hasn't met her.

"How can we help?" Lucy asks, sitting up straight at her desk.

"You can stay calm and be careful," Eleanor says. "We're not the heroes here. And, in my experience, that's the *best* thing you can do."

And now Astrid is thinking about Kat Robinson, and Eleanor's memorial wall, and the permanent wrinkle in her forehead.

"Now," Eleanor says, turning back to the PowerPoint projected behind her, the colored lights hitting the edge of her shoulder. "Any guesses for the most common superpower?"

And none of them have any guesses, because this is where Molly would have the right answer.

She should be doing homework.

Story of her life, title of her sex tape, write it on her goddamn tombstone.

Half the reason the Program was something feasible was that she could read for her Women in Lit class or desperately try to take a pre-lab quiz on her phone while taking the subway to and from. But after this class, she's not.

She can't do anything, not even listen to music to calm herself down and productively recharge. She's just sitting tense as a rope in a tensile force physics problem, eyes scanning over every single person in the subway car, flinching every time someone grabs their phone from their pocket.

Why doesn't she know what supervillains look like?

She rules out the old Hispanic lady and the white guy with the toddler, but anyone else seems fair game to be either someone with nefarious purposes or someone Eleanor hired to ruin her day.

Her heart just keeps pounding. When the subway jerks to its station stop, she holds her breath, watches people shuffle in and out.

She hasn't been this skittish on the subway since the first few times, back in middle school, heading into the city to hang out with friends, and staring at the world with wide eyes like it would swallow her whole.

Halfway between stations the train stops and it's not like this is new. Rush hour is starting up, she knows, she knows, she knows. The subway starts and stops and it always traps you when you're late. Someone falls onto the tracks or some train stops working or some station gets evacuated because of some subterranean evil scientist making a big stand. And then hours pass in the dark. And you wait.

But suddenly, even though she knows this is what New York City does, she can't breathe. She's just clutching her backpack to her chest and trying to figure out if the girl in the pleated Catholic school skirt is actually about to hit her with some sort of ray gun.

She has homework to do, so much homework, she doesn't have the time, not for this worry, not for this train traffic, not for another test. She has things to read and she has an Orgo midterm in two days that she hasn't had enough time to study for and it's Orgo so it's going to be hard and if she's not ready—

Oh. Oh, wait this is an actual problem now. The subway is moving again but her vision is a little hazy around the edges, she can't . . .

She squeezes her eyes shut.

Vulnerable, now you're vulnerable. Oh, great, there's a voice in her head that sounds like Eleanor now. *Pay attention to your surroundings at all times, you want to be the first person to know when shit hits the fan and you can't do that with your eyes closed, you—*

Okay, okay, says another voice that sounds like Wally. *Here's what we're gonna do, we're gonna breathe because if we don't breathe we're gonna die.*

Inhale. Hold. Exhale.

The subway stops again. "This is . . . 116th street— Columbia University."

She opens her eyes and hops to her feet, and swiftly joins the trudge of commuters out onto the platform.

No one is looking at her. No one is going to kidnap her. She's feet from her dorm room. She has studying to do.

Inhale. Hold. Exhale.

She follows the flow of people to the stairs.

FRESHMAN SPRING
WEEK EIGHT

"I DON'T THINK YOU'RE A ROBOT," MAX SAID.
He was pretty serious about it, so she made sure to really sell it when she waved the whole sentiment off.

"Sometimes I wish I was a robot."

Even though they were deep into spring, 2:00 a.m. was a sort of perpetually chilly time of night, her windbreaker barely staved off the crisp breezes as they strolled along a silent side street.

He shook his head. "Even back in high school, when they would say shit like that . . ." He grimaced, eyes darting over to her. "I mean, not in a bad way. No one was ever mean about it they would just—"

"It's really not a big deal," she said. "I know what I'm like. I live in my head."

"Yeah, but you aren't," he said. "You care about things. A lot, and you're so motivated and you always know what you're doing."

"Just takes a little research," she offered with a shrug. She sipped on her milkshake and shivered a little. "Like there are answers out there if you know where to look."

He rolled his shoulders back. "I've never known where to look. I think I wake up every single morning and have no idea what I'm doing. And every morning it feels like I'm choking, and I keep asking my brain, 'What are we gonna do, Max? It's another day and there'll be another one after it, just hours and hours, Max, and you gotta fill 'em. What are we gonna do about that?' And I never really know."

She stepped carefully over every crack in the sidewalk ahead of them.

"Sorry," he said, rubbing at his forehead. "I just mean to say that it's cool that you know what you want and exactly how you're going to get it. It's reassuring. That maybe I can figure something out, too."

She leaned to the side so her arm bumps along his.

"Some days I think I don't want to be a doctor at all," she said. The words just left her mouth and floated through the air, becoming property of the polluted city air. "It's just been that thing I've been planning my entire life around and I don't know how to want to do anything else. And I'm too deep in it now to turn back. So, I guess I'll just be a doctor."

"You want to be a doctor," he said. A car next to them

honked and he jumped a little, shoulders tensing and relaxing in less than a second.

"Some days," she said.

"I have chemistry with you, Astrid," he said, shaking his head. "You love it. I sit next to you and you're just so into it. You stare at that textbook like it's the love of your life."

She took a long sip of her milkshake, letting her hair fall over her face.

He has chemistry with her. David would laugh.

If he was here. Which he wasn't. Because she and Max have been doing this thing a lot this semester where they hang out alone, just the two of them, talking and laughing and not really addressing the fact that they spend most of their time together these days.

"Now if only I could have sex with a chemistry textbook," she said.

He smiled. Her chest glowed warm.

"You're smart enough to figure it out," he said.

"But the paper cuts, Max," she sighed, and he laughed, short and sudden but wonderful. It sang in the air, made the streetlamps brighter.

"I think I'm an asshole," she whispered, like this quiet side street is a confessional.

"I think you are maybe being a little hard on yourself," Max offered, trailing his hand along the side of a bike rack.

"I never think about other people," she said. "I'm always just focusing on myself and doing what I want."

"You got me that coffee that one time," he said. "You save me a seat when I'm late to chem."

"That doesn't count," she said.

"Why not?"

It's inherently selfish because I want to spend time with you, and I want you to think I'm worth knowing.

"Because it doesn't."

"You volunteer with sick children," he said.

"For my résumé," she protested, shaking her head.

"Because you care about sick people and you want to help them," he continued. "You know? Like doctors do."

She neatly sidestepped a gyro sandwich massacred in the middle of the sidewalk, moving away from Max for a few steps.

"I want to make money," she said.

"So does everyone," he shot back. "You're fine."

"I don't feel fine," she said. "I feel gross."

"That's good," he insisted, nodding heavily. He swayed toward her. "Trust me, I've met selfish people. They don't care if they're selfish or not. They certainly don't feel gross about it."

She shook her head. "I don't know what I'm doing."

"Yes, you do," he said. "It's just two thirty, and you're getting all despondent and maudlin. You'll be fine."

She didn't have to check her phone to know it was just about 2:45, but that wasn't what was jarring.

He knew. He hadn't checked his phone either but somehow, he knew that it was around that time every night where her brain folded in on itself like a house of cards.

"Let's stay out," she said, breaking New York's cardinal rule and stopping in the middle of the street. There was no one around anyway so she didn't care.

Max kept going for a few steps before stumbling to a stop and turning around.

"I think everywhere is closed," he said.

She shrugged. "Let's just walk then," she said. *I'm not ready for this night to end*, she didn't say. *I think I'm seeing you for the first time and I don't want to look away. I feel like you're seeing me, and I've never wanted that before, but it feels addictive when it's you.* "I'm not tired yet. Are you?"

He smiled. "Not even close."

She started walking again, closing the distance between them, sliding right into place by his side. "Well, then, let's go."

SOPHOMORE SPRING
WEEK NINE

M   Cell Bio Problem Set 7; BioChem Pre-lab; Beth Israel Volunteering 5-7

T   Cell Bio Pre-lab; Physics Pre-lab; Orgo 2 read ch. 24; LAB 1-5

W   BioChem Problem Set 8; BioChem read ch. 12

Th Orgo 2 Problem Set 8; BioChem Lab Report; Physics Lab Report; Women in Lit read Woolf, "22 Hyde Park Gate"; LAB 1-5

F   PHYSICS MIDTERM 2; Physics Problem Set 8; LAB 3-5

TIP OF THE WEEK

"It's very important to see a therapist. Just in general, but for this especially. Just before you confide in a therapist about dating a superhero, make sure they aren't a powered person of any kind because . . . well, it gets a little awkward."

—*Penny Parsons*

SHE COMES INTO THE LAB ON TUESDAY AFTER-
noon, so determined to get right to work to impress Vaughn while she waits for Max to find more concrete evidence about the thefts, that she walks directly by Ben at his desk with Molly. She manages to drop her backpack at her work space before realizing anything is out of place.

"Uh," Astrid says, spinning around. She's almost too stunned to react. "Hello?"

"Hi," Molly says, waving. She's all smiles and ponytail and a pastel puffy blouse, but there's dull pink marks on her wrists like a rope burn, and a redness around her eyes.

"What are you doing here?" she asks. She almost forgets about Ben—because Molly is there, in her lab, not kidnapped, not missing, not dead. "Are you okay? What happened?"

"I'm fine," Molly says, like she's never had a reason not to be. "I stopped by to see you—and to see the lab you're always talking about!"

"I showed her the big microscope," Ben offers. Astrid stares at him for a second.

"Cool," she says. "Molly, let's go out into the hallway and talk."

"Sure thing," she says, grabbing a small bag from Ben's desk and following Astrid to the door. "It was nice meeting you, Ben."

The hallway is weird and exposed but the lab with Ben is an equally bad choice.

"What are you doing here?" Astrid asks again.

"I came to talk," Molly says slowly.

"How did you get here?"

"The subway. And the Columbia undergrad research website says what lab you're in. That Ben guy is cool. Did you know he's sixteen like me?"

"Yeah, sure," Astrid says, not even remotely prepared to talk about Ben with Molly. "Are you okay? What happened? Eleanor said that . . ."

Molly smiles sheepishly and shrugs. "I spent the weekend in the hospital." She holds up her left hand, displaying a splint on her two middle fingers. It's pink. "My mom was very freaked out and my dad grounded me for like a month, even though it's totally not my fault."

"Jesus," Astrid says, and pulls her into a hug. "Well, I'm glad you're okay." Molly pats her back with her good hand.

Molly nods. "Yeah, about that. Can we talk? About . . . uh, stuff."

Astrid steps back, glancing around the lab. Dr. Vaughn is in his office and Ben is tapping away on his desktop.

"Okay, c'mon," she says, taking Molly's wrist on her uninjured hand and leading the way to the girls' bathroom on this floor.

Molly hops right up onto the counter between the sinks, kicking her legs back and forth. She stares down at her hands in her lap.

"What's up?" Astrid asks, keeping her eyes on Molly's ponytail and not the cast on her fingers.

Molly shakes her head, exhaling shakily. "Okay, it's not like I've been looking forward to being kidnapped by some super-villain. But I feel like I've always wondered what it would be like, sitting there and being scared but knowing . . . that some-one was coming for you, that there's this literal tangible action that's proof that you are loved and protected. So for a second at first, I was sitting there, in a warehouse, tied to a chair, and I could barely breathe because there was . . . b-blood dripping into my eye, but I took a breath and I told myself that it was okay because Arthur loved me and he was coming for me." She swallows hard and closes her eyes. "But it was a long time. Like, longer than I thought, longer than it seems in the movies and on the news." Her voice shakes and cracks and breaks—it takes the soft place in Astrid's chest along with it. "I kept say-ing, I should just wait it out. Cuz Arthur was going to find me and save me and it would feel so good. But I got scared and I wanted it to just be over. I tried using some of the tricks that Eleanor taught us but the rope knots were tighter than they were when we practiced."

Molly casually rubs a hand along her face like she's not wip-ing away tears.

"I mean, the stupid thing is that he showed up." She shakes her head. "And it felt just as good as I thought it would. It was almost better, you know, that it took so long, that I got scared and stuff, because when he showed up it was such a wonderful relief."

"Um," Astrid says slowly. "What?"

"But," she says, pressing a hand over her eyes. "Then he flew me to the hospital and while I was waiting for my parents to show up, he . . . he broke up with me."

"Oh." This is not where she thought this was going. It takes her a second to catch up, to move past the horrifying rest of it and pay attention to what Molly is saying now, her hands twisting in her lap.

"He said it was to keep me safe and everything," she adds quickly. "And I tried to say all the things that Wally said you should say in response, all the points about how I can make the choice for myself and that the Program is making sure I'm prepared, but he didn't listen. And I don't know if I'm allowed back at the Fridge or how to tell Eleanor or Wally because if they make me leave the Program it'll be real and I don't know what to do."

And then Molly's crying. Like fully sobbing, snotty and shaky and loud. Astrid's shoulders go tense for a moment as she contemplates how to intervene. She wishes everyone was like her, and would just prefer to be left alone when distraught, or she at least wishes that everyone wanted to be comforted the same way, that way she could just have a process in place, maybe a little speech ready to go where she could swap out the necessary specifics.

Instead she just has these brief moments of silent horror that stretch on forever where she has to spontaneously decide how she'll try to comfort someone this time, and pray it actually works instead of making things worse.

"Uh, okay," she says, steeling herself and stepping in, touching Molly's shoulder and rubbing. It's all the prompting Molly needs to throw her arms around Astrid's shoulders and bury her snotty face against her neck.

Well, at least she's forward about what she needs.

Astrid rubs at the spot between her shoulder blades. Molly's whole chest shakes, and her lungs rattle with every shaky, desperate inhale, the noises echoing off the tile walls. Astrid makes eye contact with herself in the mirror, seeking assistance, but the mirror Astrid is no better at soothing than she is. Why would she be? These days it's a toss-up if she can even soothe herself.

"Hey," she says, eventually, when she can be heard over Molly's sniffling noises. "It'll be okay."

Molly shifts back and glances up at the ceiling like she's embarrassed. Astrid grabs a crumpled handful of one-ply toilet paper from a stall and hands it over.

"Eleanor says this happens all the time, right?" Astrid offers as Molly scrubs at her eyes. "She's not going to kick you out. And . . . with Arthur . . . who knows."

She nods. "Right." She struggles into a small smile that fights her the whole way, but it is slightly reassuring to see. "Right, of course, this happens all the time. We'll be fine."

Astrid nods, patting her on the arm.

Molly slumps back against the sinks. "I hope it doesn't feel like this every time." She sighs. "But Astrid, you can't imagine . . . when Arthur swooped into that warehouse. Knowing he was there. For me. It almost felt like . . . like I was the one with superpowers."

Max sends her a Snap at 3:17 on Wednesday morning.

It's a blurry picture of the refrigerator in the common room and a caption that's mostly gibberish.

She's awake for reasons. (Including but not limited to: insomnia, chronic anxiety, existential dread, early onset quarter-life crisis.) So just in case he's dying or something, she might as well go check on him.

It's college so someone somewhere is awake. Just in case she puts a bra on. She doesn't put real people shoes on though, for fashion and convenience, just struts out of his dorm in her slippers.

Turning off the lobby of the building toward the common areas, she can faintly hear Carly Rae Jepsen from down the hall, finds herself already smiling as she rounds the corner. Which is a dangerous thing. Just going around smiling at the thought of Max, doing something foolish and endearing. Who even is she? She's supposed to be sleeping right now.

She steps into the kitchen and amazingly, there's also dancing, if the wild explosive flailing of limbs can even be classified as such. Out on the counter, there's a whole carton of milk, a bag of baby carrots, two eggs, and a chocolate bar.

"Do I want to know?" she asks.

He nearly trips as he spins around to face her, grabbing on to the kitchen counter for balance and leaving three fingerprint dents in the marble.

"Astrid," he says, breathy, beaming, and beautiful as ever. Sweaty, his hair in damp curls and sticking to his forehead. There's a bruise on his jaw, already faded, and a line of blood across his forehead but no visible cut. He's not wearing the suit, thank God, but she can see even more incriminating scrapes along his arms that his T-shirt does not cover nearly well enough.

She exaggerates rolling her eyes and steps up to the island, planting her palms on the edge.

"Hi," she says, raising her eyebrows. She is also a little breathless, potentially close to beaming. "How's your night going?"

"Fantastic," he says. He jumps over the counter between them, remarkably graceful and fast, in the blink of an eye.

"Whoa." Up close he's vibrating, thrumming, some radiant energy practically glowing out of every pore. His eyes dance and his arms wrap around her waist and she's even closer to him, warm and sweaty and breathtakingly alive.

"I have had a great night," he announces, kissing her cheek. She grabs on to his shoulders, bunching up the rough fabric underneath her fingers as he spins her around.

He's infectious, the energy just pouring off him and making her feel floaty and light and happy, like she's flying, like she has powers beyond her own belief and nothing can hold her down, not gravity, not physics homework, not insomnia.

It's terrible. She should be asleep. She doesn't have time for this. But he's doing that magical Max thing, where he makes her feel like she has all the time in the world.

He sets her down, looking a little sheepish, face flushed pink. "Man, you have no idea," he says, spinning around and heading for the cabinets. She follows along behind him like a stupid happiness magnet, like she needs to stay in the little bubble of positivity around him. "Sometimes, going out there just sucks, it sucks *so hard*. And you just see how terrible people can be and it feels like you're not actually accomplishing anything. But tonight." He punches the air, spinning around again and grabbing her hand. "It was wonderful. I was unstoppable, I was killing it, I was helping people. Five muggings, this piece of scaffolding that almost fell on top of this pregnant lady. I even got some asshole harassing a girl at the park to apologize."

He exhales in a loud, long, relieved sigh, his head tipping back, his eyes closing as he smiles at the ceiling.

She thinks she could potentially maybe understand why someone would do this if it feels half as good as just watching the high.

"That sounds great," she says, lacing her fingers between his, rubbing her thumb along the back of his wrist.

He bounces on the balls of his feet and glides over to his collection of ingredients.

"Where'd you get this?" she asks, poking at his forehead.

"Mugger number three, I think," he says, batting her hand away and grabbing the milk. "Had a switchblade."

"Yikes," she says, leaning her back up against the counter next to him, bumping her hip against his.

He shakes his head. "Nah, it was nothing." He sighs. "God, I could have stayed out all night."

"We have a physics lab quiz tomorrow," she says as he pours two glasses of milk.

"I know," he says, rolling his eyes.

She pokes at his side, smiles a little when he doesn't wince. "Don't goof it up."

"I won't," he says. "I'm great at lab."

Oh no, he's getting cocky, has a little smug grin as he grabs a baby carrot and munches on it.

She shakes her head. "I guess I don't need to help you study for it then."

"Maybe you," he says, raising his eyebrows, tapping her forehead, "should be asking *me* for help studying."

Yeah, this is not going to fly. She gapes at him.

"I don't like this," she says, waving her hand around his face. "This is not working for me."

He shrugs and pushes away from the counter, returning to the fridge.

"Sorry, babe, I'm just on fire this week." He procures a bottle of chocolate syrup, tossing it and flipping it.

"I'm breaking up with you," she decides.

"Or," he says, popping the top of the syrup. "You *don't* break up with me and I'll make you some chocolate milk."

The amount of chocolate he pours into his glass is ungodly, tens of seconds of a steady stream of syrup. The milk starts to turn a light brown before he even gets a spoon to stir it. He does not need the sugar. Her insomnia does not need the sugar.

"Or," she says, pushing off the counter. "I don't break up with you and you let me make myself some chocolate milk that won't give me a blood clot."

She holds her hand out.

He smiles and she doesn't think he's looked this happy in months. This is some unachievable level of happiness, reserved for uncomplicated birthdays and moderate to extreme life accomplishments. This is a happy high, a hit so hard that the contact high alone is knocking her on her ass and making her feel like she just saved the city.

He passes her the bottle, the plastic slapping solidly in her palm.

"And," she says, taking a spoon and measuring out a respectful and optimized two tablespoons of the syrup.

"And?" he says, his spoon clinking violently at the edges of the glass.

Sleep is overrated. She has her vitamin C pills to boost her immune system and a boyfriend to pay for an extra shot in her coffee tomorrow.

"I don't break up with you, we drink some chocolate milk," she says, "and then we make out."

He looks too smug and she hates him.

"Do we?"

"Somewhere other than the communal kitchen," she adds.

"Deal."

◆◆◆

There is relatively no purpose to her being in the lab since Vaughn took her off any kind of actual lab duty. It's not like she cannot go in though, there's still work expected of her but it's sitting at her desk in the corner and staring at her desktop there, typing up codes to turn data sets into graphs.

Which . . . sucks. It really sucks.

While her stupid codes load their stupid graphs, she has time for other things. It's good for homework, of course, studying as always, and also keeping track of everyone else in the lab, even though it gets increasingly frustrating to watch Ben Barnes pour plates and look at slides while she sits in her little corner.

Today though, while she waits for her latest data set to download, she decides to put in some genuine detective work. Specifically she looks into her second ruined cell cultures to sketch out a timeline.

There's no record of the lab being broken into that overlaps with that thirty-six-hour window she left them unattended, and she has access to the lab calendar that isn't a completely accurate account of the comings and goings of people, but two days before her shift in the lab, Greg and Vaughn had scheduled—

"Hey."

She jerks and closes out of the tab in the space between her suddenly speeding heartbeats.

Raj stands by her desk, looking at her with mild concern, which honestly is how most people look at her these days. She can't bring herself to be too worried about it.

"Yeah?" she asks.

"Vaughn's had you doing the graphs of the raw data from our latest round of slides, right?" he asks.

"Uh . . . yes."

"Well, they're looking really good," he says, nodding. "Really . . . organized and helpful. So . . . keep up the good work." He taps the lab table next to him once with the bottom of his water bottle and takes a half step back. "And . . . for the record, I don't think you've been stealing things." He grimaces briefly and nods, before turning and heading back to his desk.

Astrid watches him go before turning to stare at herself in the dark parts of her desktop's screen saver.

She floats on her way back to Max's dorm. Like her backpack is full of balloons instead of textbooks. Like the red brick pathways of campus are made of that springy black tile that surrounds swings on the playground.

"You've infected me with positive energy," she announces as she swings his door open and swings herself in after it. She doesn't even know if he's in the room when she makes her announcement but that's okay because it's in part an announcement for herself that today was a wonderful day and she did great in lab and now there's Raj as this new path to redemption, and convincing Dr. Vaughn that she's not a monumental fuckup and can absolutely be trusted with regular lab work again, and maybe someday, some far-off distant day, her own research project and a glowing letter of rec for her med school application.

Max is in the room, which makes the victory that much sweeter because not only is she on the top of her game academically, she has a beautiful, wonderful boyfriend.

But there's also another person in the room, a short, very muscular girl sitting on top of his dresser. And his Johto region poster is laid out carefully on his bed because the free wall is now covered in pictures and Post-it notes and red string.

The girl on the dresser has her fists clenched and eyes Astrid with suspicion, like she's a threat. Her eyes are also yellow and glowing and Astrid blinks, stepping back for a moment.

"Hi," Max says. She's not sure if he's moving toward her or she's moving toward him, because they just gravitate toward each other because they're kinda in love even though she hasn't said it yet and he only says it over the phone.

"Hey," she says.

"Uh, this is Katy," Max says, gesturing to the girl on the dresser. "Katy, this is my girlfriend, Astrid."

"Hello," Katy says.

"Uh, Astrid . . . knows," he says, raising his eyebrows.

Katy's shoulders slump and she grins. "Oh, awesome," she says. "I'm Tiger Girl, by the way."

Max nods. "She has tiger powers," he says, as if this explains everything. "They come from this amulet, but the amulet is missing, and we think it might have been stolen by the same guy who's been stealing from the labs around here." He shrugs.

"We're working the case right now."

"Cool," Astrid says. She glances over at the explosion of papers up on the wall. "I guess I'll see if I can work at Wally's then."

"Oh my God, no," Katy says. "I would hate to kick you out of your own room."

"It's Max's room actually," she says, stepping back toward the door.

"We can be quiet," Max says, eyes going big and soft. She shrugs.

"It's fine," she says. "See you for dinner?"

Max grimaces. "Uh . . . maybe?"

She knows what that maybe means and texts Wally, asking about his dinner plans.

Astrid is in no place to waste time these days, but she's also in no place to turn down a free home-cooked meal.

Even still, she doesn't think she would miss this for the world. As she's posited a million times, in order to optimize your efficiency, in order to truly get your best work done, you need to give yourself emotional fuel so you don't run on empty.

This. This is some grade A emotional fuel.

"It's so nice to finally meet you," Henry says, and engulfs her hand in his huge one. His voice is deep and booming but smooth as honey. He's tall and broad shouldered, wearing a red button-down and a smile so neat it belongs in commercials.

"Same here," she says, trying to mimic the literal superhuman firmness of his grip and failing completely.

"So did you tell him I'm coming for your job in ten years?" she asks Wally, sitting down at the dinner table and crossing her legs.

Henry beams. "He has not actually," he says. Wally flicks him on the forehead as he makes his way to the table carrying mashed potatoes with bits of potato skins.

"Okay, know that this is only happening because you both bullied me into it, and also know that I will kick either or both of you out of my apartment," Wally announces, setting bowls on the table. He stares directly at her, raising his eyebrows with significance.

She tilts her head. *Me? I would never.*

"My name is on the lease too, babe," Henry says. He brings over a pitcher of lemonade as he takes his seat next to Wally.

"A mistake I regret every day."

"Ignore him." Henry pushes Wally's hair out of his eyes as he sits down. "We are deeply in love. He just gets crotchety when he's hungry."

Wally frowns. "You get crotchety when you're always," he taunts back, swatting Henry's hand away.

Henry just keeps on his megawatt smile, with dopey, gooey love in his eyes.

"Henry made the branzino," Wally says. "And the streamed broccoli. That's why they're all mushy and overcooked."

"Honey, you love my steamed broccoli."

"Sweetheart, you're about to gang up on me with a twelve-year-old girl."

"I'm pretty sure that's your future boss, darling," Henry

says, and shoots her a smile.

So, this is what a superhero looks like. Sure, Max is a super-hero, but the signs of it are in the bruises and the scrapes, the tired look in his eyes, the slump of his spine. (And his biceps, triceps, and more, but that's neither here nor there.)

Henry looks like the real deal. He's big and bulky and talks like that and smiles like that. He belongs on a cereal box, standing tall on a rooftop, saving a cat from a tree, punching a bad guy in the face.

His jaw is sharp and as rectangular as the frame of his glasses. His hair sweeps over his forehead in perfect black swoops, clean lines and a clean shave. His terracotta brown skin glows in the warm light of his warm apartment.

He leans over to press a kiss to Wally's temple and it's almost cinematic in how gracefully he moves, the way the light hits him, the face he makes when Wally pushes at his shoulder.

"Sucks that Max couldn't be here," Henry says, scooping potatoes onto his plate.

"Yeah, he's been pretty busy today," she says. "Something with Tiger Girl. I don't know."

"Oh, Katy's in town?" Henry says, nodding. "Probably up against the Black Cape then. Man, Wal, do you remember back when I was fighting the Black Cape?"

"I remember your awful haircut from back when you fought the Black Cape," Wally says. He still looks Soft and Fond even as he tries to be witty.

Henry launches into a thrilling tale of grand heroics and long-winded monologues, and one very convoluted plan that included a play for the mayor's life and hypnotism gas. Astrid listens intently even though it's the kind of thing that happens once every other month or so. Henry has details the news never did though, direct quotes from henchmen and the Big Bad, funny details about how the secret lair smelled like the Greek restaurant it was underneath.

The broccoli is pretty good. It all makes something in her settle after a stressful week, watching Wally and Henry go back and forth, bickering and telling adventure stories. This is their life.

After an hour Henry pushes his chair out and carries his plate to the sink, patting Astrid's shoulder before he heads to their bedroom to get dressed in his super suit and climb out the window.

"Patrolling," Wally says, rolling his eyes. "Does it every weeknight because he doesn't want to sit the hell down and watch Fallon with me."

"Well, I better go, too, then," she says, and scoops herself a serving of mashed potatoes despite herself. "God knows I don't want to watch Fallon with you."

Max trips over his laptop charger when he gets back to his room at 4:45 in the morning. He apologizes profusely as he climbs into bed.

"How'd it go?" she asks.

"Found the amulet," he says. "And some of the stolen lab stuff. Didn't catch the guy who did it, but saved a whole lot of people."

"Congrats," she says.

"How was your day?"

"Amazing actually. I did a great job in lab. Just a banner day."

"Wow," he breathes. "You're brilliant."

"Thank you. You know, you're not too bad yourself."

"Look at us," he says, and she can hear his smile in the dark and quiet. Her eyes are heavy and don't want to stay open, so she lets them fall shut.

"Look at us," she agrees, and he meets her hand in the air for a sloppy high five.

A SCHOOL BUS INCIDENT
RETROSPECTIVE

IT'S NOT THAT THE SCHOOL BUS INCIDENT changed her life.

It wasn't even the first big Max Incident she had been near. There was the Football Field Incident, really more of a Debacle if she was going to get into it. There was their junior year field trip to Rockefeller Center and she would have been actually up on the observation platform when the fire started if she hadn't gotten really bad period cramps and missed most of the excitement, bent over in a stall in the public restrooms down on the concourse level.

Those times she hadn't been too close to the action. She had followed emergency procedure, had exited the area calmly and swiftly, and everything worked out just fine, even if her heart raced and her brain buzzed.

During the School Bus Incident there were no emergency procedures. Just the wheels squealing and everyone around her screaming. Just a feeling of weightlessness and a cold panic that began in the base of her spine and shot all the way up to her skull, a twist of fear in her stomach that felt like a stabbing, a numbness behind her eyes, and she thought violently, desperately, *Wait, wait, wait. I'm not done yet; I haven't even started.*

An eternity in a second where she thought about fifteen years and how for most of them she hadn't even known what it meant to be alive, hadn't even known what she was or who she could be or that the world was round and that she was made of cells and cells were made of atoms, that there was no limit to what insane combinations of particles the universe could hold.

She contemplated hours spent waiting on line for food in the cafeteria staring blankly at the person ahead of her, summer days she let slip away, daydreaming about nothing as bright yellow sunlight shifted around her bedroom, hours on her couch scrolling through the internet but not consuming anything, just passing the time.

She had been organized before. She had wanted to be a doctor before. She had been relatively hardworking and well behaved, and had a general idea of what she was going to try to accomplish.

And then she was on asphalt, forehead to her knees, grateful for time and concrete and her squishy legs and creaky knees like she never had been before.

Never again, she decided, there on the ground, at first, not really sure what she was swearing off. But between seconds and breaths it started to crystallize. No more unplanned days. No more waiting around. No more wasted, unaccounted for time.

SOPHOMORE SPRING
WEEK TEN

M SPRING BREAK
T SPRING BREAK
W SPRING BREAK
Th SPRING BREAK
F SPRING BREAK

ASTRID IS SO DEEP INTO THE SEMESTER THAT IT
feels a little weird to not be wearing a backpack. Because she's
not—she's carrying a light beach bag over her shoulder with a
large towel and a hefty paperback she's been planning to read
since the winter of eighth grade.

It's spring break.

She's glowing with it. Pores clear, hair shining, every bone
in her body suddenly lighter. No classes, a week off from the
Program, no lab hours, no club meetings, no large assignments.

She got grades back for her Physics midterm that went great, and her second Orgo midterm that went well enough for her to not have to hate herself. David left for his plane last night and she slept in her dorm for the first time in weeks, the air in the room free of any emotional weight.

Max opens his door and she wants to throw herself into his arms, ready to be lifted and spun around like a Disney princess. But her bag would get in the way and she's not sure about the mechanics of a full spin like that—where her legs should go, if they could even fit it in the doorway without a severe injury—as much as she feels like she's in an animated movie, overflowing with color, light, hand-drawn lines, and a string-heavy score.

She settles for wrapping her fingers around his wrist and leaning in to kiss him, solidly and soundly. It's a zing that lights her blood on fire. Her heart stutters, skipping and singing.

"Hi," she says after, embarrassingly breathless. She presses past him into the room, taking in the tangled bedsheets, the ominous streak of dried probably-blood on the side of his desk, the one corner of his Johto region poster that unstuck, slipping down the wall. Better. Calmer. Okay. No need to even sit down, she rolls her bag up onto her shoulder.

"Okay," she says, and turns around, leaning up against the edge of his desk so she doesn't have to look or think about the bloodstain. "So, I've been checking the Weather app and also a lot of the NOAA radar sites, and on the bright side there's no way it's going to rain for the next three days. Unfortunately, it's not going to break sixty, but I don't think we should let that stop us, you know. I have some blankets in case we get too chilly, and you should grab your brown corduroy jacket because it is not hoodie season just yet, unless, do you ever need a jacket? Do you get cold?"

Max is staring at her, blinking with wide, doleful eyes, lips parted just a little.

She frowns.

"Have you not . . . seen the news?" Max asks, stepping toward her hesitantly. He's halfway into his suit she realizes, the top of it rumpled around his waist, sleeves hanging toward the floor.

He looks guilty which is a bad sign, very bad, she feels the dread in her chest like a weighted blanket.

"Max, I just walked from my dorm room to your dorm room," she says. "How would I watch the news?"

He rubs at the back of the neck.

"Okay, so you have to go save the world," she says, closing her eyes and letting her head tip back, straining at her neck. "Fine. That's fine." She exhales and straightens up. "Okay. Be safe and, like, good luck."

He's still grimacing, still guilty. She steps toward him, lets her hands brush over his bare shoulders, the tan and miraculously unblemished skin.

"Um . . . it's a little more than that," he says.

Her phone starts to buzz.

◆ ◆ ◆

A Code Green is one of the rainbow of emergency situations she's been quizzed on every week. It's one of the three emergency codes that require lockdown for all Hero Significant Others.

Code Shape-shifters.

Astrid has to immediately head to the Fridge for twofold reasons. So Max knows, not only exactly where she is, but that she is somewhere that is not where the shape-shifters are. And so that she won't have to encounter any shape-shifters she might mistake for Max.

A Code Green also means that her spring break plans are canceled.

She can't bring herself to do more than trudge her way down the subway steps as she heads downtown, even as everyone else on the streets seems to be moving much faster. She waits an extra twenty minutes for the 1 Train—the subways are running with extreme delays. As she waits, she reads the news with a passing interest, like she's not living the trending topics again. The whole city seems to be shutting down, except some areas of Queens that are still holding out, like this might be one of the short alien invasions. A meme about NYU catches her eye; apparently, they've canceled classes for the whole week. It nearly sparks the extremely rare anger migraine right at the space between her eyes, because goddamn, if it was any other week she could have found the beautiful bright side in a city-wide catastrophe, namely that she could actually have some time off. But this was already supposed to be her time off. And, of course, she has the Program. And Codes. And rules.

Instead here she is, turning off the avenue and walking down the side street to the brownstone.

Telepathic alien robot shape-shifters.

If anything is going to ruin her week.

She scans her finger, passes a vocal test, a DNA test, answers close to ten security questions that are deeply personal, and presents her phone as indisputable proof that she is really her. She wonders how hard it would actually be for an impostor to fake any of this, but also doesn't want to know the answer. Hailey the AI is sweet through the whole thing, but it's excruciatingly long, and even has her wondering for a second if she *might be* a telepathic alien robot shape-shifter.

Identity confirmed, she's let into the Fridge like it's some privilege and not number three on the Places She Did Not Want to Be Today right after her dorm room and the bottom of the Hudson River. The rec room is empty but she sees a little pile of bags along the back wall, recognizes Lucy's dark High Sierra backpack and Thomas's gym bag. There's also a lot of over-the-shoulder bags, a few hard-shelled suitcases, three duffel bags.

Probably belonging to any of the muted voices coming from nearby rooms or footsteps pacing along the hallway. Astrid considers meeting new people right now, on a very bad day that was supposed to be a very good day and the start to a very good week, and decides she'd rather hide here instead.

She doesn't even put her bag down with the others, just goes over to the La-Z-Boy she always thinks of as Wally's and drops down with all her stuff. The paperback in her beach bag—a symbol of relaxation and freedom, a cherry on top of her romantic day in Central Park with Max, where she could pretend that life was good and she was in control—now carries the toxic cursed energy of another absurd New York alien invasion.

She pulls it out and starts reading anyway. It feels like a chore, like homework, something she has to do now because she said she would. The fluorescent light scratches against the off-white of the pages, the way the early spring sunlight would have bounced.

The alien invasion does not clear up by the end of the day so they end up staying the night.

Molly, Lucy, and Thomas join her in the rec room, and decide to have a proper sleepover instead of retreating to the secret, sprawling, underground section of the Fridge with, somehow, assigned bunks for everyone. It makes Astrid wonder what else is down there.

Molly and Thomas knock off soon after midnight, perpendicular on the floor because they couldn't decide who should take the couch. Astrid is content to stay up another few hours, probably couldn't fall asleep any earlier if she tried since staying up late is practically ingrained into her bones, so she perches on her chair and scrolls through updates about the invasion on Twitter.

So far nothing too catastrophic has happened, just some mild damage to the Statue of Liberty, and a few destroyed (empty) city buses. Nothing new, but no end in sight just yet.

Across the room, Lucy shifts in place again, like she has been the past few minutes, and pushes her blankets off. She sighs belaboredly before she sits up straight, shoulders slumped as she reaches for her phone, the bright screen splashing light across her face.

"Hey, uh," Astrid says in a half whisper, because she's tired enough to not overthink saying something. "Everything okay?"

"I'm fine," Lucy says, shooting her a tight smile.

"Sure. Cool," she agrees, nodding steadily. "Because like . . . you know you could talk to me, if you wanted to talk to someone, about something, anything." She winces, immediately feels unqualified, and hopes Lucy will ignore her.

Lucy runs her fingers through her hair, jostling her curls.

"I can't shake the feeling that . . . she could die," she says, her eyes darting down to her lap. "And . . . I'll just be down here. Or if it's not today, it'll just be the next time something like this happens."

"Oh," Astrid says. She wonders if she should move closer, offer Lucy some patented awkward but earnest physical contact. She also wonders if this is something she should be worrying about, too.

"So, like, what's the point?" Lucy says, hands going up in exasperation, clutching the back of her head. "What's the point of falling in love with someone, with your best friend, when you know they're probably going to die?"

For a single second Astrid's mind closes around the concept of Max with some horrible injury that isn't a cut quickly fading to clean, untouched skin, Max gasping out those little pained noises, Max not breathing, chest not rising no matter how long she stares.

"She's not going to die," Astrid says. She hopes it sounds conclusive enough.

Lucy's eyes snap open. "You don't know that."

"Yeah, well, like, she's not going to so . . ." Astrid trails off, sees how Lucy's jaw clenches, her eyes narrow. She sighs. "Or, she's gonna die anyway. And you're going to die, and your parents are going to die and everyone you love is going to die eventually. Someone dies every three seconds. There's cancer and early-onset Alzheimer's. There are cars and trains and knives and guns and . . . like, large rocks that people can pick up and throw really hard. So, sure, she could die, but so could you and so could any other girl you date."

Lucy blinks and Astrid blinks back.

"So . . . what do I do?" Lucy asks.

"Don't think about it too much?" Astrid says. "Trust me, thinking about it does not help."

"That's all?" Lucy asks.

"Well, there's no real solution," she says. She offers a small smile even though she's not sure Lucy can even make it out in the dark. "But it's better than the alternative."

Despite being the last to fall asleep, she's also the first to wake up. Sometimes her infallible internal clock is a curse.

There's a text on her phone from David, an unassuming *u ok?* that makes her chest hurt the longer she stares at it. She sends off a quick thumbs-up in response before tucking her phone away and getting up to wander.

She finds Wally in the kitchen off the line of bunks, staring blankly at the coffee machine on the counter as it slowly drips.

"Where have you been?" she asks.

"Hospital," he replies, waving his hand. "Late shift. And all I want to do is head back to my apartment and take a long hot shower but alas, my apartment is not secured enough for this type of alien invasion."

Astrid frowns as she starts poking around the cabinets for food. "You were still at work?"

He nods. "All hands on deck."

"Well . . . what's it like out there?"

"Pretty tame. Not too many civilian injuries. Definitely not as bad as that time three years ago with those weird spirally spaceships. Do you remember those or were you in the womb?"

She flips him off and carries a loaf of bread over to the toaster.

The coffee machine beeps and Wally is on it immediately, grabbing the pot and pouring himself a hefty mug.

"Hey, uh . . . ," she says, after loading two slices of bread into the toaster. "Lucy's been pretty worried about Jane." She's run out of things to busy herself with so she turns toward Wally, leaning up against the counter. "I basically told her everything was going to be fine, but . . . it might help her to hear it from you."

Wally comes up for air from chugging half his coffee.

"She might not be," he says finally.

"Might not?" she echoes.

"Jane might not be fine," he says. "Sometimes with things like this . . . and she's a high schooler, this might be her first one, and the first one is always the toughest."

Astrid watches him warily. "She's a superhero."

"Yeah," Wally says. "They tend to die a lot. Especially the high schoolers. They never know what they're doing. Always get in over their heads. Why do you think you guys are all so young? We try to find the high schoolers first, since you need this help the most."

"You said Henry was in high school when he started."

"Yeah," Wally agrees. "He was in over his head. And he got lucky."

"And Max," she says. "Max made it through high school."

"Barely," Wally says with a little huff and then has the decency to meet her eyes across the kitchen island. "Sorry, not a joke. Wow, not a joke." He rubs at his temples. "I am so tired."

"What do you mean?" she asks, narrowing her eyes.

Wally blinks, tilts his head. "The really bad one. Do you not . . ." He shifts uncomfortably, drums his fingers on the countertop. "I've met Max before, you know? There was a close call like two years ago. Right after you guys graduated,

I think. Henry knew that I was in the area and called me in, couldn't even wait for a real doctor. It was that bad." He shakes his head. "At the end of the day it was fine. I mean, I wasn't even licensed yet, but I was able to get him stabilized. Accelerated healing is an absolute beauty. He was just out for a few weeks. Only a few hours were all that touch and go."

"Max almost died," she says. *Right after graduation*, she doesn't say. *When my last memory of him would have been meeting his eyes across a gymnasium and not even seeing him, just feeling a pang of nostalgia for a face in a hall that meant familiarity. When I would have debated going to his funeral and then went and felt impending dread in the face of a chaotic universe but nothing more, no real grief.*

"It's really that dangerous?" she asks. She's heard of heroes dying. She's watched the memorials on the news. But they've always been older and most of the time they come back a few months later anyway.

Wally shrugs. "Yeah."

"Why do they do it then?" she asks. "I mean, Jesus, why would anyone?"

"Because they're brave," Wally says. He comes around the counter and watches the toaster with her. "Or because they're stupid. Mostly because they're good though, I think. Because they were given some incredible gift and instead of using it for personal gain, instead of just using it casually, keeping themselves safe, they decided that they were going to protect other people, help those who can't help themselves."

"That doesn't make sense," she says.

"Maybe," Wally agrees. He scratches his eyebrow. "I mean, I'm inclined to believe it's a little bit more than just insensible, but . . ."

She turns to him, arms crossed tight.

"But?" she says.

"Henry died once," he says. Not looking at her. "I don't remember it. Someone, I think Circe, went back in time to stop it from happening. Henry told me about it. He says he remembers it vaguely, like a dream. I don't. Just remember him coming home and telling me that there was a timeline where he died today. And I think about that more than I should, I think. That there's a timeline out there where I lost him. Probably more than one considering how he's just . . . like that. In that timeline, that me probably doesn't think it's as brave or good. I probably think it's really senseless, and I probably hate him for it, for letting himself die for a bunch of other people and leaving me to mourn him."

The whole of the invasion takes about three days. They pass slowly, in the fluorescent lights of the Fridge. She works on homework that isn't due for weeks, watches movies with the other kids, finishes the paperback even when it starts to get really boring. The Fridge is filled with people Astrid doesn't know and doesn't speak to, mostly women, some children, and Molly seems to be able to rattle off résumés for all of them. She doesn't see Eleanor once.

And then, all of a sudden, it's over. Hailey opens the elevator doors, and Astrid swears they're glowing with the golden light of outdoors. She texts Max the second she's aboveground.

The sunlight is almost too much after seventy-two hours in a bunker. She squints into it as she waves goodbye and starts down the street. The air is fresh and smells like bus exhaust and garbage and weed but also street meat and sunshine and the starts of blooming flowers. It's like nothing has changed. She passes busy people on busy streets. The cars honk, the ground shakes a little with trains rushing underneath.

It's cloudy overhead but not too cold, not rainy yet either.

New York, she thinks. Resilient and always moving, always changing and shifting and never stopping for a second no matter what happens.

She'll watch the news later, and it'll probably hit her harder, the idea of the chaos that must have splattered over streets, invading lives and destroying property and wrecking days.

She'll look into it all later, when the past few days are thoroughly in the rearview mirror. For now, she just walks along the street, letting the sound of the city bury itself into her bones. She only stops moving once she reaches Central Park, stands at a midpoint between a subway exit and a park entrance.

Max jogs up, his hair dark and wet, recently showered, smile bright but eyes desperate and deep. She steps toward him, but he reaches her in a second, wrapping his arms around her waist and swinging her around.

"Whoa," she says, and tries to pretend her heart isn't pounding, her soul isn't flying. She hasn't seen him in three days.

That's the explanation for why she feels so breathless. It has to be.

"Hey," he breathes, kissing her forehead, her temple, her cheek.

"I finished my paperback," she says, running a hand through his damp, soft hair. "It was kinda contrived and I hated the protagonist."

He exhales deeply, face pressing into her neck.

There's a spot of dried blood behind his ear, behind his jaw. She rubs it away with her thumb, rubs her hand off on her jeans. It's probably not his blood, she thinks. It's probably just generic blood. Generic, non-Max blood.

"Tell me about it," he says, and she can feel his voice vibrate through her rib cage.

"Obviously."

It starts to rain about forty-three minutes after they've set up in the grass, and the forecast for the rest of the week is similarly smattered with little gray clouds.

So that's spring break.

They ride the subway together back to campus, Max leaning his head on her shoulder and swaying with the movement of the train.

"And then I grabbed the top of the lamppost and threw it at the antigravity machine," he explains in a near silent whisper, even though the car is mostly empty anyway and people are averting their eyes like she and Max are about to start making out. Which they very well might be if she has anything to say about it. "And Nightwatcher was able to make it into the building while I helped clear those people from the bus, so it all worked out."

It sounds so cinematic as he describes it, but she can't quite picture Max there, just a Max-shaped blur of color and motion.

"Hey," she says, tracing an absent series of shapes on the back of his hand. "Did you almost die the summer before freshman year?"

He sits up a little, letting out a little laugh and rubbing the back of his neck like it's something deeply embarrassing. "Oh yeah. It was . . . well, it wasn't that bad, the coma was only about a month or so."

"You say things like this too casually," she says, turning toward him but only a little, not sure if she can handle a full picture of him.

He shrugs. "I mean, it felt pretty big at the time. It scared me a lot, that I could have died or something. It's why I stopped doing the hero thing and fully enrolled at Columbia. But . . . in retrospect, it's just something that happens. In the biz, you know?"

Month-long comas and near-death experiences. Just an occupational hazard.

"I can't imagine ever wanting to risk something like that," she mumbles.

He laces his fingers through hers and settles back against her side. "It's easier than you think," he says. "If it means saving the world, helping people. You . . . do what you have to do."

He says it so casually, but Astrid feels her anxiety coiling in her gut. Because she somehow lives in a world where getting knocked into a month-long coma is something Max might have to do. And she has no idea what she might have to do.

FRESHMAN SPRING
WEEK TEN

MAX WAS ALWAYS UNBELIEVABLY EASY TO READ, like a lovely little romance novel. Fluffy and fun, leaving her with warm fuzzies and a relaxed smile.

When he rubbed the back of his neck that meant he was embarrassed. He furrowed his eyebrows together when he was feeling serious and noble. If he tipped his chin back it meant he was happy. When he was uncomfortable, he smiled with his teeth. (Only when he smiled with the corners of his mouth was he actually amused.) If he pressed his lips together and grinned it meant he was overjoyed.

And that spring, when he blinked at her and tilted his head and swallowed hard, it meant that he was pining after her but would never say anything in fear of ruining their wonderful, meaningful friendship. When he smiled just a hint while his eyes sparkled fondly and his breaths went shallow, it meant holy shit, he was feeling that kind of way and probably wanted to kiss her.

He slowed his gangly legs to walk in step with her to the building where she had her 10:00 a.m. chemistry, on the way to his 10:00 a.m. calculus. He held the door open for her because she was still working on her to-go cup of cafeteria coffee, and he tapped his shoulder against hers before peeling off to head to the second floor. All of it, all the clues, the little looks and shoulder taps, it meant he was there, he was hers for the taking and . . .

She sat down in the second row of her chemistry lecture. For four whole minutes, she forgot why she was there. She didn't take out her notebooks and her pencils and highlighters and try to fit them all on the tiny foldout desk. And that meant she wanted him, too.

SOPHOMORE SPRING

WEEK ELEVEN

M   Cell Bio Problem Set 8; BioChem pre-lab

T   Cell Bio Pre-lab; Physics Pre-lab; Orgo 2 read ch. 25; LAB 1-5

W BioChem Problem Set 9; BioChem read ch. 14

Th Orgo 2 Problem Set 9; BioChem Lab Report; Physics Lab Report; Women in Lit read Kingston, "No Name Woman"; LAB 1-5

F   WOMEN IN LIT PAPER 2; Physics Problem Set 9; LAB 3-5

TIP OF THE WEEK

"One thing you must prepare yourself for is that you might die, your significant other might die. Many times in fact. Death, like anything else, is temporary. Grief, when dating a superhero, is tricky. My biggest piece of advice is to give it about three months. If it's really sticking after that, then you can start to worry."

—*Claire Stevens*

THERE'S A KNOCK ON MAX'S WINDOW.

She's so deep into rotational kinematics problems it makes her jump out of her skin. She jolts, nearly knocking over Max's lava lamp.

There he is in the window in his stupid blue suit, squatting on the window frame, his hand against the glass. It's not an unusual sight. He's been busy the past few weeks, still following clues about the lab thefts. But even without having found the guy responsible, the stuff he found and returned has meant that there's always a second microscope for her to use. And Dr. Vaughn has stopped giving her suspicious frowns when he sees her in the lab, so she considers it firmly a win.

She raises her eyebrows at him, hoping he can see her amused expression as she pushes out from his desk chair and strolls over to the window to let him in.

The latch opens easier than the window she and David share, but the window squeaks all the same as she yanks it up and open, a strained, rubbery whine that makes her wince.

"Hey," she says, grinning at him. "You didn't throw any rocks." She leans up a little to bring them level, but can't see if he's smiling or not. "Do you have to throw rocks if it's your own window?"

His hand lands on her shoulder and she takes the hint, rolling her eyes and stepping aside.

She expects something annoyingly graceful, a weird yet poetic ninja-type movement, maybe with some flip or tumble. Instead he pitches forward, dropping in and falling flat to the floor, his hand grasping at the edge of his bed, yanking his comforter down on top of him as he lands in a heap.

"Max," she says, stepping around him and reaching down to untangle him from the blanket.

He grunts once, his hands wedging themselves beneath his shoulders as he pushes himself up.

She manages to pull the blanket away just as his arms give out and he collapses to the hardwood floor again with a thump and a whine.

"Max," she says, slower. Then she catches sight of his back and a sudden shock of cold panic cuts down into her bones. "Jesus."

A red gash runs diagonally across his back, from his left shoulder down to his right side, below his ribs. She assumes, based on the cut in his suit. It's hard to tell. His whole back is covered in blood, the fabric soaked through.

"Ow," he says, lifting his head up a few inches. "Whoa, okay . . . Sorry, I think I passed out there for a second."

"What happened?" she says. Her hands hover over his back, looking for something to do to fix it, stop the bleeding, heal the wound.

"Had a fight with Knife Man," Max says. "He has a pretty big knife." He huffs out a laugh and then winces and then coughs wetly for five seconds longer than she's remotely comfortable with. "Hey, what's the difference between a knife and a sword?"

Breathe in. The voice in her head sounds like Wally when he's using his therapist voice.

She takes a breath, holds it, exhales.

"Where's the first aid kit?" she asks, pushing up.

"Hmm?" There's another cut on his cheek but it doesn't look nearly as bad. The blood is lighter, and the skin doesn't look like it's peeling away. Which it absolutely does on his back by the way. "Oh. Oh, I'm fine."

"Max," she says again as a substitute for the way she really wants to scream into a pillow.

He twists around to look at her, grimacing and hissing when his back moves. She drops her hand to his shoulder and pushes him down, holding him in place.

"The first aid kit," she repeats. He closes his eyes, his hand coming up to close over hers.

"Astrid," he says, the light, charmed way he always does, his voice only barely shaky, his soft little smile only mildly bloody. "I'm alright. Really."

"You're bleeding," she says.

"This is nothing."

She scoffs, her breath stuttering with the panic that's rising in her throat. "It doesn't look like nothing, Max."

"I've had worse," he offers.

"That is not reassuring."

"Look," he says, tilting his head, peering up at her with a smile that's too wide for the situation at hand. His eyes are droopy, the same way he looks when he's just woken up from a nap. "It hurts, but I'm fine. I promise. It'll heal itself before you know it."

"You need stitches," she says. The skin is split open. He's

267

lost blood. She should call a hospital. But since that's not an option she's gonna get some early practice in. Not that she's trained or qualified to give stitches or to disinfect a cut like this. Not that she's ever seen this much blood in her life. She balls up the blanket between her hands and presses it against his back, leaning her weight onto him to apply pressure.

"Astrid," Max says, sighing softly. His head dips a little, back toward the floor before he seems to jerk back awake. "I don't need stitches. I never need stitches." He tries to push himself up again. She presses him back down, as firmly as she dares, watching stray streams of blood trickle along invisible paths in his skin to the rug as his body moves. "I'm serious. You should get back to work. I just need to sleep it off."

"You're bleeding out on the floor of my dorm," she says.

"I thought this was my dorm," he says, squinting, like they're just teasing around. Like she isn't breathing through her mouth because the room is starting to smell like blood.

"Well, it'll become mine if you die," she snaps.

"Then why are you even trying to save my life?" he says.

"Max," she says for the thousandth time.

He reaches over his shoulder to pat her hand where it presses into his back. The blanket, while soaked, seems to be holding. The worst seems to be over. At least, she hopes.

"I'm alright," Max says again. "Just need to get up into bed so I can sleep it off."

She shakes her head and stands, stepping over his torso to reach the desk.

"Stay," she says, when he tries to move, pointing firmly. She rifles through his drawers, her hands almost shaking as she pushes through the jumble of stuff. Nothing in his desk has a proper place, and it's exactly for occasions like this that things should have proper places, so she doesn't have to spend nearly a minute and a half almost hyperventilating before she finds a pair of scissors.

"What are you doing?" he asks, half mumbled into his elbow.

She kneels back down near his head, frowning even as he reaches out and pats sleepily at her knee.

"Don't move," she says, pulling the fabric away from the wound.

"I'm concerned," he announces. "You don't have a degree yet."

"I'm getting this absurd Halloween costume off," she says, fitting the scissors against the spandex and snipping away.

"Oh no," he whines. "How bad is it? Should I try to get it fixed or just scrap it and make a new one?"

He sounds so concerned, like it's the most pressing matter of the night, whether the goddamn dry cleaners are going to be able to get the bloodstain out.

She decides that she hates him and that she's breaking up with him when he's not gravely wounded.

The spandex is resilient, against the scissors at least. Thankfully, though, because if she could just cut through it like paper, she might be the thing that kills him tonight. As she saws away, the tear widens until she's snipping through the collar and tugging it apart.

"How do you get into this thing without a stupid zipper?" she grumbles, yanking the fabric down his shoulders.

"Honey, I'm just that good," he says through gritted teeth, his eyes shut.

It takes some twisting and a lot of patience, but she tugs the sleeves down his arms, one then the other, before getting up and heading to the sink.

"Man, I wish this was a good enough reason to not go to Discrete Math tomorrow," he says. His head is tucked into his elbow.

"I hate you," she announces and returns again to his side with a wet washcloth and a mug full of water.

"No, come on," he says. "Not the *Star Wars* mug, I love that thing."

Yeah well, I love you and yet here you are all banged up, she almost says, like a fool.

"Maybe next time you'll think about your mugs before you do something stupid like this again," she says, and starts wiping blood off his back.

"Wait, why are we mad at me? We were concerned at me a few seconds ago," he says. Along his sides the blood is already dried and flaky, dark, dark red.

"Well, apparently it's nothing," she says. "You're fine."

He shakes his head, forehead rubbing up against the floor. "No, not fine. I'm sick," he says, pantomiming a cough.

By the time she's done, carefully cleaning everything but the wound itself, the water in the mug is pink.

The cut is long, diagonal along the slope of his back, and she gags a little in the back of her throat, looking at it. With the bleeding stopped, it doesn't seem quite as horrifyingly bad, but still seems to have split the skin. By the edges it seems to be scabbing over already. Which is, a little bit absolutely the strangest thing she's ever seen, but also deeply, deeply relieving.

A few turns of gauze from the first aid kit seem to hold him together. When the improvised bandage stays white and clean, thankfully, she takes the blanket, spotted with blood patterns like a tie-dyed shirt, and wraps it tight over his back, tying it off over his chest like a bastardized toga party costume. The wound is clean. Bandaged. Held together.

She helps him stand and limp over to the bed before he completely collapses facedown onto the mattress.

"Thanks," he whispers, eyes drooping. He tugs on her hand, pressing his mouth to the inside of her wrist. "Love you."

She shivers, spares the open window a glare like that's the problem.

He's out in seconds, breath evening, back rising and falling steadily. His hair fans out against the pillow in matted tangles.

She hovers by his side for a second, watching him, watching his eyes twitch, watching water from her hands drip to the sheets.

There's this urge she has that she might have to throw up to get all these gross, concerning feelings out of her system. But her legs are shaky and she's not sure if she can make it all the way to the bathroom or if she even wants to let Max out of her sight for a single second.

So she exhales to remind herself to breathe, and moves back to the desk to finish her physics homework first. It takes twice as long as it should because she keeps glancing over at Max to make sure he's still breathing. Every time she checks, he is. She still checks all night.

This time, she's the one to climb into bed in the early hours of the morning, jostling him awake even as she tries not to.

"Just me," she whispers, moving to pat at him, but then freezing in midair, not able to decide where was safe for her to touch.

"Okay," he mumbles, rolling over a little to give her room. "Night."

She doesn't want to sleep. Hasn't wanted to sleep. But she had to draw the line at a seventh review of the problem set. Her brain is spinning still, like a hamster in a wheel, that faint metallic whining as she works herself over and over again.

"Did it hurt?" she asks.

Max huffs out a little laugh. "Uh, yeah." His hand brushes against hers beneath the sheets. "But it doesn't anymore. I'm okay."

"Why do you do it?" she presses, something tight and knotted in her chest. "If it hurts?"

"It helps people." Quick and easy. Without even thinking,

like it really is just that simple.

"There are a lot of ways to help people," she says. "You told me that."

She hears the scratch of his hair against the pillowcase as he nods. "I guess . . . well, why do you work so hard in class all the time, even though sometimes it hurts?" he asks. It's rhetorical. She swallows hard and closes her eyes. "It's why I'm here, I think. Even if it hurts, it's who I am."

FRESHMAN SPRING
WEEK ELEVEN

ASTRID KNEW HER SCHEDULE AND MAX'S WELL enough to know exactly how to corner him. Right after her Calc lecture, in the seven minutes before Chem Lab, she bee-lined for the library.

She didn't bother putting down her bag, just leaned against the table he'd seized and tapped his shoulder.

He jerked back violently, and she got a good look at his screen, a Pokémon ROM. Her heart fluttered and she raged internally at how endearing he was.

"Hey," he said, tugging at his headphones. "What are you doing here? Don't you have class?"

"Currently en route," she said. And now to the point, she squared her shoulders. "Next Thursday."

"What about it?"

There was a little pit of nervousness in her stomach, which was ridiculous. People get nervous when there is uncertainty, and she had no uncertainty about this, hadn't for a while. She took a breath, tried to banish the emotion.

"You should ask me out next Thursday," she said.

He coughed hard, and then coughed again, clasping his hand to his mouth and doubling over his laptop screen.

"Huh?"

Looking at him made her mouth go dry. Nobody should actually look that good in rumpled flannel.

"You should ask me out on a date next Thursday," she repeated. Hopefully this one would stick, but she'd prepared for at least two more rounds of this. He stared at her, eyes wide, face steadily flushing, maybe some panic and mortification but mostly stone-cold confusion. She continued, "I did the math, crunched the numbers and all that, and starting next Thursday we both have a light ten days. No midterms, no essays, no projects, no club events."

"Date?" he asked. "I mean . . . like you want to date. You want us to date."

She nodded carefully.

"I like you," she said. "And you like me."

"You know?" His voice squeaked. It should have been embarrassing but instead it was just so damn adorable, and she was exhausted with these sparkly, fluttering feelings that took stupid things like his voice squeaks and his bug eyes and the way his stupid face went red and made them into cute things that warmed her from the inside out like a hot chocolate in the middle of January.

"Yep," she said. "Since finals week last semester. You're not very subtle."

"You—you didn't say anything," he said, blinking.

"I was busy."

"And you like me?"

"Yeah. Yeah, I do," she said. "Obviously." She fought with a smile. She sumo wrestled with a smile, forced it back down because they were in the library during heavy traffic hours and she had a reputation to maintain within the BioChem department. "And starting next Thursday I'm not busy and you're not busy. So, we should utilize the free time."

He smiled, beamed. And gone was the panic, gone was the fear, gone was most of the confusion, gone was the redness in his cheeks. Just a pure sunshine smile and her heart saying, *yes yEs YES that's the shIT right THEre.*

She full-body tackled a beaming, face-splitting smile and put it in a headlock.

Instead, she patted his shoulder, heartily, like a baseball coach.

"Thursday," she said. "Ask me out. I'm going to say yes, obviously, but a little wooing is essential."

"Right," he said. Once again, his face was so very red. "Wooing."

"I have to go to class," she said, because she can feel the time ticking onward, only four minutes and thirty-seven seconds until lab starts, and the last thing she wants is to have to run and get all sweaty since she doesn't have an allotted shower time until Wednesday. "But Thursday."

"Thursday," he agreed.

"Alright, see you at dinner."

"We're still . . . dinner?"

"Yeah, I'm not avoiding you until Thursday. I'll see you at dinner with David. I have to go to class now. Enjoy your Pokémen."

She walked away, the green-gray carpeting supporting her weight oddly—it made her legs feel a little shaky.

SOPHOMORE SPRING

WEEK TWELVE

M   BioChem Pre-lab; Beth Israel Volunteering 5-7

T   Cell Bio Pre-lab; Physics Pre-lab; LAB 1-5

W   CELL BIO MIDTERM 2; BioChem Problem Set 10; BioChem read ch. 15

Th Orgo 2 Problem Set 10; BioChem Lab Report; Physics Lab Report; Women in Lit read Marshall, "Poets in the Kitchen"; LAB 1-5

F   PHYSICS MIDTERM 3; BIOCHEM MIDTERM 1; Physics Problem Set 10; LAB 3-5

TIP OF THE WEEK

"Your partner will try to break up with you. To protect you, most likely. It's annoying, but it will happen. And you just need to assure them that it's worth it. The whole messy thing is worth it, to be with them. Because who would you be without them?"

—Annie Anderson

NEW YORK IS A BIG CITY, BUZZING WITH LIFE and color and noise, people and yellow taxis and blue buses and a rainbow of trains, pushing through the same grooves in the concrete. On a night like tonight, the blood in Astrid's veins is thrumming with it, and the ground feels a little like it's shaking apart beneath her.

Her nerves feel fried. A pigeon makes her jump. She has to remind herself to breathe and that despite aliens and Max's injury and the unbelievable amount of work she still has to do tonight and tomorrow and every day until she dies, the world is not ending, goddammit. It's just another week. A week with three midterms and for some reason she was volunteered for extra hours at the hospital, but that's fine, everything is fine. She's a short subway ride away from campus and Max. Max, who is healing up and going to be fine. *Everything* is going to be fine.

She stops looking over her shoulder at every sudden movement, she relaxes into the music flowing through her headphones, and decides to dedicate more energy to appreciating the city at night, maybe squeezing a single drop of serotonin out of the glowing lights, the bustle of pedestrians. The concrete beneath her feet is so solid that she can almost feel every ridge of it through the flat sole of her boots.

She carefully does not think about weighted scores and studying sessions, just watches the street numbers trickle up and thinks of a nice warm shower and a bed hopefully with a nice warm boyfriend.

And then someone slams into her. *Max*, her brain decides, because that's how these things usually go. But of course, it's not Max at all. She finds herself teetering over, losing her balance, and where Max would have been apologizing clumsily, there's nothing. She goes sprawling toward the street. There's a tugging at her hoodie, a crackle of static as her phone disconnects and the music stops.

She's on the ground, hands and knees stinging, pain shooting down her leg and up her wrist as she watches the guy run off, baseball cap pulled low, hands clutched around a phone and wallet. *Her* phone and wallet.

"Hey!" she shouts a second after her brain starts working again and a second before her world goes white in the face of oncoming headlights.

Everything—her scream, her breath, her heart—gets caught in her throat.

Get up, get up, get up, her body says, and she pushes against the concrete, desperate to get to her feet.

She barely lifts her knees from the ground before there are arms around her waist, sweeping her out of the street and into the sky as a particularly aggressive taxi brushes by, the force of it thundering in her ears.

Back on the sidewalk, back on her feet, for a second her vision is consumed by bright navy-blue spandex before it's gone. She nearly falls over again, her knees aching and her thighs shaking.

People are staring. New York staring, though, turning to look at her as they walk by or else glancing back down the street where Max has grabbed the guy in the baseball cap by his shirt collar.

Astrid glances between the two of them and the spot on the street where she landed. A bus chugs along, narrowly avoiding running a red light.

Max pats the guy on the chest and steps back enough for him to slip away and go sprinting down the street.

"And I don't want to have to tell you again," Max calls after him, voice deeper, resounding and buoyant. He practically skips back over to her, holding out her wallet and phone.

"Ma'am," he says, chest puffed out, breathing a little heavy, his mouth at an angle that's quantifiably smug.

"What the fuck was that?" she asks. Maybe him or maybe the universe at large.

"You okay?" he asks, stepping closer and lowering his voice. His gloved hand lands on her shoulder and she can't help but lean into him.

Her heart hasn't stopped pounding. She feels fuzzy and unreal and like she's thrumming down to her cells. Here it goes again, another new little pocket of chaos that'll keep her up all night tonight.

Max glances around at the street, glances up at the sky, and then meets her eyes again. They're still his eyes, deeply rich and brown, even through little cutouts in his mask.

"Hey," he says. "Why don't you head to my room and I'll meet you in like fifteen minutes and—shit."

A terrible metallic screeching noise rips across the sky.

Max shoves the phone and wallet into her chest, backing

away as a shadow descends from above.

"Hey, Comet!" a voice calls from the sky. Black cape and red mask. She should know this, she memorized god knows how many alter egos and costumes for the goddamn Program . . . and she's drawing a blank.

"Well, good night, endangered civilian," Max says loudly. "Keep your eyes on those side alleys. And look both ways before crossing the street next time."

The black cape descends, levitating feet above the sidewalk between her and Max. "That was rude, Max," he says. "I wasn't done with you yet."

Max is doing very Max things, bouncing on his toes and shaking his shoulders out.

"I was getting bored, Kyle," he says. "I don't know what to tell you."

Max meets her eyes and raises his eyebrows, every single nuance of his expression so clear even with the mask. *Hey, uh, maybe get out of here as fast as you possibly can.*

She turns and runs, hoisting her backpack up on her shoulders and gripping her wallet and phone tight. This is new. Running with her textbooks. The practice running Eleanor required was always just on the treadmill, jogging steadily while Hailey offered steady encouragements. Here, her bag keeps slamming into her lower back, at an angle that makes her want to throw it off into oncoming traffic.

Textbooks aren't cheap, though.

More pedestrians turn to look at her while she runs, glance

behind her, and then move carefully out of the way. There's more metallic crunching noises and a few loud car noises.

She doesn't look back. One of the first rules she learned about running properly.

Don't look back and ditch the heels immediately. Done and done. She's not wearing heels.

The street ahead of her screams with more angry cars and a particularly furious bus as Max leaps through the air, stopping in the middle of the intersection she's charging toward just in time to catch a thrown minivan. He flips it over and sets it down carefully, pushing it out of the way of the traffic and waving at the driver.

Astrid skids to a stop on the street corner as the black cape shoots past her overhead.

Max takes a running start and jumps, crashing into him in midair and smashing him into the side of the building next to her. Glass shatters, showering down on the street below.

She gasps, throwing her arms above her head.

"Ma'am," Max calls down at her, not nearly as smarmily as he had the first time. He pants heavily. "You might want to try the side street!"

It's getting harder to get her feet to push off the ground, but she turns the corner anyway.

In the air Max shouts something, and another crashing sound explodes above. She doesn't look back, she doesn't look back, she doesn't look back.

"Astrid!"

And something hits her, something large and solid, and she goes sprawling, her phone and wallet slipping right out of her scraped palms. She braces for another impact but doesn't hit the ground.

Something, presumably the large and solid something, has her by the handle of her backpack and she's going up and up, her gut lurching, her limbs flailing in their search for something solid.

"So, who are you?" she hears from above. It's not Max.

Her brain skips like . . . like vinyl on David's hipster record player, like the stones on the lake in Central Park that time Max tried to be romantic. Any coherent thought slips through her fingers as she stares down at the black asphalt and realizes she's just entered a sort of long-distance relationship with the ground and she doesn't care for it one bit.

They're moving fast, cutting through the sky, wind whipping at her face, flyaways beating against her cheeks.

She doesn't scream. She imagines she will on the way down.

Do something, her brain screams. It's not used to being this absolutely powerless.

There's protocol for this. There has to be.

Right, one of Wally's weeks. *Tuck your arms and legs*, he had said in that Wally tone, light and jovial. *Ride it out. Any villain worth his salt will land somewhere to engage in a verbal confrontation, which is a better time to plan an escape.*

So, protocol sucks.

She tucks her thumbs into the little pockets the straps of

her bag have. She stares straight ahead at the row of concrete buildings, the yellow glow of offices still at work.

A blur of dark blue flies by on the right. She stops breathing.

"Alright," Max shouts, landing crouched on a nearby windowsill. "Let's put her down." His voice shakes. She thinks she'll blame it on the wind.

"You never said you had a girlfriend." Kyle sounds amused. She gets shaken briefly like a rag doll.

She decides she does not want to throw up and starts focusing on that.

"Like I have time for a girlfriend when I spend all my time kicking your ass, dude," Max says. "C'mon. Let's put her down and get back to it."

"Fine."

The deep elephant weight of fear starts to ease off her chest. She knew Max was probably pretty good at the hero thing to have made it this far, but she's almost genuinely impressed—

The thought cuts out with a sudden lurch. Her stomach drops.

After a solid heft, Astrid is thrown into the air by her backpack, arcing through the sky like a projectile motion practice problem.

This time she does scream. Not intentionally—the sound just rips itself out of her throat as she tumbles over herself, the world a sudden incomprehensible blur of lights and colors.

Through the haze of panic, she feels the moment she

reaches maximum height, pictures the parabola graph in her head. And it's one thing to know that there's no vertical velocity or acceleration acting on an object at its peak; it's another to feel that split second of weightlessness, her breath caught in her throat, feeling light as a feather and thinking that maybe if she felt like this, it wouldn't even hurt to hit the ground.

And then she starts to fall again.

The fantasy of floating forever is lost to the wind along with her screams. She's left grasping at nothing except for the force of gravity and the friction of the air. Negative 9.81 meters per second squared. Solve for time of descent. Solve for vertical velocity at impact. Solve. If she was falling on Jupiter, with a gravitational force of negative 24.79 meters per second squared—

And then Max slams into her from the side and she's yanked off that perfect, sloping graph. Rotational motion now, they spiral around some arbitrary center of gravity between them like a two-headed football. His arms go around her waist and he twists, slowing the spin, with practiced ease.

They land on another building's ledge, Max rammed up against the hard concrete, the breath punched out of him as her body lands on top of his.

"Okay," Max says, almost a gasp. She blinks through the rapid encroach of black spots. He's smiling faintly, like it's for her, a tiny kernel of reassurance that she clings to even though his eyes are wide and his chest heaves, running gloved hands over the back of her head. "We okay?"

No. Probably not ever again, actually. She's forgotten what a resting heart rate is supposed to feel like. Her insides feel scrambled like all her organs have decided to flee the country.

She tries to open her mouth to tell him, but her mouth is too dry, and her throat is congested with heavy emotions she doesn't have names for.

"Max," she says, because his name is practically default to say. It's easy as breathing, just exhaling and finding his name right there on her tongue. "Max." And then when she can blink again. "I have . . . I have three midterms this week." And he knows her, so he knows that she means, *I'd really like to not die tonight. Please don't let me die tonight.*

His eyes go soft. He grabs her hand.

"Trust me?" he asks, tapping his forehead to hers.

She's not sure what kind of question that is at a time like this, but she nods anyway, breathing shakily through her mouth.

"Okay," he says, and kisses the tip of her nose. "Hold on." He pulls her in and breathes in deep.

"Max," she says because she does trust him, but she'd prefer if he didn't—

He doesn't even take a running start, just one second they're balancing on this thin little ledge ten stories up and the next they're slicing through the air again.

She doesn't scream, blessedly. It doesn't feel scream-worthy this time. She just claws at the back of his shoulders. Her legs wrap around his waist in a feat of flexibility she didn't know she was capable of.

It's like clipping through a video game, like a bad VR gimmick, as they shoot up and she can see into random apartments, a million little lives that look much nicer than hers right now.

However, unlike a video or a dream, everything is so crisp, and she can feel the wind in her hair, stinging at her eyes. She feels the pressure on her shoulders and the motion in her chest.

He lands on the edge of a roof, barely a bend in his legs.

"Okay," he says, and somehow, miraculously, as she leans back and blinks her eyes open, he's beaming. "Here we go."

She is deposited gently back onto her shaky, frightened legs, barely a foot away from the fifty-story drop.

"I'll be right back," he says, squeezing her shoulder, eyes on the sky. "Just hang tight."

"To what?" she asks as he hops off the side of the building, flinging himself at Kyle. Through this, he's been approaching them casually, cape blowing in the breeze.

"Jeez, Kyle, take a breather, buddy. You work yourself too hard," Max says, and then he's off, tumbling through the sky, wrestling Kyle into a choke hold.

She takes a step back from the edge of the roof and then takes another ten until her back hits a solid stone wall and she almost has a heart attack and dies.

There is nothing up here. Just the black void of the night sky, devoid of stars. Just a smattering of other buildings rising up from the concrete bedrock, flickering with lights from within. The black hole of Central Park to the far left.

The edge of the roof has a gravitational pull, the drop-off tugging at her heart and soul, and she feels like she's falling already. The bottom of her stomach is empty, just empty, and her legs shake, down to the bones her legs shake, a cold tremble that spells uselessness and numbness.

Her breath comes fast and loud, echoing like gunshots across the silent, empty, dead rooftop.

She thinks of the bridge during the School Bus Incident and how solid it had felt against the skin of her knees. This building feels like it'll collapse, like even if she doesn't fall off the edge of it, it will just crumble beneath her feet and she'll drop and drop.

She thinks of the School Bus Incident and how it was all motion and noise, and she couldn't see a single thing, just feel.

This is different. This is quiet and still everywhere except for inside her brain and body. This is not being able to see but not because there's too much going on, but because there's no light on the rooftop, just the dark, just the night that yanks at her, trying to eat her alive, and the distant lights of the other buildings.

She thinks of Max as he dives in and out of her vision, leaping and flying and smiling. Always smiling, like it's not only easy for him, it's also fun. Only he's not exactly Max right now, is he? He's a little bigger and a little louder and a lot faster, zipping around and bouncing like he weighs nothing at all, throwing out zingers, witty little one-liners.

This doesn't matter to them. This is the most terrifying moment of her life and for him it's just another weeknight.

A different world. A different scale.

There is a world that exists on top of hers. A world where things like this happen in the sky every single night, and people with mind-melting powers put on masks and fight it out. Where things are larger than life, and stakes are high, so high that they feel like nothing at all.

She's not scared anymore. She's just angry, that the world is large and chaotic, and she is small and powerless. She's no hero, and she's not even a civilian anymore. She's a bargaining chip for this pompous douche to hold over Max's head in a game they're playing with stakes she can barely comprehend.

She thinks of Wally getting kidnapped fifty-three times. Molly and her pink finger splint. Eleanor, with a bruise expertly covered with full coverage foundation, saying, "Two supers don't cancel each other out. Just doubles the number of enemies to keep track of."

Her entire semester gone, because she had to prepare for someone like this to look at her and not even see her, just see some quantifiable hurt the loss of her would have on someone else. And not just someone. On Max.

She feels it all so suddenly, weighing on her shoulders, making her weak in the knees. It's all piled up, every single time she's wanted to cry for the past twelve weeks, every bit of stress and loss, the bone-deep exhaustion she never stops feeling, living her boring, small little life that will end before she's ready for it to.

She looks out at the city, not for the first time, but doesn't see the whole city, doesn't see a huge, untouchable thing. She sees every pinprick light along the skyline and thinks, that's a person. That's a person living a life. There's a world of small people and small lives down there.

I want to be a doctor, she thinks, and it feels different from every other time she's thought it. Because it's not about the science and her own fears and her own need to understand every chemical reaction that creates her.

There is a world above the world where the small people and their small lives are gambled with messily. Where they are like ants and the city becomes a unit, something to save and protect.

She wants to save those small lives. She wants to make them better. She wants to live a small life, down there. A life that will never mean something as big or grand as the world up here.

Astrid Rose is not going to save the world. She's not going to change the world. She will not be the best doctor, she will not be remembered forever, no matter how hard she works for a 4.0. The city will churn and the world will turn, and she will live a life that is small and not exceptional in any measurable way.

But it will be her life. Even if small. Even if simple. Even if messy and sometimes boring and sometimes bad. And she'll do things that matter in their small, little ways, help in the ways she can with her feet on the ground.

And she can't have that life if she dies in this world of giants that live and fight on top of the city.

She can't do that because Kyle is trying to kill her. Suddenly he's barely a few feet away, swooping in like a large bird, metal claws extended.

She still feels a paralyzing fear, like moving a muscle will send her falling.

Use what you have. That's what Wally and Eleanor had said. *Be prepared but use what you have. Play dirty. There are no rules and nothing is off-limits.*

She rolls her shoulders back, letting her backpack slide off her shoulders. She grabs a strap of her bag in her right hand and turns and throws it as hard as she can.

On the one hand she doesn't miss. On the other, it's because the goddamn guy is close enough to her that he doesn't have time to move out of the way.

It hits him on the side of his head, sends him careening away from her. Her backpack disappears over the edge of the roof and she can feel every inch it drops, can see the textbooks, the notebooks, her traveling stationery bag, her to-go planner spinning wildly in the air and crashing into the alley below.

"Nice one!" Max calls, zooming back into the action. Like it was a grade on a test or a mildly successful Frisbee toss. "Hey, Kyle, go home, pal!"

They both go tumbling off the side of the roof, reengaging in their fray.

It might be seconds and it might be hours, but it ends even though she doesn't see any of it.

Max lands in front of her on the roof, literally bouncing a step forward like the ground is rubber.

"That was awesome!" he says, bright and vibrant and loud. "Wow, you were incredible. Perfect aim and everything."

He drags her into a hug, and she takes a moment to cling. She still doesn't feel entirely settled in her body, but Max feels hot and alive in her arms, his heartbeat steady under her ear.

Her backpack is gone. She can almost picture it hitting the ground at terminal velocity and exploding on impact in a tornado of the papers that make up her life. Books and notes and planner. Her phone and wallet are gone. She needs a shower and something passive-aggressive to say to her ex-best friend when she gets back to her room. She needs at least four hours of sleep to be remotely functional tomorrow and it's looking more and more unlikely. And she still, someway, somehow, has three midterms.

"Alrighty, let's just—" He tightens his arms around her waist and spins her around. Rom-com, animated movie spin. He holds on to her and hops off the side of the building.

Her stomach leaps to her chest, the drop tingling along the inside of her spine.

He lands easily but she feels it through her entire body. She takes a moment to try to locate her internal organs and then unceremoniously gives up.

"I can't do this," she says, and then the words are out there in the space between them in this little dark alley between these two giant apartment buildings.

Eleanor was wrong. Astrid knew—a part of her always knew—what it meant that Max was a superhero. She's not a genius but she's not a fool. She knew things like this could happen, had to happen, were going to happen. With every deep talk with Wally, every warning, misanthropic speech Eleanor gave. She knew it was probably going to happen.

She had rationalized it. In some deep corner of her brain, she had accepted that it would happen eventually, maybe even worse than it was tonight. And in that same place she had made argument after argument, brushing it away. It wouldn't be as bad as she thought, as it sounded. It wouldn't be that time-consuming, it wouldn't be that scary, it wouldn't be everything she feared it would be, feeling like an ant and feeling like she was dying and losing pieces of herself left and right to cold, sharp fear.

But of course, it did.

She only thought it wouldn't be because she loves Max. She is in love with Max, and if not having to give him up meant lying to herself, then she would lie to herself. She would self-sabotage, ruining her life because her brain had been highjacked by this unruly, fiery passion in her soul for this miraculous person and the way he made her feel.

Max sets her down on top of a pile of old and damp newspapers, and it feels like the inches of spaces she reclaims between them are miles.

"Astrid?" he asks, taking her hands in his. "You okay?"

"I can't do this," she repeats because that's all her brain is spitting out, *ERROR ERROR*, *recalculating sans rose-colored glasses.* "I'm sorry."

"Hey," he says, rubbing her arm soothingly. "Sorry about that. It got a little out of hand. But you're okay, right?"

"Max," she says, because he isn't hearing her somehow despite all his superpowers. "I can't do this anymore. I can't . . . I'm done."

"It can be a lot, I know, but you were safe the whole time, I swear," he says, moving his hands up to her shoulders and squeezing just a little, just enough. "I promise. The whole time I had an eye on you. I would never let anything happen to you."

The universe is branching into these multiple realities, and she is standing at its crossroad, staring at him, barely able to see his deep, tired eyes in the dark of the alley beneath his bright blue mask.

"*Let* really isn't a part of it, Max," she says. "You can't control—we can't control these things. *Let* doesn't factor into the equation."

"I had everything under control, though," he says. His voice is pitching upward, getting faster and more frantic. There's no easy slide into this conversation, no gentle landing. "I've done it a million times before and I don't take senseless risks, not anymore, not after . . . I know it was a lot and we can—can we talk about it? Try to talk through it?"

Yes, she wants to say, could say, technically. *Let's go back to your room and I can use your shower and watch* Scrubs *on your bed and talk about it and make out about it, and I can wake up in the morning with my life in pieces all around me but next to you if nothing else.*

"I was scared," she says. "I was more scared up there than I think I ever have been in my life."

"I know. I'm sor—" he says.

"But it wasn't just that," she continues. "I'm not even afraid of heights, Max. I just . . . can't balance this. I don't have the time to overcome this fear, or to stand on rooftops or hide away in safe houses. I can't even remember the goddamn names of your super-evil enemies who might try to kill me. I can't fit any more in, there isn't enough room to keep shifting this stuff around and I love you—"

They both freeze, and both inhale sharply, and both go completely still.

She could laugh. Months of trying to figure out how to say those three words, how to communicate what he means to her without falling apart with how much she feels, how to say it without it sounding fake and forced, but now she can let it just slip out when she finally realizes the depth of what he does to her, the lengths she'll go to be with him, the absolute irrationality of it all, and the fact that she has to break up with him.

She's breaking up with him.

She could probably also cry.

He doesn't say anything to that. He just stands there, hands on her shoulders, mouth hanging open just a little.

"I love you," she says. It's so easy. Too easy, and it makes her wonder if it was ever really that hard or if she's always been too selfish to even try. "I really do, Max."

Leave it at that, she thinks. She could. Just leave it at that. They're not at the point of no return yet.

"Astrid," he says.

"This isn't my world. This whole hero thing isn't my world and I don't want it to be. I don't know how to be in it, actually. I can't straddle the line. I can't be the type of person these circumstances are asking me to be. And I can't be the kind of person who dates a superhero. At least not at the same time that I'm trying to be the kind of person I want to be."

"Astrid," he says again, and saying her name is suddenly his default, like it's all he can do to prove he's still breathing.

"I can't lead a double life," she says. "I barely have a handle on a single one."

"We can figure something out," he says, nodding to himself. "We can. It doesn't have to be so messy. It doesn't have to be dangerous. I love you. You love me. It can be as easy as that."

She shakes her head, places her hand on top of his where it clings to her shoulder.

"Max," she says. "I wish it could be." So much that she fooled herself into thinking it could be. Just that easy. Like things are easy.

"Please," he says. "Just . . . give me a few days. I can talk to some people. We can ask for advice."

"I don't have a few days," she says. "I have to go back to my room now. And I have to take a shower because I've sweat through . . . everything. And I have to explain to the Barnes and Noble bookstore that I just threw five rented textbooks off a roof and then buy them again. I need to get a new planner and ask a lot of people for notes since I just lost a semester's worth of them and I have three midterms this week."

She feels each sentence, each realization like gunshots tearing through. Searing hot pain and then cold.

He winces, glances around the alleyway like he might spot the tattered remains of her backpack.

"I lost my wallet. I need a new phone and to cancel every one of my credit cards and get replacements. I need a new non-driver's ID," she says. The words feel numb, their meanings lost as they pile up. "I need to rebuild my entire life, and I don't know how I'm even going to start because all I have is the spare key I keep in my shoe. Thank God because I can't text David to let me into the room and I'm not sure if he even would right now."

"I'm sorry," he says, voice breaking.

"It's not your fault," she says. "None of this is your fault. I'm pretty sure you saved my life tonight. But I can't do this again."

He steps back, a little staggering step like he can't find his balance. Just out of arm's reach he sways dangerously. His hands drop away from her shoulders and she feels the loss of him keenly, already misses his warmth and the physical comfort he radiates in spades.

"I'm sorry," she says. He steps back again and turns around, facing the back of the alley, the grimy wall lined with garbage bags. It's fitting that this is happening in a place that is the antithesis of romance.

She racks her brain for anything to say that can help. It's like the funeral all over again as she pulls out cliché after cliché. *It's not you, it's me. You deserve better.* A hug isn't exactly something she can offer this time.

"Max," she says instead.

"I can . . . I'll take you home," he says. She can feel the tension of his shoulders, the tightness in his chest.

"I can walk," she says.

"Astrid," he says, still turned away, still curled in on himself.

"I'm not gonna ask you to do that right now," she says. "And I need to walk home. I need to be on the solid ground for a little while."

He wraps his arms around his center.

"Okay," he says. "Okay. I'll just . . . I'll . . ."

"Max," she says before she turns away, before she embarks on the long, cold walk back to her cold, empty dorm room. "When I'm rebuilding my life tomorrow." Jesus, she has to rebuild her life tomorrow. "I'll leave room for a friend. If that's something you'd be comfortable with."

He nods jerkily but doesn't turn around. "Okay," he says.

She leaves because she doesn't think there is anything to say that makes this not suck, that makes it not hurt. And even if there was, she wouldn't know how to say it.

◆ ◆ ◆

Her legs shake. The entire walk back, she can't feel her knees, and her eyes burn.

She feels it in her chest, the entire goddamn day like an anvil sitting in there, pressing down, trying to push all her emotions out until she's an empty husk. She can barely breathe, she can barely walk, but she pushes and pushes through. Because that's what she does, isn't it? Just pushes and pushes until she breaks something.

Her hands keep fumbling with her key, keep almost letting it slip through her fingers but it's just a key, she's not going to cry about it. It's just a key and she's got it all under control.

She finally shoves the door open, pushes herself inside, and shrugs her jacket off right there in front of the door. She'll find time to put it where it belongs tomorrow. Or maybe she won't. Maybe she'll just leave it there forever.

David is lounging on his bed, laptop on his chest, fingers poking around the touchscreen. Thank God there's no girl. She's not sure what she would do if there was a girl.

She can't look at him and doesn't want him to see her right now. She barely wants to exist right now, the last thing she wants is another stilted conversation, a passive-aggressive nightmare reminder of her first warning sign, the first red flag that she was in over her head and should have just given up. Why doesn't she know when to give up?

She should have broken up with Max that first day, the second he said he was a superhero. She should have. She just wanted so much. She wanted *him* so much, wanted everything, med school, best friend, boyfriend. Because he was Max. He was impossible not to want, not to love.

She claps her hands over her eyes, letting her knuckles dig into the sockets even though it hurts. How is she supposed to stop loving him?

"Astrid?" David asks.

"Can I have the room?" she asks. It's going to be bad. She knows in that moment that it's going to be so bad. This whole time she had thought of it like juggling or Jenga or . . . games, nonsense, something simple and without stakes. Really, she had been walking a tightrope over the Grand Canyon and she let go weeks ago and she doesn't want to hit the ground, but it feels like she's been falling forever.

"What?"

"I'm sorry," she says. "I'm sorry, I just really need the room for, like, a few minutes and—and then . . ." She doesn't know, actually. She needs a few hours, probably longer, to gasp and ache and cry and fall apart, but she's not sure what comes next, what she does after, how to sweep up the pieces and break out the Gorilla Glue.

"Hey," he says, and the laptop closes with a click and his bed squeaks. "Are you okay?"

She shakes her head violently, presses her knuckles in and down like she can force it all back down, push it all back down and under until she can get a grasp on anything.

"Please," she says. Maybe to David, maybe to the universe, maybe to herself, maybe to Max.

"What happened?" David says, and his hands land on her shoulders.

She shakes her head again.

"I . . . Max and I, we . . ." She's gasping for air, her breath stuttering, her chest shuddering. She chokes on a sob but the next one just bubbles out. She doubles over and thinks she might just tumble to the floor and fall right through it and fall forever.

She doesn't fall. David wraps his arms around her shoulders.

"Hey," he says. "Okay, okay. Just breathe, okay?"

Right. Breathing. That's a thing she used to be able to do instead of just gasping for air and choking on tears and exhaling in sharp sobs.

"Astrid?" he asks again. "Breathe, okay?"

David pats the back of her head, shifts around so he's hugging her properly.

"I'm sorry," she says. "I'm really sorry. I couldn't do it, I couldn't . . ."

She pulls her hands away from her eyes, digs her nose into his shoulder until it hurts and grasps at his shirt.

"Just breathe, okay," he says, hushed against her ear. "That's all you gotta do, right? Just keep breathing."

Breathe. It's the one thing she's never had to plan out. It feels now like the hardest thing she's ever had to do. Just keep existing.

FRESHMAN SPRING
WEEK TWELVE

IT WAS THURSDAY. THE THURSDAY, THE ONE SHE had told Max about, the one she secretly drew a little heart around in her planner like a fourth grader, and the world was ending.

"Change of plans," her Diff Eq professor had called it, like it was something simple, something easy, like Astrid didn't live her life according to every syllabus like they were religious texts. Like this new, unplanned problem set and quiz to "make sure the whole class really understood Fourier transformations" due end of day tomorrow wasn't actively going to ruin everything.

She left the lecture hall in a horrified daze, half expecting the ground to open up beneath her feet and swallow her whole, half expecting the sky to fall. She pushed open the heavy glass doors and stumbled out onto the quad path, nearly tripping down the stairs.

Two months. She'd spent two full months working through every concern she had about feelings, messy breakups, making time in her busy schedule to keep the romance alive. The amount of magazines and psychological studies she'd consulted could probably qualify her for a marriage counselor's license. (Which wasn't, she thought, a bad backup plan if the MCAT went terribly.)

She had pored over intensive calculations, color-coded Excel spreadsheets, carefully formatted graphs, just to pick this goddamn week and a half, just to fit this into her schedule.

And now it was ruined.

Maybe she could rearrange everything, fit Max in sometime next week, but all her weeks are front-loaded this semester, so it probably won't be until later in the week, and then she'll already be worrying a little bit about the week after that, which was busy again, and then end-of-year projects and then finals and then the semester would be over and they'd be heading home for the summer and . . .

And what if this whole thing was a mistake?

This week was supposed to be perfect for a start, to have some time to set some foundation before the semester kicked into gear again, but if she couldn't even count on the security of one week . . .

Preparing for the MCAT was going to be a nine-month process, utterly and all-consumingly intense, that had to start about a year and a half from now. Did she even have room for a relationship in those nine months?

Max was wonderful and understanding, but he was also sweet. He wouldn't survive the level of detachment that deep a study binge would require.

Three months max probably before he got tired of it and broke up with her. And that would be the end of a two-year relationship, an even longer friendship. She'd probably try to swallow it all down, and the first free moment she would have to feel the full implication of the loss would be in one of the ten-minute breaks between test sections during the actual MCAT, and then she'd have a complete breakdown and completely lose her focus. Goodbye MCAT, goodbye med school, goodbye ten-year plan, goodbye Max.

She passed someone on the quad walkway and their shoulders bumped, but it was New York, and it happened all the time, but she did stop and turn because . . . hello, Max.

"Max?" she said, and he nearly tripped turning around.

"Astrid," he said, breathless, eyes wide. "Hey—"

"What are you doing here?"

He gestured over his shoulder vaguely. "I was, um . . . going to meet you outside of your class to . . . well . . ." His hand came up to rub at the back of his neck, and he let out a loose laugh.

Oh God. Oh, she was going to have to do this here.

"I have to reschedule," she said quickly, and embarrassingly felt her eyes heat up.

"Oh," he said, eyebrows knitting together in confusion and disappointment that she felt in her chest.

"There's this problem set that I didn't—We weren't supposed to have any . . . but now I . . . and—and the MCAT is nine months and—" Her brain spun and spun, built and destroyed schedule after schedule in microseconds, moving and shifting everything like tectonic plates just searching and searching for some kind of neat slotting together where everything balanced together.

"Hey," Max said, his voice soft and steady. His hand was on her arm, she realized, lightly, the warmth of it almost settling her back into her bones. "It's okay. We can reschedule."

Reschedule. Just reschedule and reschedule forever. And she realized deep in her gut that she didn't want to, she was so tired of it.

"Look . . . okay, here's the thing," he said, swallowing and smiling softly. "You are the coolest person I've ever met in my life and I regret every second of high school that I didn't spend hanging out with you. You're so . . . powerful and assured and yourself. You make me want to be like that, to have direction and purpose and to know so clearly what I want and to not be afraid to go get it. And you work so hard and you're so, so brave and you never hold anything back. I'm around you and it's like I'm unstoppable. I can laugh and breathe and not worry about the million and one ways life is crashing down on me. And I hope that I give you something, that there's something about me that makes you feel powerful if you don't already, or makes you . . . I dunno, feel half of the things you make me feel. Any of the things you've made me feel this year. And like, being your friend is the best thing I could have ever asked for, but the thought of being more, doing more together seems like, unspeakably great. So . . . today or tomorrow or a week from now or whenever it works for you, do you want to go on a date with me?"

She shivered a little. There was a breeze. She was fine. Her heart was not hammering, her stomach was not sweeping and dropping out, and she was not light-headed, and she didn't . . . she was fine.

She had no recourse for this. No thing to say that could compete with that. So instead she fought against that fear in her, that evolutionary instinct that said don't step off a cliff, don't embrace a free fall. She tugged him down with a loose hand on the back of his neck and his eyes went wide but he met her in the middle and she kissed him.

She wasn't sure what she expected kissing Max would be like, or even what she even expected kissing to be like despite the excessive research she'd been doing for the past month and the general cultural osmosis, but it exceeded those expectations. His mouth was warm and a little wet, and it was easy as breathing to meet him in the middle, to close her eyes and feel her lips part and move with his.

This was it. Max, as he was. Simple and sweet and somehow always in sync with her. It was less of a kiss, more of a steady push and pull that said *I know you and still like you and I like you and I want to know more.*

She pulled back to breathe, and he followed her like gravity, like magnets, like magic, like science, and she couldn't help but kiss him again.

"Alright," she said after really pulling away. "Where are we going?"

"Going?" He looked punch-drunk and dazed.

"For this date," she clarified.

He nodded, blinking a few times hard. "That café on Amsterdam with those cookies you like."

She grabbed his hand and started leading him along the path. He followed without question.

He gripped her hand like he needed support.

"It's your smile," she said when they reached the edge of campus. She was kinda hoping the bus that sailed by might drown her out.

"My . . . smile?"

Nothing really got by him, though. Supergood hearing.

"Your smile kinda . . . jeez. Your smile makes me feel like I'm like floating or something, like it's easier to breathe. It's a good smile."

He heard that too, even though she mumbled and even though they were embraced by the rumbling noises of a New York street corner.

And he smiled, dopey and happy. And yeah, that was worth whatever else in her schedule would get shoved out of the way. A smile like that was worth all of it.

SOPHOMORE SPRING
WEEK TWELVE

???

ASTRID WAKES UP AT 6:30 A.M. DESPITE HER-self. She doesn't need the alarm on her phone; it's conditioned deep in her. She couldn't sleep in even if she tried.

God, she wants to try. She's so tired. Deep down in the marrow of her bones, the weight of exhaustion presses down on her chest. Or maybe that's a heart attack, or a panic attack.

She has class in three hours. She has an hour-long midterm in five and no notes, no phone, no planner.

Oh yeah, and now she has a panic attack. She sits up and clutches at her blankets.

"I don't think so," David says, pulling up alongside her bed and shoving a plastic cup of water at her. "Drink."

She's never seen him awake this early.

She chugs, squeezing her eyes shut. There's a pain in her palms, crescent-shaped bruises from tightening her fists all night, unable to release the tension even while asleep.

The water is a godsend—her throat is sore and dry and aching from screaming and shivering on a rooftop for however long. David takes the cup back. It's his favorite, the red one from the health center about STDs.

She thinks she might cry some more, even though she still feels more dehydrated than she's ever been in her life, and her eyes are swollen and puffy from last night, and there's an ache right in the middle of her forehead.

"I'm sorry," she croaks. "I'm sorry we've been fighting. I don't want to be fighting."

"We've been fighting?" David asks, setting the cup down on the windowsill and handing her a pint of ice cream.

She squints at him. He shoves a spoon of ice cream into her mouth. Cherry Garcia.

She grumbles through the mouthful.

"We haven't spoken in weeks," she says. "I haven't seen you in weeks."

"Yeah, because you're never here," he says. "And then when you're here, I'm not here."

"We had that argument," she says. He shrugs.

"Yeah, I dunno, I got over it," he says. "You're busy and you have a right to privacy."

"I was an asshole," she says.

"Probably," he agrees. "I was mostly likely a little shitty

myself, but whatever, right? We're best friends. We get over this stuff."

She blinks at him. That might be the first time he's said it. Best friends.

"Every time I've seen you you've been super angry."

He exhales, glances down at the bedspread. "I've been having a rough semester," he says. "So . . . sorry, if I've been distant."

"Oh," she says.

"I mean, not physics hard, obviously," he says, ducking his head and exhaling.

"Oh no," Astrid says. "Don't . . . don't say that."

"Nah," he says, shaking his head. "It's nothing. I just . . . have not heard back from a single one of the internships I've applied to. And I've applied to a lot of them. And I'm doing really badly in my Brazilian history class. Like I've never done this bad in a class ever and I don't know why. It's not even . . . And I thought I was going to get vice president for *lit mag* but I didn't. So it's been a bummer."

"I'm so sorry," she says. Her chest feels tight. "That sucks."

He laughs a little and nods. "It does. But you know, today is about your tragic breakup."

"No," she says. "Hey . . . I don't have to monopolize the tragedy in this room. I shouldn't."

"You just broke up with your high school sweetheart."

"We weren't dating in high school. And you have had a rough semester that I've been ignoring because I'm an asshole, and I've been having an equally rough semester."

He sighs. "It really sucks, right? This whole life thing."

She nods.

"But it's gonna get good eventually," he says. "It's gotta, right?"

"I dunno. Does it?"

"No. It does. It *is* good. Sometimes. Not today. But some days, we're happy."

She wishes she could remember a time when she was happy, really happy, and not just stressed about what she had to do when she was done being happy.

"Here," he says, dropping his clunky headphones over her ears. "Got a breakup playlist for you. Listen to it while I go run for some hot chocolate."

"I hate your music," she says, batting his phone away.

"I know," he says, tapping play. The sound is immediately loud and overwhelming, because David hates his sense of hearing and has proclaimed on multiple occasions that he wants to lose it by the time he's thirty. "It's your terrible emo trash and some Taylor Swift songs. I made it while you were crying in the shower last night."

If it wasn't impossible for her to cry again in the next ten years, she would cry right now.

David slips out the door just as an angry drumbeat is hammered out, higher quality than she's used to, just loud and powerful enough that it makes her start to feel something, just a little in her chest.

The world is shaky all around her. But she clings to a pillow and a pop punk song she knows better than she cares to admit, and breathes, like it's enough.

There are extra planners.

Of course there are.

She sits in front of a blank page, two hours before her first class, with her home set of markers and pens, and tries to find that magic in her schedule, that rush of power she feels when looking at a blank page. Her heart thrums. She picks up a purple pen and feels her eyes burn again with tears. A breath, swallowing it down, and then she tries to feel out a starting place.

She has a copy of her schedule on her laptop (thank God, she left it home, thank God, thank God, thank God), it's just a process of copying things over (and adding in time to get a new ID, get a new phone, replace her debit cards and credit cards and everything else on her ever-increasing to-do list).

She can't make herself do it. She can't get her brain to calm.

She places the tip of her pen on the page and tries desperately to pick anywhere to start.

Max, she writes. Loopy, perfect cursive. *Max, Max, Max.* Because it's all that her hand wants to write, all her brain can repeat.

A whole lot of everything gets caught in her throat, and she aches and burns and wants him so bad her shoulders tingle with it. She wants him, loves him impossibly, irrationally. It's going to destroy her. Missing him, wanting him.

She has a midterm in four hours. There's no time for this.

God, she's been such an idiot.

She tears out the page, shuts the new planner and tucks it away.

Why has she ever needed so many planners and schedules to begin with? She has a perfect sense of time.

Breathe in. Breathe out.

The classroom smells like chalk and stress, silent except for an echoing of other students taking occasional deep breaths and the scratch of pencil on paper.

Every problem on this test has been of mild difficulty but she's dedicated almost two weeks to preparing for problems of extreme to "mercy-kill-me-now-please" difficulty.

She should have it in the bag, and has been moving pretty easily through the questions. In a way, being numb to the world is a perk, because she literally can only focus on the step-by-step process of manipulating equations and plugging in numbers. Anything else hurts too much to think about or is too stressful to consider, sending her heart pounding or her breath shaking.

As it is, her numbers are sloppy on the page, her grip on her mechanical pencil weak.

She feels loose and untethered, using a smaller, lighter backpack that doesn't have her textbooks or wallet or phone.

The world is hollow and all that exists in her universe is the test in front of her and the seat beneath her. The rest is all cold and empty, hard edges she bumps up against if she moves too much.

Breathe in. Breathe out.

She pinches the bridge of her nose and digs her nails into her palm and empties herself out.

There's a phone on her desk when she gets back to the dorm.

It's a fine rectangle of gaudy high-tech and it's obviously from Max.

She carefully moves around her desk, places her smaller, emptier, sadder backup backpack on her bed. All she has are keys, so she stuffs those into her back pocket before she grabs the phone and heads out to lab.

"Hey, Astrid, it's Wally. Listen, Eleanor told me that you . . . that things have been pretty chaotic for you lately and I just wanted to reach out . . . see how you were holding up. Yeah . . . um, call me back."

"Hey, Astrid, it's Max. I know you probably don't want to hear from me right now, but I just . . . shit, okay . . . Just wanted to make sure you got back alright and that everything is okay with David. You don't have to call me back, but like a text or something. Sorry. Jesus. Yeah, sorry. Um . . ."

"Hey. It's me again. Max. It's Max . . . again. Still haven't heard from you—because your phone . . .

fell . . . right. Shit. Okay, please ignore the last seven voice mails I've left. I'm so sorry."

"Astrid. This is Eleanor. I'm so sorry to hear about you and Max. If you need someone to talk to, feel free to reach out. I'm available Monday through Friday before ten and after six. I know breakups like this can feel very permanent, but I've found for people like us it often isn't. So I would still highly encourage you to continue coming to our weekly meetings. There's still a lot to learn."

"Hey, kiddo, it's Wally. Haven't heard from you but have heard about you. Just thought I'd check in, see how you are . . . right . . . um, call me back."

Without a boyfriend and without weekly meetings in the Fridge and with no homework in three of her classes after her last midterm of the week, Astrid finds herself with a few hours of actual free time on Friday for the first time in months. David is at the library, working on a history essay, and not to be disturbed even if he said she can absolutely feel free to disturb him at any time.

A part of her wants to give in and just head to her dorm and sleep it off, or watch YouTube videos for too long—something mind-numbing and meaningless.

But on her way back from her last class, as she hurries across campus, she passes Lerner Hall and remembers her first week of orientation, and the student services in the building and . . . then she's heading inside.

On the top floor is the lobby for the student counseling services. She steps in and finds the room almost empty. When the woman at the front desk looks directly at her, she almost leaves.

Instead, she heads over to the corner of the room and starts looking over the different pamphlets.

(She'd almost done therapy once before. But it was pretty clear after some research that she just had some post-traumatic stress and generalized anxiety, so it seemed easier to just skip the whole thing and rely on the online tips and tricks she found.)

There are a lot of services. Mostly group sessions with various themes.

Including one pamphlet: "Post Super-Incident Recovery Group."

She flips through it, glancing at the front desk lady to make sure she's still clicking away at her desktop and not looking over.

She tucks the pamphlet in her pocket before leaving.

There's a knock on the door Friday night.

She has somehow survived the worst week of her life, all three midterms, and while she'll anxiously wait for the results of those midterms to the point of a thirteenth mental breakdown of the week, they're done.

She has a phone. She has keys. She has a wallet and has one replacement debit card, has canceled her other cards. Her notes are lost to the ages. Her planner is too, which hurts a little more. It was a recorded history of the past nine months, everything she did every day captured in neat colored boxes.

But she is still alive.

That being said, if Max is knocking on her door tonight, her soul might just give out.

David gets the door because he must recognize the look on her face, like a rat looking up as a subway train comes screaming around a corner.

"Um, can I help you?" he asks, in a tone light enough that it's not Max, it can't be Max, please God, she still has dried flaky skin around her eyes from all the goddamn crying she's been doing.

"We're looking for Astrid Rose," a voice says, low and feminine and demanding. She knows that voice.

"Lucy?" Astrid asks, sliding off her bed and dragging her blanket cape along behind her.

Lucy is in the doorway. So are Thomas and Molly, a little behind her.

"Hi," Thomas says, waving timidly.

"Do you know these people?" David asks, raising his eyebrows.

"Yes," she says, blinking at the three of them. "I . . . tutor . . . them."

"In math," Thomas offers.

"And chemistry," Lucy says, nodding.

"Right," David says. "I should go."

"You don't have to—"

"I'm going to go," David decides and slips out the door. And he's off.

"You forgot your—" Astrid attempts, holding up his keys. He's gone.

"How did you guys find this place?"

"Molly," Lucy says, pointing with her thumb.

"It was scary," Thomas says. Molly shrugs sheepishly.

"It wasn't hard, I just had to compare pictures from your Instagram to the pictures of the dorms on the official Columbia website. The floor was mostly a guess," she says.

"Right, well, what are you guys doing here? Is everything okay?" Astrid asks as they close the door and lean up against the wall. Lucy crosses her arms over her chest and bites her lower lip.

"We missed you," Thomas says, as Lucy says, "We heard about your breakup."

And Molly just frowns and nods along sympathetically. Which is surprising, because it's Molly, she usually has the most to say about anything and . . . well, this is something she definitely has experience in, though. . . . Astrid barely wants to think, let alone think about the fact that she and Max have broken up, and she doubts that'll change in the next million years.

"Oh," she says. She wonders if she should go after David with his key chain.

"We just wanted to make sure you were alright," Thomas says, stepping forward. "And we missed you at the Fridge and at lessons. So, we wanted to stop by."

"Right," Astrid says, and pulls her blanket close over her chest like it does anything to cover up the way her voice is scratchy and weak. "Well, I'm doing alright. I appreciate the concern though and it was nice to see you guys. I have, um—"

"We brought popcorn," Lucy says, dropping her bag on David's desk. "And a movie."

"*Inception*," Thomas adds. They move farther inside and drop down to sit on the floor.

"I picked the movie," Molly says, excited, and Astrid has no choice but to offer up her laptop and sit on the floor with them. When David comes back—they have to let him in, since Astrid is still holding his keys—she also has no choice but to join them in throwing popcorn at him.

And somehow, even though she didn't think it would, even though she can't really understand why it does, it helps, for just a moment.

SOPHOMORE SPRING
WEEK THIRTEEN

M Cell Bio Problem Set 9; BioChem Pre-ab
T Cell Bio Pre-lab; Physics Pre-lab; Orgo 2 read ch. 21; LAB 1-5
W BioChem Problem Set 11; BioChem read ch. 8
Th Orgo 2 Problem Set 11; BioChem Lab Report; Physics Lab Report;
       Women in Lit read Yamamoto, "Seventeen Syllables"; LAB 1-5
F Physics Problem Set 11; LAB 3-5

SHE ENDS UP GOING TO THE GROUP THERAPY
session.

They sit in a circle in a colorful back room off the main lobby of the student services office.

The session is led by a young-looking psych postdoc fellow who mostly lets them talk and nods along. She hears a lot of stories. Bridges collapsing, Roosevelt Island tram rides gone wrong, falling debris in Union Square, Herald Square, Times Square. The session leader makes them all jokingly swear off ever taking the N or W past Queensboro Plaza, because aboveground trains are just asking for trouble.

Astrid feels a pressure in her chest building as more and more people speak. She's going to have to say something and she doesn't know how to talk about last week without talking about Max. And she can't talk about Max for obvious reasons, and then also because this therapy session shouldn't become about her breakup.

So instead, when the room goes silent and she's the only one who hasn't spoken, she swallows hard and says, "I was on a school bus in high school that almost fell off a bridge." And the session leader and a lot of the rest of the group nod encouragingly, and she actually feels very encouraged. "We were saved by Kid Comet. And it was only a few minutes total. But it was a lot. I was fifteen. I didn't really have any close friends, I was mostly just a really good student but when I wasn't doing homework, I was just doing nothing, letting the time pass. Uh, after, I got really existential. And ever since, I think I've been waiting for another near-death experience, but like, to go worse. So, I keep pushing myself to make myself something before I run out of time. And I don't think I know how to slow down anymore."

Her words float up into the room, into the space in the middle of the circle. She's not crying, which is a small miracle. There's a silence after she finishes, that feels like breathing on a cool spring day.

"Thank you for sharing," the session leader says. "Astrid, right?"

◆◆◆

She sees Max everywhere on campus.

Not literally because then maybe she'd get used to it. But every head of dark brown tufty curls sends her heart racing. Every graphic tee stabs at her soft underbelly, her weak spot, her heart. She buys an extra coffee Tuesday morning before remembering they're not going to meet up in the library to study and ends up downing both and having her hands shake while she works on problem sets, because the thought of throwing one out or giving it to David makes her chest ache. She walks past where his classes let out because it's muscle memory, and then sprints away because she thinks if she sees him, she'll break again, irreparably.

But other than that, she's doing just fine.

"Hey," Greg says, hovering by the side of her desk, swinging a Hydro Flask between his fingers. "What are you up to right now, because I could use an extra set of hands prepping some gels?"

"Oh," she says, grimacing. "Uh, I'm not sure if I'm allowed to?"

Greg frowns, confused.

"Vaughn has me on computer stuff for now, because of . . ." She looks up at Greg and thinks very hard for a long second. She tries not to think about how Max solved all that. She tries not to think about Max. "Actually," she says. "Since the thefts have stopped, maybe I can—"

Greg frowns. Again. Deeper somehow.

"Yeah, well, we thought they did," he says. "But then . . ."
He shakes his head.

"Sorry," he continues, "I forgot you were . . . on time-out or
whatever. I've been forgetting what you all do around here."

Which isn't boding well for her chances of having any
kind of productive mentorship conversation with Greg in the
future, but does sound vaguely suspicious.

"What do you mean? Who else has been doing mysterious
stuff around here?"

Greg shrugs. "You. Ben. I never know what you're up to."

"Isn't he doing that independent project?" she asks.

Greg leans his weight back into his heels. "No, he finished
and presented in the fall. He actually was supposed to graduate last semester, wasn't he?"

"I think he's retaking some classes."

"Right," Greg says, nodding. "Yeah, apparently somebody
destroyed the curve on the final in one of his classes, and he
ended up with like an B plus or something. He complained
about it all winter break. He had to push back his MCAT date.
Lost like four hundred bucks."

That was her. She did that, ruined the Calc 2 curve and
destroyed Ben Barnes's GPA.

"So, he was working over winter break?"

Greg shakes his head. "No, his project finished before
Thanksgiving. I have no clue what he's doing around here,"
he says. "I should probably ask Vaughn about that . . . that's
weird."

"Right," Astrid says, glancing carefully around the lab even though she hasn't seen Ben all day. It feels like he could jump out from any corner, now that she knows.

Knows what? It could all just be some coincidences, perfectly natural reasons for why Ben is still hanging around the lab. Vaughn probably knows exactly what he's working on and just didn't tell Greg.

It's just coincidence that she ruined his GPA and her experiments have been stolen or sabotaged, because sometimes things just happen and they aren't a part of some big plot. Some things are just coincidence.

Okay, so turns out Astrid doesn't believe in coincidences anymore, and should have actually stopped believing in them when Max disappeared on a school trip and showed up to school the next day with biceps.

"I need a favor," she says upon entering her dorm room.

It feels very good to do this again, come in hot to their dorm and see David there, and interrupt whatever he is doing because he'll listen.

He raises his eyebrows. "What's in it for me?"

"Pride, glory, heroics," she offers.

He closes his laptop. "Now that's a pitch."

"Do you have any weapons?"

"How have I never been in your lab before?" David asks, making himself at home in Greg's desk chair. Astrid doesn't think about how Max said almost the same thing. She definitely doesn't think about it.

"I'm not allowed to just bring people in here," she says instead, taking in the dark lab, assessing possible projectiles and long swingable objects just like Eleanor taught.

"So we're breaking the rules," David says with a faux gasp.

"Yes," she says.

"Because you think the sixteen-year-old in your lab is a supervillain?"

She sighs, leaning against a table before realizing she still has energy to burn and begins to pace.

"I think he's trying to sabotage me," she says. "Because I wrecked that curve and ruined his life."

David sighs, deep and long-suffering. "Or maybe you're just a little paranoid."

"He's a premed. You don't know what he's capable of."

He scoffs. "I've lived with you for the past year. Last finals I watched you eat raw ramen noodles and then drink the flavor mix with a glass of water."

"That's called depression, David."

"So are we just waiting for him to show up?"

"Yes. The only security cameras are at the entrances and they don't record, just feed to the security desk."

"He's sixteen."

"He's potentially a mad scientist."

"He doesn't even have a degree, how is he—"

"Just please humor me and wait over here in the dark in case he shows up."

David stands. "Fine," he says. "I will humor you, if you admit that this maybe is less about Ben and more about your breakup with Max."

"Why would this be about my breakup?" she asks, a little too loud for the quiet lab.

"Look, I'm not an expert in how deflection works," he says. "But maybe, instead of this guy deliberately sabotaging you, you're just looking for an outlet at an increasingly tense time in your life."

"This isn't about Max."

"Are you sure?" he asks.

She shrugs. "I dunno. Look I've been going to . . . therapy, group therapy, like once a week."

He pauses and she can't make out his expression in the dark, but she feels his hand close around hers.

"That's amazing."

"Yeah, well . . ." She sighs.

"No, seriously," he says. "That's so good, dude. Is it helping?"

"It isn't hurting."

"I'm oddly proud of you, roomie." He punches her shoulder lightly and steps away a little. "Okay, here's what we're gonna do."

"Uh?"

"We're gonna not wait here all night for this guy. I'm gonna phone a friend, and you are going to not be weird," he says, pulling his phone out of his back pocket.

"What are you talking about?" she asks.

"You need to promise you're not going to be weird," he says. "Okay, promise?"

"I promise," she says, rolling her eyes.

"Hi," Astrid says, a little breathless, face aching as she keeps herself from smiling too bright.

"Hi," Priya says, setting her bag down, eyes wide as she takes in how deeply weird this is. "You're David's roommate then? Astrid?"

"Yep," she says. "And you are Priya, David's . . . friend from the musical."

David has a crush. Which is new and exciting because David doesn't usually have crushes—David has ridiculously gorgeous female friends who he sleeps with and never sees again.

David's eyes say, *You're being weird and I want to kill you.* His mouth says, "Priya is a film major. She's really good at tech. So she's gonna set up some little cameras to watch your dorky science stuff."

Astrid nods and Priya nods and they stand there for a second, Astrid scrutinizing every detail between the two of them together like she'll be able to see the chemistry pinging off if she looks hard enough.

"I'm . . . gonna get started then," Priya says, glancing over at David. David smiles widely and rubs at the back of his neck awkwardly. Astrid is stupefied.

"Yeah, yeah, sounds great," David says. "Uh, do you like need help with anything?"

"Probably," she says, and hoists her bag up again, heading over to the incubators. David follows along behind her, like a puppy, all excited steps and tripping over his own feet.

Astrid looks around the lab for someone to exchange a look with, no, not just *someone* but someone who knows and could appreciate this moment.

After a moment, she sighs and follows after them, because she realizes she's just looking for Max.

"So that was Priya," Astrid says when they're back in their dorm room, eyes glued to the little tab on her laptop that's recording a live feed from the back of the lab.

"I hate you," David says, but passes her a spoon and a Ben & Jerry's pint over the space between their beds.

It's getting late. Like *late* late, so she's feeling more maudlin and sad with every passing minute.

"Can I ask . . . What makes her different?" she says. "For you. For your whole thing with relationships. Are you not scared?"

David slumps back onto his mountain of pillows.

"I think I'm more scared than I've ever been," he admits. "I don't even know if she likes me back. Which is bizarre because usually I can feel the vibe with these things, but with her I'm always too distracted. She's just wonderful. I'm still scared but I know even if it isn't what I imagine it's gonna be, there's a chance it might actually be better."

"Goddammit," she mutters, swiping at the corner of her eye

violently so no other tears get any ideas.

"Why did you break up with Max?" David asks quietly. "Did something actually happen or was it just you self-sabotaging again?"

"We have fear for a reason, you know?" she says, stabbing the spoon into the cold, stiff mass of ice cream. "It's evolution, it's biology. It's every single sentient creature that we came from, warning us to not do the thing that will make us die."

"Oh, come on," David says. "Not everything is evolutionary. Our society has developed far past a lot of those instincts."

"I know," she says, rolling her eyes. "Obviously, but that doesn't mean that fear doesn't come from a survival instinct. And that maybe it's okay to listen to that instinct."

"What about anxiety?" David asks. "What about a five-year-old being scared of monsters under the bed because some great-great-great-ancestor was afraid of the things that could eat us that were hiding in the dark? But there is no actual monster under the bed."

"Sometimes there is!" she says, voice pitching sharp and high. "Sometimes you are afraid because your bus is going over the side of a bridge and you're about to die."

"Jeez," David says softly. "That incident really fucked you up, huh?"

She laughs a little, rubbing a hand over her forehead. "Yeah, it did."

"Astrid," he says. "Being afraid when you're already falling won't stop you from hitting the ground."

She sticks her spoon into the pint and pulls out a glob of ice cream, watches it slide against the metal.

"But what if I avoid heights. Then I won't fall at all."

David sighs, sneaking a peek at the screen, her empty lab filled with dark corners and sharp edges.

"Fair enough. But you're gonna miss some incredible views."

David passes out about an hour later.

She puts his ice cream in the fridge before it melts onto his comforter. Then she stays up on her bed, studying and studying and studying even as her eyes burn and her hand cramps and her brain feels oversaturated with facts and figures. She keeps glancing back at the lab feed again and again. Until 3:39 in the morning when Ben walks into the frame.

It's quiet in her room, David breathing quietly feet away. There's a chill from the window and her eyelids are heavy, but she keeps watching as Ben Barnes opens the incubator and starts pulling out cell cultures. The labels on them aren't clear but she's pretty sure they're hers.

He splits them up on the table, half and half.

He pulls a syringe full of some clear liquid from his backpack and carefully portions it out between one group, closes them, and then puts them back in the incubator.

He abandons the others on the table and leaves the room.

She scribbles down the time stamps into her notebook and lets her heavy eyelids carry her down.

In the morning she pulls the clip together and emails it to

Dr. Vaughn with some bullshit phrasing, "Attached please find evidence of lab safety code violations and improper handling of my cell cultures."

It doesn't feel like a victory, or like redemption, or like anything. It feels hollow and boring. Like turning in a homework assignment that she just did with no fuss at all, just because it was due and she had to.

She sends the email and then closes the tab and then starts on the next pre-lab she has for physics.

Molly shows up at her dorm on a rainy afternoon sans Thomas and Lucy. She shakes out a polka-dot umbrella and props it in the corner, hopping onto Astrid's bed and crossing her legs.

"So," Molly says, resting her elbow against her thigh and her chin against her fist.

"Hi," Astrid says, raising her eyebrows, but feeling a sort of peace and amusement settle over her.

"You broke up with Max," Molly says.

Goodbye peace and amusement, have fun on your very long, cross-country trip.

"Uh," Astrid says. "Yeah."

"Eleanor didn't really give us a lot of details, but *you* broke up with *him*, right?"

Astrid nods, glancing briefly at the problem set on the desk in front of her like she can disappear into the numbers and hide there until Molly leaves.

"Why?" Molly asks.

"Well," Astrid says. "I almost died." Molly nods like she's

prompting her along. "And I don't really think I have time for a regular boyfriend much less a superhero one."

"You guys were fine last semester."

"He wasn't exactly a superhero last semester," she adds. She also didn't have lab last semester, or the Program, or extra volunteer hours and three lab classes. It's been a bad semester.

Molly bites her lower lip, brushes a strand of hair behind her ear. "Okay, I mean, I think it's good that you guys are taking a little break. I think it's healthy, you know, so you can come back even stronger than before."

"Molly," she says, pressing a hand hard into her forehead. "I think this is more than just a little break."

She can hardly admit it to herself, even though she was the one who pulled the plug. She doesn't know how to explain it to Molly, especially Molly who's been growing more frazzled by the week, the longer she goes without Arthur responding to any of her texts.

Molly sighs. "See, that's what I was scared of," she says. She turns on the bed so she has her knees under her. "I thought maybe I could offer you some perspective, you know."

"Alright," Astrid says slowly.

"When I was five I had an Olive O'Neil-themed birthday party," Molly says. Astrid pauses. The name sounds vaguely familiar, and she tries to recall if it's some alter ego she should know. "Not her boyfriend, like all the other kids who were into superheroes. I was *obsessed* with Olive. I did a school project on Margaret Mallory in the third grade. I wrote Eleanor fan letters like once a month all of middle school."

"Oh," Astrid says. "Um, wow."

Molly leans up on her knees, moving in place with a strange, frenzied energy that builds as she talks. Astrid watches with mild concern as Molly keeps going, her hands getting into it too as she starts talking even faster. "I think you're misunderstanding this whole thing. Dating a superhero is far from a burden. It's something I've always wanted." She takes a deep breath, ducking her head like she's a little embarrassed. Then, quieter, "It's why I started dating Arthur."

She says it like it's some big revelation, but Astrid can't quite figure out what exactly she's revealing.

"What does that mean?" she asks.

"Um . . . it means . . ." She leans back onto her heels and her voice goes a little quieter. "There was this . . . incident last year at one of the football games. This villain, he showed up and started flying around and throwing things with his mind powers. I was trying to get back to the locker room with the other cheerleaders, but he grabbed me and flew me way up and then dropped me. It was terrible, but before I could hit the ground . . . Arthur was there. Not as himself obviously, as the hero. And he saved me, caught me and brought me to safety, and it was so wonderful. And he must not have had a lot of time to change because when he went flying back up, I saw he was still wearing these red Vans and . . . " She smiles, shrugs a little helplessly. "So, I thought, it's a sign, you know? *He goes to my high school, and he saved me.* I started looking, and sure enough, after a few weeks, I saw the shoes and I knew it was him. So I bumped into him after school one day and we started talking and he was so sweet. And I . . . bumped . . . into him again. And again. And then . . . you know."

"You . . . knew?" Astrid says like saying it out loud will help her make sense of it, and maybe more importantly how she feels about what she thinks it means. "Does he know? That you knew?"

She sinks back into her heels a little. "I . . . he knows now. I told him, and it's kinda the reason he broke up with me, but that's not the point and I'm working on it." She says it in a single breath and waves her hand like that settles the whole thing.

"What?" Astrid says.

"*The point is* . . . I think you should give Max another shot," Molly says. "Because dating a superhero is, like, the purest form of love we have access to. There is adventure in this world and we have the chance to be a part of it, as normal people, as . . . symbols of love."

"Symbols of love?" Astrid echoes. "You mean, we get to be collateral damage." She crosses her arms over her chest.

Molly shakes her head vigorously. "No," she says. "No, everybody else out there in the city, they are the collateral damage. We are different."

"What? Because we're the love interests, because we're the damsels in distress?"

"Yes," Molly says emphatically, almost leaning forward, that buzzy Molly intensity in her eyes. "Because we are the ones who get saved. We're important. This makes us important."

Astrid steps back.

She doesn't want this to be what makes her important, she realizes.

Molly runs a hand through her hair and sighs quickly, like she's distressed. "You just . . . you just don't understand."

"Does Eleanor know about this?"

Molly's head snaps up, eyes wide. "No," she says. "No, you're the only person I've told and you can't tell anybody else, they'll—they'll get the wrong idea."

Right now, looking at Molly, her muscles drawn tight, arms crossed, shoulders squared, practically the textbook definition of defensive, Astrid isn't sure what idea she's supposed to get.

"Right," Astrid says. "Um . . . I think you should go."

And then Molly is back again; with a sigh the tension slips out of her shoulders and the clench of her jaw. She smiles tightly.

"No, it's fine," she says. "I didn't mean to get that heated, I just need to think of a better way to explain . . . what I mean."

Like night and day. Like Molly lives a double life too, fits two people inside her and keeps one a secret. Apparently, everyone does now.

"It's fine," Molly repeats brightly.

"No, Molly," Astrid says. "I think you should go."

"Oh," Molly says. She sits very still for a second and then slides off Astrid's bed. "Okay. I, uh, I hope I've given you something to think about."

Well, she absolutely has.

Ben gets expelled.

Astrid finds out in an email back from Vaughn who apologizes for the misunderstanding and offers her any opportunity to continue with practical lab stuff should she want to, and maybe even start an independent project in the fall. He also sends her a glowing rec letter. And then he sends her the emails of some colleagues on campus and off, looking for summer lab assistants.

Greg stops by her desk on Thursday with wide eyes, shakes his head, and says, "What a wild world."

She doesn't know how to feel about Ben getting expelled. She doesn't know how to feel about a lot of things right now. She thinks she'll keep going to therapy, but for now she decides to feel nothing, and just nods at Greg as she gets back to work.

SOPHOMORE SPRING
WEEK FOURTEEN

M Cell Bio Problem Set 10; BioChem Pre-lab
T Cell Bio Pre-lab; Physics Pre-lab; Orgo 2 read ch. 22; LAB 1-5
W BioChem Problem Set 12; BioChem read ch. 16
Th Orgo 2 Problem Set 12; BioChem Lab Report; Physics Lab Report; LAB 1-5
F ORGO 2 MIDTERM 3; Physics Problem Set 12; LAB 3-5

"I DON'T HAVE TIME," ASTRID WHINES.

"But you do," David says, and keeps yanking on her wrist.

"David, finals are coming," she says. "Coming fast. Two weeks. That's fourteen days. I needed to start studying for them last Tuesday."

"You were going to watch a movie with me tonight anyway," David says. He manages to pry her out of her desk chair. She goes limp, but he's used to her tactics. (Hailey's lessons on self-defense sit right below her skin, and she wonders what

David would do if she kneed him in the solar plexus. She thinks she'll save it for the next time he hogs the shower and cuts into her carefully scheduled thirteen minutes.)

"I was not," she says. "Because I don't have time."

"C'mon," he says. "Support me. Support the arts. Be a good friend. Get some culture."

"No culture, only science."

He pulls her an inch along the floor and she kicks out at him weakly.

"I'll let you talk to Priya," David offers.

"Max is in the ensemble," she says.

"You'll barely see him," David assures her. "Hell, I barely see him he's so far upstage."

She closes her eyes and wonders if it's worth it to explain that if Max is there, the only thing she'll be able to do is see him because she's in love with him and it has hardwired her brain to go absolutely nuts.

She hasn't told David why she broke up with Max, though. She doesn't think she could get through an explanation without sobbing. Plus, there's all the superhero stuff too that she technically can't tell him about.

"Fine," she sighs instead and lets David pull her off the floor.

After it's over, she pushes her way through the throngs of people waiting in the hall toward the backstage area. She knows she won't be allowed in and that David will mock her for not being allowed in, but she has to wait somewhere.

Her shoulder brushes with someone else and she turns her

head for a split second to check and apologize maybe, and that's all it takes. Just less than a second of not looking where she's going and she bumps into Max.

Because who else would it be.

"Sorry," he says. "Sorry." Probably before he even knows it's her. Probably before they even crash, just preemptively because he's always crashing into people and things as he stumbles along through life, a little cyclone of chaos.

"Hey," she says, and he freezes, staring after her.

"Hey," Max says, eyes going a little wide and a little wet. He's wearing makeup, stage stuff. It covers the bags under his eyes.

"You were really great," she offers, like it's something approved to say to your ex. Ex. She's too young to have an ex, or maybe too old or too dense or too ugly, but there's definitely something about it that feels wrong.

"Not really," he says, his hand going up to the back of his neck. Fair enough, he's far too clumsy to be a good dancer and barely had a single line. "Can't really sing or dance or act. It's a miracle they even let me in the ensemble."

"I did notice you were pretty far back," she allows. He smiles and she smiles and it's a moment.

"I liked it though," he says. The sound of his voice pushes its way into her chest and starts shoving shit around. "It was fun. I'll probably see if they let me back in next year."

She wants to step into him, wants to press herself against his chest and stay there forever. His eyes are so brown that she can't help but feel breathless.

"Or I dunno," he says, because she isn't saying anything, just staring at him. "Maybe try something new. Did you know there's a tabletop role-playing club here?"

"Sounds like fun," she says. She pats his shoulder because she needs to touch him, and it seems like the only way she's allowed to.

"Um, how are you?" he asks, throat bobbing.

She shrugs. "Doing okay. How 'bout you?"

He shrugs. "You know me. I land on my feet."

She can recall. The rest of that night is so blurry and coated in sticky panic, but she remembers him, the way his body moved and the way he would just float and leap and always land perfectly on his feet.

"Well, I'm just waiting for David," she says. "But he's probably taking his time."

"Right! He was great," Max says, stepping back. "I gotta go, but let him know that he really killed it tonight."

The hallway exists again. For a moment it hadn't and all that was real was Max and his voice, not the chatter and the push and pull of the crowd or anything else that ghosted across her senses. It's all back now, as he moves around her, returning to the throng, about to fade into the mass of people, just another face on campus or another person in New York City.

"Max," she says, catching his arm before he can disappear, spinning around to face him.

"Yeah?" he asks. "You okay?"

No, I miss you. No, I love you. I'm sorry. I didn't mean it.

"You should do this again next year," Astrid says.

He blinks, like maybe he was hoping for any of the million other things she wanted to say.

"Yeah . . . yeah, okay," he says. "I think I will."

"Are you going out tonight?" she asks because she can't let go of his arm, not yet.

"Nah, performing was kinda exhausting and the cast party isn't until next week. Are you?"

Oh, that type of going out.

Don't think about him dancing. Don't think about the lights and the heat and how free he'll look, free like he did on that rooftop. Don't think about him.

"No," she says. "David and I are gonna have a quiet night in probably."

"Right," he says. "Well, good night, Astrid."

"'Night, Max," she says, and then she doesn't watch him walk away.

Thomas and Lucy end up coming over for another movie night. David excuses himself.

The movie is on in the background to not-watch, and Astrid is feeling the pressure of finals around the corner so she pulls up her laptop and starts making study guides while they talk.

"I'm just so glad that Eleanor had us go over knot untying for like two weeks," Lucy says. "Because Jane just left me tied up in the middle of the warehouse while she was fighting those mobsters. I mean, I couldn't go anywhere after I broke out, but it was nice to be able to scroll Twitter while I was waiting."

"Right!" Thomas says, shoveling another handful of microwave popcorn in his mouth. "Look, I love Allie, but she was fighting this Dark Force guy and he like almost dropped me off . . . which is the tall bridge, the Williamsburg or the Manhattan?"

"Manhattan is right next to the Brooklyn Bridge," Astrid offers. "Williamsburg is further north."

"Right," he says. "I guess it was the Manhattan Bridge then. Allie, of course, has her big hero moment, but then she leaves me right on the bridge, like right on the road. Luckily it was around five so traffic was all gridlocked, but she was, like, gone fighting. I had to walk the whole bridge before I could call an Uber."

Astrid looks up from the computer at the two of them on her floor, passing the popcorn bag back and forth.

"Max left me on a fifty-story rooftop in the middle of the night for like twenty full minutes," she says, and for some reason saying it out loud right now almost makes her snort.

Lucy rolls her eyes in solidarity. "Fucking superheroes, man."

Astrid nods, because it's all a little ridiculous, isn't it? "Fucking superheroes."

SOPHOMORE SPRING
READING PERIOD

Study for FINALS

"MAX," SHE SAYS, BECAUSE IT'S MAX, SUD-
denly. He's just right there in the door, shifting from foot to
foot, curls and eyes and all.

"Hey," he says. His eyes home in on a fixed point on her
cheek and he blinks, worrying his lower lip with his teeth. "I'm
not interrupting anything, am I?"

"No," she says. Technically yes, she's in the middle of an
hour of Orgo 2 studying, but she's trying to be a little more
flexible with things like that. Also, he does look really bummed
so she's willing to make the exception. Right, that's why. Not
because it's Max and he's always the exception for her. She's
still lying to herself, apparently, trying to find any other reason. She steps back, letting the door creak open. "Come in."

He follows her in, hands fiddling by his stomach, like there's an invisible fedora hat and he's a forties detective with bad news.

"Thanks," he says. She still knows him, can still read the way his shoulders shift, the way he inhales sharply. He has something important to say, working to build the courage to get it out there.

"You okay?" she asks, because it's good to give him a gentle prompt when he's like this, carefully invite the confession out.

"I'm giving up the mask," he says. And exhales. And looks up.

"No, you're not," she says.

He blinks. She blinks.

"Yes, I, uh, am." It sounds a little less sure, pitched up like a question.

She steps farther into her room, pressing one palm flat against her desk. There's a pressure building between her eyes.

"I'm not asking you to do this," she says. "Don't do this because it's what you think I want you to do. Because it's not what I want you to do."

"I'm not," he says, carefully and assured. A bullet point on an outline of an argument. He's pacing, just a little. He shoves his hands in his pockets. "I'm doing this for me. Because I want to be happy."

"Being a hero makes you happy," she says. She thinks of the rooftop, of his smile cutting through the dark, and his laugh carrying in the air all the way up there on top of the world.

"Yeah, sure for a few hours, when it's a good night, when things are going well, which they usually don't," he says. His shoulders are up by his ears. He stops moving to meet her eyes. "And every other minute it's taking away everything else that makes me happy. So . . . I think I need to find a different way to help people."

He looks a little shaky, and she feels that, she knows that, that anxiety, that loss of identity, that spiral of "who am I," "why am I," "why do I feel so empty."

She wants to go to him. To hug him, rub little circles on his shoulder, and feel his back stutter and shake until he can be calm and whole again.

"And," he says, shifting again, tossing his weight between his feet. "And I thought I'd tell you because you make me happy. Made me happy. I've already lost so many people to things that are permanent and unchangeable, and it feels stupid to lose you over something I can fix."

His voice slices through her, down to her core. She scratches at her eyebrows, closing her eyes for a half second of relief from the pounding drum that's right there between her eyes.

"I can't," she says. "I can't have you do this for me because that's no way to have a relationship, based on some ultimatum or sacrifice—"

"This is my choice. I want—"

"I still don't have time for a relationship," she interrupts. "With you or with anyone. That's a choice I made."

"I don't care," he says. He steps forward and then overthinks it and steps back again, hovering awkwardly in the doorway. "I mean, I do. I care about you and your choices and if you don't, then we won't . . . but you said you love me, and I love you. I don't need your time. I don't care if being with you means sitting on the floor next to your desk while you study for the next nine years."

"That's not fair to you," she says, crossing her arms over her chest, drawing herself in and tight, squeezing every emotion into a dense little marble behind her sternum. She presses her palms over her eyes. "Max, I love you—"

"I know." He steps closer. She doesn't see him do it, but she doesn't have to. She can feel it, his warmth cutting through the air. "I love you, too, so much."

And it's not fair. He shouldn't be able to say it like that when he's looking at her like that, while his eyes and his hair and his entire self looks like that. It should be illegal for him to use all his Max-ness against her, to weaponize it and just cut right through her.

"I have lab and volunteering hours," she says, for both of their benefits because she's not allowed to make this mistake again. *Fool me once, universe.* "I'm the PR chair for Women in Medicine, I'm copresident of the premed society. I start studying for the MCATs next month, and I'll be working that PhD prep program up at CCNY. I'm pretty sure I'm gonna get those extra research hours with Professor Vaughn next semester." It's not about him, it never was. He's this perfect temptation. And maybe it's sad that she never could have made this work, and that she is the problem, but she's almost glad it is, because it means she doesn't have to consider this offer Max is laying forth, wonder if she should let him stop being a superhero just for her, damn the world and damn himself because she's a coward.

"I don't care," he says gently. "I don't need to be a priority. I understand—"

"No." He doesn't. "It's not that—" She barely does and it's her goddamn thought process.

"What?" he says pleadingly. "Then what is it?"

She swallows hard. "It's that I can't stop myself from making you a priority," she says, and she has to look away, eyes locking on the sharp corner of her desk like it's a port in the storm. "I tried and I can't, so I can't do this at all."

She trails off, watching him shift in place out of the corner of her eye. The silence that settles is heavy and humid. It crackles with tension, the way concrete does under pressure.

"I don't understand you," he says. He barely raises his voice. It fills the room anyway. "Some days I think I do, I think I look at you and see all the things you refuse to say because you don't have time, all the things you would feel if you weren't too afraid your head getting messy, when you need it to just be facts and answers. But . . . maybe I don't at all. Maybe you just—" He cuts himself off, shakes his head, and steps away like he's physically abandoning wherever that sentence was going. "I can't understand why you never let yourself be happy. Sad, scared, angry, sure, I get why you push through those. Who wants to feel any of that. But happy. I've seen you do it. Every time something good happens. Every time we're enjoying ourselves, a beautiful day, a good movie, a smile. I can count to ten and watch you realize that you're actually happy. And then you shut it down."

"Max," she says, feeling the panic rise inside her. She steps toward him hesitantly, but can already feel her knees starting to shake. "Don't." Because it's Max. He's known her longer than anyone she actually talks to. He's seen parts of her that nobody else has. She's spent two years telling him hopes and dreams and thoughts and fears, as they discovered each other little by little, inside and out. His eyes are moving around the room, around her face, like he's putting it all together. He knows her so well—probably better than she knows herself—and if he says something, some deep psychological analysis of her, some deconstruction of who she is, it will be like a bullet to the gut. It will define her. There'll be no erasing it, no reevaluating, no redefining. He has that power: the power to tell her who she is.

"Astrid," he sighs, hand stuttering in the air, half reaching for her before he shakes his head again and pulls back. "When you talk about happiness, when you talk about living your life, it's always in the future, nine years down the line, when you're a doctor. But . . . I've been worrying that it won't change a damn thing. You'll never let yourself be happy. You'll just keep scheduling it in for later."

It lands softer than it should, the blow of his statement like that. It doesn't feel like getting shot, it doesn't jerk her back, it doesn't burn, it doesn't tear. Maybe because it's Max, and he wouldn't know how to hurt someone if he tried. But she still tastes salt at the corner of her mouth, anyway, can't breathe even though the air wasn't punched out of her.

"Max," she says, wincing when her voice breaks on his name, just giving out completely as her chest shudders.

"I'm sorry," he says, and it's softer. "I'm sorry. I'm not try-ing to—I didn't come here to—to—Jesus, make you cry. I'm sorry." He steps forward quickly, but again his hands freeze, hovering in the air, like he's not even sure if he's allowed to touch her anymore. Maybe he isn't.

She wants him to. She wants him to hug her because he's so good at hugs and comfort, warm and soft, his heart sure, his chest firm.

She also, in a very real and more present way, wants to dig her feet into the ground and say something half as devastating right back, give as good as she's got, prove that she knows him, too.

"You need this relationship because you don't know what else to do with yourself," she says. The words slip out and for a second they feel good, like power, something she has control of. Max steps back and losing him by even inches makes her heart aches. "Because you've spent years living a double life and dedicating more time to being a hero than anything else, that you forgot to make Max Martin into a real person and you don't know how to start now."

And there's some response on the tip of his tongue that she's ready to hear, ready to respond to, but the door slams open.

"Someone take *The Last Five Years* soundtrack away from

me!" David says, kicking his shoes off, flinging his keys halfway across the room until they bounce on his bed. He is unbearably loud, shouting over his headphones, shattering through the room. Bull, meet china shop. He seems to realize what exactly he's walked into in the next second, freezing in place like he's staring down a velociraptor. "Oh."

For a moment, maybe for the first time in years, there is stillness in Astrid's entire life, the three of them standing in the leftover energy in the room, the emotional carnage still scattered across the floor. Nothing moves, not a muscle, not a thought.

And then . . .

"Max," David says stiffly, a parody of a greeting.

"David," Max says in reply, smiling politely like David is his second-grade teacher he just ran into in a Stop & Shop.

"Um . . . ," David says eloquently. "I could—"

"I should leave," Max says.

No, *don't*, she almost says, on pure driven instinct. She's playing Jenga with her insides again. She needs to keep everything in place and perfectly still, there are already too many holes in the tower. It'll fall over if someone breathes.

"I'm . . . sorry," Max says, barely able to look at her.

And he's fast. Superfast, slipping around David and then he's already at the door. There's a vacuum at her side. She feels like she might fall over.

She stares at him as he hesitates in the doorway.

She's not good at saying things, explaining how she feels, but

Max could always tell, always read exactly what she wanted to say but couldn't. Only right now she doesn't know what she feels. So, they stare at each other, with David in the middle like a frozen statue, and not a single thing passes between them.

And then Max is gone.

"Bye, Max," David says, turning his neck around at a dangerous angle to watch him go, before his attention jerks to Astrid with the resounding abruptness of a snap bracelet. "What was that?"

"That was Max," she says, amazed she's able to speak, amazed she's able to say his name. There are tears still trickling down her cheeks, but she doesn't feel like she's actually crying anymore. It's just water leaking.

"And?" David says, toeing the door shut behind him.

"Wouldn't you like to know, weather boy?" she says, and she's not bleeding out internally or anything.

She takes a breath, to remind herself that she can.

"Do you want to . . . talk?" David asks, hovering a few feet away from her, like there's a line or something that marks off the splash zone.

"I gotta study," she says, and staggers over to her desk, sliding into her chair at an angle that won't jostle the wound at her gut, even though there's not anything there.

SOPHOMORE SPRING
FINALS, WEEK ONE

M
T   ORGO 2 FINAL
W
Th BioChem FINAL
F   Physics FINAL

SHE HATES AFTERNOON FINALS. THEY ALWAYS feel wrong. Mornings were made for tests, when your brain is fresh and clean, not sticky from too much time awake. So, she sleeps in and doesn't look at any material that might overload everything she has stored up, and has breakfast/lunch at 12:05 while fighting every instinct to panic-make five dozen more flash cards.

Thankfully she has David as a distraction.

"Give them back," Astrid says, crossing her arms petulantly, wondering why she thought giving David her flash cards was a good idea.

"What are the three main angular velocity formulas?" he asks.

"David," she says, stern, stretching her hand across the table, nearly knocking over the plastic cafeteria cups. "I am in lockdown. No studying the morning of the test."

"Phone," David says, tossing the flash cards at her and grabbing her buzzing phone from next to her cutlery while she's distracted.

"David," she says through gritted teeth, scrambling for the cards before they tumble into her applesauce and salad brunch power meal.

"Hello," he says into her phone. "This is Astrid Rose Bot; please enter username and passcode."

"Fuck you," she says, carefully restacking the cards, ordering them and straightening the edges against the table.

"Uh-huh," David says. "One second." He pulls the phone away from his ear. "One of your tutorees is freaking out. Maybe they're nervous about finals, too."

"I'm not nervous," she says. Not excessively nervous. She's average finals nervous, which is a good place to be an hour out. "Give me the phone."

He jerks the phone back when she reaches for it, so she throws a spoon at him and snatches the phone while he's ducking the cutlery.

"Rude," David says as she pulls the phone to her ear. "You could have killed me."

"Hello," she says, flipping him off.

"Astrid." She glances at the caller ID. Lucy. Which makes no sense because the voice on the other end of the line sounds scared and Lucy doesn't do scared.

Her stomach sinks.

"Lucy," she says. "What's up?" She really doesn't want to know the answer.

"Something's happening," she says, voice shaking, hushed, with staticky breaths like she's pressed up to the phone. "I think . . . Thomas and I are at the Fridge and . . . there's someone else here."

"Someone else?" She pushes back from the table, stares at a mysterious stain on the floor, clamps a hand over her other ear to muffle the chatter of the cafeteria. "What do you mean?"

"Thomas and I were just down here, hanging out cuz we had a half day for APs, and then there was this loud crash and an alarm started going off. We went for the elevators, but there was someone there going through Eleanor's desk so we turned around and found this—this broom closet."

"What's wrong?" David asks, smiling nervously. Astrid probably looks as sick as she feels.

"Well . . . uh . . . have you called Eleanor?" she asks, waving David off.

"We tried," she says. "But the call wouldn't go through and—"

Astrid starts rubbing at her forehead like that'll make her brain do something.

"Have you tried . . . I don't know, anyone else? Your

355

girlfriends?" *Anyone else. Anyone besides me. What in the world do you want from me?*

"What was that?" Thomas. He sounds just as shaken, but it's still good to hear his voice until—and there's a sudden and faint clanging noise that rips through the static of the call.

"Astrid," David repeats. But she can't really hear him right now while also trying to will her ears to pick up on anything on the other end of the line.

"Thomas?" she calls. No answer. Breathe in, breathe out. Focus.

"Shhh." Lucy again. Another clang. There's a short century of crackly breathing, echoing in Astrid's ears despite the buzz of the dining hall at high noon.

David's hand lands on her wrist. "What's happening?"

She shakes her head, trying to communicate desperately with her eyes that everything is not fine, but she needs another goddamn second to figure this out.

"Okay," Thomas says. "Okay, I think—"

It's hard to say what kind of sound explodes across the line, her phone's tinny audio just screaming some terrible metallic nonsense.

"Thomas," she says, slapping a hand to the cafeteria table to brace herself. *Please, please, please, please, please, please.*

The static clears.

"Get Max!" It's Lucy again. There's air rushing around her, a great whooshing muffling her words. Running, she's running. Right?

The line goes dead. Call ended, her phone snaps back to the lock screen, a picture of her finals schedule.

"I can't," she says. To David, because the call is over.

"Is everything okay?" he asks.

No.

"Max is at his final," she says. David frowns at her.

"Um, yes."

"He won't be out for two hours," she says, still holding the phone. Lucy and Thomas can't hear her. "I couldn't get in there. I don't even know where the Ab Psych final is. Do you know where the Ab Psych final is?"

David shakes his head. "Why would I know where . . . ? Why do you need to know where the Ab Psych final is? What's happening?"

She stands up, her chair scraping against the linoleum. Her flash cards tumble out of her lap and onto the floor.

"*I* have a final," she says, bouncing on the balls of her feet. She wants to run. Run where? Just run, like if she keeps running then Lucy and Thomas will keep running and not die.

"Yes," David says. "You have a final. Astrid, you're scaring me. Is everything okay?"

She needs notes, she needs PowerPoints. She needs . . . she needs Max. This is Max's world. Missing finals and saving people and knowing what to do when the world is ending. She needs to hand this off to Max as soon as possible, and get to her final fifteen minutes earlier with her number two pencils and her water bottle and her TI-85 calculator.

"Astrid?" David says again.

She grabs her backpack and slings it over her shoulders.

"David, if I even seem remotely interested in anyone ever again, please slap me across the face," she says. Then she marches out of the cafeteria with fifty-six minutes until her final, heading in the opposite direction.

She paces the length of the quad, listening to her phone buzz out a dial tone again and again.

No Eleanor. No Wally. She texted everyone she knew, asking where the Ab Psych final was. She googled which building hosts the Psych department.

She tried calling Max.

Nothing. She has nothing. It's been five minutes.

She's running out of time. Her final starts in forty-seven minutes.

Thomas and Lucy are running out of time . . . They're . . .

The quad is mostly empty. Finals are in full swing; the library's probably crowded. It's lovely out. A little cloudy, but a bright and beautiful May afternoon.

She reaches one corner of the quad again and turns on her heel, stalking back down the concrete path.

Okay, one last person to try.

"Hello?" Molly answers on the second ring, sounding very confused.

Astrid freezes. She's forgotten what it's like to have a phone call actually go through.

"Molly, it's Astrid," she says. "I think something is going on at the Fridge and I can't get in contact with . . . anyone else."

"What? What's going on at the Fridge?" Molly asks.

"I don't know." But it feels so good to be explaining it to someone else. "Lucy called and said it looked like there was an intruder and then the line went dead."

Molly gasps a little. "He didn't," she breathes, but Astrid hears it loud and clear over the line nevertheless.

"Who didn't?"

"What? Nothing," she says quickly. "I've got it under control, it's fine. Don't even worry about it, just go to your final."

Which . . . yes, she's been waiting and waiting to reach someone who could take charge of the situation and tell her just that, except . . .

"How do you know about my final?"

The line goes dead.

The quad is empty enough that Astrid gives a strangled scream without fear of judgment. A few pigeons startle, abandoning the splattered remains of a tuna salad sandwich.

It's not her job. What could she even do anyway? She doesn't have superpowers or decades of martial arts training or alien DNA or any of it. She has nothing. She is nobody. She's a broke, depressed, clinically anxious college student with a very important final in under an hour.

"It's not my job," she says aloud, breathing the words frantically as she speeds over to the other end of the quad path. "It's not my responsibility. There's nothing I can do." She pulls at her hair, like she can drag the answer out by her own scalp.

It's getting harder to breathe. She's spiraling, down, down, down toward a panic attack when she needs to be clean and cool and locked in for this three-hour final worth 30 percent of her grade.

"There's nothing I can do," she whispers. "What do they want me to do? There's nothing I can do. I tried. I called everybody. Nobody's answering. What can I do? What else can I do?"

She needs this final. She needs this physics grade in her GPA. She needs a 4.0.

Nothing else should matter.

Why? Why does she keep letting herself get distracted with nonsense instead of trying to become the best doctor she possibly can be? Didn't she make a promise to herself to use every second of her short time in this chaotic, unpredictable, cruel, and spontaneous universe exactly the way she wanted to?

She barrels over to the next fork in the path, turning toward the streets of New York, dread and fear pounding in her blood, regret already settling in her stomach.

She hates superheroes.

She walks fast. The farther she gets from campus and the room where her physics final is, the more untethered she feels. The city is quiet because it's just past noon and everyone is in school or at work, doing the things they're supposed to be doing. And she's not. Astrid is not where she's supposed to be for maybe the first time.

There's been something in her for her whole life—since that first time her parents left her alone and talked to her about responsibility and doing the right thing and not jumping on the couch—that makes her always do the things that are expected of her. She's had a path, she's known rules, she's planned days and places to be, and even in college without a curfew, on her own, she goes to class, she goes to lunch, she goes to tests, review sessions, clubs, from point A to point B in a straight line, not stepping on the grass, not leaving the red brick paths or straight gray sidewalks.

And now she's walked right off the path, hopped on a rocket ship, and jettisoned as far away from the path as possible.

Deep breath.

Her phone rings.

"David?" she asks.

"Okay, uh, where are you? Because I'm back in our room right now and your finals emergency preparedness bag is still here and you are not here and your final is in like ten minutes and why aren't you at your physics final?" he says quickly like it's the run-up to a joke but he's not laughing.

"I'm fine," she says, even though no one who has ever said that has meant it.

"Look, I know I've been making you watch *Ferris Bueller* every month since the day we met, because you know you're totally a Cameron and you've needed to crash a Ferrari through a glass wall since way before I met you, but this isn't what I meant," he says. "Like as free and wonderful as you feel right now, you're gonna hate yourself and maybe me forever if you miss this final. Or if you're having a breakdown right now just like let me know, okay, and I'm on the way. I know it's been a rough semester for you, but we're so close to finishing it and I don't want to watch you self-sabotage, because there's a difference between self-care and self-sabotage even though it's not clear sometimes and I—"

"David," she says, and grimaces. "There's no easy way to explain this fully. I am fine, but I can't talk right now. And I need to go, okay?"

"Is this about Max?" he asks.

"No, it's just . . . it's nothing," she says, and almost gets hit by a car as she tries to cross Fifth Avenue, because she's on the phone and still walking, and also maybe having a small panic attack. "Uh . . . but if you see Max, tell him to check his voice mail, please."

David sighs on the other side of the line, a big staticky gust of breath. "Could you at least tell me where you are?"

"Uh . . . I'm . . . ," she starts, trying so desperately to remember every second of Wally's Excuses Week. There was making excuses for your SO, keeping track of your SO's excuses, coming up with excuses for why you were missing from important work events because of various superhero shenanigans. "I'm . . . at a doctor's appointment."

The second it's out of her mouth she winces.

"Um," David says, sounding incensed. "What is happening?"

"I gotta go, David," she says, because she literally does: she's turning down the last block before the Fridge now. She hangs up before he gets his next sentence out.

She takes a deep breath and tries to switch her brain on, to put it into threat-analysis mode. It's not hard; her brain is hardwired that way.

The brownstone looks the same.

It's quiet and calm, like it's just another apartment building on a residential street in New York City. Like there isn't a sprawling underground labyrinth, spreading like roots from this very spot, like there aren't two scared people that Astrid cares about down beneath the ground.

Another deep breath.

She tries one more call.

"Hey, Max," she says, and for the first time in her life doesn't feel weird recording a voice mail. Her voice is already shaking, and her head feels cluttered with worry and fear and excuses for why she doesn't have to do this. The words come easily though, like she's had them prepared. "It's me. Again. You might want to check your other voice mails for context, but something bad is happening." It's all there but hard to get through with the golf ball in her throat. "If for some reason, things go badly here, I just wanted to let you know that it's not your fault. At all. This one is all on me. I love you and I'm sorry I didn't say it every time I thought it because I thought it so many times, like an unreasonable amount of times. I'm sorry that I'm a hypocrite. I want you to know that . . ." She moves the phone away from her ear and closes her eyes. "When I'm around you, I lose track of time. And I never thought—"

The phone beeps, the message stops recording.

She swallows, lowers her phone, and walks up the steps of the brownstone.

"Astrid!" The voice comes from down the block. Molly comes jogging toward her, ponytail swinging. "How did you get here so fast?"

"How did *you* get here so fast?" Astrid shoots back, hovering awkwardly in the doorway.

"I said I had everything under control." She takes the steps two at a time.

"Believe it or not, I didn't exactly trust you after that phone call," Astrid says. Molly has the audacity to look offended.

"This whole thing is just a misunderstanding. I can fix it."

"What did you do? Who is down there?"

Molly sidesteps around Astrid and around the question, and pulls the door open, no security code at all, no fingerprint scan, no welcome from Hailey.

"You don't have to come," Molly says. "I've got it."

Astrid rolls her eyes and follows Molly into the brownstone. "What happened to the security system?"

"It's been disabled," Molly says, still walking fast like she can get away in a dead-end hallway. "Did you know Eleanor built in a complete security override? Because I think it's a huge design flaw."

They reach the elevator.

"Hailey," Astrid calls. "Could you get the elevator, please?"

"Uh," Molly says. "Hailey's gone. Complete security override. A design flaw, right?"

The hallway is completely silent and overwhelmingly small.

Molly steps forward and sticks her fingers into the place where the two elevator doors meet. Astrid watches her try to wedge them apart unsuccessfully for a second before sighing and joining her. Astrid has never been very strong but grip strength was a huge part of training. Still, even as she leans her whole weight into it, the doors barely budge.

Molly gives up first, stepping back and fixing her ponytail.

"Okay," she says. "Looks like we're taking the back entrance."

Molly leads the way across the avenues.

"What?" Astrid asks. "Why? Why would a hospital elevator take us down to the Fridge?"

"I know about the lab, Astrid," Molly says. For a second she thinks Molly's talking about Vaughn's lab but that makes no sense.

"What?"

"And I know Eleanor showed you like a million weeks ago, because you do science-y stuff."

"Wait, are you talking about the Rotunda?" she asks, jogging forward to keep up with Molly at the first crosswalk. The light is red so they have to stop and wait.

"Look," Molly says, turning. "I've spent eighty hours a week in the Fridge for the past dozen weeks. I know who comes in and out. I know that Dr. Midnight comes by way too often. I know that sometimes he comes in and never comes out, and other times I don't see him come in but I see him leave. So, I did my research. The furthest east room of the Fridge is right underneath the hospital. He uses the elevator to bring down his stolen medical supplies in a more discreet way."

The light changes. Molly charges ahead. Astrid has to remind herself how to walk.

"You think Eleanor's supervillain boyfriend has a secret lab in the Fridge?"

"Yes," Molly says defensively. "I even think it's pretty sweet that Eleanor lets him work there."

"It's not a lab," Astrid says. Medical supplies, she thinks. You need medical supplies to maintain a coma patient. "It's a memorial. And . . . it's Kat Robinson's hospital room."

That stops Molly short. Her eyes go big and she goes pale.

"Oh . . . ," Molly says slowly. "Oh God."

"Who did you tell?" Astrid asks. Molly leads them through the sliding glass doors to the lobby of the hospital. "Who is down there?"

"This way," she says instead of answering the question, walking quickly past the front desk with her head down.

Astrid trails after her, her shoulders tensing until they make it past the lobby without being stopped. It must be some Molly thing, the ability to walk right into places she's not supposed to be with the confidence to not be stopped.

Astrid finally catches up, pulling up to her side when Molly stops and leans into her leg casually in the elevator hall.

"Molly," she says, as stern as she can manage with her brain swirling in panic and bewilderment.

"We need to go," Molly says, grabbing Astrid's wrist and dragging her into the next car that opens.

It looks like an average elevator when they get in, but Molly approaches it with a confidence that is stunning and terrifying, but in this moment a good thing. She punches in a series of numbers on the floor buttons.

"Molly, who's down there?" Astrid asks again, pitching her voice low.

Molly meets her eyes and swallows hard.

"Ben Barnes," she says.

"Ben Barnes," Astrid echoes before stunning clarity sets in. The elevator dings, accepting the code Molly somehow knew. And it feels like the floor falls out from under her. Of course it's Ben Barnes.

He was using her cell cultures but doing something to them, accelerating growth. And what was it Jenny Chen said? Her lab had been hit up too. Every enhanced-bio research lab across campus. The guy Max had been trying to find. It wasn't sabotage. It wasn't about her. The conclusion spills out of her, her mouth working while her brain catches up: "He wants superpowers. And you want him to get them because you want to date a superhero."

"When I came to your lab that morning after my breakup, I saw Ben in there injecting himself with something. He wants to help people. Our . . . relationship just grew from there."

"Sure, it did," Astrid says, pressing her knuckles to the space between her eyebrows.

The doors open and the first thing Astrid notices is Kat Robinson. She hasn't seen the hospital room from this angle before, but Kat looks just the same as she did all those months ago. Serene and peaceful, like a Disney princess in a perfect romantic slumber.

"Ben!" Molly says.

The second thing Astrid notices is Ben Barnes on the other side of the room, spinning around to face them with wide eyes and tense shoulders, and an Erlenmeyer flask full of some clear liquid. There's a lab table behind him covered in glassware, a whiteboard covered in various scribbles of chemical equations, and a veritable wall of vials with a rainbow of glowing substances.

"What are you doing here?" he asks, and then seems to notice Astrid stepping out into the room too. "What are *you* doing here?"

"What are *you* doing here?" Molly shoots back, standing tall, looking angrier than Astrid's ever seen Molly. "I told you to wait and let me handle it, not do this."

She waves her arm to the Rotunda across from them.

The third thing Astrid notices: Through the broken glass door of Kat Robinson's hospital room is Lucy and Thomas with their hands tied behind their backs, sitting next to each other on the floor. Lucy has a red stain on the shoulder of her blouse, and Thomas has a cut over his eyebrow, but other than that the two look unharmed and bored.

Don't be the hero. That was Eleanor's big rule. Protect yourself but don't make things worse. Seize any opening but wait for help.

Fuck, that means she's the help.

"I can't wait anymore," Ben says, gritting his teeth. "Because *she* got me expelled. I need to figure this out now." He reaches for the table behind him, grabbing a thin black box and holding it out threateningly in front of him. He flips a switch and it starts buzzing in a slightly menacing way.

And Astrid recognizes it.

"Is that from the Watts Lab?" she asks. There had been a meeting for BioChem undergrad lab researchers two weeks ago to present on different labs, though she spent most of it doing flash cards in her lap. All she remembers about the Watts Lab was that they were looking into the viability of short-range laser tech. "Were you stealing from there too?"

"Look," Molly says, holding her hands out. "Ben, just let Thomas and Lucy go and you can finish what you're doing."

"Uh," Astrid says, turning to Molly. "I don't think we can let him do that."

Molly frowns.

"Shut up!" he says, stepping forward and leveling the little box at Astrid. The buzzing is definitely menacing now, louder and higher, and his finger hovers over another switch. She thinks she should be as terrified as she was standing on the roof, but a quiet calm starts to spread over her. This is much less scary than being thrown around above the city. This is just Ben Barnes and a laser that she's trying to deeply remember the details of. But that's all it really feels like, a problem that she's going to solve, that maybe she can solve. "You ruined my life, two semesters in a row. You ruined my med school applications and you got me expelled."

"Hey," Molly says slowly, a little shaky. She steps deeper into the room, and Ben watches her warily. "How do you expect to be a superhero if you're gonna kill people?"

"A superhero? I don't want to be a superhero," he says. "I want to be super *smart*. That's all that matters. And that's what you showed me, Astrid. I'm not smart enough. Not if someone like you can do better than me."

"Someone like me?" Astrid echoes. "What does that mean?"

"Just in general!" he snaps. Did she think the box was buzzing before? It sounds more like a whine, like angry hornets. And it's growing higher and higher pitched. And louder. "Just in general . . . if someone else can do better than me on a Calc Two final, I'm not smart enough. So, I clearly need to make myself smarter."

"What about helping people?" Molly demands, yelling over the noise of the definitely-evil-laser-box.

"God, you're such a groupie!" Ben screams back, rolling his eyes.

And then the box goes silent.

Astrid barely has time to duck, instinctively, before Ben

presses a button and a beam of red light explodes from the end. It shoots across the room. Astrid, from her crouch, watches the beam in slow motion. It zags a bit, Ben's hand unable to hold it steady, before pinging, with deadly accuracy.

It hits Molly square in the chest. She sprawls to the ground.

Astrid gasps, the air yanked from her lungs. The hum is back, the device gearing up again. A buzz. A whine.

Ben turns the box as it screeches back to dog-whistle levels, but Lucy is there suddenly, crashing into him like a linebacker. They go tumbling to the ground in a mess of limbs, the box skidding across the linoleum, still shrieking demonically.

Thomas appears next. He's usually the last to finish in their knot-untying exercises. And he goes diving for the box on the floor between them.

Where time has been slipping out of her grasp for the past few hours, it seems to stop completely for Astrid now. Not in the wonderful calming way it used to with Max, but in a dreadful paralyzing way, like she's watching from afar, only able to absently take in the scramble for the black box, and Molly on the floor, and Kat Robinson in the bed behind her.

And then Molly starts to seize.

No. No more thinking about time, no more thinking at all. Astrid snaps back into herself and drops to her knees next to Molly. There's a large and bloody and charred-looking gash down the front of her chest and Astrid goes to apply pressure with her hovering, useless hands.

The seizing stops, but then so does all movement. Including

the rise and fall of Molly's chest. She's completely still.

"Oh no," Astrid chokes out. "Oh . . . let's—let's not."

She reaches down for Molly's wrist like it's second nature, fingers finding the groove between tendons where her pulse should be. Where it currently isn't.

Astrid swallows hard.

CPR. That's the move. Obviously, she's not breathing, so CPR. That, at the very least, Astrid remembers from high school gym, even though she lost the free plastic mask you're supposed to use for mouth to mouth. It's fine. Chest compressions can work just fine.

Only her chest is where the injury is, bloody and angry.

"Shit," she breathes. "Shit."

She doesn't know what to do. She doesn't know what to do and there's nothing she's ever memorized or problem-solving process she's learned for this moment. There's no right answer and she's just kneeling here, feeling the cold splash of an anxiety attack starting to paralyze her. She's just stock-still, struck speechless, all the while Molly isn't breathing and her brain is losing oxygen and . . .

Here's the thing. She took a class last semester about the super type of serums as a 200-level biochem elective, because it fit best in her schedule and went to her major requirements, and literally no other reason.

And, as always, she did really well in the class.

Well enough that she knows to look back to the board above the little lab table and take it in again. And it's not for any super serum. It's about cell growth, specifically brain cell growth, targeting cell receptors that control healing. She thinks about her overgrown cell cultures, and superpowers, and Kat Robinson and comas.

She dashes for the lab table, carefully dodging around the tangle of flailing limbs on the ground.

Careful, she reminds herself. *Let's be careful and safe.* She—*carefully*—pulls two latex gloves from a box at the back of the table before anything else. Whatever Ben had been doing before they showed up was still laid out on the table; a mixture in a beaker, the Erlenmeyer flask, and a halfway finished titration. He's following the serum outlined on the board, but replacing the superhero's blood sample with stem cell samples from Vaughn lab.

"What are you doing?" Ben asks. He sounds furious and strangely muffled (Astrid assumes she has Lucy to thank for that) but she ignores him. She doesn't have time for him.

It's sloppy work, but she doesn't have time to correct any of it, just starts finishing the titration and mixing the rest of the serum. She checks the board again and scans over the vials in front of her before measure out five milliliters of the blood sample labeled "Dr. N, US+—5/1." The final step seems to be to put the mixture in a vortex mixer for fifteen seconds, but with the extra organic material from Vaughn's samples, it'll need more time to mix and settle, so she leaves it in for thirty seconds, feeling each single one tick away slowly.

"Astrid—" Ben tries again, and is again silenced.

She moves to the glass cabinet holding other equipment and unwraps a clean syringe. Somehow, despite it all, her hands are steady as she moves back to the lab table and sterilizes the needle before attaching it.

She taps it off, pushes out the air, and walks back to Molly.

A quiet calm crashes over her. An emptiness in her brain, that doesn't think of things before doing them. She can't even hear whatever tussle the others are having. It's just her, Molly, and this syringe.

She kneels next to Molly and inhales once, and finds a vein in Molly's elbow and sticks the needle in.

For better or worse, this is what she can do. She crosses her fingers and closes her eyes and presses down on the plunger.

It'll take time, she reminds herself, for the compound in her bloodstream to reach her heart or brain and start to do something, but hopefully—

Molly sits up with a start, eyes snapping open. That's good, except for her eyes, which are so wide. And they're glowing blue.

"Molly?" she says, leaning back. Molly jolts upright to a standing position. Her feet are only on the ground for a moment. Then she's hovering.

The equations on the whiteboard didn't say anything about that.

Molly shoots right into the tangle of limbs on the other side of the room and right at Ben Barnes, grabbing him by the collar of his shirt and throwing him against the wall, the entire lab table and all the equipment on it crashing to the ground and shattering. Thomas and Lucy tumble back as Molly swings at him, a solid right hook that lands with a crunch. His eyes roll back in his head as blood blossoms from his nose.

"Molly?" Thomas says.

She moves back, dropping Ben. He slides down the wall with what can only be described as an undignified squelch. Her feet touch the ground again and she blinks, the lights in her eyes flickering.

"Oh," she says. The red burns across her chest start to fade and she sways on her feet for a moment before falling like her strings have been cut.

Astrid swallows hard, her weight leaning back onto her hands.

Thomas and Lucy turn toward her slowly, before their eyes drop to the empty syringe still in her hands.

The nurse has a perfect poker face as she makes her way across the hospital waiting room.

At the sight of her, Thomas grabs Astrid's hand on top of the geometric gray couch and squeezes. He's been having a particularly rough time of it, pacing around the waiting room every few minutes, knees shaking when he sits, a perpetual motion machine of worry.

He'd finally fallen apart when they made it to the lobby of the hospital, nearly hyperventilating on the spot when the man at the front desk asked for Molly's contact information.

Miraculously, some backup generator in her brain kicked in, and Astrid snapped to attention, pulling information out of Molly's wallet, following the careful instructions she memorized weeks ago with Eleanor to get them to the doctors to handle this sort of thing.

Once Molly was situated and Thomas and Lucy received some first aid, mostly for bruises and a few shallow cuts, every bit of left-over adrenaline evaporated, the stress and the worry slipping off Astrid's shoulders. She collapsed into the first available couch in the waiting room and hadn't moved for the half hour they'd been waiting.

Despite it all, and even though it makes her feel like a bad person, she's still worrying about her physics final, but in an abstract sense, like maybe she's trying to distract herself from the way her hands have been shaking and her mind has been racing. It's one way to stop feeling the syringe in her hands, the feeling of Molly's skin beneath her fingers as she searched for a pulse that wasn't there.

Or she might just be a terrible person.

The nurse stops in front of them and presses her lips together.

"She's stable," she says. Thomas sinks back into his seat, his eyes shutting slowly. Lucy pats his shoulder and nods to herself. "We're just waiting for her to wake up."

Astrid squeezes Thomas's hand back, but it's a reassuring squeeze. They're actually going to be okay.

◆◆◆

Astrid lets her phone ring, but only twice before she answers.

"Hey," she says, grateful she's alone. Lucy is grabbing a coffee and Thomas is in the bathroom.

"What happened?" David demands. "Do you know what time it is? You missed your physics final. Where are you?"

"I'm fine," she says. "Everything's fine, I promise."

"You scared me," he says, blowing out heavily. "And Max looked freaked when he went off."

"Wait," she says. "What?"

"I found the Ab Psych final," he says. "Went right in and grabbed him. The second I mentioned something was wrong . . . he took off without me, said it was dangerous. Why would it be dangerous?"

"Uh," she says. "He was being dramatic. I just . . . I had a little freak-out, but he calmed me down. That's all."

"You're killing me here," he says. "That's such a weak sauce lie, but I trust you, okay? Even though you scared the hell out of me again."

She smiles, pressing a hand to her forehead. "I'm sorry I can't tell you everything yet."

"Whatever," he says, even though she can tell he's a little annoyed she's not saying more. "I'm just glad you're okay. And I bought us a literal gallon of ice cream, so hurry back, cuz it's not fitting in our mini fridge."

"You're my best friend, David," she says.

"Gross," he says, but it's not even close to being convincing. "Same."

She feels a shift in the air before he even says her name. "Astrid!"

Max. She doesn't need to turn to know it's him.

Her heart stutters out a response. A part of her has been thinking about Max for hours, since the second she got the phone call, since the moment she woke up this morning, since the minute she last saw him when he super-sped out of her dorm room. This whole time a small section of her brain has been thinking about him, wondering if she would ever see him again.

She sent him a text once they had wheeled Molly into a hospital room. *All ok, pls ignore voice mails.*

From the look in Max's eyes he had ignored the *text* and hadn't ignored the *voice mails*. How he found her here, she has no clue, but just seeing him has something deep within her settling; something like peace sweeping through her.

She stumbles up to her feet, swaying and shaky.

"Max," she croaks. Wow, she's already crying, huh? She's not sure if she expected it sooner or much, much later. Therapy-ten-years-from-now later. She feels like everything inside is pressing outward, desperate to make her explode, to have her splatter and leak all over the patterned carpet right here.

She wonders if he's listened to every voice mail or just the embarrassing ones. She wonders if there were any non-embarrassing ones.

"Astrid," he says, and she barely gets a step forward. He moves faster than her eyes can follow, on her like a windstorm, crashing into her, and catching all of her weight. She hadn't realized how tired she was from holding all of herself up.

His hands brush over her arms, along her shoulders, down her back. One sweeps up along her cheek, fingers getting tangled in the greasy flyaways spilling from her ponytail.

She thinks maybe her knees give out because she's clinging to him, arms around his waist, hanging off him. He pulls her in, one hand moving to cradle the back of her skull, the other pressing into her lower back.

"Are you okay?" he asks. "What happened? I've been looking everywhere for you and—"

It's all background noise, like the buzzing in the back of her head. She closes her eyes and presses her cheek against his, digging her fingers into his back, and doesn't let go.

"Don't ever do that again," he says, forehead pressing against hers, eyelashes fluttering. It's hard to focus on anything when they're this close. She's given up, just lets her eyes skirt off every centimeter of space on his face. "Please."

She's not sure if this is allowed. Like she's pretty sure the whole breaking-up thing comes with rules, and this has to be flouting a bunch of them. She can feel each breath of his against her lips. She has her nose touching his nose. Literally it would only take a strong sudden gust from the air conditioner and they'd be kissing.

That being said she's not going to do something foolish like pull away or set clear and appropriate boundaries.

"Trust me," she breathes. "I have no intention of doing this again."

"Because," he says, swallowing hard. "Because this is not allowed. Voice mails like that? Not allowed. Okay?"

The fucking voice mails.

She nods, which is weird since she's just rubbing her forehead against his.

"The voice mail was a mistake," she agrees.

"The voice mail was not a mistake," he says, shaking his head. "The opposite of a mistake really. But highly unpleasant, like you were ripping my heart out of my chest."

"And how would you know what that feels like?"

He closes his eyes, breath hitching.

She hopes it's a laugh. "Please tell me you don't actually know what that feels like."

This time she's 83 percent sure it's a laugh.

"No," he says. "No, I do not."

"Thank God," she mutters, shaking her head.

"I still love you, too," he says, running his fingers along the back of her neck, sweeping the hair aside.

"Obviously," she says.

"Really?"

"I mean you were begging for me back a week and a half ago," she says. "It's kinda obvious you're still carrying that torch, pal."

"I meant . . . ," he says, sighing, deeply and passionately. "Are we really doing this whole thing again? The whole joking-around-our-feelings thing?"

"Hey," she says. "I have had a very traumatic day. All I have left is my humor. To cope."

"You're an asshole."

"You love me anyway."

"Yeah, because you tricked me," he says. "Here I am thinking you're an asshole with a heart of gold."

"Who's to say I'm not?"

"I hate you."

"Sure you do."

She can't really see his face from this angle, can't really get a full view of his eyes, the slope of his nose, the cut of his chin, his perfect cupid's bow. But she can picture it in her mind. Picture his wonderful eyes and the smudge of purple beneath them from being out all night. His tight smile, like he's trying not to break, and failing because he loves breaking, loves laughing, and somehow, miraculously, loves her.

"Hey," she breathes, already closing her eyes.

"Yeah," he replies.

"Kiss me?"

He nods. "Of course. Why?" He rubs his thumb along her cheekbone. "What's the plan, Astrid?"

"I don't know yet."

She just really wants to kiss him right now.

"But," she says, swallowing hard. "I know that I love you. And I know that I was almost killed today by Ben fucking Barnes who became a supervillain because I did better than him on a final."

"Holy shit," Max says. "Really?"

She nods. "So . . . Fuck it, right? Life is unbelievable enough as it is, so kiss me."

He's a man of his word.

It feels like the first real breath she's taken all day, maybe all week, maybe all semester. It feels the same as every time she's kissed him before, before knowing what it was like to lose him, before knowing what it was like to walk into danger unblinking and determined. Same mechanics, same dip to his lips, same press of his nose against hers, same hands on her waist and in her hair.

But through it all her brain keeps saying, *thank you, thank you, thank you.*

She's not sure for who or to what.

She'll figure it out later.

It's been a pretty long day so she can't exactly be blamed for dozing in the waiting room.

These gray couches are more comfortable than they have any right to be. It's not hard to lean back against the assortment of bright pillows, and close her eyes for just a second.

She doesn't really deserve a granola bar in the face.

"Jesus," she says, jolting up, the bar bouncing over her nose, tumbling into her lap.

"You're welcome," Wally says, standing in front of her, popping open a bag of chips.

She blinks at him and thinks she'd hug him if she wasn't sitting down with her knees up at her chest.

"Where were you?" she asks.

"On vacation, you prick," he says. "Next time you're going to risk your absurd, silly life, wait until I'm not on the gorgeous

382

Hamptons beach I've been begging my masochist husband for years to take me to."

"Gee, I'm so sorry that the worst day of my life didn't happen when it was convenient for you," she says. "It wasn't all that convenient for me either, you know? I kinda just ruined my entire career."

He rolls his eyes and drops onto the sofa next to her, bouncing lightly. She feels it through her entire back. Her whole body is hovering between an exhausted numbness and overexaggerated soreness, but this stiff couch is somehow killing her back worse than her cheap desk chair.

"Yeah, well, imagine turning your phone back on after a luxurious midday beach walk to literally a hundred missed calls. It was stressful. I had to Uber back here. It was very expensive."

"Wow, I can't imagine," she says. "That must have been so hard for you."

"It really was," he says, nodding. He holds the chips out to her, lets her stick her hand in and steal a clawful. "I have a family history of heart issues. I'm at high risk for stress-induced medical emergencies."

"Thanks for letting me know," she says, and carefully extracts one chip from her hand with her teeth. "Next time I won't call you."

He shakes his head like that's the step too far.

"How're Thomas and Lucy doing?"

"Better than expected."

"How are you doing?"

She shrugs. "As expected."

"You know, the last time we spoke was four weeks ago," he says.

She didn't know exactly how long it was. Time doesn't really work like that for her anymore. There were just days and days, and any time longer than that was separated into Before Max, Max, After Max.

"I broke up with Max," she says.

"I knew that," Wally says. "Because I heard from Eleanor when she said you had quit the Program. And I haven't heard from you since."

Right. The phone calls.

"I'm sorry," she says, letting her head drop back. Her neck cracks alarmingly loud.

"Good," he says. "You should be."

"I didn't have the time." *And if I talked to you about it then it would all be real, then Max would really be gone, and hanging out at your apartment and having dinner with you and Henry would only remind me of how much I've lost.*

Wally raises an eyebrow. "Yeah, I figured. But you could have said that. Trust me, I'd understand. I was premed once."

"Yeah, at NYU."

"Hey, it's just as hard, you elitist snob."

She thinks she's laughing. It's been a while. It feels great and freeing and light.

"You know Henry had this awful joke the entire time we were in undergrad," Wally says, taking a chip delicately from the bag and popping it in his mouth. "What do you call the guy who graduated med school with all Cs?"

"What?" she asks, raising her eyebrows.

"Doctor."

He grins smugly. She exhales hard and nods. "Fair enough."

"I get it," he says, tapping her wrist. "I get all of it, kid. Just text next time. Or whatever you youths do."

"Next time I break up with my boyfriend and quit the relationship training program you were interacting with me through, or next time there's some extreme crisis I need adult help with so I don't have to stage a one person rescue mission." She downs another chip. "Cuz I'm pretty sure I *did* text you about one of those."

"Don't get smart with me."

"Sorry. I can't turn it off."

"Henry wants you to come for dinner tomorrow. Probably gonna give you a big hug and a long-winded hero speech."

"Sure. But I'm peeling the potatoes this time."

When Molly wakes up, they all go in together. Astrid follows at the back of the pack, unsure if she should even come. She's not sure what she might have to say to Molly or what Molly might have to say to her.

And yet, she files into room 616, hovering in the threshold as Thomas and Lucy reach the bed.

Molly smiles, a sad, wilting thing.

"Hey, guys," she croaks.

"Thank God you're okay," Thomas breathes. "What happened back there?"

"Yeah," Lucy says, a little less forgiving. "What happened back there?"

"I'm so sorry," Molly says, tears springing to her eyes so suddenly they must have always been there. "I had no idea that Ben would . . . I didn't want anyone to get hurt, I just thought—" She presses her lips together hard and blinks against tears.

Astrid still hovers in the doorway, watching this tableau like it's something distant and unreal. She wishes she could say that Molly was the same as she has always been, or maybe different than she'd been. Just something, just one, instead of both, instead of a messy, complex thing. She sees the hopefully smiling Molly and she sees the defensive and ambitious Molly all in one and doesn't know how to parse it.

"How are you feeling?" Astrid asks, because that's something she thinks she wants to know, more than anything else.

Molly's breath hitches when they lock eyes.

"You saved my life," she says, sniffling.

Astrid shrugs. "I didn't know what I was doing," she says. "I could have just as easily killed you."

"But you didn't," Molly says, smiling weakly. "You're going to be a good doctor."

Astrid's not sure if she thinks good doctors inject people with risky, unknown substances for a chance at saving their lives, but she'll take the compliment.

She steps deeper into the room.

"The doctor says you have powers now," Thomas says, eyes darting between them, testing out the tension in the room. "You really knocked that guy out. Probably superstrength or something else cool like that."

"Which is unfair," Lucy says. "That you get to be a super-hero now."

Molly winces. And Lucy responds in kind with a wince of her own, like an echo chamber of uncertainty.

"I just meant that . . . I mean what's a gal gotta do to get some powers around here," Lucy says with a tight smile.

"I thought you said education and political activism were the real superpowers," Thomas says, raising his eyebrows. Lucy rolls her eyes.

Astrid comes to stand at the foot of the bed, loosely holding the railing.

"Uh, didn't Wally say that female superheroes usually date in-house?" she offers, patting Molly's foot lightly. "You could . . . still date a superhero if you play your cards right. Without all the lying and stuff."

Molly shrugs like it's nothing, but Astrid can see all the hope and gratitude in her eyes.

"I think I might need to take a break from dating for a little while," she says.

Lucy exhales a startled laugh. Thomas squeezes Molly's shoulder.

"Yeah," Astrid says, smiling slowly. "Maybe."

◆ ◆ ◆

Eleanor arrives late. After five, hair falling out of a bun, still carrying a work bag. She flits around the waiting room until she's laid eyes on each of them, and then is off talking to doctors, talking to Wally, and then disappearing into Molly's room. After she comes out, she seems calmer, and moves to stand in front of the window, overlooking the city at night, the streetlights spotting the avenue, the little clumps of pedestrians.

She looks like a superhero, head bowed, shoulders straight, overlooking the world and wondering about large, existential things.

Astrid steps up next to her and tries to see what she sees.

"What a horrible excuse for a day," Eleanor breathes.

Astrid has nothing to add so she just nods.

"You did good," Eleanor breathes. "Amazing, actually. I can't believe—" She shakes her head. "I'm never turning my phone off at work again."

"What did you say to Molly?"

"Oh," Eleanor says. She exhales, an empty sound that's trying really hard to be a laugh. "That I was glad she was okay. She's sort of out of my jurisdiction now that she has powers, but we're putting her in contact with the right people."

"Is she in trouble? For telling Ben about the Fridge?"

Eleanor shakes her head. "Different people for her than for Ben, some friendly advisers to help her figure out her next steps. Power and responsibility and all that fun stuff. She didn't try to kill anybody today so . . ." She turns out a little, her shoulder angling toward Astrid. "Do you think she should be in trouble?"

"I dunno," Astrid says, tucking her hands into the pockets of her hoodie. Technically it's Max's hoodie—he gave it to her before they separated, her off to Molly's room again, him to the Chinese place down the block to grab them both some dinner. It's warm and smells like him. "We're all alive."

"The Fridge is compromised," Eleanor says. "I have to move Kat. I have to find a new base. I have to tell my boyfriend that pretty much all of his research samples were destroyed by a teenage boy being thrown across his lab."

Astrid lets her breath puff out and blow some frizz away from her eyes.

"He was trying to figure out how to heal Kat," Astrid says.

"Yeah," Eleanor says. "Yeah, he was. Using my other boy-friend's alien blood." She shrugs as if to say, *Life.* "Apparently, it can work though. That's a good thing. A really good thing."

"I'm sorry. That the Program is compromised," Astrid says, not sure if it's the guilty sort of apology or just the empathetic sort. "And that Kat was in danger."

"That's the way things go," Eleanor says, looking over at her. Astrid feels it even as she keeps staring down at the city street, watching a couple walk by, swaying in and around each other, like orbits, like gravity holding together cosmos and molecules. "You work hard on things and they fall apart, because that's how the universe works. Chaos, entropy. You're the scientist, right?"

"Then what's the point of doing anything at all? If it's just going to get destroyed?" Astrid asks.

Eleanor pauses. "You get to try again. Rebuild it again, but better. Maybe move your friend to a real hospital. Maybe . . . offer a summer session of your Program? For those with busy school schedules."

The couple turns down the street, two silhouettes in the night, two people she'll never see again.

"Well," Astrid says. "I'm free Tuesday and Thursday afternoons after May twelfth."

"Yeah? I'm pretty sure you just passed any test I could give you now."

Astrid nods. "There's always more to learn, right? And it, uh, looks like I'm dating a superhero again."

SENIOR SPRING
WEEK ONE

TIP OF THE WEEK

"How do you date a superhero? You don't. No one in their right mind should. They could die, you could die, again and again in increasingly painful ways. You will be kidnapped and dropped from buildings and held at gunpoint, knifepoint, unidentifiable-alien-weapon-point. Hours of your day will be gone to being tied up somewhere and waiting to be rescued, with worrying where an attack might come from, with replacing irreplaceable things like keys and IDs and books and laptops, paying out of pocket to repair your window when it's smashed in for the fifteenth time. So, you shouldn't date a superhero. Although, of course, you already are, aren't you? Maybe without even knowing. And you might have even gone and fallen in love with one like an idiot. And why did you fall in love? Because they're kind and noble and beautiful? Because they make you laugh? They make you happy and

*full and more you than you've ever been. And you can't just give
all that up, right? And, of course, because all of those things, all of
that danger, that happens anyway. You could break up with your
superhero today and get exploded by some new alien tomorrow,
or have your bus go off a bridge, or discover your coworker is some
evil scientist with no qualms about killing you. And, of course,
you could get hit by a car or trapped in a fire or get diagnosed with
some terminal disease. That's life. It's dangerous. So, date that
superhero. Because that's life and because you love them. Because
life at its worst is fear and life at its best is love. So you might as
well embrace both. And listen to everything Eleanor and Wally
say because they know what they're talking about. And when all
else fails, an MCAT test prep book is a hefty projectile."*

—*Astrid Rose*

IT TAKES ASTRID THREE MINUTES AND TWENTY-
seven seconds to unlock the pair of handcuffs, which coinci-
dentally is a new record for her.

She lets the cuffs fall to the rooftop and stands, stretching
her arms out over her head before grabbing her phone from
her back pocket. Below, the city is a midday quiet, with all the
people indoors to work or escape the mild late January cold.
She breathes it in as her phone rings.

"Hi," Max says in a second over the line. He sounds like he's
smiling. She smiles right back.

"Hey," she says. "So, I'm on a roof around Fifty-ninth and
Fifth from what I can tell."

"Oh," he says, and there's a sudden rushing on the other end of the line, like he's already on the way. "Are you okay? Are you safe?"

"I'm fine," she says. "Take your time. It's a great view."

And it is. The sun is high in the sky.

"Who is it this time?" he asks.

"I dunno. Some guy in purple with a bird theme. You might want to catch him first, he's heading downtown, but I missed the whole monologue so I'm not sure what exactly he's up to besides the wanting-to-kill-me part."

"Nah, I'm coming to you first, you've got that class at one, right?"

She does, Dev Bio, but it's week one. She won't miss too much and she knows like three people in the class to get notes off. Plus, she TA'd for the professor in junior year so she'll be fine.

"I can miss it."

"I'll be there in five."

She rolls her eyes because there's nothing else to do against the stupid, wonderful swelling in her chest.

Or . . . okay, well, there is one other thing.

"Love you," she says, because she does and because it feels as good in her lungs as the fresh air does.

"Love you too. Bye."

The call ends and she shoots off a text to Eleanor with her new time, before tucking the phone away again, and staring out over the city.

◆ ◆ ◆

"I cannot believe you," David hisses. She shoots him a look and tries to take deep breaths to keep from wheezing.

"I . . . ran . . . here," she shoots back between gasps for air as if her hair and the sweat stains running down her back aren't enough proof. Everything burns. There are spots dancing across her vision, but she tries to take in the entryway to the apartment around the blotches. "Should I be concerned with how out of shape I am?"

"You should be on time for things," David says. "You know, like how you sent me fifteen reminder emails about today."

"I am a busy premed student," she says, crossing her arms tightly.

"It's been four years. That doesn't work on me anymore," he says. "Where is he?"

"How am I supposed to know?"

"Keep tabs on your man," David says. He hands her a stack of papers. "Here, you do something with this."

"I'm so sorry!" Max trips his way into the room. He's breathing heavy but she knows it's a show. He hasn't even broken a sweat.

David shoots her a look, one blatantly calling her out for the fond smile she gets just being in a room with him.

"Honestly, Martin," David says, shaking his head. "I expect more from you of all people."

"I had a . . . ," he starts. Max stares at the ceiling for a moment. "Class?"

She drifts toward him on instinct, raising her eyebrows. He winces and shrugs.

"How are you still so bad at that?" she asks in a whisper, pressing a kiss to his cheek and fixing his collar to cover a scrap of blue suit poking through.

"Honestly, I don't know how I've made it this far," he replies. His hand lingers on her waist as they both turn to face David.

"Disgusting," he says.

"Okay," she says, rolling her eyes. "Give us the tour."

"Maybe if you had been on time—"

"*David.*"

"Fine, right this way," he says, gesturing widely with his arm.

She follows, skimming through the printouts from Street-Easy. It's not a great apartment. It's New York City and they are about to be college graduates, Astrid with a career that will start in approximately ten years and David and Max with internships or, if they're lucky, minimum wage, entry-level jobs. It's small and has three windows and is on a low floor. But it has two bedrooms and is solidly in their likely budget. (They also have safety and reach budgets. *They* being Astrid, who commandeered the project early. It's resulted in some of her best spreadsheets.)

"Do you think he suspects anything?" Max whispers, leaning into her as David peeks around in the bathroom. One bathroom. That'll be fun.

"No," she says. "Good job staggering arrivals."

"Nice," he says.

"You're getting better at predicting how long it takes regular people to get places," she notes. He smiles, turns into her hair.

"Stop flirting," David snaps. "Since you guys are late, I have given myself the larger bedroom."

Astrid shakes her head. "Bastard. We agreed since there are two of us and one of you, we should get the bigger—"

"Oh, I'm sorry. Is someone talking? I can't hear them because they were twenty-three minutes late to this apartment tour. Anyway, my bedroom is this door."

She glances over at Max, pressing her lips together. He grins, and the cool winter light streams in one of the three windows, and lights up his face. She can almost picture living here.

"Now imagine if he knew," she says. He nods and takes her hand as they start down the hall. "You're going to tell him soon, right? I mean, if we're living together, he's going to find out eventually."

"Yeah. I've been expecting him to find out the past three months. Do you wanna do the honors?"

"How about . . . ," she begins. They turn to enter the larger bedroom. David starts moving around the room, sizing it up, announcing loudly where he plans to put his furniture. Astrid smirks and whispers the rest to Max: "You throw a supervillain through his bedroom window in the middle of the night, and I tell him about it after."

"So?" Henry asks, leaning back in his chair. Astrid helps herself to another scoop of mashed potatoes. "Do we know what medical school is being gifted with your wonderful brain next fall?"

"Laying it on a little thick, honey," Wally says.

Astrid does not smile smugly but it's a close thing.

"I don't know yet," Astrid says, and takes a breath. "Actually, I'm taking a gap year, so it might be a while before I know for sure."

"Kids these days with their gap years," Wally sighs. "Back in my day, we had to pay off student loans."

"I paid off your student loans," Henry says.

Astrid raises her eyebrows and presses her lips together, giving Wally a look that very specifically says, *Tell me again that you're not a gold digger.* Wally shoots back a look that says, *Next time I'm poisoning the chicken meatballs.*

"What are you going to do during a gap year?" Wally asks. "Die of boredom?"

"Max wants to travel for a month or two," she says. "He couldn't figure out how to fit going abroad into his semester so we just started planning a hypothetical trip. And then it became less hypothetical."

"Where are you going?" Henry asks.

She shrugs. "We don't know yet. Just gonna see what happens."

Wally rolls his eyes. "Insufferable."

"David went on exchange to Amsterdam last fall, and he has some friends there we could crash with, but . . . we were also thinking about heading out to Japan, maybe."

There's a tapping on the window. Astrid feels her heart skip, hand jerking and nearly spilling red wine on the table-cloth. Wally hisses through his teeth. Henry gets up and walks to the window and throws it open.

Max tumbles in, breathing heavy, pulling his mask off.

"Sorry I'm late," he says, running his hands through his hair like that'll make it less of a tangled mess. It makes it worse. She rolls her eyes and stands, meeting him for a kiss when he walks past her for the seat to her left.

Henry shuts the window. Wally pushes the green beans toward him. Max helps himself to a heaping.

"What's it like out there?" Henry asks.

"Calm night," Max replies. "Some muggers. Uh, you ever tangle with Worm-Man?"

"Who?"

Max waves his hand. "Never mind. He's . . . yeah, just held me up for a second."

He's halfway through scarfing down the five servings of green beans he helped himself to before turning to Astrid, eyes widening.

"Hi . . . hello," he says. "How are you?"

His eyes are so warm and wide. There's a bruise forming under his eye that will probably disappear by the after-dessert coffee Wally always insists on serving.

His hand reaches across under the table and brushes hers.

"I'm good," she says, like she hadn't seen him that morning warm and drowsy over a cup of coffee from the pot David brewed with his Ultimate Starbucks Barista Skills, that afternoon at lunch between class and lab, and before he had to run off to the admin office.

He beams.

"Disgusting," Wally says. "Where are you traveling for your gap year?"

"Traveling?" Max repeats. He looks over at her, raising his eyebrows.

She had only just decided earlier that day. Not when she was with him at lunch, watching him laugh at one of David's ridiculous jokes until he almost choked on a baby carrot, but in the middle of her Genetic Evolution section when she had stared out the window for a second while the TA went over a homework problem she had already gotten. The sun had been so yellow, even though it was still late-winter chilly out. On the street below cars honked, buses huffed their exhaust, pedestrians walked by. It was 3:07, schools nearby letting out, little kids with bright backpacks and swinging lunch boxes about to come screaming into the playground down in Morningside Park. Still too cold to take her homework out on the quad, but not too cold for those kids to be racing around, young and free.

And just like that she had decided that she didn't want to spend her year stuffed up in her apartment, only getting fresh air from when Max spilled into her window or when David physically dragged her to Starbucks to abuse his discount. ("Sabotage the capitalist system from within," as he would say. "Eat the rich, but also this banana nut bread.")

She could pack her MCAT prep books in a carry-on.

"Yeah," she says, reaching her ankle out so it brushes against Max's foot. "Where are we gonna go?"

SOPHOMORE SPRING
FINALS, WEEK TWO

M
T   CELL BIO FINAL
W
Th
F

"YOU HAVE THREE HOURS," THE TA SAYS. HE'S not her TA, but one of the other sections', the useless one if she remembers the hot gossip correctly. He sounds bored already. "If you have any questions, you can raise your hand and we can come over to clarify things. If you finish early—"

She tunes it out. She knows the drill, has memorized this little speech, could recite it back. This isn't her first rodeo.

But it is her last of the year. Three hours and six pages of questions sit between her and the end of this semester. This semester that felt so much like something she just had to get through, classes and lab hours and the Program like check marks on a list that she could cross off. This semester that felt like it would break her, throwing her off roofs and exploding in her face over and over. And yet here she is, in a quiet, sunny classroom with two dozen other exhausted premeds, the AC chugging along, and one final test in front of her.

She stares at the blank back page of the test, waiting for someone to say start.

Three hours and she'll leave this room, light as a feather, finally free. She'll meet David and Max for a very late lunch, brush off David's teasing that she probably failed, brush off Max's earnest assertions that she probably did fine because she's a beautiful genius.

She'll rope both of them into helping her carry her boxes of clothes, textbooks, stationery equipment down to the cart she procured, up the hills and down the valleys, twenty blocks to CCNY where she'll be working in a lab this summer.

David will inevitably protest.

Max will pretend that he's struggling with the heavier boxes, or maybe forget entirely because he's the worst at the secret identity thing. David will make snide side remarks about her jacked nerd boyfriend.

Max will end up sitting on the floor of her new dorm when David ditches her for some frat party with Priya. With the two of them alone, Max will make eyes at her until she sits down next to him. And in the privacy of the room, boxes stacked high, room bare and new and clean, they might make out, or maybe now that the semester is done and she has time and he promised to take the night off, they might do a little more.

Or a lot more.

They don't really have a schedule. No plan, which makes her feel exhilarated like a high-speed roller coaster, but also weird and scared like her harness is a little too loose and there's a weird clunking noise during the lift hill that could mean any number of disasters.

"Your time starts now," the TA says, and scribbles out the stop time on the chalkboard.

She doesn't need it. She has her own watch, her own mental ticking clock that works even better than the TA announcements.

She turns the exam over, writes her name on the first page, signs the statement that she isn't cheating.

She opens the test, folds the corner off precisely along the staple.

She should probably be stressed about the test in front of her. Her 4.0 is gone forever, her physics grade barely salvaged by a semester of hard work, and her fate hangs on her ability to fight this entire second half of her college education to inch it back up.

But, the good thing is, she has time.

ACKNOWLEDGMENTS

Ever since I was child, I would rehearse book acknowledgments in the shower like an Oscar acceptance speech, running down a list of names and getting teary-eyed at a journey I hadn't even gone on yet. But here it is, this book and these acknowledgments, and I barely know what to say.

I started writing this book the summer after my sophomore year of college, right where we leave Astrid, and I'm writing this just a few months after graduation. This, my wonderful college book, would not exist without the people who made college wonderful for me. To Mickey, my favorite premed and my favorite person to sleep five feet away from, you are the smartest person I've ever met and for some reason you let me borrow your genius for this. I owe you my life and also probably a Subway sandwich. To Marjorie, you make me a better writer with every hours-long conversation we've had about popular media franchises, whether on the phone or standing outside the bathroom after midnight. Every bit of my love for college that I channeled into this book comes from the two of you.

To my mom, who is always my first fan and my first critic, and who never lets me drop the ball. To my dad, who has always encouraged me to work hard and play harder. To Nicolas, who has been forced to listen to my stories since birth and has only rarely complained. And to the rest of my family, who have loved and supported me and believed that I would make it here even when I didn't.

To Siena, my writing partner for over a decade and the first person to read pretty much all of my attempts at books, I would not be the writer I am today without you. To Yanick, for forcing me to read all of Brian Michael Bendis's Spider-Man run, and getting me to Comic-Con every year, and seeing every Spider-Man movie with me, this book would definitely not exist without you.

To my amazing agent, Abigail, who believed in this project and in me and loves Astrid almost as much as I do, for being the best cheerleader and champion and showing me all this story could be. To my incredible editor, Sara, for knowing exactly what I was trying to say with this book and helping me say it a million times better than I could on my own. To my copyeditors, Lindsay and Ronnie, for finding every timeline hole my non-Astrid brain created. To Molly, for this beautiful cover that I have cried many tears over. And to the rest of the Katherine Tegen team, my proofreaders Chris and Sonja, production editor Rye, and managing editor Gwen for bringing this story from a lowly Word doc to an actual book.

Looks like they're playing me off the stage, so I'll be fast: Id like to thank Carly Rae Jepsen for releasing her seminal album *Dedicated* the summer I wrote this first draft; every single person involved in the creation of Michelle Jones; Stan Lee; Jack Kirby; Steve Ditko; and anyone else over the years who has dreamed about superheroes.

Thank you and goodnight!